MW01041305

And the Beat Goes On

And the Beat Goes On

by

Tracy Krauss

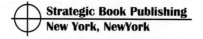
Strategic Book Publishing
New York, NewYork

Eloquent Books
An imprint of AEG Publishing Group
845 Third Avenue, 6th Floor - 6016
New York, NY 10022
www.eloquentbooks.com

ISBN: 978-1-60693-199-8   1-60693-199-7

Printed in the United States of America

Book Design: SP

Prologue

"And God saw that the wickedness of man was great in the earth, and that every imagination of the thoughts of his heart was only evil continually..." Genesis 6:5 KJV

Tom-tom . . . tom-tom . . . pulsing . . . throbbing . . . the earth reverberated. Dancers leapt to the ancient rhythm, their half naked bodies glistening with sweat in the firelight, twisted and arched, as the primal beat called to the pulse within. Overhead, the display case of heaven sparkled, the diamonds large and brilliant against their black velvet nest. Accompanying this was a symphony of sound; a full choir of heavenly voices carried on the solar winds through the crystalline canopy of heaven to the sons of earth below.

The heavy scent of giant orchids that bloomed along the outer perimeter of the temple gardens mingled with the spices and perfumes that were thrown into the fire by the temple priestesses. It had all been set in place for his honor; soon to be absolute ruler and son of the gods himself.

High above the ornate alter, around which the dancers poured their carnal worship, a handsome, young, would-be king watched from his seat of honor. His heartbeat quickened, for he knew what was coming next. He had once before witnessed the ancient ritual as a child, when his own father had been crowned king and had become god.

Abruptly, the drumming ceased. A hush swept through the crowd of onlookers that circled the stone platform. The dancers and priestesses scattered. From out of the shadows marched twelve beasts. They were human in appearance except for the gigantic wings, leathery like those of a bat, that were folded across their backs and whose tips nearly touched the ground. Each man was tall and well muscled—the finest and bravest in the kingdom. They were the king's guard, specially chosen and groomed from boyhood; a privilege for only the strongest and bravest. They would accompany the king wherever he went—even to the grave. As descendants of the Nephilim—the race of giants born from the union of the gods and mortal women—they feared nothing, not even death.

The guards lined up on the large platform facing the king, as the chief among them solemnly ascended the flight of stone steps that led from the platform and alter to the king's throne. From here he would have a good view of every spectacle. The guard saluted, turned, and gave the signal to the others.

With precision, the guards stepped back to form a corridor. The here to fore silent crowd could not help but murmur. A wave of "oohs" rippled through the masses as six burly slaves led the captive forward, shackled, hobbled, and muzzled. Even then, it was a struggle to get the huge beast prostrate upon the altar of sacrifice. Its beady eyes glistened as its leather wings twitched.

A priest came forward, gilded knife held high over the creature's heart. A slave released the muzzle that had kept the creature silent and the knife plunged directly into the heart of the animal as a piercing scream echoed through the forest, seeming to rebound from the canopy of the brilliant sky.

Other skilled workers moved quickly into place, and with a few precise cuts, the huge leather wings were removed. Next, the head was severed, the brains neatly extracted, leaving only the long pointed beak, majestic red crest, and beady eyes intact.

Blood dripped from the newly hewn crown as it was placed reverently in the hands of the chief guard. With dignified solemnity, he carried the grisly trophy up the long stairway to the king. The priest followed closely on his heels. The prized headpiece was placed on the king's head, even as blood continued to drip from its depths onto his hair and beard. The priest, who had brought with him a goblet of the animal's blood rendered from its jugular vein, presented it to the sovereign. He whispered the ancient words of the deity into the king's bloody ear, an incantation meant only for the gods, not mortal ears. Slowly the new sovereign raised the goblet to his lips. Without wavering, he took a swallow from the cup, letting the blood trickle from the corners of his mouth. Lowering the goblet, his handsome face was suddenly spoiled by a malicious grin.

The priest stepped back as four others came bearing the wings, still attached as one piece by the skin of the creatures back. They were strong men, but even they let out a grunt as the heavy cape was settled onto the shoulders of the monarch. He thought for a moment that he wouldn't be able to bear the weight of it. Once the wings were properly cleaned and tanned, they would weigh much less and he would be expected to wear them for all public ceremonies. But for this night, he must bear the full weight of the mantle, blood and all.

The blood that the priest had mixed with some special herbs was giving him new strength, however. And the words . . . those secret words passed down from the outer world of his ancestors . . . words that no human could hear . . . these also gave him power. He was one of them now. A god among men. He straightened

7

majestically in his seat as if the weight on his shoulders was nothing more than an ordinary cloak made of woven material. He smiled his bloody smile again, flashes of white peaking through the glistening red, and raised his hand in salute.

A cheer went up from the crowd. The heartbeat of the tom-tom was revived. People rushed forward to clap and dance around the flaming torches that skirted the perimeter of the platform, as the dancers resumed their gyrations around the altar of incense. The tempo became frenzied as dancers and spectators alike became more agitated. Some began screaming and wailing; others tore at their clothing, leaving themselves exposed. Just when it seemed the festivities were about to turn into a full-fledged orgy, a trumpeting signal brought the writhing crowd to a standstill.

The guards remained steadily at their posts, circling the outer edge of the platform. The tom-tom took up another beat, this time methodical and solemn, as a priestess, waving a fragrant branch of flowers before her, led a procession from the darkness of the forest into the light of the torches and then up into the centre of the platform. With her were twenty-four maidens, all beautiful in their delicately fluttering garments; all virgins, never even setting sight on a member of the male gender before. They had been raised for this purpose; innocent, yet knowing that their lives held great significance. Now was the time for the fulfillment of that purpose.

The air was heavy with perspiration and heat. The tension and anticipation of the coming spectacle were almost too much for the crowd to bear. The priestess finished her brief words of blessing. One word from the king now was all it would take.

The newly crowned king surveyed the virgins with relish. Beautiful, innocent, and ripe— every one. His own lustful desires rose up and he grinned widely. He would have his pick, but at a later time, and in the privacy of his own chambers.

Suddenly, a flashing sheet of light swept across the sky to the east, followed by a deep rumbling much like the mighty cascading noise of a waterfall. The crowd gasped in fear. *Perhaps it was a sign of approval from the gods,* he thought. He hoped. Somewhere deep within, he heard another voice. His father had told him once about a man—a lunatic—that had been building a boat from before his grandfather's time. He was a self-proclaimed prophet and said that the earth was to be destroyed by a flood. It seemed ridiculous then, and even more so now. The crazy man had been giving his warning for hundreds of years and nothing had happened yet.

Besides, he was a god himself now. He was absolute ruler, at least in this part of the world. His own ancestors had left the area where the lunatic lived long ago, partly in search of treasure, and partly to get away from his teaching. They had settled far away in a prosperous and fertile land, and here they had been met by the gods.

As if in answer to his thoughts, another amazing spectacle lit the sky. This time it was a giant forked bolt of lightning, followed by an even louder crash. The people gasped again, and someone screamed. He must take control. With a lion like roar, the king lifted his arm, giving the signal. "The gods, my fathers, are pleased! Let the ceremony continue!"

The guards, who had previously been standing at attention around the perimeter of the platform, suddenly jumped into action. Without any delicacy or ceremony, they charged at the group of maidens, grabbing their chosen prey and proceeding to rape them with violence and brutality right before the gaping crowd of onlookers. The mob cheered in encouragement as the fetid orgy continued before their eyes on the platform. Potential escapees were thrown back into the arena for more, as each man exercised his rights to the full. Before long, many onlookers joined in the debauchery, some willingly, others not. It didn't matter. This was one night when anything and everything was acceptable. The king looked on in sadistic pleasure, hungry lust burning within his own loins. But the gods had control over their desires. He must remember that. His time would come later.

Another sheet of lightning crashed along the horizon, illuminating the spectacle below. Some of the people started to scatter in fear, but others seemed to be spurred on. The king ignored the uncertainty in his own heart. With another roar, he stood with outstretched arms and shouted his approval.

"And God looked upon the earth, and, behold, it was corrupt; for all flesh had corrupted his way upon the earth. And God said unto Noah, the end of all flesh is come before me; for the earth is filled with violence through them; and, behold, I will destroy them with the earth." Genesis 6: 12-13 KJV

Chapter One

The African sun beat down on his head in the open jeep as Dr. Mark Graham and his companion bumped along what could hardly be called a road. A local man from the Nbedele tribe, hired on as part of the archeological team, drove the jeep along the hazardous path up the mountain. Hair raising switchbacks and steep inclines didn't seem to faze the driver as he maneuvered the vehicle with one hand. Some pebbles cascaded off the trail's edge to the ravine below. Good thing he was used to it, Mark decided, or he might have been tempted to bail.

As he braced himself for the next jarring pothole, Mark thought about yesterday's meeting with the Zimbabwean government officials. Everything had gone well—on the surface, at least. They had agreed to continue their sponsorship, and renewed their pledge of faith in his abilities as a leader in his field. Yet there was this nagging sense at the back of his mind that something rippled beneath the surface—something hidden either by neglect or design of which he wasn't aware. It was an uncomfortable feeling, probably just his general distaste for dealing with administrators. As meticulous as he was, it rankled when unnecessary red tape seemed to get in the way of real progress. Added to that, it was not

11

a trip he relished unless absolutely necessary.

His crew had been meticulously digging under the site of an ancient temple—a sacred site stringently protected by the government of Zimbabwe. The temple site itself had been unearthed decades before, but legend had led to speculation that an even older civilization had once used the spot. Mark had been honored when asked to assemble a team of specialists to investigate the possibilities without compromising the original excavations. It was painstaking work. But already, after only five months, the team was rewarded with signs that the legends were indeed rooted in fact. Under the temple mount they had discovered an even more ancient burial ground with an intricate system of tombs that seemed oddly more technologically advanced than the layer of simple graves directly above it. This wasn't entirely unexpected; history often bespoke of a more barbarous people supplanting a superior civilization. But there was more . . . so much more. There was a sense that they were on the verge of something big—monumental, even.

And then the authorities had the audacity to question whether there was any use continuing! They said they were running out of money and it was taking too long. Fools! Didn't they know there was no way to unearth secrets that had been buried for millennium in just a few short months? These things took time and care. And money.

That was the bottom line. Always was. Mark wished he had the benefit of some nice multi-trillionaire benefactor right about now, instead of a crumbling third world dictatorship. Oh well. For now he had managed to secure another four-month contract, having convinced them of the importance of the find to the economic development of the region. But in the end, he doubted that it would be enough time and he was a scientist, not a politician.

As the jeep rounded the last corner, Mark spotted one of the tents that had been set up on site as a lab. The archeological site extended over a fairly large area. Several tents and simple wooden structures had been erected to house the necessary work stations and accommodate the crew. Various roped off areas were meticulously squared off for the painstaking process of uncovering tidbits of information, one grain of sand at a time.

Mark jumped from the jeep into the cloud of gathering dust and strode directly to the quarters where he expected to find his coworker, Laura Sawchuk. He left his bags for his Nbedelian assistant.

He had left Laura in charge during his brief absence. Laura Sawchuk, Doctor of Anthropology, was very capable at giving direction and leadership. She had been his colleague on more than one job before, and he trusted her judgment and skill for the task at hand. She was also, at present, his girlfriend.

Girlfriend had a somewhat adolescent ring to it, Mark decided. His "partner" would be a more appropriate phrase—it was the terminology Laura used, anyway. Mark wasn't quite sure how their relationship had advanced to more than just colleagues. Close proximity did that to people sometimes. And loneliness.

He found Laura sitting at a corner along one wall, examining a fragment under a microscope. She didn't look up when he entered. At thirty-six, she was a couple of years older than Mark. Her career always came first, a fact that suited Mark since he shared her passion for delving into the past.

"Laura," he greeted her. "What have we here?" He tried to get a glimpse over her shoulder at the tiny fragment she was scrutinizing.

She ignored the question. "I thought you were going to be back yesterday," she said, still not taking her eyes from what she was examining.

13

"I was delayed an extra day in Harare," Mark explained as he pulled up a stool and sat down beside her.

"Oh? That good news or bad?" she asked.

"Good. I managed to convince them to give us another four months."

"Four months?!" Laura asked sharply, straightening and looking at Mark for the first time since he had arrived. There was a powdering of dust on his skin and hair that almost made him look like he had stepped out of one of those old fashioned sepia photographs— all monochromatic brown. "We can't possibly be finished in four months." She reached over and flicked a stray twig from his unruly mass of dark curls.

"I know that," Mark shrugged, running a hand through his hair, creating a small cloud of dust. He rubbed his chin thoughtfully. Two days growth of stubble had begun to form. "But for now, I had to take it or leave it."

Laura leaned forward and placed a quick kiss on Mark's nose, her streaked brown and blonde ponytail bobbing. "Good to have you back, in any case. Mnanga didn't kill you with his reckless driving, I see."

"Still in one piece, miracle as that is," Mark nodded with a grin. "What you looking at anyway?"

"A fragment from some of the plaster leading into the antechamber I told you about," Laura replied, turning back to the microscope. "It seems to have some kind of metal alloy embedded right in it."

"Plaster?" Mark asked uncertainly, his brows furrowing.

Laura nodded. "I'm not sure what else to call it. A coating of some kind. Unusual, I know."

"Very," Mark agreed. "Most tombs are simply hewn from the rock, not plastered over. Mind if I take a look?" Laura relinquished her seat and Mark took his turn peering into the microscope. "Hm.

14

I see what you mean. I've never seen anything like it." He couldn't help keeping the disappointment from his voice. He had wanted to be the first into the chamber himself.

Laura picked up on the tone in his voice. "Don't worry. We haven't made a breakthrough into the chamber itself yet. I knew you'd be disappointed not to be here, so we've held back a bit."

"Oh. Thanks. I appreciate it," Mark nodded. There was obvious relief in his voice as he continued to peruse the tiny fragment.

"Besides, there's been plenty of other excitement to keep us busy."

"Like…?"

"Like the bone fragments," Laura offered.

"Still no word from the lab?" he asked. He already knew the answer. He'd checked back in Harare.

"Nope. But we're starting to see a pattern emerging," Laura said.

Mark's curiosity was really pricked now. He looked up. "What kind of pattern?"

"Come and see," Laura said, leaving the plaster fragment behind for the time being. She led Mark to a computer station. She sat down in front of the screen and clicked several icons with the mouse. A large blueprint of the dig appeared on the screen. "The strange bone fragments we found first were located here," she pointed to the location with her finger, "alongside the human remains that appear to have been disturbed—either by some type of seismic activity, or by other humans."

"Mmhm," Mark nodded. It was nothing new to him. He had been present during that discovery. "Go on."

"The next grave we uncovered also contained unidentified bone fragments. Only this time," she paused for effect. She glanced over at him, ready to gauge his reaction. He raised his brows in question. "I'll bring up a digital photo," she said, clicking the mouse deftly once again. Several windows opened. "Ah, here we are." She punched one more key and a color photo came up of a long curved bone. It was broken in two places, with part of the inner section missing. She hit another key and a second picture came up. This time it showed Laura and Rocco, one of the crew managers, holding the bone between them.

"That's one big chicken wing," Mark whistled.

"Then you do agree that it looks like part of a wing?" Laura asked, surveying him closely.

Mark blinked and peered at the image again. "Yes . . . it does, doesn't it?"

"The humerus is almost entirely intact, with parts of the ulna attached. It looks to be from a very large winged creature. The parts that are left clearly seem to have been placed with the body intentionally."

"Large," Mark mused. "How large?"

"Pretty damn big, that's all I have to say. Bigger than an albatross or any present species of bird that I know of."

"You know what this means, don't you?" Mark asked expectantly. He looked over at Laura, obvious excitement burning in his eyes. "We've discovered another Troy—an ancient legend thought to be nothing more than myth." He pounded the computer table and the monitor flickered momentarily. It was the most emotion he had displayed thus far.

"Watch it," Laura warned with a smile. "No hitting the furniture! You're forgetting our power supply isn't the most stable."

"What else you got?" Mark asked anxiously.

"Rocco's team has been continuing on those same graves. He may find the other "wing," so to speak, and by the look of the placement of those two graves, we're speculating that there could be a whole ring of graves surrounding the entrance to the antechamber. Providing you want to disturb them."

"Hmm. Like guards," Mark commented.

"Right. Here's another interesting find from the same grave," Laura said, referring to the next photo. "It appears to be some kind of head piece or mask, probably worn expressly for burial. It's pretty badly decayed and was in danger of disintegrating into dust if we tried to remove it."

Mark just stared at the screen. "I know what you're thinking, okay?" Laura interrupted his thoughts. "About that legend—don't go spreading rumors until the lab has done a full analysis. I've had a hard enough time convincing Rocco to keep his feet on the ground. You know how he can be. We could all be discredited if we aren't careful. First, we need solid lab work as to the type of bone, then solid dating on both the human and non-human fragments."

"You don't need to remind me about procedure, doctor," Mark stated in a business-like tone. "I am still chief archeologist on this dig."

"Of course," Laura agreed, giving Mark a sideways glance. "I wasn't trying to offend you. You seem awfully touchy."

Mark sighed and ran a hand through his thick, unruly hair. "My apologies. I guess I'm just tired after the trip."

"More like your nerves are shot after Mnanga's driving," Laura offered.

"Right," Mark agreed with a chuckle. "Plus, I hate being out of the loop. I feel like all the important discoveries are being made when I'm gone."

"You need to relax," Laura said, coming up behind him and kneading his neck with her fingers.

"Hm . . . that feels good," Mark said, closing his eyes.

"Of course. And I'll make it feel even better a little later on,"

Laura promised with a suggestive smile.

"Oh? That's definitely worth coming back for," Mark said with a smile of his own. He closed his eyes and allowed her fingers to do their magic on the stiff cords in his neck. Suddenly he opened his eyes. "I'd like to take a look, myself," he said, all business once again. "At that bone. It's been stored and numbered with the rest of the artifacts?"

"Of course," Laura shrugged, dropping her hands and walking away with a sigh. She turned back to the computer. "I expected you'd want to have a look at everything. I just thought you might want to wait and start fresh tomorrow."

"With only four months grace, I don't think we can spare the time. I better be off to inspect the rest of the work in progress," he said with obvious relish, rubbing his hands together. He rose and turned to leave.

"Mark," Laura stopped him.

"Hm?" Mark turned.

"I missed you."

His nod of acknowledgement was barely perceptible. He was already out the door.

Mark strode to where he hoped to find Rocco Cortez, one of the crew chiefs. He'd been talking to various other crew chiefs along the way and was brought up to date on most of the developments already, so it was just a matter of seeing it for himself. He was physically weary from his trek, but his mind was on high alert.

By far, the dominant feature of the entire site was the ancient temple ruins. It had been reconstructed in places and consisted of an outer and an inner courtyard, with the chambers of the temple itself in the center. Much of the building had been constructed of rock quarried from the surrounding area. Mostly what was left, after being uncovered, was the foundation, with only a few walls

18

remaining intact. But the location of the altar and several other important features could be clearly identified from what remained. The original archeological excavations had taken place over thirty years ago. What Mark and his team were interested in now was not the temple itself, but what lay hidden far beneath it.

This type of excavating was very painstaking and precise. In order to get at the layers beneath without disturbing the top layer, the team had to tunnel underneath using an elaborate system of braces, all the while ensuring that they didn't destroy a potentially important find. They started well away from the temple mound itself, creating a crater-like moat around one side of the site. From here they could open up the side of the hill underneath, exposing subsequent layers as they went. It was backbreaking work with an element of risk, but the thrill of discovery outweighed the drawbacks.

"Rocco," Mark greeted his colleague, pumping his hand vigorously. "I hear there have been some exciting discoveries in my absence." Rocco was a short, somewhat stocky man of Puerto Rican descent. He wore his graying hair in a haphazard ponytail, and sported a thick, black mustache.

"Hey, my friend," Rocco responded enthusiastically. "She showed you the photos?"

"Yeah. Pretty amazing," Mark nodded.

"See the real thing yet?" Rocco asked, surveying his boss out of the corner of his eye.

"Just heading over there now," Mark informed. The two men started walking together toward the storage and cataloguing compound. "So what do you think?"

Rocco shrugged noncommittally. "You probably don't want to know."

"Come on, Rocco. I trust your judgment." Rocco looked skeptical and kept his mouth shut. Mark smiled encouragingly and slapped the older man across the back. "Don't let Laura scare you off. She even warned me about keeping the discovery under wraps until the final analysis report comes in."

Rocco considered his answer for a moment. "Seems obvious to me. In keeping with local legend, plus the size, shape, and wing span . . ."

Mark nodded. "I know. I just can't quite wrap my brain around it yet. It seems impossible."

"Wait until you see it," Rocco responded.

"So you seriously think we've unearthed the remains of a long extinct variety of flying dinosaur?"

Rocco nodded. "Very Pterodactyl like. I've seen them before."

Mark grunted and let out a small disbelieving laugh. "No wonder Laura is so paranoid. The sooner we get a positive ID, the better. I just wish I'd been around to personally document the whole thing."

"You don't trust us?" Rocco asked.

"I didn't say that," Mark explained. "It's just that this could either be the biggest scientific discovery of the century or the biggest hoax. We'll either be famous or made to look like laughing stocks. Any slip in procedure and we could be completely discredited."

"They'll try it, don't even fool yourself into thinking they won't."

Mark glanced sideways at his long time friend and trusted colleague. "You sound pretty skeptical. And who are 'they'?"

"The establishment."

"The establishment," Mark repeated sardonically.

"In this case, the scientific community," Rocco clarified.

"Oh?"

"Sure. They accept only what fits into their own pre-conceived theories. Anything outside the box gets tossed."

"That's hardly fair," Mark laughed. "If that's the case, then what's the use? We might as well pack up right now and go home. Discovery is what this is all about."

"There, my friend, is where you are sadly mistaken," Rocco replied knowingly. "It's really about the capitalist regime that rules us all. Money. Profit. Bottom line. That's where the real power is. We're all just pawns in a big game of chess, fed whatever information the powers-that-be think we can swallow. Just enough to keep us quiet and satisfied. It's a conspiracy."

"Someone definitely put something nasty in your cereal this morning," Mark said with a laugh.

"I'm serious," Rocco responded.

"I know," Mark said, sobering. "That's what worries me."

They had reached the compound, a large canvas-walled structure. Mark greeted the guard with a perfunctory nod and entered without comment. Rocco followed closely on his heels.

"It's numbered and documented right along with everything else from my quadrant. I did it myself," Rocco said, leading the way in the dim interior of the make shift compound. It consisted of rows of metal shelving lined with labeled trays and clear plastic bags of artifacts. "Right here," He searched the area with his eyes, squinting. "What the . . . it was here yesterday. I knew you'd want to do the preliminary lab work yourself. What did she do with it?!" he blurted, letting out a string of expletives in Spanish.

"Whoa, whoa! Who do you mean?" Mark asked. "Laura?"

"Has anything been crated for transport to the States yet?" Rocco demanded, ignoring the initial question.

"Is that what she suggested?"

"Yep. I told her to wait until you got back. I told her you'd want to see it for yourself," Rocco spat, shaking his head in frustration.

"I take it you two had some disagreements on the subject,"

Mark noted.

"You could say that," Rocco admitted.

"So just what else has been going on in my absence?" Mark wanted to know. He wasn't feeling too happy at the moment. Laura had just finished telling him she had saved the bone for him to look at. Why would she lie to him about it?

"Go ask your second in command," Rocco directed with a wave. "She'll tell you what ever you want to hear, I'm sure."

"I don't like the sounds of this. The last thing I need are my two most valuable crew members at logger heads with one another."

Rocco just shrugged. "Talk to her about it. I just did my job. Numbered and documented, just like it's supposed to be."

"I intend to talk to her about it," Mark said in no uncertain terms. He turned and strode from the compound.

Chapter Two

"I think we need to have a talk," Mark announced as he strode into the lab where Laura was working.

"Oh yeah? About what?" Laura asked casually, continuing with her work. She was calibrating some measurements on a chart that was spread open before her.

"I think you probably already know," Mark said. "I just came from talking to Rocco."

"Oh," Laura said with a depreciating snort. "And what kind of hype is he spouting now?"

"He seemed surprised that you'd sent away the bone sample. He said he'd already catalogued it and had advised you to wait for me." There was just a hint of accusation in his voice.

"Sent away the sample? What are you talking about?" Laura asked.

"You didn't send the bone away for detailed testing yet?"

"No. Why would I do that? I knew you'd want a look at it," Laura shrugged in bewilderment. "Besides, that's not procedure. We'll crate up the items we think can't wait until later on and send them together. Although, I'm not sure I want that particular item to get out of my sight." Her eyes narrowed in sudden understanding. "I suppose Rocco's been making up nonsense again," she said angrily. "That man definitely has an authority issue."

"Really. I hadn't noticed," Mark replied coolly.

"Because you're a man. He doesn't like taking orders from a woman," Laura explained.

"I heard you two had some disagreements while I was away."

"Nothing I couldn't handle," Laura assured. "Although, by the sounds of it he hasn't let it go. What's he accusing me of now?"

"The wing bone. It's not in the compound," Mark replied.

"What?" Laura gasped, looking over at Mark sharply. "Where is it?"

"I was hoping you could tell me," Mark said.

Her face hardened. "And he said I sent it away?" she asked. She shook her head angrily. "That figures. He's definitely on some kind of a vendetta. The guy is a nut case." She looked at Mark, betrayal in her eyes. "Thanks for believing in me, by the way," she added sarcastically.

"Sorry," Mark replied, breaking eye contact. He sighed and rubbed his chin. "There must be some explanation for it. I'll go back through the compound myself with a fine-toothed comb. He probably just forgot where he put it." Somehow Mark doubted it; Rocco was always thorough and professional. A mistake of this magnitude wasn't typical of him. But what other explanation could there be?

Laura interrupted his thoughts. "He's gone way over the deep end this time. He was carrying on about dinosaurs and proof of the coexistence of people. Then he got on to international conspiracies and cover ups—it was starting to freak some of the crew. You know how tenuous our position is here with the Zimbabwe government. One bit of bad press and they'll shut us down."

"I hardly think it would come to that."

"No? Well, I don't trust Rocco. The guy is nuts. I seriously have doubts about his stability—and his credibility. As head of this thing, you might want to look into it."

"Are you suggesting I fire him?" Mark asked.

"You do what you think you have to," she stated firmly, her eyes not wavering from his.

"Rocco's been an important part of the team from the beginning. He's experienced and knows his stuff. I'll bet he's worked on more digs that you and I combined—and seen a lot more, too."

"He's seen too much," Laura scoffed. "In fact, I think he's starting to see things, as in hallucinations."

"You mean all the dinosaur stuff," Mark stated.

"Exactly. I mean, who in their right mind would even entertain something so ridiculous?"

"Well, Rocco says—"

"Stop," Laura interjected, putting up her hands. "Just stop. I will not stand here and listen to this kind of crap. Dinosaurs and man did not coexist, okay? We're scientists. We know that. It's been proven. So don't even go there. You're scaring me," she added, turning and crossing her arms over her chest.

"Hey," Mark said, coming up behind her and rubbing her arms. "I'm not going nuts, okay? I didn't say I believed it. Besides, as a scientist, I'm not afraid to test my own theories. It's what science is all about."

"We'll let the evidence speak for itself," Laura said.

The sun rose and set abruptly in the Zimbabwean mountains, and darkness meant one thing. Suppertime. Mark crunched his way over the sand and gravel to the large army-style tent that was the kitchen and dining hall. A string of electric light bulbs hanging limply in front of the tent helped to light the way. The pulsing of diesel generators was a constant sound in the background. It disturbed the peace of the otherwise remote location, but was necessary to keep power up and running.

Mark greeted several crew members as he took his place in the cafeteria line. Local cooks had been hired for the task, and the food was not fancy—standard backwoods fare that filled your stomach and kept you going through the long and physically taxing days.

He found a spot at one of the long tables beside Laura. She still seemed angry with him, and he couldn't blame her. Rocco joined them a few minutes later.

"Hello, boss," Rocco said as he eased in beside Mark. "Laura," he added with a nod. Laura barely acknowledged him. The tension between the two was palpable.

"Tomorrow I'll get some of my men to open up another Joe," Rocco said, referring to the human remains still encased in their burial cells. "You'll be busy with the chamber, no doubt, but we'll be close by one another."

"Is that necessary?" Laura asked lightly. "You know the policy about leaving as many graves undisturbed as possible."

"I think, under the circumstances, yes, it is necessary," Mark said. Rocco fairly beamed.

"You're the boss, after all," Laura shrugged. "And keeping that in mind, maybe you should be the one to open the 'Joe', as Rocco so eloquently puts it. At least with you in charge, there shouldn't be any questions about procedure." She gave Rocco a scathing glance.

"What about getting inside that chamber?" Mark asked. "I had hoped to be present for when we break inside for the first time."

"There's plenty of time," Laura reasoned. "The place has been there for a few thousand years already. I'm sure a few extra days won't make much difference."

"True, although we need to get as much accomplished before the rainy season," Mark said. "And we only have four months, remember?"

"How could I forget?"

26

Mark decided to leave the subject at that. There was way too much tension between Rocco and Laura—far more than a mere disagreement over whether to send some bones away for analysis would warrant. "Oh well, I guess we'll decide on a plan of action in the morning. I think I've made too many miles today to make any more decisions tonight."

"So, did you hear that Sam is getting married next week?" Rocco asked conversationally, referring to one of the local men they had hired on.

"No," Mark replied, taking a bite of the rather watery mashed potatoes that were on his plate.

"Apparently," Rocco nodded his head. "I guess he only had to promise two cows instead of the traditional three for the bride."

"You're kidding, right?" Laura asked.

Rocco just laughed, a wily grin appearing under his bushy moustache. "You know what they say about these local girls . . ."

"That is so racist and you know it," she objected with disgust.

"What about you, boss?" Rocco asked slyly. "Why don't you pick yourself one of the locals for a bride? With your reputation, you could probably get away with only one cow."

Mark tried to smile, not really enjoying Rocco's obvious sadistic pleasure in the turn of the conversation. "I'm not ready for marriage." He avoided Laura's gaze and concentrated instead on his meal.

"I don't know," Rocco said reflectively. "I always figured if I was to fall in love, it would just hit me. Smack!" he clapped his hands together. "Right between the eyes and I wouldn't know what happened."

"Trouble is, who in the world would return the sentiment?" Laura asked dryly.

"Hey, look at this face. Who wouldn't fall for this face?" Rocco argued. He looked from one to the other. "What? It could

27

happen."

"The idea of love at first sight is absolutely ridiculous," Laura stated. "It just doesn't happen. It's a myth."

Mark considered this for a moment. "I don't know about that," he mused. "Take my own folks. That's the way it happened for them, or so I'm told."

"Really?" Laura asked scornfully. "I could hardly believe it, with you for a son. You're about as romantic as the dead bones you like to study."

"Thanks," Mark said with a rueful grin.

"Speaking of dead bones," Rocco piped in.

"Oh, no you don't," Mark put up a hand. "Enough shop talk for tonight. I'm beat. I'm heading straight to bed."

Later that night, as Mark lay beside Laura on his narrow cot, he was surprised by his inability to sleep. He had been physically exhausted even before they'd made love, but now he was wide awake. He eased his arm out from under Laura's head, and carefully stood up. He was just pulling on his jeans when she stirred.

"I guess I should go back to my own tent," she mumbled, turning over. She didn't seem in any hurry. Everyone knew about their relationship, and even though things were a lot more casual out in the field, they still maintained their own quarters.

This change in the status of their relationship had only recently developed. They had been acquainted for a number of years. The archeological field was a fairly tight community, even worldwide. Laura came from Australia, but they had met first at a site in Arizona. It was a Navajo burial site—Mark's personal specialty. They remained connected through conferences and various other job related functions until Mark had requested Laura's expertise on a particular dig in South America. She had agreed and now this was the third job site that she had joined him on.

They'd been together so much in the past few years that it just seemed inevitable that their relationship take on a more personal nature. He just hoped she wouldn't read too much into it. Then again, this was Laura he was talking about. If anything, he should be more worried about his own sense of emotional attachment.

Mark sat down on the one folding chair and reached for the saxophone case that sat propped against the tent wall. He gently removed the instrument and fingered it fondly in the darkness.

"What you got there?" Laura asked, sitting up half way.

"Hmm?" Mark asked absently. "Oh. My saxophone."

"Oh. I didn't know you played a musical instrument."

There was a lot she didn't know, Mark brooded silently. "I don't really. At least not well. It belonged to my grandfather. Jack Burton." He checked to see if the name meant anything to her. Apparently not.

"I see. So you keep it around for sentimental reasons," Laura nodded.

"I guess. It's my one connection to home," Mark shrugged, carefully putting the instrument back in its case and shutting the lid with a click. "You mean you never heard of him?"

"Who?"

"My grandfather. Jack Burton. He used to be a pretty famous jazz musician in his day."

"I was never really into music much," she said. "He still alive?"

"Last I heard," he replied with a wistful smile. It struck Mark suddenly how very little they knew about one another outside the field. He looked over at the woman sitting on his cot, wearing nothing more than a sheet. "What's your take on marriage? Commitment?"

Laura blinked in surprise. "Whoa! Where did that come

from?"

Mark shrugged. "I'm not sure. Maybe thinking about Jack got me thinking about home which got me thinking about my folks . . ."

"Ah," Laura nodded, "The love at first sight pair."

"Yeah," Mark laughed, feeling somewhat bashful about his earlier comments.

"I can hardly believe they spawned the likes of you," she teased.

"Well they didn't, really. Deanie is my stepmother. My dad married her when I was about twelve. It was just he and I before that."

"What happened to your own mum?"

Mark shook his head. "I'm not quite sure. Apparently she took off when I was quite young. Never met her."

"Oh. I see," she said.

"What about your family?" Mark asked. "Any brothers and sisters?" He was amazed that they had never had this conversation before. What kind of a man expected sex, but didn't even know anything about the woman who shared his bed?

"Nope, just me," Laura said. "My mum and dad were quite a bit older when they had me, so I don't have any other known living relatives. Maybe a cousin in Sydney, but I've never really kept in touch. You?"

"I have one sister, Harmony. She's quite a bit younger than me, obviously. I used to have to do my share of babysitting—her and the other musicians' kids while they were out doing concerts."

"Concerts? What do you mean?"

"My step mother used to be in a band. I used to get stuck babysitting a lot while they were out rehearsing or performing."

"Interesting."

"I spent a lot of time with Jack in those years, too. My

grandpa. Well, he's my step grandfather, actually. We became very close, though." He paused, remembering the days that he had treasured with family and friends like they were a million years ago. Sometimes it felt like they were. He hadn't had much time for family recently. Too busy digging into the past . . .

"You're scaring me with all this sentimental bull," Laura stated.

"Sorry," Mark muttered, letting his eyes roam elsewhere.

"You're still worried about that missing bone," she said, more a statement that a question.

Mark latched on to the excuse gladly. "Shouldn't I be? It's not like Rocco to be so careless."

"I told you. Rocco's beginning to slip in more ways than one."

Mark thought about that for a moment. "What if it is some kind of conspiracy, like he says? What if someone is out to sabotage the site?"

"I really doubt that," Laura said, shaking her head. "Although I have heard some of the local workers talking about the dangers of tampering with the dead. Maybe someone is trying to scare us off for superstitious reasons."

"Hm. I hadn't considered that. But who? I can't work like that, worrying that someone is watching and waiting. I can't be suspicious of every local worker that I take my eyes off of."

"It's probably nothing," Laura assured. She rose from the cot, pulling the sheet around her like a toga and strolled around behind his chair. "You're way too tense," she said, massaging his shoulders with her hands. She bent over and kissed his neck suggestively.

Mark turned his head sideways and gave Laura a quick peck on the cheek, then disentangled himself from her hold as he rose from the chair. He wasn't in the mood for any more tonight. "What about the fact that that wing bone looks a lot like a Pterodactyl?

But it was found with human remains?"

Laura sighed, coming around to sit on the chair herself as she reached for her errant clothing. "There's probably a very logical explanation for it," she said, pulling on her own jeans. "Whoever belongs to those human remains probably also had access to some dinosaur bones. They were probably used as part of their burial ritual and aren't contemporaneous. Dating will clear it all up, I'm sure."

"If we find those bones," Mark added.

"I thought you were going to supervise another excavation of one of the graves tomorrow?"

"I am, but not if I don't get some sleep," he said with an over exaggerated yawn.

Laura took the hint with discretion. "Right. I'd better get back to my own bed before dawn and get some sleep myself."

Mark flopped onto his cot after she'd gone and crossed his arms behind his head. Too many conflicting feelings were running around inside of him. Laura, Rocco, dinosaur bones . . . What was really happening here?

Chapter Three

At 6:00 am sharp, God turned the light bulb on. At least that's how it seemed. There were no drawn out dusky shades to the morning. Near the equator it was either night or it was day. Mark rose at his usual 5:45 and met Rocco shortly after he'd had his breakfast.

"Hey, boss. You're up and ready early, I see," Rocco commented.

"Absolutely. Your team ready to go? I'm anxious to get started. Show me where you uncovered those first set of bones."

Rocco led the way into the side of the crater that had been created beside the temple mound. Elaborate cross beams held the hill intact as they went deeper into the wide tunnel that led below. Legend had it that a mighty race of kings had been buried here, long before the ancients that had built the temple. It appeared that they might have found evidence to prove it was true.

The team had uncovered an elaborate system of tombs carved deep into the side of the mountain. The main tunnel had been blocked off by what appeared to be a mud slide. A thick layer of sediment had hardened over the entrance and it was only by chance that Mark and Rocco had noticed enough irregularity in the pattern of the swirling layers of rock to investigate further. Once this had been cut away, the tomb appeared to be part of a natural cave, the height and breadth of which varied substantially from one part to the next. Branching off from this main artery were several smaller tunnels, only high enough to crawl through. These all led back to the main tunnel, but within each were carved shelves upon which human remains had been laid and then sealed with tightly fitting rock plugs. Rocco and his team had opened the first encasement while Mark was away. It's where they'd found the surprising contents.

Rocco led the way to the open grave. The remains hadn't been removed yet, and were lying in grim testament to a former life long since expended. Mark wasn't ready to make an estimate on the age of the find yet, but the skeleton was in surprisingly good shape, considering. He took note of the large frame—at least seven feet tall—and the strange headdress, which, as Laura had pointed out, was very fragile.

"You've taken all the measurements?" Mark asked.

"Naturally."

"Just checking," Mark said, noting Rocco's defensive tone of voice.

"And the wing bone? Where was it?"

"Here. Exactly," Rocco pointed. "You can still see the depression of the wing itself in the dust. I've taken all those measurements, too."

"Good," Mark said, peering more closely at the indentation the bone had made and the soft markings around it that implied more than just a bone had rested there. "Nothing seems to be disturbed. Like there hasn't been a breath of wind in here for millennia."

The rest of the crew was waiting quietly. There was a general hush, like the place was sacred and they were afraid to talk out loud. Mark felt it too. The place hadn't been visited for a long, long time.

"You ready to open the next one?" Mark asked.

"Ready when you are."

* * *

"I'm worried about Mark," Laura confided to another member of the crew over breakfast.

Anthony peered at Laura over the tops of his wire-rimmed glasses, his mouth full of toast. His slightly ruffled appearance belied the intellectual brain underneath the surface. Anthony Vanguard was the resident expert on legends of the Southwestern regions of Africa. He washed the toast down with some coffee before replying. "About what? Mark seems to be the same take charge guy we all know and love."

"Sure, around you guys, but I can tell he's under a lot of pressure."

"Of course he's under pressure," Anthony shrugged. "This is a pretty important dig we're on. Not to mention that we're stuck out in the middle of nowhere with a less than stable government wielding the power to shut us down."

"Last night he seemed all sentimental. Did you know he plays the saxophone?" she asked, as if that meant something.

"No," Anthony responded without concern, taking another bite of toast.

"Well, neither did I."

"So? The fact that you just found out he's a closet musician is no cause for alarm," Anthony reasoned.

"I know. That's nothing in and of itself," Laura tried to explain, "but it just goes to show that he's obviously got a lot on his mind. He's never been one for sentiment."

"And that's a bad thing?"

Laura gave an irritated sigh. "Oh, just forget it. You obviously wouldn't understand, being a man yourself."

"Okay, now I'm really confused. What does me being a man

35

have to do with anything?"

"Oh, you know. Pretending like you don't have any emotions and then broad siding a person with a whole lot of sentimental mumbo jumbo."

"I don't appreciate being lumped into any of your categories, thanks," Anthony announced. "It seems to me that you and Dr. Graham have some personal issues to work out."

"Maybe," Laura conceded.

"Well, count me out. I'm no shrink."

"No," Laura conceded. "But you are supposed to be an expert in your field. What about all that romantic crap you were spewing off the other day?"

"What?" Anthony asked.

"You know. You were quoting some ancient text or other, all about the prince finding his true love out in the orchard or something, and then she turned into a wolf."

"What has that to do with anything?" he asked again, bewildered.

"I don't know," Laura shrugged in exasperation. "Just that you obviously have some sentimental bones in your body, so maybe you might know why Mark is acting so strange."

"Love?" Anthony offered with raised brows.

Laura dismissed that with a wave. "The doctor? Please! I have more romantic bones in my little finger. And that's not saying much."

"True," he agreed.

Laura considered the revelation for a moment, her brow furrowed. "Ya think?" she asked, a look of concerned disbelief on her face. "Nah. I vote for stress."

Anthony nodded. "Me too."

* * *

The close quarters in the tunnel made it difficult for more than

36

a few people to work together at once. Rocco, Mark, and another local man worked together to carefully unseal another tomb, chiseling away at the mortar around the stones used to block the opening.

"So tell me more about your theory. What do you think we've actually discovered here?" Mark asked curiously.

"It's obvious," Rocco stated without hesitation. "Those wing bones are from a dinosaur.

"Pterodactyl, or some other type of large flying reptile."

"Well, for starters, dinosaurs died out long before humans," Mark countered.

"Maybe, maybe not." Rocco shrugged.

"What makes you say that?"

"I've been on digs before and seen things," Rocco replied. "Things that nobody wanted to face up to."

"Give me an example," Mark prodded.

"Okay. Like the time I was working on a dig in Texas. Found dinosaur tracks and human tracks in the same valley."

"I heard about that," Mark replied. "I thought it was established that the human tracks were a fraud. Somebody carved them."

"That's what they want people to think," Rocco explained. "And who knows, maybe some funny guy thought he'd sabotage the dig that way. Maybe it worked, too."

"And your point?"

"That was only one set of tracks. I saw others with my own eyes. I helped uncover and measure them," Rocco said with a glint in his eye. "But who is left to believe it except those of us who were there? Too many skeptics were just looking for a way to discredit the site."

"Okay, so that's one example," Mark conceded. "Certainly not proof enough on its own. There could be any number of explanations for that occurrence."

"Yeah? Like what?" Rocco challenged.

"Well . . . in any case, you can't build a case like that on one site alone."

"There are others. Lots of them."

"If that's the case, why aren't they documented?"

"They are," Rocco replied, "but nobody in the scientific community wants to touch them."

"I can see why," Mark said wryly.

"Which is exactly what happened the last time."

"What last time?" Mark asked.

"The time they found actual skeletal remains along with dinosaur remains."

"You mean human skeletal remains," Mark clarified.

"Of course. What'd ya think I meant?"

"Just being sure," Mark said dubiously.

"I've been doin' my research. Ever since the time in Texas, I've been keeping track. There are a lot more of these types of finds than you'll ever read about in a scientific journal." Rocco hesitated. "I can see you think I'm nuts. Loco in the head."

"Which is why we have to be so careful. So meticulous in our documentation," Mark replied pleasantly, with a grin.

"I'm no religious wing nut, you know," Rocco defended.

"Never said anything about religion," Mark shrugged.

"Most people do. The two seem to go hand in hand."

"I think this is loose enough to move, boss," Sam, their soft-spoken assistant cut into the conversation.

Mark waited anxiously as Rocco and Sam carefully lifted the last remaining block from its place. He directed the light beam from his hard hat into the chiseled alcove.

His breath caught in his throat. "Oh my God," he whispered.

"Pretty impressive wing span, eh?" Rocco commented with a

grin, joining him as they both knelt before the freshly opened tomb.

It was just how Laura and the others had described it. The human skeleton lay perfectly intact, horizontal with hands folded over the rig cage. It was a very tall specimen, Mark noted; even longer in length than the last had been, and perhaps even eight feet tall. Remnants of a headdress clung to the skull; perhaps bits of tanned leather, and a long, fragile armature that could have been a beak. Most impressive, though, were the set of wings, long since disintegrated to nothing more than the bones, that had been obviously folded over the body like a shroud. They would have covered the man, as large as he was, from chin to toes.

"I think we'll have to remove the remains in their entirety for analysis," Mark decided. "I think this is unusual enough to warrant opening more tombs as well. All of them if we have to, to get to the bottom of this."

"Boss, check this out," Rocco said, lifting a gold chain and pendant from the chest cavity with some long tweezers. He held the piece of jewelry up for examination. Though covered with dust, it was definitely gold.

Mark examined the pendant then looked into Rocco's eyes, which were shining with vindication. It looked like a perfectly fashioned flying reptile, wings outspread; beak open. "It doesn't prove anything," Mark cautioned. "We'll wait for the analysis."

"You'll send these away?" Rocco asked.

"Not till after I've examined them thoroughly myself," Mark assured, "and not until I have another set locked away somewhere for safe keeping. I'm not letting anything else get out of my sight."

Rocco agreed with a nod.

"And Rocco," Mark added, "just for security sake, you know, in case this does turn out to be something . . . unexpected . . . let's not sound any alarm bells. I want everything perfectly and precisely documented, without any questions until we know for sure. Get it?"

"Gotcha," Rocco nodded.

Mark had time later to examine the bones carefully himself. They were hollow, like a typical bird's, but had the distinctly elongated fourth finger of a flying reptile. They were also very large, with an estimated wingspan of twenty feet, although in comparison to the human, "large" was a relative term. Maybe things just grew big back in those days. As to the age of the find, that was still a mystery. So far no other artifacts lined up with any other known eras in human civilization. He was anxious to do his own set of dating tests on the bones themselves.

"I hear you're opening up the entire burial site, wholesale," Laura said as she sauntered to Mark's work station.

"I think, considering the unique quality of what we've been finding so far, it would be pure negligence not to," Mark offered as explanation.

"The Zimbabwean government might not see it that way," Laura noted. "Part of the agreement was to keep disturbance of the original temple to a minimum."

"I'm well aware of our agreement," Mark stated, "and so far have complied. We're digging under the temple, not through it."

"But the agreement also states that graves must not be unduly tampered with beyond what is reasonable for finding out—"

Mark cut her off. "I know what the agreement states. Under the circumstances, I feel I am doing only what is reasonable," He sighed then noticed the worried look on Laura's face. "Look," he said, standing, "this could be the biggest find in the history of modern archeology. What if those are Pterodactyl bones? The people of Northern Zimbabwe have a long-standing oral tradition that includes reptilian like flying creatures. Legends also abound of gods coming to earth in the form of giant birds. What if they didn't die out with the rest of the dinosaurs? What if some dinosaurs did survive to coexist with men? I mean, think about it. Every culture has legends about giant reptiles, dragons, and such. What if there's some truth to it? Most legend has at least a small basis of truth to it somewhere. We'd never have discovered the ancient city of Troy without believing the legend first."

"Sounds like you're trying to convince yourself," Laura said skeptically.

"What if the lab results come back and verify Rocco's claims? What if they are Pterodactyl bones?"

"Rocco!" Laura fairly spat. "The man is a lunatic. If not for him and his crazy ideas, nobody would have even considered anything of the kind."

"So what's the problem?" Mark asked reasonably. "The lab results should clearly show that. Nothing to worry about. Once those bones are sent, it's out of our hands anyway."

Laura looked nervous. "So why bother opening more tombs? We've got all the evidence we need."

"All the evidence you need, you mean," Mark stated. "But not near enough evidence to satisfy this cowboy." He turned back to his work, clearly closing the subject. With an exasperated sigh, Laura left the lab.

Chapter Four

Several more tombs were opened, revealing a distinct pattern. Each grave housed a very large human specimen with the same "wing bones" and headdress carefully placed with the body. A few other pieces of gold ornamentation were also found, usually depicting a winged creature of sorts, either in flight or standing at attention.

Progress had also been made at unblocking the entrance to the inner chamber. It appeared as if an earthquake or some other natural disaster had blocked the entrance itself. Several members of the team had been working diligently around the site with brushes and baggies, lest they find any tidbits worth bringing to the surface. The day finally arrived when they were ready to break the final seal to the entrance and investigate the inner room itself.

A reverent hush enveloped the crew as the last stone was carefully removed. Laura, Rocco, and Anthony stood ready as, with careful movements, Mark stepped over the portal and shone his lantern into the depths of the room. Gasps were heard all around as they entered the chamber.

"Look at the walls," someone breathed. The walls themselves seemed to give off an eerie glow, similar to the florescence of white walls under black light, only green in hue. Elaborate paintings covered every surface, the images seeming to jump forward spatially. It was certainly not the primitive cave paintings they had expected.

"What's making it glow like that?" Anthony asked.

"Must be the metallic alloy we found traces of earlier," Laura suggested. "I was never able to identify it."

Mark touched the wall tentatively, not wanting to cause damage, but unable to stop himself. It was indeed plaster, applied masterfully to create a remarkably smooth surface. When he removed his hand, traces of the green glow had transferred to his fingers.

"I knew it," Rocco said under his breath.

They all turned to examine the story depicted on the wall. A monarch of sorts, clearly wearing royal attire and sitting on a throne, was presiding over a throng of ordinary subjects. Startling, however, were the numerous guards surrounding this kingly figure. Humanoids with massive wings outstretched and long, pointed beaks.

"Kingly guards," Anthony stated. "Just like we suspected."

Other parts of the mural showed Pterodactyl like creatures flying through the air, while others were shown being sacrificed on elaborate altars.

"So these creatures, whatever they are, were part of an important religious ritual," Laura noted factually. "Obviously symbolic as well. There's still no proof about what they were."

"I'd say the artist's rendition is pretty clear," Rocco said cryptically.

They turned to another wall.

"Our lanterns seem to be activating this illuminating effect," Mark noted. He pointed to some ceramic jars placed along the perimeter of the room. "What do you suppose these are?" he asked no one in particular.

"Boss, check this one out," Rocco said, embarrassed amusement clearly evident in his voice. Mark and the others turned to look at the opposite wall. Anthony whistled. It was a graphic depiction of grotesque winged creatures having sexual intercourse with human women. The whole scene was presided over by another Pterodactyl-like creature.

The room itself was not that large, only about ten feet square. In the far wall, covered by more of the glowing plaster, were the clear signs of another door. "The king himself?" Mark asked.

"Probably," Laura agreed. "We'll need a specialty team to open the door without damaging the plaster."

"What do you make of it, Anthony?" Mark asked.

"It clearly supports the local stories of a mighty race of kings that inhabited the area. Notice the ornamentation and signs of superiority. And the guards . . . Well, I think we've seen evidence enough that they were more than just legendary."

"And the flying creatures. What do you make of them?" Mark wanted to know.

"Clearly reptilian," Anthony mused. "You know, doc, I'm not so sure that Rocco's so off base on that one. Of course, legend abounds, especially to the north, about Pterodactyl like creatures living in the Jiunda Swamps. Kongamoto, they're called. Locals have reported sightings as recently as a hundred years ago."

Laura let out a scoffing grunt. Anthony continued, unphased. "Now this one here has some interesting possibilities." He pointed to the last depiction. "There are numerous accounts from various cultures all over the world of god-like beings coming to earth and copulating with humans. It's often a way that ancient cultures justified a certain line of rulers. If the king descended from the gods, ordinary folks were afraid to question him. It's interesting that this particular one also includes the strong reptilian bird imagery that is so prevalent."

45

"Seems logical, given the reverence and symbolism the creatures seem to evoke," Mark commented.

"True," Anthony agreed.

"Well, we'd better get busy gathering our stats," Mark said. "I want detailed photos from every possible angle. I also want another sample of that plaster, as well as the pigment, for further analysis. And one of these ceramic containers. We'll want a crew down here as soon as possible to open that next door."

"I'm on it, boss," Rocco offered, already heading out into the narrow passageway that led to the surface.

"Laura, you'll look after the photos?"

"Of course. Don't I always?" she asked somewhat petulantly.

"Good. I have a couple of ideas I want to check out."

Mark did have something to check on—a hunch, really. The ceramic jars that had been placed around the perimeter of the antechamber brought back some vague recollections of something similar he'd seen in a museum somewhere. It took some time to locate the information on the Internet, but, sure enough, it was there. Several years back, similar ceramic jars had been found in an ancient Mesopotamian site. Encased in the jar was a smaller copper cylinder suspended within its mouth. Inserted into the length of the cylinder was a length of iron ore. Apparently, when grape juice was added to the jar, an electric current was generated.

The jars recovered from this site were similar in design, although more sophisticated in appearance. Perhaps they were a power source to help illuminate the chamber. Imagine! Early electric lamps!

Now he just needed to find out what was in that plaster to make it glow. He'd already sent a sample, along with some other bones and artifacts, to a personal friend and colleague who worked in New Mexico. John would know what to do with them.

For some reason, however, Mark decided to keep that little bit of insurance a secret.

Chapter Five

"Here's something that you might find interesting," Anthony was saying. A group of workers was sitting under the shade of one of the tent flaps, taking a break from the African heat. "I've catalogued over 250 stories from every continent about gods coming down to earth and sleeping with our women. Seems they don't make them as good looking in the 'ether' world. Either that, or the gods are always horny."

There was a round of ribald laughter. Besides the expert on folklore and legend, Anthony considered himself the resident entertainer. "Hey, doc," he called, as Mark walked by. "Did you know I even found just such a reference in the Bible?"

"Huh? What's that?" Mark asked, stopping. He'd been on his way to talk to Laura and hadn't been listening.

"In the Bible. A story about gods getting it on with our women."

"Really. I don't recall anything like that," Mark replied.

"Sure. It's in Genesis. 'The sons of God had relations with the daughters of men', or something like that. Started a whole race of giants, who were apparently very evil, since after that God sent Noah's flood and killed them all. Part of His judgment on the earth, I guess."

Mark nodded absently. "Interesting."

Anthony continued on with another story as Mark moved on. He found Laura sitting in front of her computer. "I was wondering if you'd made any progress with the photos," he said.

"Oh, yes. Fine. It's coming along fine." She closed the email she was composing, and looked up with an unnatural smile.

"Well, it's just that I was looking for them in our photo folder and I didn't see anything. I thought you were making some hard copies as well."

"I am. I just haven't gotten to it yet," Laura said lightly. "They should be there. I downloaded them myself."

"Well, they aren't there," Mark repeated, more irritably.

"Are you sure?"

Mark gave her a murderous look. "Check for yourself."

Laura brought up the photo folder on her screen. "That's funny. They were here yesterday."

"Look what else is missing," Mark continued. All of the photos of the wing bones had been deleted. "Somebody is sabotaging our data," Mark ground out.

"Are you accusing me?" Laura asked haughtily.

"I haven't ruled anyone out."

"I may not agree with Rocco's assessments of those bones," Laura said. "In fact, I admit that I'm a little uncomfortable with the way this whole dig is progressing. But I'm a professional anthropologist. I don't go around sabotaging sites."

"Then who is?" Mark asked blackly.

"I don't know. Maybe it's just a computer glitch. They probably got put somewhere else and we'll find them later. In any case, I'll go down and take more pictures immediately, if it'll make you feel better."

"Don't bother. I'll do it myself," Mark said. "But from now on I want everything, I mean every scrap of information, to personally pass my inspection. I intend to email every single dash and comma to a secure location." He strode from the room.

Earlier that day he had confronted another crew member about the bone analysis. He'd called the lab in Harare, and apparently they had sent the information back almost two weeks ago. They would have to check their files for a copy and get back to him. No one on site remembered receiving the registered package. Not even Laura. She suggested that it got lost in the mail. After all, this was Africa.

It could happen, he supposed, but too many such slips were starting to arouse his suspicions. He didn't like the feeling. He felt as if he was looking over his shoulder at all times, like he couldn't trust anybody any more. He had already started compiling notes and evidence on the side that he was emailing to himself, as well as to his friend John Bergman at the university in New Mexico.

He sat down at his work station with a heavy sigh and flipped open his laptop. Good. There was a message from John now.

'Analysis complete on those bone samples. One of the most perfect examples of a Pteranodon I've seen. Probably dates to the late Cretaceous period about 65 million years ago. Like to know where you found him. As to the human sample, we did Carbon dating only, since you sent no other reference info. It is definitely male and appears to be about 40,000 years old, give or take a few thousand. As to Carbon dating the Pterodactyloid, we were not able to get an accurate reading. The sample was contaminated and was giving a much younger reading than is possible. Analysis also came back on the metallic alloy samples you sent. Although, I'm not a specialist in geochemistry, it is apparently a very unique combination of copper and tungsten. All the official specs are being sent 'as we speak', both by web and hard copy via registered mail. Just thought you'd be interested in a sneak peek. JB.'

Mark let the contents of the message sink in. It was confirmed then. The strange bones were Pterodactyl. As to their age, Mark had to laugh. Naturally, the scientists at the lab wouldn't have accepted their findings as accurate. Dinosaur bones couldn't be dated contemporaneously with human remains. It was unthinkable, even when the evidence was staring them right in the face. Wait until he proved that the two sets of bones had been found together —placed there on purpose. But he realized from the opposition that he'd been facing on site, as well as the easy disregard in his friend's email message, that he must be very careful about how the facts were presented.

As to the metal that was suspended in the plaster, Mark had some other theories that were developing. Tungsten was used in the filaments of electric light bulbs, while copper wire was the main conductor of electricity used in most modern appliances. What if the ceramic jars were small generators, like the ones found in Mesopotamia, and were used to actually power up the wall itself? It would be an astounding example of advanced technology never before seen from an ancient culture. Then again, nothing should surprise him about this dig anymore.

The real dilemma now was, how much should he share with Laura?

"You sent specimens to New Mexico?" Laura asked incredulously. She was definitely put out. "That seems a bit unorthodox. Besides, you need more than one signature to verify the location from which the specimens came. You can't just go sending off bone samples without anyone else knowing about it. No matter what your friend's conclusions, if you can't prove where you found them in the first place, his findings are useless."

"I'm getting the feeling that you're working against me, here, Laura," Mark stated. "What do you mean 'verify where I got them'? You were there! You saw them with your own eyes, placed along with the human remains. So were Rocco and Anthony, and I don't know how many others."

"Of course I'm not trying to deny that fact," Laura defended herself. "I was just pointing out that you didn't follow procedure, and therefore, if it came to it, your findings could be considered suspect. There might be plenty of people out there who would like nothing better than to sabotage this dig and make us all look like fools."

"So that's what you're worried about. Your own reputation."

"And yours."

"Thanks. I think I can look after myself in that department," Mark quipped curtly.

"I'm worried about you," Laura said quietly. "You're becoming almost—obsessive."

"You would be too, if every time you turn around something else went missing."

"Look, I already apologized for the photos and for the delay in getting the sample results. Although, neither one of those was my fault. What more do you want? A pound of flesh?"

"Of course not. Just forget it," Mark replied blackly. He really didn't know who to trust anymore.

The mental stress was starting to take its toll. Mark hadn't had a decent sleep in weeks. He lay awake now, unable to relax. He turned over on the narrow cot. He almost considered sneaking over to Laura's tent. They had never renewed their relationship in that way since their disagreement over opening more tombs. He wondered what she would say if he just showed up on her doorstep.

He thought better of it. Things were too complicated as it was, without making them worse. He thought again about the tests he'd been running in the lab with the ceramic generators. He was

51

anxious to try them out in the antechamber itself.

The whole camp was asleep as Mark emerged from his tent and looked around. The sky was inky black and clear. Stars twinkled boldly overhead as the moon shone at half mast. He used his pocket flashlight to illuminate the path to the lab where he retrieved some supplies, before heading to the mess tent. He was sure he'd find what he needed there.

He continued on toward the entrance to the tomb excavations, careful to listen for wild animals along the way. It felt eerie entering this home for the long dead alone and so late at night. Although it was pitch black inside, even during the day, there was something about the stillness of the night that sent a shiver up his spine.

Once well inside the cave, Mark switched on his head lamp. He passed by the various tunnels leading off to the resting places of the guards, and approached the entrance to the antechamber. Suddenly he heard a noise. He stopped dead in his tracks, listening intently. After a few seconds of silence he continued until he heard it again.

"Is someone down here?" he called.

Nothing. The noise had come from the antechamber itself. With measured movements, Mark snuck forward and peeked around the narrow entrance.

"Laura!"

"Mark! What are you doing down here! You nearly scared me half to death," Laura panted, hand over her heart.

"I guess I could be asking you the same question." He emerged fully into the glowing interior of the chamber.

"I couldn't sleep," Laura replied. "I thought I'd come down and take those pictures we lost. A peace offering," she added.

Mark looked around, but didn't see any camera. As if reading his thoughts, she pointed to the backpack resting on the floor.

"Camera's still in my pack. I was just admiring the artistry when I heard something. I must say, you pretty much had me freaked there for a second. I thought I was in a bad horror film."

"That thought also crossed my mind," Mark admitted.

"And what are you doing down here at this time of night?" she asked. "The boss needs to get his sleep so that he can be alert for all the crises that happen in a day."

"Couldn't sleep either," Mark stated. "Come over here for a second." She complied and joined him where he was extracting some items from his own backpack.

"Wine?" Laura asked in surprise. "Planning on having a romantic dinner party?"

"Closest thing I could find to grape juice," Mark replied. "I've been working on this theory, see? Based on some artifacts found in the Fertile Crescent. The theory goes, the ancient Babylonians were able to construct these simple generators made out of iron ore and copper and 'fueled' them with nothing more than simple grape juice."

"Really? Fascinating."

"Now, my hypothesis goes something like this," Mark continued. "We have here several examples of potential generators —ceramic jars that also contain iron ore and copper filaments. Thus, we have our power source. Now, also note that the plaster in the walls contain a delicately balanced mixture of copper and tungsten."

"You figured it out?" Laura asked.

Mark simply continued with his discourse, lecture style. "Potential 'light bulbs', if you will. Witness that the jars are all connected to the wall by this small, almost imperceptible, copper wire protruding from the base of the jar and imbedded in the plaster itself. 'Plugged in'. Now, when I fire up the generator…" He carefully poured the wine into one of the ceramic containers.

The wall nearest to the jar began to glow a brilliant fluorescent green. "It works," was all Mark said, amazed.

"You're a genius," Laura cried. "But why were the walls glowing slightly to begin with?"

"I haven't figured that out yet. Maybe just some residual effects. Maybe the electricity coming off our gear, or even our bodies. It does appear that the elements used in the plaster are very sensitive to any energy source. Certainly different technology than anything else I've ever encountered."

They stood back, looking at the mural for several minutes.

"You gonna drink that?" Laura asked suddenly, pointing at the half empty bottle of wine.

"Huh?"

"Well, it just seems like a waste now that it's open," she reasoned.

Mark shrugged and handed her the bottle. She took a long swallow, then handed it back to him, wiping her mouth on her shirt sleeve. "Not bad," she commented looking around. "Nice atmosphere too. Although the company's not very talkative."

He smiled and followed her lead. The wine was warm, but full-bodied with the taste of ripe, juicy grapes. They sat down on the floor, sharing the rest of the wine in silence as they surveyed the glowing room.

"You know," Laura said, "I do realize that I need to apologize for all the stress I've caused. I've been meaning to bring it up for days, but I'm rather proud, you know."

"I know," Mark agreed, but cracked a smile.

"I mean, the screw up with the lab results and then the photos. I don't blame you for thinking the worst. You just need to know that none of it happened intentionally. And if I've been a little uptight, well . . . it's only natural. When you see someone you care about being put under so much pressure . . . " her words trailed off as she placed her hand on Mark's thigh.

"I guess we've all been under a bit of pressure."

"I know. We need to relax, I think. Let off some steam." She was rubbing his leg now, coming dangerously close to his privates. "I've missed you," she breathed, leaning forward for a kiss.

Mark felt his libido surge in response. It had been awhile.

"I think it would be exciting to make love here, in this place," Laura was saying.

Mark was about to acquiesce, shifting to a more comfortable position. His eye caught a glimpse of the grotesque demonoids, swooping in the act of possession over the helpless women. He froze.

"I don't know," he said, disengaging himself and standing. He couldn't look at the picture again. "It's getting pretty late. We'd better get some sleep."

Laura's face had turned hard. "Suit yourself," she said tightly. She grabbed her bag and led the way from the chamber. It only took Mark a minute to gather his things and catch up.

"About those photos," he said, coming up behind her. She stopped in her tracks, but didn't turn around. "Don't worry yourself about it. I came and took plenty earlier on today."

Chapter Six

It was the moment they had all been straining toward. The inner chamber had been opened to reveal an elaborately carved casket.

"Careful," Mark cautioned with a grunt, as it took four of them to lift the heavy lid and slide it off to one side. He frowned. The container seemed to be full of charcoal.

"A common method of preservation," Laura commented.

"I know," Mark snapped.

"Just anxious to get to the king, himself, eh?" Rocco laughed.

"Okay. Well, let's get this packing swept away. I want every bit of it bagged and sent to the surface for analysis," Mark ordered.

"No staying clean on this dig," Anthony commented. It was true. The crew had emerged from the excavation over the last few weeks like coal miners from a pit.

With surgical precision, the charcoal packing was gently swept away into storage containers, until enough was removed to allow the unveiling of the corpse itself. In slow motion, the fragile shroud was lifted.

Gasps and "ahs" echoed throughout the chamber. Before them lay not just a skeleton, but a perfectly preserved human specimen. His skin, which was of an olive complexion, still appeared pliable, with only some slight recession around the mouth where a hint of gleaming teeth could be seen. His hair was intact, seemingly still attached to the scalp. It was a handsome face, probably no more than thirty years of age. He was also enormous in proportions.

"The Nephilim," Anthony breathed.

"What?" Rocco asked.

"A race of giants," he explained. "Born of the union between gods and men."

"I wonder what embalming technique was used," Laura wondered. "The preservation is remarkable."

"We could make millions selling it as an anti-aging cream," Rocco laughed.

"The layers of charcoal and clay are probably a factor," Mark noted. "We'll have to make a careful analysis above ground. Let's get some preliminaries first. Rocco, Anthony, let's remove a little more of this shroud. See if the king here, has a crown."

They gently lifted back more of the shroud. All eyes widened at the treasure beneath. This was no crown of gold and jewels. Tucked along the top of the casket, lying on its side, was a ceremonial headdress similar to the remnants found with the guards. However, this specimen was perfectly preserved. Dark leather, pointed skull, gleaming eyes, long, sharp beak . . . a textbook Pterodactyl.

"What've you got to say now, doc?" Rocco directed at Laura with satisfaction. She remained speechless.

"There's no denying it now," Mark stated. "Flying dinosaurs didn't all die out."

"Just like the legends say," Anthony offered with a whistle.

"Once we get all the evidence together, this could be the biggest discovery of the century," Mark said reverently, still in awe himself at the magnitude of what they'd just uncovered.

"As long as you get the evidence together," Rocco cautioned.

"Don't worry," Mark said. "I've been taking precautions, especially since our little conversation the other day, Laura. Everything is absolutely well documented and in order. Nobody could possibly deny the findings we've made here."

Rocco grunted.

Mark continued, "Besides, there are enough eye witnesses to verify the findings even if every shred of evidence was lost, although that's not going to happen, I assure you. I won't let it."

"I'll get some photos," Laura finally spoke, opening the camera case. Mark gave her an intense stare, before giving her the nod. "Don't worry," she added icily. "I won't let anything happen to them this time."

"Good," Mark stated in a business like tone. "Now, we all better get to work gathering our stats. I want this entire casket removed to a safe location as soon as possible."

The "king" was wearing a suit of leather armor, and clutched a scepter of bronze that had intricately carved images of various animals on it. Included with the lion, boar, and elephant was the now familiar Pterodactyl. Rocco whistled as he and Anthony took some measurements. "Big sucker. Must have eaten his Wheaties."

Anthony agreed, "Yeah, that's for sure. Here's our proof of that legendary race of giants."

"There are probably basketball players just as tall," Laura noted.

"True," Anthony conceded, "but the average height has increased over time, not the other way around. For this time period, these men would have been considered giants."

"We haven't established a time period yet," Laura pointed out. She seemed intent on being argumentative.

"What did you call them again?" Rocco asked Anthony.

"Nephilim," he replied.

"I don't recall hearing that reference before," Mark mused. He thought he had read up on all the Nbedele legends that might have a bearing on the dig.

"Oh, it's not from this area," Anthony explained. "It's a Biblical reference."

That surprised Mark even more. "Really. Fill me in."

"'And the sons of God saw the daughters of men that they were fair; and they took them wives of all which they chose. There were giants in the earth in those days; and also after that, when the sons of God came in unto the daughters of men, and they bare children to them, and the same became mighty men which were of old.' Some manuscripts say 'Nephilim' instead of 'giants'," he added.

"How do you do that?" Rocco interrupted.

"What?" Anthony asked.

"Repeat it like that. Like you were saying it word for word."

Anthony just shrugged. "Photographic memory. Anyway, the story goes on. People became very wicked in the sight of God. And it was at that point—"

"That he sent the flood," Mark finished for him.

"Exactly," Anthony verified with a grin. "I'm proud of you, doc. You must've attended Sunday School after all."

"A few times," Mark agreed dryly, but he smiled nonetheless.

"So it all comes back to a fairy tale about gods coming down to earth to have sex with the local women," Laura said with disgust. "That's the best you can do?"

"Hey, don't shoot the messenger," Anthony said defensively. "I'm just telling the story."

"As enjoyable as your story was, we need to get to the facts," Laura stated. "Who were these people and where did they come from?"

"I think the pictures on the walls speak plainly enough about what they believed," Anthony said.

"Or what a few powerful people wanted them to believe," Laura countered.

"Now, that's true," Anthony conceded. "I think we all realize that those in power have to have some kind of hold over their subjects. Being a descendant of the gods would be a good way to keep your opponents in check."

"I think there is more to it than that," Laura said. "Notice how the power is in the hands of the males, which only goes to show that males have consistently felt the need to prove their dominance over females, especially sexually. It's a basic insecurity built into the male gender."

"Now, them's fightin' words," Rocco laughed.

Laura continued, "However, they have overlooked the fact that females have always had the real power—they've historically been able to make men do whatever they want simply by enticing them with sex. Men just don't have control of themselves in that department, so they've had to make up stories with themselves portrayed as super human in both strength and power."

"Better watch yourself," Rocco cautioned with a grin. "Any of that true, boss?"

Mark just shrugged. He, for one, wasn't going to be manipulated by any female's games.

"What you say has some truth to it," Anthony admitted. "Women have been the downfall of many great men. Napoleon and Josephine, Samson and Delilah."

"Did I say that?" Laura asked. "It seems to me the real downfall was in the weakness of the men themselves. The women were just proving the point."

"Give up. You can't win," Rocco advised Anthony.

"No, no. I agree with much of what Laura is saying," Anthony said. "But to get back to the legend. There might be a connection between the Biblical account and what we have here."

61

Laura rolled her eyes before taking another picture. "You think that this race is the real thing. Descended from gods who came down and raped the women of the area. Please. This is even more ridiculous than dinosaurs and humans coexisting."

"Which proved to be true," Rocco pointed out.

Laura ignored him. "If we were worried about our credibility before, this is sure to take the cake."

"Now, you're not listening!" Anthony complained. "I never said I believe that actual gods came down. Maybe it was a race from a different place—another part of the globe with different technology—that seemed god-like. Certainly these are not typical proportions for any human beings."

"There are other African tribes that are unusually tall," Laura said logically.

"But not in this area. The legends all clearly point to a race of men from 'elsewhere'."

"I think you put too much weight on your legends."

"Most legends, although usually embellished, have some basis in fact."

"So I've heard."

"This is one site where we actually have more than just the legend," Anthony pointed out. "We have actual specimens that point to a race of giants, however they were 'begotten'. We also have the very unique location of the burial caves. Not only were they far underground, but, if you recall, we had to dig through a layer of sediment and fossilized material which suggests a catastrophic flood of some kind."

"That's right," Mark nodded.

"Pre-Noah. Get it?" Anthony said with a grin.

Laura rolled her eyes. "Now I've heard everything."

"These tombs were buried and preserved by some such natural disaster," Anthony explained. "You can't deny that."

"He's right," Mark agreed.

"Yeah," Rocco added. "We dug through and catalogued it just like that. 'Catastrophic flooding'.."

"Now, I'm not saying it had to be Noah's flood," Anthony quickly raised a hand before Laura could say anything else. "Or that such a world wide event even took place. But we have here evidence that clearly follows the Biblical legend: giants inhabited the land before the flood."

"I'm getting tired of this three ring circus," Laura said. "I'm surrounded by people who are supposed to be scientists—experts in their field! And all I keep hearing is fairy tales."

"But wait! There's more," Anthony said enthusiastically.

"Oh joy," Laura replied dryly.

"There are also Biblical accounts of dinosaurs roaming the earth. Most scholars think that the story of Job takes place chronologically before that of Noah. It's in this account that we find references to dinosaur like creatures—the Behemoth and Leviathon, to name two. For those interpreting the Bible in a literal fashion, this makes sense, since God created everything. It stands to reason that he also created dinosaurs."

"I see where you're going with this," Rocco said. "If this cave dates back to pre-flood days, then the presence of Pterodactyl bones would be nothing strange."

"You've got it!" Anthony enthused. "Even if there was a world wide disaster, miraculously, evidence got preserved in these caves. This could be the greatest find in history. It could prove much of the Biblical mythology as true."

"You sound like you're already convinced," Laura noted skeptically. "Next you'll be asking for an altar call. 'Repent! Then send that donation!'" she said mockingly.

Mark winced. Her words were cutting a little too close to home.

"Just think about it," Anthony continued, undaunted. "There has been a lot of research done already and some very interesting finds have been documented. For instance, several archeologists have sighted an ark-like structure in the Middle East, right where the Bible says it was grounded."

"I've heard about that," Rocco verified.

"This could be the missing evidence that would blow the whole thing wide open," Anthony said.

"Mark, what kind of operation are you running here?" Laura interrupted.

"It seems to me like Anthony's just offering another possible angle," Mark shrugged. "I don't think there's any need to be so defensive. Right, Anthony?"

Anthony agreed, "Right. Geez, Laura. Lighten up a bit. It was just a thought. An idea that I came up with. You know me, always ready to delve into one more good folk tale."

"Stick to your story books, Anthony," Laura advised. "Leave the science to somebody that knows it."

"You about done with your photos?" Mark asked Laura, changing the subject. She nodded. "Good. We'll take more detailed shots after we take him up to the lab."

"You gonna do the testing yourself?" Rocco wanted to know.

"You bet," Mark affirmed.

"You know we don't have the best equipment here on site," Laura mentioned. "You'll have to send him out for proper analysis."

"I know that, but he's not going anywhere without me," Mark said.

"You're going to leave the dig?" Rocco asked.

"Only temporarily," Mark assured them all. "I think this is one of the most important finds so far and I don't want anything to happen to it. We've still got plenty of work to finish up here, though. I'll be back once our king is safely analyzed and stored. Rocco, we better get some men down here to get this casket up to the surface."

"Right, boss," Rocco said, turning to leave.

Mark turned to Laura, "Laura, you'll have to start on the curatorial end of things. We've got lots of documentation to do."

"I know my own job," Laura cut in testily.

Mark considered her remark for a moment, and then motioned with his head for her to join him at a distance. Anthony was occupied examining the king's scepter, but Mark spoke in a hushed voice nonetheless. "Please don't let your personal biases get in the way."

"What? And what is that supposed to mean?"

"I'm more than just a bit concerned about the tension on site these past few weeks."

"And it's all my fault?" she asked haughtily.

"I never said that," Mark clarified. "Maybe it's no one's fault in particular, but there does seem to be some bad blood between you and a couple of other key people."

"Oh. The boys club?" Laura snapped. "Seems to me Rocco and Anthony have all the answers. I guess you don't need me anymore."

"See? That's exactly what I'm talking about. You're so defensive these days. What happened? You never used to be that way," Mark noted.

"And you never used to be the way you've been acting either," Laura countered. "If Rocco and Anthony were women, I'd be jealous."

"Is that what this is about? You and me?" Mark asked. "Look Laura, I know we haven't been, you know, seeing everything eye to eye lately, but we need to put our personal lives aside for a moment and pull together as a team."

"How nice. Just 'put your personal life to the side.' I'm glad to see our relationship means that much to you."

"Laura, listen," Mark tried to mollify her. "You know what I meant by that. This is important, for both of us. It could be the biggest discovery of our careers."

"Or make us laughing stocks," Laura commented.

"In any case, I expect you to work closely with Anthony," Mark said reasonably. "It doesn't matter what you believe or don't believe. We aren't making any suppositions about the origins of these people just yet, but I do think it is important to include all the possible links to past legends. Biblical or otherwise."

"Naturally," Laura agreed with a pout. "I do know my own job."

"What's all the whispering about?" Anthony asked.

"None of your business," Laura said sweetly.

"Ah. Lover's quarrel," he said knowingly.

Laura was about to make another remark when she stopped suddenly, listening. "What was that?" she asked.

"What?" both Mark and Anthony asked, looking around.

Laura held up her hand for quiet and they all listened again. They all heard it this time— a distinct rumbling.

Just then, a crew of four men arrived with moving harnesses.

"Did you hear anything on your way in?" Mark queried.

"I heard some rumbling noises, but nothing else," one of the men offered.

"The tunnel looks okay though? No sign of a cave in?" Mark asked.

All the men nodded.

"Where's Rocco?" Mark asked.

"Don't know," another man answered. "He sent us down ahead. Said he'd be coming in a few minutes."

"Well, let's get this thing loaded. I don't like those sounds,"

Mark ordered.

The crew skillfully loaded the now closed casket, and balanced it between them on shoulder harnesses as they edged toward the chamber entrance leading into the main tunnel. Suddenly, sediment sprayed down from the ceiling as the earth emitted another distant groan.

"Anthony, Laura, you go on ahead," Mark barked. "Let's see if we can get this thing out into the main tunnel," he said to the moving crew as he helped them with their load.

"Leave it behind," Laura advised. "I think we're in for a cave in!"

"No! I'm not leaving it behind. Now get going," Mark fairly bellered. He was answered by another tremor and more rocks.

Laura and Anthony scurried ahead, out of sight, as the crew moved as quickly as possible with their precarious load. Another large rock tumbled from above, hitting one of the men squarely on the head. He let out an exclamation of pain and surprise as he momentarily lost his balance. The casket swayed on the shoulder harnesses. The shear weight of it caused another man to bump against the tunnel wall.

"Steady!" Mark yelped. "Ron, let me take over that harness."

But it was too late. The heavy treasury landed with a crunching thud on one corner, crushing the man's foot beneath. He let out an agonized cry. "My foot!"

"Take it easy, Ron," Mark said, jumping forward. "Steve, help me get his harness off. Ron, take some deep breaths."

They worked quickly to take the harness off the injured man. There was another rumble, only this time closer. Another barrage of rocks and pebbles rained down. Mark shielded Ron with his back, then continued with the last buckle.

"We'd better hurry," Mark commented. He was strapping on the harness. "Now on my signal, lift."

67

Ron let out a gasping groan as the men hoisted the heavy burden off his shattered appendage. They shuffled their way a few feet down the tunnel and carefully set the cargo down.

"Looks like we might have to leave the casket behind," someone commented.

"I know. I hate to do it, but . . . " Mark was interrupted by another spray of sand and sediment. "Come on. We'd better hurry."

Ron was helped to his one good foot and assisted on either side by two of his colleagues. They limped as quickly as possible down the tunnel.

"I hate to leave you behind," Mark said to the casket as he and the other crew member followed. "But I'll be back."

They hurried as fast as they were able down the tunnel toward the entrance. Here and there fallen debris made their passage more difficult. At one point, Ron had to be lifted through an opening while the others had to crawl on hands and knees. Mark noticed several beams that had been used for bracing, leaning drunkenly or fallen all together.

They could see the natural light at the entrance now, and strained even more urgently toward the goal. Mark was the last to emerge, just as another rumbling crash could be heard, filling the tunnel completely just yards behind them. He looked back and covered his face with his t-shirt as billows of dust clouded the entrance. All of the men were covered from head to toe in grey, powdered earth.

"Mark! You're alright!" Laura cried, running forward to embrace him. "Thank God! I was worried there for a few minutes."

"Only a few minutes?" he asked with a relieved grin. He turned to shout some orders, disentangling himself from her embrace. "Get a stretcher! Ron's been hurt."

"What happened?" she asked with concern.

"His foot got trapped under the casket. Might be broken. He'll

68

be alright though."

"Thank God that's the extent of it. You could've been killed! You scared me half to death. I told you to leave it behind, but I thought you just might be stubborn enough to try and get it out with you."

"I probably would have too, if Ron hadn't gotten hurt," Mark said. "Maybe that was a blessing in disguise."

"I'll say," Laura agreed.

He barked some more orders as people began scurrying to Ron's assistance. Others gathered to see what was going on. "Just a cave in," he called, trying to sound unconcerned. "Let's move away from the entrance, everybody. Give them some room. Ron's going to be alright. Come on, back to camp. We'll start in first thing tomorrow and dig our way back in."

"Are you serious?" Laura asked. "After that you'd risk going back in? It might not be safe."

Mark continued to wave the onlookers back to the main camp. He took Laura's arm and maneuvered her in that direction also. "I'm not just going to leave it there," he said firmly.

"But it might be too dangerous," Laura persisted as they walked. "You have to think of the lives of your crew. One dead king isn't worth the life of a living crew member."

"No one else is going to get hurt. I'll make sure of it—triple the safety factor on the bracing, if necessary. Obviously, it wasn't done properly in the first place. Should've been made to withstand unexpected seismic activity. I'll have to speak to Joey about it."

"You mean, speak to Rocco," Laura supplied.

"Rocco? That's not his department," Mark said, puzzled.

Laura just shrugged. "I'm pretty sure I overheard him telling Joey that he would handle it."

"That explains it, then," Mark said angrily. "He had no business. I have experts in place for that job. Joey is an engineer, for goodness sake. Somebody could have been seriously injured or worse, down there. I'll have to speak to them both about it. It seems like there have been way too many glitches on this job."

"Could be a bad omen," Laura suggested. "Maybe you shouldn't go back in."

Mark looked at her with disbelief. "That coming from the least superstitious person on the crew? What happened to all your scoffing at Anthony's legends? Don't tell me you've become a believer?"

Laura laughed, "Hardly. But as you say, there have been a lot of problems arise since we first discovered those bones."

"I'm not giving up," Mark stated emphatically. "I don't care how long it takes. We're getting that casket out of there."

"What if the money dries up?" Laura asked. "You know how sponsors can be. Enthusiastic one day, off the next. If there are too many delays, they just might lose interest."

Mark shrugged. "Then we'll find another sponsor. I'll finance it myself if I have to."

"You got a few hundred thousand tucked away somewhere you haven't been telling me about?"

"I'll do whatever. Mortgage all my assets, take out a loan. Whatever it takes. Besides, it's not going to come to that. This is big. Once they see what we're dealing with, we won't be going anywhere."

"How much has the government seen so far?" Laura asked.

"Enough," Mark hedged.

"Meaning?"

"I've kept them informed. They've seen the photos and my weekly reports. I admit, I've laid low on the Pterodactyl thing. Taking your advice and not trying to scare anybody off until we had solid proof."

"Probably wise," Laura agreed.

"Once we show them the photos you took today, there should be no question about continued support." Mark stopped and looked at Laura. She had become suddenly silent and there was a pinched look of apprehension on her face. "Laura? What? What is it?" He waited, not wanting to believe what he already knew. He felt himself beginning to shake with anger. In a tightly controlled voice he managed to bite out, "The camera. Where's the camera."

"You don't have it?" Laura asked weakly.

"No! Of course I don't have it! You were the one taking the bloody pictures!" he cursed again loudly. "How could you do this? We need those pictures! It could be weeks before we dig through to the casket. How could you?!"

"I don't know!" Laura defended herself hotly. "I guess I thought you were looking after it. You did say you wanted to make sure everything was in order, remember?"

"But you're the one who's supposed to take the pictures. You brought the camera in, you take it out!"

"Stop yelling at me!" Laura yelled herself. "People are staring."

"I don't give a damn! I need those photos!"

"Well, sorry for being human," Laura spat sarcastically. "In all the confusion, with the cave in and everything, I guess it got left behind."

"The cave in? There was no cave in when we left the chamber!" Mark said accusingly.

"Oh, so now you're implying that I left it on purpose, is that it?" Laura fumed.

"I just can't believe you would be so negligent," Mark countered.

"Negligent? Me? Who's the one talking about risking the lives of the crew? You're more concerned about 'your' big find than about anyone else around here."

Mark could've gladly throttled her. He was about to make another scathing remark, but he thought better of it. He clamped his mouth into a tight line, and strode away in the direction of his own quarters.

Maybe this dig was cursed.

Mark stayed in his tent alone until darkness fell like a curtain over the African mountain. He knew he had things to do. He should be checking on Ron, confronting Rocco, talking to Joey . . . apologizing to Laura. But for some reason, he couldn't force himself to face any of them. He wanted to go to bed and wake up the next morning and find that it had all been a dream, that they had gotten the casket up to the surface safely. He should be on his way to New Mexico the day after tomorrow, accompanied by the most astounding archeological find imaginable.

Instead, he was sitting here. Alone. In a dark and dusty tent with no one to talk to, while a whole crowd of people waited outside for his next order.

He wondered what his next move should be. Of course, he wasn't even going to consider leaving the casket and its precious contents behind. They had to re-dig that tunnel. There was just too much valuable evidence lost down there not to. He had some slight misgivings about the safety factor, despite what he'd said to Laura. There were risks involved, but he had to remain confident. The less of a big deal that was made about it the better, not only for the psyche of the crew, but also to keep any government officials off his back. He didn't need Laura's reminders about the tenuous agreement they had with the Zimbabwean government. He needed to keep a low profile, get back in, and get out before his permit to excavate got yanked.

Confronting Rocco was going to be another thing. He was a trusted colleague and a good friend. Out in the field, Rocco was one of the most knowledgeable and practical people he knew. He knew his stuff, and had a good rapport with the other crew members. He was able to maintain productivity without dampening their enthusiasm for discovery. But he also had the humility to know when something was out of his league. Mark just couldn't believe that Rocco would have been so careless as to go over his head and take care of the bracing himself. Or that Joey had let him. Getting the facts sorted out tomorrow was not something he was looking forward to.

Mark sighed and glanced around the darkening room. His eyes rested on the saxophone case. He wondered what advice his grandfather, Jack, would give. Jack was never one to give up. He was the very embodiment of tenacity. Mark didn't relish the thought of having to dig back into the tombs, once again. But he knew he would do it. There was no other choice.

He went over to the battered instrument case and picked it up. He clicked it open and gently lifted the saxophone from its crushed velvet bed. Attaching the reed, he put the mouthpiece tentatively to his lips, but didn't blow into it. He closed his eyes and fingered the pads in a silent song from the past, one that Jack had taught him long ago. Someday, when he had the privacy of more than just canvas walls, he would attempt to play in earnest. For now, he must be content with the memory of the song as it played in his head.

There was a "knock" on the outer flap of his tent. There was no hiding, Mark realized. If he didn't take matters into hand, matters would come to him. "Yep," he called gruffly.

It was Anthony. He bent to step through the inner door flap, letting it fall behind him as he straightened. "Sorry. Hope I'm not interrupting." He gestured at the saxophone still sitting on Mark's lap.

"Oh, no. That's alright," Mark said, nestling the sax back into its case where it sat on the floor.

"I didn't know you played the sax," Anthony commented. "The way sound travels around here, it's funny I never heard it before."

"I don't play, really," Mark admitted. "Only in my dreams. The sax belonged to my Grandfather. Sometimes, I just like to hold it. Helps me think."

"Hmm. And I guess you've got plenty to think about right now," Anthony commented.

"Yeah. You could say that."

"That's a real bummer about the cave in."

"No doubt."

"Rocco's going to be in some pretty deep kaka, I would imagine."

"Who told you that?" Mark asked. He didn't like the fact that people were already talking, but he supposed he shouldn't have expected anything else.

Anthony looked surprised. "It's common knowledge. I must admit, I had doubts about letting Rocco take charge of the refit in the first place. But I figured you were the boss, so you must have had your reasons."

"I never gave Rocco any such instructions," Mark stated emphatically. "Safety and engineering are Joey's portfolio. Why would I change that?"

Anthony shrugged. "Beats me. Sorry, man. I just assumed . . ."

"I need to get to the bottom of this, once and for all," Mark said abruptly, standing.

"Um, hey, if you've got a minute . . . " Anthony interrupted before Mark could leave. Mark turned sharply, looking at Anthony impatiently as he continued. "Well, that is, I came here to talk to you about something else. That is, I mean, I can see you've got other important things to look after, so it can probably wait."

Mark let out a pent up breath. He could see that Anthony was clearly agitated and had come expressly to get whatever it was off his mind. What did it matter if a little gossip continued to fly for another half hour? The damage was already done.

"Probably not a good idea for me to confront anybody right now," Mark acquiesced. "I might do something I might regret. Come in and sit down. Get what ever it is off your chest. I'm listening."

Anthony seated himself on the one folding chair while Mark lowered himself onto his cot. "Okay," Anthony began hesitantly. "It's about what we were talking about earlier, in the chamber before the cave in."

"We talked about a lot of things. I'm afraid you'll need to be more specific."

"Right. Well, about the legends surrounding the site, and how they seem to line up with our findings. More specifically, the Biblical ones—about the Nephilim and the Flood and that." He stopped, waiting for a comment from Mark. When Mark gave none, he continued. "See, it's like this. I've been doing a lot of reading. Researching all the angles. Obviously, that's my job. It's what I do. I've studies hundreds, possibly thousands, of manuscripts from every culture and country. But there's something about this particular story, this Bible account. It's different, somehow, but I can't quite put my finger on it. It's far fetched— way out there—yet I find myself wanting it to be true. Almost believing that it is. And then the evidence we've found—it's almost too much. Not to mention all the weirdness. Techno glitches, cave-ins, artifacts gone missing . . . like we aren't supposed to tamper with it. Like the whole site is cursed, or something. It has me feeling spooked."

"What do you mean by artifacts gone missing?" Mark asked, picking up on that point.

"You know. That first set of Pterodactyl wing bones. Then no results came back, records went missing . . ."

"Why did you say 'set'? That first site contained only one wing. There was no 'pair'. It's what made the subsequent tombs so important. We were able to verify a 'set' of wings had been placed around the bodies."

"Yeah, there were two wings in the first one."

"How can that be? I saw the photos from that first excavation. There was only one, badly damaged and incomplete. And Laura and Rocco clearly stated that, that there only was one specimen." His stomach was beginning to clench spasmodically. Were Rocco and Laura in on this together? And others?

Anthony shrugged. "Hey man, I know what I saw. I was there during the initial opening of that tomb. The first one was damaged —a cave in, I guess. But we definitely dusted two wing fragments. The indentations made by the bones were right there after we removed them. You must have noticed it yourself."

Mark thought for a moment. He recalled the stillness of the shallow tomb and the perfect indentation left in the sand of a large wing. It had filled him with awe, but there had only been one. The sand on the other side of the body had been perfectly smooth. Too smooth, perhaps. "You're sure?" he asked.

"Photographic memory, remember?" Anthony laughed, tapping his head. "Ask Rocco. He'll verify it. He and I were together."

Rocco. Again. Mark felt an uneasiness rising in the pit of his stomach. Rocco's name was connected with a few too many incidents for comfort.

"Anyway, about that legend thing," Anthony picked up where he left off. "I just needed to bounce it off someone. To talk about it out loud instead of play it over in my head. Kind of de-mystify, so to speak, so I could sleep tonight. Sounds kind of crazy, I know, but—"

"No. It's not so crazy," Mark said. "I must admit, I've been entertaining some of the same speculations myself."

"Yeah?"

"I mean, I've always been one to look at the evidence. Verifiable facts only. But some of what we've uncovered does not fit in well with what I've assumed to be true up until this point. There's the rub, for all of us. If we take the evidence before us, it means throwing out a whole lot of other evidence that we've come to believe as fact. The new evidence doesn't fit into the old framework. The two simply don't mesh."

"So what do we do about it?"

"Create a new framework," Mark suggested. "I just haven't figured out quite how to do that, yet. But I know for a fact that I can't deny what I've seen."

"Ditto," Anthony agreed.

"Which is why it's so important for us to get back down there and recover that body. It could be the key to the whole mystery."

"Or not. Maybe it's like I said, and we're not supposed to know the truth."

"Back to the curse thing?" Mark asked wryly.

"Precisely."

"I'm not willing to go that far yet. It's taken a leap of faith for me to accept that dinosaurs coexisted with man."

"Hmm. Rocco's been telling me some interesting things about that. I thought he was off his rocker at first, but now that I've seen it with my own eyes . . . I guess that's why it suddenly doesn't seem so far fetched to just jump in and believe the whole thing. The Bible thing, I mean. Noah's flood, everything. The works."

"I know a lot of people who believe every word of the Bible as the literal truth. They wouldn't be at all surprised by what we found here," Mark said.

"Oh yeah?" Anthony asked speculatively. He surveyed Mark

for a moment. "You another one of those prodigals?" he asked.

Mark's eyebrows shot up in surprise. "What do you mean?"

Anthony laughed self depreciatingly. "It's okay. Takes one to know one. I'm the son of a preacher man myself."

"No kidding," Mark said.

"Mmhm," Anthony replied. "The fire and brimstone variety. You?"

"My family are all believers," Mark admitted.

"But not you," Anthony stated.

"The prodigal son," Mark laughed dismissively. "You said it yourself."

"Why?" Anthony asked. "What happened that you don't believe the same way your family does?"

Mark shrugged. "I just don't know," he replied honestly. "I mean, I definitely saw a positive change when my own dad got 'saved', as they say. But it was like I was on the outside looking in. I just never really felt the need for that kind of thing, I guess. What about you?"

"Now mine's a real prodigal story," Anthony laughed. "I had to try extra hard to play the part of the bad boy so that the other kids wouldn't think I was a wimp. You don't know the pressure of being the preacher's kid. Everybody expects you to be perfect all the time. And then of course, I had to endure the double retribution of my father's shame. He kept warning me that I'd cross the line someday. I guess I believed him. We haven't spoken in eight years."

"Eight years," Mark repeated. "That's a long time. I haven't seen my family in three, but it's not because we aren't speaking." *It's because I've been too preoccupied with myself,* he added inwardly, but didn't say it out loud.

"Well, good to know I'm not alone in my waywardness," Anthony quipped. "I suppose I'd better head back to my own tent now. Think of a way to reconcile what I think this is all about and what people want to hear." He waved good-by and ducked out through the canvas flap.

Well put, Mark mused blackly. How did one present the facts in such a way as to not be lumped with a raving bunch of religious fanatics?

Chapter Seven

"I want round the clock digging to get at that casket," Mark informed in his most commanding tone. "That's got to be number one. And this time I want double the bracing under Joey's direction. You got that?" He held Rocco's gaze pointedly.

"That was a misunderstanding," Rocco defended. "I thought —"

"I don't want to hear your excuses," Mark clipped. "It cost us big time. Now we're under the gun. All I expect from you is to deliver. Get me that casket."

"Gotcha," Rocco nodded. Apparently he wasn't going to stick around for anymore. With a salute, he turned and scurried away. The rest of the crew followed.

Mark watched them for a moment before turning in the direction of the lab.

"Mark, wait a minute," Laura called. He stopped short in his tracks, waiting for her to catch up. "So, you're still going ahead with the dig?" she asked, almost accusatory.

"Of course. You don't think I'd leave a find like that buried, do you?" he countered. He didn't slow his strides. Laura was tall, but she still almost had to run to keep up.

"But the safety issues—"

He cut her off. "Taken care of. I'm still the boss out here, remember?"

"Of course," she said coldly. "I'm not questioning that. I just thought—"

He did it again. "Don't you have work to do? Cataloguing? Analyzing data? Something?"

She looked at him mutely, setting her mouth into a grim line. She turned and strode off in a different direction.

Mark sighed and ran a hand through his already unruly mass of dark curls. This was going to be one bad day.

"What's up with the boss?" Rocco asked Anthony a little later, as they were working together at the sight of the cave in. Every available able-bodied person, even resident experts on myths and legends, were enlisted for the task.

Anthony shrugged. "Beats me. He has a lot on his mind, I guess. I mean, you and I have the luxury of stating our minds, but he has to think about what the scientific community at large is going to say about what we've discovered here."

"If they ever find out," Rocco stated skeptically.

Anthony gave Rocco a sideways look. "What do you mean?"

"With all the goings on around here, I have my doubts about whether this dig will even make it to the media, let alone scientific journals."

"Yeah?"

Rocco nodded. "I've seen it before. Nobody wants to admit it when things don't fit neatly into their own preconceived theories."

"So you think there is a conspiracy? Somebody has been sabotaging the sight? Maybe even caused this cave in?" Anthony asked.

"Seems pretty obvious to me," Rocco said.

They worked silently for a time, grunting under the stress of using the shovels and their backs. Anthony stopped and leaned on his shovel, wiping his forehead with the sleeve of his shirt. "You a religious man?" he asked Rocco speculatively.

"I have my own beliefs," Rocco shrugged, still digging doggedly.

"Oh? Like what?"

"You're here to dig, not talk," Rocco said.

"Right." Anthony dug in to the mixture of sand and rocks with his own spade. "I was brought up in the church, myself," he offered conversationally.

"You don't say."

"Yep."

They dug for a few more minutes. "I'm Catholic," Rocco informed, deciding to pursue the conversation after all.

"You don't say," Anthony repeated Rocco's own words with a grin. "Well, I won't hold that against you. My dad was a Baptist preacher. Still is, I guess."

"What do you mean? You don't know?" Rocco asked, eyeing the other man suspiciously.

"We don't talk much," Anthony shrugged.

"That's too bad."

"What do you think about the worldwide flood?" Anthony asked, still digging. "You believe in it? Noah's ark and all that?"

"The more I see, the more it makes sense," Rocco replied with a grunt.

"Hm," Anthony nodded speculatively. "Me too."

* * *

Mark squeezed his eyes tight, resting his forehead against the coolness of the saxophone. What was he supposed to do? Leaving the site now was unthinkable! But . . .

Jack.

He had just received the email that morning. Jack Burton, jazz great, had passed away peacefully in his sleep. Jack Burton, his mentor, friend and confidant. Dead.

Mark drew in a shuddering breath, willing himself to get control. He had a job to do. The biggest discovery of his career—perhaps of all time, lay buried under a pile of rubble deep in an African cave. And time was not on his side. He couldn't afford to go gallivanting off, half way across the globe, to Winnipeg.

No, he would just have to take it on the chin—another one of life's left hooks—and carry on here. He rose from the rickety folding chair, stroking the gleaming metal instrument with gentle fingers before placing it reverently back in its carrying case.

"So?" Rocco asked Anthony at the dinner table later that night. "Your muscles stiff, or what?" He gave his colleague a slap across the back, which brought a brief spasm of coughing.

"Watch it, man! I was just about to swallow. You almost made me choke."

"Not used to real 'man' work, huh?" Rocco continued with a grin.

"Either of you two seen Mark?" Laura interrupted, coming up behind them with her own tray. Both men shook their heads. "That's funny. I haven't noticed him in the lab or out on the site all day." She sat down uninvited beside Anthony.

"Check his tent?" Anthony suggested.

"I did," she replied.

"Oh. Then I'm out of ideas," he shrugged. He winced slightly at the movement. "I think you're right, Rocco. My shoulders are feeling kinda stiff. Although, that crack about real man work . . ."

"A lot different that having your nose in a book, eh?" Rocco chuckled.

Anthony just nodded his acquiescence and took another mouthful of food.

Mark entered the mess tent. There was no line up anymore, so he was able to fill his plate quickly and walked over to join the group.

"There you are," Laura began. "I've been looking for you practically all afternoon."

Mark nodded an acknowledgement, but turned to Rocco instead. "You have another crew working the night shift?" he asked perfunctorily.

"As we speak," Rocco replied.

"Good. I want back in there in less than a week."

"It might take a little longer, considering the damage done to the bracing. But don't worry. Joey's on it this time. By the way, Joey says there was nothing wrong with the initial refit. Seismic activity of that nature would have caved almost any type of bracing," Rocco supplied, vindication gleaming in his dark eyes.

Mark looked down at his plate, his stomach suddenly rebelling at the thought of food. He speared a minute piece of meat and popped it in his mouth, moving it around thoughtfully, trying to swallow.

"So where have you been all day?" Laura asked, eyeing Mark speculatively.

"Here and there," he answered vaguely. "Why? You need something in particular?"

"There were a few inconsistencies in some of the lab work that came back from Harare," she explained. "Plus, I've made some progress on those photo comparisons from the antechamber. I thought you'd like to know."

Mark nodded. "I'll take a look as soon as I'm done here."

"I thought you were going to check on the progress at the excavation?" Rocco asked.

"Right," Mark said, nodding absently. He turned to Laura. "Actually, I'll take a look at that information you mentioned after I go down and check on the dig."

"Okay," she shrugged.

"I might even join the crew for a bit later, myself," Mark added. "Every bit of man power will help."

"You don't need to do that," Laura protested. "You've got work crews for that sort of thing. You need to be available in case something else comes up. Besides, you can't work day and night. You're going to wear yourself right into the ground."

"I can't expect my men to take a night shift without doing one myself," Mark reasoned. "Besides, the sooner we get that casket out of there the better for everyone."

There was a lull in the conversation. It was obvious from Mark's stiff tone and manner that he wouldn't be swayed one way or the other. The doctor had obviously made up his mind and there was no use trying to change it.

"Um . . . are you alright?" Laura finally asked. "Obviously, you're under a lot of stress, but I just wondered . . ." She trailed off.

"I'll be fine," he clipped.

"Say, did I tell you about the latest theory Rocco and I were discussing this afternoon?" Anthony piped up, hoping to lighten the mood.

Mark suddenly pushed his chair back from the table, his plate of food remaining almost untouched. "Let's have a look at that information right now," he said to Laura.

Anthony and Rocco exchanged a bewildered glance as Laura scurried after Mark's already retreating figure.

It took about half an hour for Mark to look over everything Laura had to show him. He rubbed his neck wearily as he clicked the laptop shut.

"Thanks," Laura offered. "I'm glad things aren't looking as bad as I feared. After so many problems, I was really beginning to think that this project was jinxed. I guess I over reacted to what I thought were more glitches in the lab reports."

"It's okay," Mark said. "Better safe than sorry."

Laura surveyed him for a moment. His sunken shoulders and glassy eyes made him appear a lot older than his thirty-three years. "You look beat," she observed. "You're not seriously going to go help dig, are you?"

"I most certainly am," he replied without hesitation.

"Mark, you're working yourself to the bone," she said. "You'd be a lot more useful to the entire operation if you got a good nights rest instead."

"I doubt that. Besides, I wouldn't be able to sleep anyway."

"Mark, what is it?" she asked. "And there's no use saying 'nothing'. I can tell there's something else bothering you. Is it some other news about the dig that you're not telling me? More issues with the government? Or another misplaced artifact?"

He took a deep breath and expended the air in a gust.

She narrowed her eyes, trying to figure out what was the matter. "Stubborn," she muttered.

His own eyebrows shot up in surprise. "What did you say?"

"You heard me. I said 'stubborn'. You. That's what you are. Trying to carry the whole weight of this dig on your own shoulders when you could share the load. This excavation is just as important to some of us too, you know. You're not the only one who feels the magnitude of what we've discovered here."

Mark considered that a moment. "It's not only the dig," he admitted finally.

"No? Then what else is it?"

Mark shut his eyes for a few seconds, squeezing tight, then expended another burst of carbon dioxide. "I got news today from home," he said.

"Oh? What news?" Laura asked tentatively.

"About my grandfather," Mark answered, finally deciding it was time to come out with it. "Jack Burton. Remember I told you about him a while back?"

"Yes," she nodded, waiting for more.

"He died," Mark stated flatly.

"Oh Mark! No wonder you've been so . . . so owly."

Mark shrugged, feeling a certain amount of release now that he had told someone. "My father emailed me this morning. He died peacefully, in his sleep. So that's a blessing."

"But it's still hard," Laura supplied.

Mark nodded.

"So, are you going out to the funeral?" she asked, always practical.

"Of course not," Mark said. "How can I? I couldn't leave the site now. Not at this critical time."

"Why not? You think we can't handle it?" she asked.

"Of course I don't think that," Mark denied. "But the cave in. The casket. The tight time frame we're under . . ."

"Exactly why you should go," Laura reasoned. "It'll be at least a week until they get back into that tunnel. In the mean time, you'll be roaming around like a caged lion making it difficult for the rest of us to do our jobs. You'd be better off to take that week and visit your family. Grieve with them."

Mark frowned. "You really think so?"

"Of course," she replied. "You'll get the closure you need and arrive back just in time to open the King's casket. After that we'll still have some time to finish everything up here, crate what we need to send, maybe even get an extension once the government sees what we're sitting on."

"Hm . . . you really think you can handle it?" he asked again uncertainly.

"Of course," she said confidently. "Trust us for a change.

You've got a great team assembled here." She paused. "Well, except maybe for Rocco. But other than that, you've just got to trust us. Trust me."

What she said was making sense. Maybe he did need some closure if he was ever going to be able to continue on this project without going crazy himself.

Chapter Eight

Mark glanced out the tiny port hole. Nothing but swirls of cottony whiteness could be seen far below. The jet flew too high above the earth for there to be any other sights in view. They were somewhere above the central plains of the North American continent by now. It had been a long and physically taxing trip from the dig, first by jeep, then Cesena 185, and finally jet, making several transfers along the way. It was quite a trek from the back country of Zimbabwe to Winnipeg, Canada.

It seemed like forever since he'd seen them last. How long was it anyway? Three years? It had been for his sister's graduation from High School. Harmony was almost twelve years younger than he was. In many ways he felt like he had been part of the parenting team, rather than just an older brother. It was hard to believe she was now twenty-one. It would be good to see her again—and the rest of his family.

Well, almost the rest. Jack wouldn't be there. The realization hit him again, in the gut like a punch when you hadn't tightened your muscles against it. Of course it was bound to happen one of these days. Jack was getting old. But for some reason Mark had always thought he'd get back one more time before . . .

"Excuse me, Dr. Graham," a pretty flight attendant with a

French accent interrupted Mark's thoughts. "The Captain has asked that all electronic devices be turned off. I will have to ask you to shut off your computer."

Mark blinked at her absently for a moment. "Oh, of course," he acquiesced as her words registered. He may have heard just such a request over the intercom only moments before, but he couldn't be sure. He had been lost in his own thoughts.

He scanned the screen of his laptop once more before shutting down, then clicked the lid shut with finality before zipping it into its carrying case. He sighed heavily. Jack Burton had been more than a grandfather. He had been his mentor and his friend.

The familiar monotone melody of the seat belt sign broke into his thoughts, and Mark concentrated on the changing view out the window as the airplane began its descent. They broke free from their cottony cocoon and were suddenly thrust into a clear expanse of blue sky. The curvature of the earth stretched out beyond the horizon of flattened landscape; a patchwork quilt of brown and gold and green pocked frequently with small, irregular marshes and ponds that spoiled the precise grid of man's claim to the land. On the table flatness of the prairie he could already see in the distance the heart of the province of Manitoba, its capital city of Winnipeg. The downtown core rose like a multifaceted steeple among the sprawling parish of suburbia. At its core, the city was sliced by the meeting of two mighty rivers, the Red and the Assiniboine. The forks of these two water highways had been the centre of commerce during the early days of the fur trade, the birthplace of a revolution, and afterwards, the seed of a province.

He felt bone weary as he joined the other passengers in the tunnel leading out of the plane. The travel home had been long and arduous, and the emotional stress that he was sure to face already had him feeling drained.

As he walked through the gates from International arrivals, he scanned the crowd for the familiar faces of his family. Then he spotted them. His father, Russ Graham, an older version of himself, stood beside two red-haired women. When they made eye contact, his sister Harmony and his stepmother Deanie both came rushing forward.

"Mark! Oh, Mark, you look terrific! So tanned!" Deanie burst out, squeezing the daylights out of him. "Look, honey! Isn't he tanned?" she directed at her husband. "It must be all that hot African sun." Harmony joined in for her share of hugs and the two women chattered excitedly for a few more minutes while Mark's father, Russ, held back.

Finally, Mark was able to extract himself from their embraces and turned with an outstretched hand to his father. "Dad."

"It's good to see you, son." Father and son shook hands firmly, before Russ pulled Mark into a quick embrace, slapping him on the back. There had been a day when he wouldn't have showed such a public display of affection. His wife had been working for over twenty years to free him from that reserve.

His parents hadn't changed all that much in the past three years, Mark noted. Russ Graham had aged slightly, adding a little more grey at the temples to his dark hair. He still kept it closely cropped in an effort to keep the unruly curls in order. Mark's hair had the same propensity, but Mark usually didn't have time to worry about such things, and at present his hair was rather bushy, curling over his collar. Both men had dark and intense blue eyes, well-chiseled features, and solid builds. There was no mistaking the resemblance, except for the quarter century difference in their ages.

His stepmother, Deanie, looked almost as young as ever. She was almost fifteen years younger than her husband, but even regardless of that fact, she looked younger than the early forties that she was. People often mistook her and Harmony for sisters, rather than mother and daughter. "I'm so glad you came, Mark," Deanie was saying as they gathered his baggage and headed for the exit. "Jack will be pleased, I think, looking down from heaven. It's such a comfort to know that he's gone on to be with the Lord."

"That it is," Russ agreed.

"I mean, when I think of how he used to be so skeptical about spiritual things, it's so awesome to know that he came to know Jesus before he passed on." Deanie smiled.

Mark felt a familiar tightening in his chest. Naturally. His family couldn't pass up an opportunity to talk religion. He had kind of forgotten how much it irritated him sometimes.

Deanie continued, "I guess we have your mother to thank for that, Russ. She just wouldn't give up on Jack. He didn't stand a chance!" Even though she was Jack Burton's daughter, she had always called him by his first name. It was something Mark was also used to. That's just the way it was in this family. His father's mother was "grandma" or "mother" depending on who was addressing her, but Jack had always just been Jack, even to his own daughter.

"Grandma Graham can be stubborn," Harmony commented.

"Probably as stubborn as Jack ever was," Russ agreed with a fond grin.

"You're a fine one to talk!" Deanie laughed, giving her husband a playful nudge. "If I recall, you wrote the book on stubborn. You're as immovable as they come."

"Hardly," Russ scoffed. "I married you, didn't I?" He slipped an arm around Deanie's still slim waist and she leaned into him. It was obvious they were still very much in love, even after twenty years of marriage.

"You've got to be stubborn in order to survive in this family," Mark cut in lightly. "And Harmony, here, got a double dose from both sides of the family."

"Thanks," she shot back. "Nice to have you back in the country, big brother. And when were you leaving again?" she asked with sarcastic humor. They continued the good-natured banter as they reached Russ's sedan and piled in.

The warmth of the summer sun beat down on the heads of the mourners, as they gathered to pay their last respects to friend, father, and grandfather, Jack Burton. Mark scanned the graveside as the minister pronounced the benediction. There were more people here than he would have imagined, including some people from the press. Jack had more friends and followers than Mark had realized. He was once again struck by the simple humility of the man that was also known as one of Winnipeg's favorite sons. He would be sorely missed.

The minister talked about Jack's faith in Christ at the church service. It was surprisingly upbeat, considering that someone had just died. A musical tribute was played by the surviving members of Jack's band, and several other friends and dignitaries gave short testimonies about Jack's life and character. Mark's own father, Russ, read the eulogy. He could tell that it was difficult for him, but Russ was a man of stalwart disposition, and carried it through despite the eruptions of tears coming from Deanie and Harmony. Now they stood huddled together at the graveside, along with Jack's closest friends.

They continued that way for several more minutes as the general mourners began to disperse. "Goodbye daddy," Deanie said softly, blowing a kiss toward the lonely coffin. She'd never called him that. Russ's arm encircled her shoulders a little more tightly.

The intensity was almost too much for Mark. He let out a pent up breath and stepped back for a little more air.

"Mark," someone addressed him, hand out stretched. "So good to see you. I didn't get a chance to say 'hi' earlier. It's been awhile, eh?" Brent Walters pumped his hand vigorously. Mark was glad for the friendly diversion.

"Good to see you, Brent. How are Holly and the kids?"

"Great, just fine," Brent responded. "Around somewhere," he waved vaguely. Mark caught a glimpse of Brent's wife, Holly, hugging Deanie.

Brent and Deanie went back a long ways. Brent was the son of Jack's best friend and fellow band member, Benny Walters. He and Deanie had grown up on the road together, more like siblings than anything else. They had quite a history, both good and bad. Mark had been awe struck by Brent in the early days when he had led a rough looking rock and roll band. Twenty years later, Brent no longer looked like the Bohemian, longhaired artist. He was a regular looking middle-aged man with trim, graying hair and a moustache. The rest of the band had pretty much gone their separate ways, but Deanie and Brent had remained connected, partly due to their long history, but mostly due to their mutual faith in Christ.

Apparently, there was a time when Mark's father, Russ, had been jealous of Brent's friendship with Deanie. But Brent's conversion to Christ had been a factor in bringing both Russ and Deanie to the Lord, as they put it. The two men had become solid friends since.

"Here's Bryan, now," Brent said, waving his son over. Mark was surprised at the difference in the young man that stood before him. Last time he'd seen Bryan, he was a gangly teenager with a cracked voice. Now he was a young man of about eighteen, who was filling out in muscle and stature, and who addressed him in a decidedly mature tone. Certainly not the same kid whose diaper he'd had to change on occasion!

"I didn't see your dad around," Mark commented to Brent.

"Nope. He passed on about two years ago. Cancer," Brent

informed.

"Sorry to hear it," Mark said with genuine sympathy. "He and Grandpa Jack made quite a team."

Brent laughed. "Kind of like Oscar and Felix," he noted.

"Who?" Bryan asked.

"The odd couple," Brent explained. "Oh, never mind. You're too young. In any case, there's only Toby and Mike left of the old group."

Mark nodded. The aging musicians had played their tribute at the service, and had been gathered with the family at the grave. They still stood talking with Russ and the others, Toby Rantt's white head starkly contrasting against his leathery black skin, while Mike Colinsky's gangly height stood out above the rest of the group.

Mark saw his sister in the tight embrace of another young woman as they rocked back and forth for a few minutes. When they stepped back from one another, he was surprised to recognize Brent's daughter Amy. If he thought that Bryan had changed, he was shocked at the transformation in the older sister as well.

Last time he'd seen them was at Harmony's graduation three years earlier. He had flown in especially for the occasion from an archeological site that he'd been working on in New Mexico. In fact, the job had led to a profitable career connection with one of the universities there. In any case, he had only been able to spare a couple of days, and what with the necessity of spending the majority of the time with his immediate family, he'd had little more than a quick reacquaintance with the Walters and company. What he remembered was a small, unremarkable adolescent—a shy girl who was somewhat underdeveloped and had dirty blonde hair. She was only one year younger than his sister, but at the time she was still the annoying little girl whom he'd had to read the same story to over and over again in order for her to go to sleep.

What he was presented with now was a very pretty young woman, still petite, but certainly not underdeveloped. Her blonde hair was piled loosely on her head in an attractive style, and she wore just enough makeup to enhance the green of her eyes without covering the sprinkling of freckles across her nose.

"Mark, you remember Amy?" Harmony said, slipping her arm through the crook of Mark's elbow.

"How could I forget?" Mark smiled at Amy. "Still enjoying 'The Little Train That Could'?"

"What?" Amy asked, looking puzzled.

"If I recall correctly, you made me read it to you at least 100 times before agreeing to go to sleep," Mark replied.

"Part of the science I was developing to punish my parents for leaving me with a babysitter," Amy replied.

"More like punishment for the poor babysitter," Mark said with an amused grin.

"Excuse me," Russ interrupted the exchange. "A few people are going up to the house. I wonder if you and Harmony could catch a ride over with Brent and meet people as they arrive? He said he wouldn't mind squeezing you in. I think Deanie would like to spend a few more minutes here alone."

Mark looked around. More and more people were leaving the cemetery. A few of their closer friends and family were gathering at Russ and Deanie's home afterwards. Mark nodded his agreement. "No problem."

Mark, Harmony, and Amy walked across the grass to the tree-lined driveway where Brent's car was parked. Brent, Holly, and Bryan sat in the front, with Holly in the middle, while the other three squeezed into the back seat. Harmony sat in the middle between Mark and Amy.

"So I hear you've been in Africa this last while," Brent said conversationally.

"That's right."

"It must be fascinating," Holly observed. "What exactly is it that you're working on?"

Mark went into a simplified explanation of the temple site in Zimbabwe and the layers of burial sites that had been hidden underneath. Although normally not verbose, archeology was one topic that Mark had no trouble talking about.

"Mark's always liked rocks and old pottery better than people," Harmony teased when she got a chance.

They arrived at the Graham house just minutes before the first visitors. Deanie had arranged for a caterer to provide refreshments, so all Mark and Harmony had to do was act as host and hostess.

Mark's Uncle Ken and Aunt Kathy arrived first. They had escorted Ken and Russ's mother, Dorothy Graham, to the funeral, but due to the elderly woman's mobility, they had not gone to the cemetery. Mark allowed Harmony to open the house while he helped his uncle get his grandmother out of the car. They proceeded along the sidewalk and up the wide front steps at a snail's pace.

"You were always such a good and helpful boy," Grandma Graham noted. She was panting once inside the house, quite out of breath.

"A long way to come for a dead man," Ken commented to Mark with a grunt.

"Ken! That was rather unfeeling, don't you think?" Kathy scolded.

"What was that?" Dorothy asked. "I can't hear out of my right ear."

"It was nothing, Gran," Mark assured her. Mark could see that his Aunt and Uncle hadn't changed much since last time he'd been home. Still bickering and complaining. There had been a time when the whole family thought they would change. It was true, they had both gotten help with their alcohol problems, but AA hadn't been able to fix the negativity and bitterness that still seemed to define their lives together. It was a wonder they bothered to stick it out, especially now that their two children were well away on their own. Perhaps for some people the familiar, no matter how unpleasant, was preferable to the unknown.

"So what are Sam and Greg up to these days?" Mark asked conversationally once they'd gotten Grandma settled in a comfortable chair.

"What's that?" Dorothy asked loudly.

"I was just asking Uncle Ken and Aunt Kathy what Sam and Greg are up to," Mark repeated, loud enough for her to hear.

"Oh, I'm still praying for your cousins," Dorothy responded.

Ken rolled his eyes. Kathy piped up, "Samantha lives in Brandon now. She moved there last year and is doing quite well in real estate. I'm sure she would have come to the funeral if she wasn't so busy all the time," she excused.

"Finally left that stiff of a husband," Ken added. "About time, too. The guy was no good."

Mark found it ironic that the same thing had often been said about Ken, himself. Sometimes it was hard to see the log in your own eye.

"No need to bring that up," Kathy chided her husband. "Sam is doing very well these days. She's got the children in a very nice daycare. They're benefiting so much from the extra socialization."

"Learning how to swear, cheat, and steal," Ken muttered. "I couldn't wait for them to go home last time they came for a visit. At least now we don't end up babysitting them all the time like before."

"There you go again!"

"What's Greg doing?" Mark interrupted before his aunt and uncle could fan the argument into a full-fledged fight.

"Who?" Dorothy asked, straining to be part of the conversation.

"Greg," Mark said loudly.

"Greg's doing very well in the oil patch," Kathy said proudly.

"So you think," Ken muttered, taking a sip of his coffee.

"He moved out to Alberta a couple of years ago," Kathy explained. "Of course, we don't hear from him very often. You know how young men are about calling home."

"I don't know about that," Ken mused, looking at Mark. "Mark, here, flies half way around the world to attend a funeral. Bet he calls his folks a little more often too."

"I haven't been home much these last few years either," Mark laughed, trying to deflect some of the attention off of himself. The last thing he needed was to have his relatives start an argument over comparisons between their own children and himself. He'd been down that road enough times as a child. As he recalled, his cousins had always caused their parents their fair share of grief. They had been irresponsible and ungrateful, even then, and apparently things hadn't changed.

Harmony was greeting more people at the door and Mark used it as a way to excuse himself. "I'll talk to you a bit later, Gran," he said into his grandmother's ear before departing.

Several people that Mark recognized from his parents church had arrived. Toby Rantt, the drummer from Jack's jazz ensemble, had arrived with his wife, children, and grandchildren. They had all been close with Jack Burton over the years. Mark shook hands with various people and made some small talk as he made the rounds with the ever-increasing number of guests.

Finally, his father and Deanie arrived. Deanie didn't appear to be in any shape to play hostess, and Harmony was engaged in conversation with one of the younger members of the Rantt clan. With a sigh, Mark went to see if his grandmother needed anything.

His time for grieving would come later. For now, he needed to be strong for the rest of them.

He sat quietly beside his grandmother for a few minutes watching the rest of the people chat. She reached over and grasped his hand with a surprisingly strong grip. Her skin was very soft and fragile feeling; paper thin and loose on the knotted chords beneath.

"Did she tell you about how your grandpa came to accept the Lord Jesus?" Dorothy asked. Mark didn't respond right away, and she went on. "I'd been witnessing to Jack for years. Ever since his heart attack, oh, twenty years ago, at least."

Mark remembered the time well. He had just gotten close to Jack, and felt like he had finally found someone who really understood him. Then Jack had suffered a heart attack and Mark thought that he would never see him again. He'd cried many nights into his pillow when no body else was around. Jack had eventually recovered, although a much weaker man, and he and Mark had renewed their relationship. It had made Mark appreciate him even more, knowing that he'd almost lost him.

"Stubborn man, though, he was," Dorothy mused, "he'd always just laughed and started in on one of his own stories, as if he hadn't really heard what I had to say." Mark smiled. He could see Jack doing just that. "Then, about six months ago, he startled me with a question. 'Dorothy,' he said, 'where do you think a man goes when he dies?' It was an open invitation for me to share the gospel once again, just as I had done before. But this time he really listened. He never said anything, which was unusual for your Grandpa Jack, as you well know. He just listened like so," she demonstrated by cocking her head to one side. "He must have known something; that his time was coming soon. He never said any more to me about it. Probably didn't want to hear me say I told you so. But he told Deanie just a week before he died that he had accepted Jesus as his Savior. My, what a blessing for her to hear those words, once he passed on. Just died in his sleep, real peaceful like. It's a good way to die, I think. In your sleep."

Mark was more affected by the short discourse than he was willing to admit. Once again he sensed a growing uneasiness. It was fine to talk about God and Jesus in relation to any one else. For most of his family it was the way they defined themselves. But Jack . . . he had been such an independent thinker . . . such a free spirit. To know that he had put his faith in something so illogical was unsettling somehow.

Mark excused himself and went out onto the back deck for a breath of fresh air. There were a few other people out enjoying the late afternoon sun, conversing in small groups of two or three.

Mark leaned against the railing and surveyed the rooftops of the neighborhood. This was the home of his boyhood. He used to know every family by name for blocks around when he'd had his paper route. Now he doubted that there were any familiar faces left. People had moved in and out in the last twenty-five odd years. His own parents had remained one of the few constants.

"Hi," a female said, joining him. He looked down to see Amy Walters, at least a head shorter than himself. She looked soft and feminine. Laura was tall and athletic, hard and tanned from working in the African sun. He felt embarrassed that his mind had made the comparison, unbidden.

"Hi, yourself," Mark replied with a friendly smile. He turned back to stare at the rooftops once again.

"I know you were probably much closer to Jack than I ever was," Amy began. "I mean, he was your grandpa, not mine. But sometimes I felt like he was my grandpa too. He and my real grandpa were so close."

"You probably saw more of him in these last years than I did," Mark said. "And he wasn't really my grandfather. Not by blood, anyway. But he was one special guy. I'll miss him."

"Me too," Amy agreed.

They were silent for a few moments before Mark picked up the conversation again. "So tell me, Amy. What do you do now that you're all grown up?"

"Nothing as exciting as the infamous Dr. Mark Graham," she laughed.

Mark scoffed, "Hardly."

"Oh, I don't know about that. Harmony's got a whole scrap book of articles about you and your discoveries."

"Really? From where?" Mark was genuinely surprised that his work had gained that much notoriety.

"Science journals, 'Archeologist Today', or something," Amy shrugged. "Pretty impressive for someone so relatively young."

"The operative word is 'relatively'," Mark laughed. "Compared to someone your age, I'm pretty ancient."

Amy just shrugged again.

"So you still didn't tell me what you're doing these days," Mark prodded.

"I just finished my second year of nursing," Amy said.

"Following in your mother's footsteps," Mark nodded. "Makes sense."

"I guess it's what people expected," Amy answered.

"You don't sound all together pleased," he noted.

"I don't know," Amy said. "I mean, I'm not musical like my dad. Harmony and I used to pretend that some day we'd start our own band when we got old enough. Kind of like our parents and our grandparents. Carry on the family tradition and all that. Only an all-girl band, since we didn't want Bryan involved; my stipulation, totally! But when we finally got big enough, I had to face the truth that I couldn't carry a tune and had a terrible sense of rhythm."

"A terrible fate for someone with your lineage," Mark stated with humor.

"Exactly!" Amy agreed with a grimace. "So my next best alternative was nursing."

"A fine and noble profession if it's what you want."

"What I really want to do, what I dream about, is going into missions," Amy said dreamily. "To go to some remote part of the world where they've never heard about Jesus, and teach them to read the Bible and pray . . ."

"Do places like that still exist?" Mark asked doubtfully.

"You tell me," Amy shrugged. "You're the world traveler."

"In my line of work, our only contact with locals is with some of our preliminary work crews or in dealings with the governing authorities. We're more interested with the cultural aspects of any past civilizations, not the present one," Mark explained. "In any case, if that's what you really want to do, you should go for it. It's what Jack would have said."

Amy smiled. "I suppose he would have, wouldn't he?"

"Sure he would have."

"I just keep telling myself that nursing could be a useful skill if I ever did go into missionary work."

"True. It would probably be very practical," Mark agreed.

"Although, I really don't like the sight of blood," Amy mused.

"Hmm. That could be problematic," Mark said dryly.

"Ya think?" Amy laughed. "My mom keeps telling me I'll get over it."

"Remind me to keep an eye out for you, just in case I end up in hospital before you've conquered that one," Mark laughed.

"Amy! There you are!" Holly Walters said, coming through the sliding glass patio doors. "I think we're going to get ready to leave soon. Deanie's looking awfully tired. I think she needs some solitude. Nice to see you again, Mark," she added before retreating back indoors.

"Nice talking to you, Mark," Amy said as she turned to follow her mother back into the house. "Hope it all goes well for you back in Africa."

"Thanks. And likewise. It was nice talking to you too. You've grown up a lot since last time we met," Mark said. And how. "Hope you figure out what it is you want to do," he added. He watched as she stepped through the opening and closed the glass behind her. Amy Walters had indeed grown up.

Chapter Nine

All of the guests had gone home. Deanie was in the family room listening to some of her father's old LP's, Harmony was talking on the phone, and Russ was loading some glasses into the dishwasher. Mark decided it would be a good time to check his emails. He wondered if any new developments had occurred at the site.

He scanned through several messages before opening one from Laura.

Bad news. You need to hurry back. Zimbabwe government wants to shut us down due to risk factors. Sorry to rush you.

Laura

Russ frowned. It was just like Laura to make it short and to the point. No details what so ever. He knew his family would have a hard time understanding, but he would have to take the next flight back to Harare. He couldn't risk not getting the casket out of that tunnel.

Harmony found him in the study a few moments later, still in deep contemplation. "Looks like some serious thinking going on," she commented, perching on the arm of Mark's chair. She put her arms around his neck and gave him a quick squeeze before standing up and sauntering to a row of framed family pictures on a shelf. "What's up?"

"Just work," Mark shrugged, shutting off his laptop computer and snapping the lid down. "You know, all that same old stuff you find so boring."

"Did I say that?" Harmony asked, picking up a picture of herself and Mark. He was wearing a cap and gown; she was at least half his height. "Remember that?" she asked, showing him the photo.

"Of course. It was my graduation day," Mark smiled.

"Obviously," Harmony laughed. "I mean what you told me that day. Remember?"

"Refresh my memory."

"I was worried because you were going off to university in the fall and I thought that when you moved out I'd never see you again. You said that no matter where you went in the world, you'd always come home again. You said that family was family forever, no matter what."

"Hmm. Pretty sage advise, if I do say so myself," Mark commented. "I guess I haven't quite fulfilled it as often as I should have."

"I don't know. You've done okay. Your work is pretty important to you. I'm fairly proud of my big brother."

"So I've been told," Mark said. "Amy Walters tells me you've kept some kind of scrapbook. I might like to see it sometime. Just to see what the experts are saying about me."

"I can go get it now, if you like," Harmony offered. She left the room and came back a few minutes later with a large, hard covered album.

Mark flipped through the pages. He was surprised by the in depth discussion of his life and work that he saw. He vaguely remembered talking to some reporters at the various sites portrayed, but hadn't really paid much attention to what was being done with the information. He was also dismayed by the misrepresentation that he caught on occasion. "I don't recall making that comment," he said under his breath, flipping to the next page. "I was hardly implying that my discoveries rivaled those of Machu Picchu. If they would have checked my own final dissertation on the topic, they would've seen that." He closed the book.

"So what had you looking so puzzled a few moments ago?" Harmony asked, taking the album from her brother's hands. "They can't hold down the fort without you?"

"I've got an excellent crew," Mark replied. "It's just that we're running into some issues with the government authorities. I'm afraid I'm going to have to leave as soon as possible."

"But you just got here!" Harmony protested.

"I know. Sorry, kid," Mark said sheepishly.

"So tell me more about this great archeological dig of yours that you have to go back to it so soon."

"We've come across some pretty spectacular discoveries, if I do say so myself," Mark said.

"Like what?"

Mark stopped for a minute, considering just how much he should tell her. Finally he leaned forward in a conspiratorial fashion. "Actually, little sister, we've found some dinosaur remains. Pterodactyl to be exact."

"So what's the big deal in that? There've been lots of dinosaur bones found."

"Not among a human burial site," Mark clarified. He smiled, waiting for her reaction.

"Really?" she asked, her eyes getting wide. "Now, that is cool!"

"I thought you'd think so," he nodded with satisfaction.

"Well, that just proves it then," she said triumphantly.

"What?"

"Since God created all living creatures, it follows that dinosaurs and people lived at the same time. Believe me, I've had this discussion with my Biology teacher more than once. Now, thanks to you, we have scientific proof!"

"Hold on, there," Mark cautioned. "You're forgetting that's it's also been scientifically proven that dinosaurs died off millions of years before human life existed. Though I am very excited about this discovery, we're still waiting to piece together all the information. There's got to be a plausible explanation. Maybe one type of flying reptiles survived in isolation; we don't know. But don't go jumping to conclusions."

"Proven by who?" Harmony asked. "Some scientist somewhere that doesn't want to entertain the existence of a supreme being? There's been plenty of evidence to show that dinosaurs and people coexisted. The scientific community just doesn't want to take a serious look at it because it would blow all their precious beliefs in the theory of evolution out the window. They've spent too many billions brainwashing the general public to admit that they could be wrong after all."

She was beginning to sound a lot like Rocco, he noted. "They, as you say, are also highly educated professionals, trained in scientific methodology," Mark pointed out. "You also forget that I'm one of them."

"Hey, nothing personal. I'm just laying it on the line for you."

"And where did you get all your wisdom?" Mark asked.

"You sound kind of defensive," Harmony noted. "I've been reading up on it. It was a subject that always kind of bugged me.

110

Somehow, what I'd been taught in school didn't sit well with my personal convictions about God. But I never really found any very satisfying answers."

"Until?" Mark prodded.

"Well, I found several sites on the net," Harmony explained. "Mostly all trained professionals and scientists, too. They've got all kinds of scientific evidence that's never made it into the major scientific journals."

Mark was skeptical. "There's probably a good reason for that."

"Hey, what ever happened to you?" Harmony asked. "I remember a day when you had as much faith in God as I do. You're one of the people who said I had to be myself, who God created me to be."

"I guess I grew up," Mark said. "It's all well and good for you, if that's what makes you happy. Personally, I prefer to put my faith in things that can be seen, not some invisible benevolence."

"But that's just it, Mark. Don't you see? You can't see, or prove evolution any more than you can prove creation. None of us were there to witness it first hand. But the evidence is overwhelmingly in favor of intelligent design. It takes a lot more faith to believe that this whole world, so delicately balanced right down to the most minute detail, could have happened by chance." Harmony could see that he wasn't convinced. "I'll send you some information sometime," she said.

Their father walked into the study where they sat. "It's been a long day," he commented before sitting down himself.

"Where's mom?" Harmony asked.

"It's been a pretty stressful day for your mother," Russ said. "She went to lie down. She'd gotten a bit of a headache."

"Hmm. Maybe I'll go see if she needs anything," Harmony decided. She gave her father a kiss on the cheek, then turned to her brother before leaving the room. "Think about what I said, Mark.

'The heavens declare the glory of God; the earth proclaims the work of His hands.' It's all right there for you to see, if you'll just open your heart to see it."

Russ looked amused. "Your sister been lecturing you?" he asked.

"You could say that," Mark replied with a smile. "She's certainly not lacking in conviction."

"She never was," Russ agreed. "She's like her mother. Once she's decided on something, she goes for it 100 percent. What was she trying to convince you of?"

"We'd been talking about some strange discoveries at the site I've been working on." He almost didn't want to say anymore. His father was sure to side with his sister on the matter.

"What kind of discoveries?" Russ asked the inevitable.

Mark swallowed. How was he ever going to explain this to the scientific community if he couldn't even tell his own father? "We've found something pretty—unusual, dad. Human remains purposely buried with the remains of what appear to be Pterodactyl." He waited for the response.

Russ didn't say anything for a moment, then rose and went to his bookshelf. He took down a volume and handed it to Mark. "Here. You might be interested in this."

Mark scanned the cover. Great. A book about God. Just what he was afraid of.

"I'm not asking you to believe what I say," Russ said. "Read it for yourself. With an open mind. It's written by a scientist who'd made some discoveries himself that he couldn't at first explain. In the end he came to one conclusion. God created the heavens and the earth. He's put years of research into that book. I think you'll find it fascinating, if not enlightening."

Mark turned the book over and read the back cover. He raised his eyebrows at the author's credentials. Maybe he would take a peek later, just to satisfy his curiosity.

"Yep, your sister has her mother's enthusiasm for adventure, and the ability to see the silver lining in everything. Now you, you're more like your old man. Don't take any one else's word for anything. You want to figure it out for yourself, to test all the angles and mull over all the possibilities. I wish I could convince you to see things my way based on my own experiences. But I know that's not the way you tick. I understand that perfectly, and I respect it."

Father and son sat silently for a time until Mark spoke up. "Ever wonder what our lives would have been like if you'd never met Deanie?"

"Sure. Lots of times. And I've come to the conclusion that I'd still be stuck in my own self-righteousness and bitterness over your mother. It's because of Deanie that I gave my life to Christ."

Mark thought of the woman who had given him birth. He'd never met her and his father did not talk about her. From the bits of information he'd been able to piece together, she had abandoned them when Mark was just a baby. Apparently it had been a marriage of necessity, which she was not ready or willing to commit to. She had never attempted to contact him or establish any kind of relationship. Mark had only seen one picture of her at his grandmother's house. It was taken the day of the wedding. His father hadn't kept any reminders of that painful period in his life. His baby pictures started at about four months of age, shortly after Miranda Graham had left. Mark had held secret resentment toward her as a child, as well as a sense of inadequacy. What mother would abandon her baby unless he didn't measure up in some way? Now, as an adult, he was over those feelings. He felt nothing but remote apathy that occasionally bordered on the curious.

"So what are your plans now, son?" Russ asked.

"I need to get back as soon as possible," Mark replied. "I

know it hasn't been much of a visit, but there are some important developments that I really need to get back to attend to."

Russ nodded, understanding full well the driving need to keep one's commitments.

Later that night, in his bed in the spare room, Mark flipped through the book that his father had given him. Petrified tree trunks running directly through several layers of the geologic record; human and dinosaur footprints found side by side; evidence of catastrophic flooding throughout the earth; countless flaws in carbon dating and cover ups galore, some of which never got removed from science text books . . . Fascinating, if not credible. He might enjoy reading the book after all.

A light tapping sounded at the bedroom door. "Come in," Mark said, setting the book aside, and sitting up a bit in the bed. It was Deanie.

"Your dad tells me you're thinking of leaving sooner than expected," she said, sitting on the edge of the bed.

"Yes. There are some . . . problems on sight that need my attention. I really can't stay," Mark explained.

"I understand," Deanie said. "I just wanted to say how much it's meant to me, for you to come all the way for Jack's funeral. I was a bit out of it today, and I just wanted you to know that I really appreciate it."

"No problem," Mark shrugged. "Jack was pretty important to me. I wanted to come."

"He always looked on you like his own grandson, you know," Deanie smiled.

"And he was, and always will be, my grandpa," Mark offered.

"You know, he said some things before he died that I think he wanted you to hear."

"Like what?"

"He said that he was sorry that in all the times you spent

together, he never gave you any real advice that mattered."

"That's not true," Mark disagreed. "He always gave me lots of good advice. Why, I came to him with everything, and he always delivered."

"I think he meant about spiritual things," Deanie said gently. "He never was one much for religion, you know that. And I think toward the end he felt bad about that, like he had somehow turned you off God because he had never believed. You were always so willing to listen to whatever he said."

"I think I eventually grew up enough to make up my mind on most things," Mark laughed. "No need for him to worry on that account."

"But he realized he was wrong near the end. That he did need Jesus. I think that's what bothered him the most. That now he knew Jesus and maybe you didn't."

"So my whole family thinks I've turned away from God," Mark mused.

"Have you?"

"I don't know. Maybe I never really belonged to Him in the first place."

Chapter Ten

Mark had plenty of time to ponder the question on his flight back to Africa. He had believed in God as a child because he'd seen the evidence of change in the lives of the people around him. Mark remembered the turbulence of those early years well. His father, normally a conservative and self-controlled individual, had veered off course in an uncharacteristic fashion and begun a relationship with Deanie, an ex rock and roll junkie and daughter of jazz great, Jack Burton. When Deanie ended up getting pregnant, she and his father had married. The early days of their union had been anything but peaceful. Mark recalled the harsh words that were exchanged when they thought he wasn't listening, covered by pretense when they knew he was. He remembered the times that Deanie had snuck him over to her rock and roll friends' rehearsal studio to listen to them play. His father hadn't been pleased. Then Deanie had run away for a short while. It wasn't until she went into premature labor and she almost lost her own life in the process that things started to turn around. Through it all, Grandma Graham had been praying, and apparently her prayers had paid off.

After that, his parents turned to God and started attending church. The change in their behavior and outlook was truly remarkable. Not to say that they never had problems, but somehow they managed to work it out. His father was still the conservative accountant he had always been, but without the judgmental perfectionism. Deanie remained her flamboyant and fun loving self, but she too learned to trust God instead of her own resources when the going got tough.

Mark had witnessed these changes firsthand. He had been about twelve at the time, and although he had always been sent to Sunday School before that, and had been ministered to by his grandmother, he had never really experienced a living faith like what he saw in the lives of his parents and their friends. Certainly the evidence of positive change in his own family was proof enough of the existence of God. But sometimes he'd felt more like a spectator. He'd seen dramatic conversions and even healings, but for himself, had never really experienced anything life shattering. His grandmother said it was okay, that not everyone had the same emotional response to God. He was naturally reserved and reflective like his father, so he accepted his lack of emotionalism as normal.

His scientist's mind opened up to other possibilities as he grew older and went on to study at university. Some of the things that he had witnessed as a child were just not logical. Added to that his own lack of spiritual connection with any unseen forces, and he came to the conclusion that most of what he had witnessed was human emotionalism, pure and simple. Not that there was anything bad in that; as emotional creatures, people needed an outlet of some kind, and he was glad for his parents that they had found something that seemed to work for them. But he'd long since dismissed any need that he might have himself for such an outlet. He had his work, and the fulfillment that he felt with each new discovery was enough to keep him going for the time being.

Or was it?

He wondered, then, at the unsettled feelings he had experienced when Deanie had brought up Jack's faith. Mark had always looked up to Grandpa Jack as the imparter of wisdom and giver of sage advice. To find that he had succumbed to the same kind of blind faith as his parents was news that left him feeling strangely upset.

The journey back to Zimbabwe also afforded Mark plenty of time to read the book his father had given him. It was surprisingly well documented in its attempt to undermine the pervasive theories on the origins of the planet and life on earth. It also presented some interesting alternatives a.k.a. creation, which, if not altogether convincing, were food for thought. Certainly, the concept of intelligent design, be it by a benevolent Creator or by some other form of advanced being, explained many of the discrepancies that the more accepted theory of evolution only seemed to exacerbate. It pricked enough of an interest in Mark, at any rate, to have him wanting more. He would have to do some research of his own.

* * *

"So? What do you think of this find Mark was taking about?" Deanie asked her husband.

"Sounds like quite the deal," Russ said, scanning his newspaper.

"I think it sounds very exciting. If they find solid proof that backs up the Bible, nobody will be able to deny the truth any more."

"Don't be so sure."

"You're encouraging," Deanie noted sarcastically.

"Just a realist. You know me."

"Know and love," Deanie smiled, coming up to hug her husband from behind. "I think Mark's got some questions of his own in that regard. God isn't finished with him yet, I don't think."

"I agree with you there."

"How could He be? I haven't stopped praying for him. He doesn't stand a chance."

"Tenacity," Russ said, setting his paper down and pulling his wife down on his lap. "It's what I love about you."

* * *

Mark arrived back at the archeological dig armed with new insight into the possibilities of creation theory, and plagued with his own resistance at believing it. He felt like a man being pulled in two directions at once. At some point, joints and muscle would be severed, as neatly as if he were on one of those ancient inventions of torture. Only this time, it was his brain and his heart.

He had also stopped in Harare, and secured the remaining time they had left from the original four-month contract he'd negotiated last time. At least that was something.

"So? What news?" Rocco asked, joining him the moment he'd stepped from the jeep.

Mark took out a hanky and blew the dust from his nose. "We're back to the same time frame as before," he replied, stuffing the hanky into his back pocket. "That gives us less than six weeks."

Rocco swore in Spanish.

"I know, I know," Mark agreed. "But it's better than nothing. Your work crews still going around the clock?"

Rocco nodded. "Another day or two, maybe. That's it. We'll rescue the king, don't worry, boss."

"I'm counting on it," Mark quipped.

Mark strode to the tent where he knew he would find Laura. There she was, leaning over the microscope as usual.

She looked up, relief at seeing him obvious in her eyes. "What took you so long?" she teased.

120

He didn't smile back. "I want all, and I mean *all*, of the artifacts crated and ready for transport to the States. Only do what cataloguing is absolutely necessary. Any other analysis can be done later."

"What's going on?" she asked.

"We've only got a couple weeks to wrap this up," he explained. "I'm afraid the government isn't taking too kindly to what they consider unnecessary disturbance to the temple. I've explained the magnitude of our latest discoveries, but they seem adamant in their original time frame. And I don't want to take any chances with what we've discovered here, either. I got wind that some of the more nationalistic minded in the government don't want any artifacts leaving the country. Before they come in here and start asking for access, I want everything safely on its way. We can always plead ignorance and return it later. Once it's safely at the university in New Mexico we can piece it together then."

"I had the feeling something like this would happen," she said knowingly. "I'm already on it."

"Good." He turned to leave.

"Um, Mark?" Laura asked tentatively.

"Yes?"

"Aren't you glad to see me?" she asked, a hopeful smile softening her lips.

He blinked. He had been so focused on the task at hand he hadn't even stopped to consider niceties.

"Oh. Oh, yeah." He waved awkwardly, then turned abruptly and strode from the room.

Later that night, Laura snuck into his tent. It had been awhile and he was only human . . .

They lay now on the narrow cot, his arm behind her neck, her head cradled against his chest. Mark laid there, his eyes fully awake, staring at the ceiling.

121

"So how was your family?" Laura asked quietly, playing with some of his chest hair.

"Huh? Oh, okay. As good as can be expected, I guess."

"It's hard to lose someone you love," she noted with sympathy.

"Yep. That it is," he agreed.

"You were close to him. Your granddad."

"Yes. I learned a lot from him," Mark stated.

"About what?"

Mark shrugged. "Life in general." Jack had opened up a whole knew world to Mark. He'd sat in on countless jam sessions with Jack's cronies, never realizing the musical genius to which he was so casually privy, or the celebrity status of those with whom he had been allowed to hobnob. He was simply allowed "in," and was witness to a creative passion that in retrospect filled him with amazement. To say that Jack Burton had influenced his life would be to grossly underestimate the powerful bond that had brought them together. He was his grandfather, not merely by chance, but by choice.

"Hm. That's nice." She seemed to snuggle in further and sighed contentedly.

Mark's arm began to ache, like the circulation was being cut off. He shifted uncomfortably.

"Sorry. Am I too heavy?" Laura asked, sitting up slightly.

"Probably just the long trip. I didn't sleep much on the plane . . ."

"Oh. Well, I suppose I could go back to my own tent and let you get some rest," she said somewhat petulantly.

Mark knew she was trying to get him to ask her to stay. But he kept his mouth shut. Right now he needed some space.

Laura rose from the cot, which made a creaking noise as soon as the added weight of her body had been released, and grabbed for her clothing. Mark could see that she was hurt. He couldn't do anything about that right now.

"Bye," he offered lamely as she lifted the tent flap. She turned and gave him an angry stare, but didn't say anything. He watched her leave and heaved a great sigh of relief.

What was he doing, sleeping with a woman he didn't really have any feelings for? He knew it was not something he could admit to his father, or Jack for that matter, with comfort. Jack's commitment to passion, and his own father's unwavering adoration for his stepmother were examples that made him now feel ashamed. But he was a man, after all. It was pretty hard to say no when it was offered so casually. And Laura didn't seem to mind— she usually didn't demand a lot in return.

No, Laura would never fit in with his family. And she was no Amy Walters either. Thoughts of the petitely curvaceous blonde, just barely an adult at twenty, brought a smile to his lips and a softening to his jagged nerves.

He froze for a second, his mind having a knee jerk reaction to its own train of thought. Now where had that come from? She was just a kid—his little sister's friend. Someone he used to babysit. And what kind of man was he anyway, to be thinking of one woman after having just made love to another?

His family would indeed be disappointed if they knew just how far he had fallen.

Chapter Eleven

"Looks like today might be the day," Anthony said in greeting a few mornings later.

Mark nodded. "Yeah. I was worried we'd never get that casket out in time. But it looks promising. Now I just have to make sure the final arrangements for the air lift are in place. Our mystery man is about to make his first overseas flight to Albuquerque."

"You're going with?" Anthony asked.

"You bet I am," Mark replied with certainty.

They were walking together from the storage compound, which had also emptied out considerably in recent days.

"Say, Anthony," Mark said off hand. "Before I forget, I have a book I think you might be interested in."

"Oh yeah?"

"My father gave it to me," Mark explained.

"What kind of book?" Anthony asked.

"Come on and I'll show you."

They strode with purpose to Mark's quarters and stepped in through the flap. Mark found the book where he'd left it right beside his bed and handed it over to Anthony for inspection. "A pretty interesting read, if I do say so myself," Mark said.

Anthony perused the cover and nodded. "Thanks, man. I'll

return it when I'm finished."

"Some of the accounts in there are fascinating. According to this man, our find isn't so unique after all. There have been lots of dinosaur remains found with more, so called, modern species."

"Just like Rocco said," Anthony mused.

"Right. But not only that, human remains have been found around the world in layers that have been labeled millions of years old; certainly before the development of homo erectus as scientists have now come to recognize him. Fossils of modern horses were found alongside their accepted ancient ancestor; all kinds of discrepancies in the geologic layer that are either ignored, hidden, or otherwise explained away by elaborate means."

The two men stepped back out into the African sun, which was already shining hotly on their backs. Mark continued his discourse with enthusiasm. "I tell you, Anthony. After reading that book, I don't feel so alone anymore. I think Rocco was telling the truth about a conspiracy. Did you know that scores of fraudulent 'missing links' that were documented as fact and then found to be untrue are still being used in reference books?"

"Really? You don't say."

"Absolutely. Take for instance, Neanderthal man. Although the scientific world has long since dismissed that discovery as a fake, most of the general population still believes it to be a fact. And get this. Modern DNA testing has even proved the impossibility of any link between bipedal primates thus 'discovered' and man. Yet there are some less scrupulous scientists out there, with federal backing I might add, that are willing to tweak their findings just a bit in order to fit them into acceptable theories. As a strict follower of scientific methodology myself, that really irks me! That's not even science."

"Sounds like a pretty fascinating read," Anthony noted with upraised brows. "Certainly caught your interest, anyway."

Mark shrugged and laughed slightly. "I guess I was getting

pretty excited there, wasn't I? It's why I thought you might want to read it. I'd appreciate your thoughts on the subject once you're through."

They parted ways with a wave and Mark entered the lab where Laura was still hard at work.

"You're looking much more chipper this morning," she noted, looking up from her computer.

"Thanks. I'm feeling better too," Mark replied. "Probably the fact that we should be able to recover that casket today."

"That is good news," she nodded. "Say, what were you and Anthony having such a heated discussion about just now?"

"You heard that?" Mark asked.

"The walls are only made of canvas," she reminded him.

"Oh, just some research I've been doing." He looked over her shoulder at the computer screen. "What are you working on?"

"I think I have a plausible explanation for the Reptilian remains," she said.

"Okay," he nodded. "I'm listening."

"Well, since there is a fair bit of seismic activity in this region, that well preserved headpiece we saw in the casket could well have been buried and almost instantly freeze dried during one of the ice ages. Eons later, more seismic activity reopened the long-buried remains that the people of the region must have come across. Then they used them in their ceremonial burials. It's probably how the whole legend started."

Mark raised his brows skeptically. "That seems a fairly elaborate explanation. What's wrong with just accepting that there could have been a Pterodactyl-like reptile alive at the same time as the humans living in the region? Scientists are discovering new life forms in the jungles of South America practically every day. Why are we so reticent to admit that there could be dinosaur like creatures that lived contemporaneously with man?"

127

Laura gave him a withering look. "I thought we'd been through this."

"What?" Mark defended. "Did you know that there are numerous documented cases of human remains found in geologic layers where they're not supposed to be? Take for instance, a site in Germany where a human skull was found buried in the layers of coal. Coal! You know how many millions of years old that's supposed to be? Or in Texas, remains that are clearly human were found in the same geologic layer as long extinct fossil remains. There are dozens of discrepancies. Recognizably modern birds have been found side by side with, oh . . . what's the name of it," he frowned, snapping his fingers. His face cleared. "Archaeopteryx, that's what it's called."

"Pardon me?" Laura asked with disbelief. "What are you talking about?"

"Archaeopteryx. The supposed link between flying reptiles and birds," Mark explained.

"Listen to yourself," Laura interrupted.

"What?"

"You're spouting off a lot of very questionable 'facts'. If these finds are so well documented, why aren't they common knowledge? Come on. Just think about it. You've been doing a little reading from a book written by whom? Some quack that has a questionable background in science, with degrees from some obscure university that nobody's heard of, and who obviously has a religious agenda behind it all."

"How do you know what I've been reading?" Mark asked defensively.

"I saw the book by your cot," Laura answered. "I have been in your quarters since you've been home, just in case you've forgotten," she added sarcastically.

It was a low blow—the kind of catty remark that Laura didn't usually bother with. "And you made all those deductions when?" Mark asked angrily. "While we were screwing?"

"That was rude," Laura remarked.

"Well?" Mark asked.

"I took note of the author's name," Laura explained nonchalantly. "You'd already mentioned your 'reading' a couple of times, so I thought I'd check it out. I did a little research of my own on the net."

"And?"

"Like I said, the credibility of the author is iffy, at best."

Mark felt suddenly deflated. And foolish.

"I'm worried about you, Mark," Laura said. "You've got your reputation to think about."

"So what you're saying is, I should just turn a blind eye to anything that might raise a few eyebrows and pretend it never existed," Mark said tightly.

"Well, no. Not exactly," Laura replied.

"No? Then what are you saying, Laura? I'm a little confused here," Mark said irritably.

"Don't go making any claims that you can't verify 100 percent," Laura pleaded.

"I've never done that," Mark retorted. "It's not my style. You know that."

"Well, don't go looking for trouble either."

"You mean, ignore the finds and the facts if necessary."

Laura let out another exasperated sigh. "You're impossible!" Turning, she stormed out of the lab.

* * *

"I got a strange email from Mark," Russ Graham told his wife as he crawled into bed beside her and shut out the bedside lamp.

"Oh?" Deanie responded with a yawn.

Russ's expression was troubled. "He asked me to make sure I

129

put everything in a safe location and to download everything from my computer onto discs, but not to leave anything on my hard drive."

"Hm," Deanie frowned. "What do you mean put everything in a safe location? What's he talking about?"

"Mark's been shipping small crates to me over the last month or so since he went back after the funeral," Russ replied. "I haven't opened them. He gave me specific instructions to store them, untouched, in a cool, dry location."

"And you didn't tell me?" Deanie asked incredulously, suddenly becoming more alert.

Russ shrugged. "I didn't think it was any big deal. It's not the first time he's sent things here for temporary storage. Besides, I didn't think you'd care about a few extra cartons in the garage." Deanie was not known for her housekeeping abilities. If left to her own devices, the house would have been a total disaster, and she completely oblivious to it. Russ had long ago resorted to hiring a housekeeper to keep his home in the kind of immaculate condition he preferred.

"True," Deanie mused. "But what do you think it means? Why is he asking you to keep it 'safe'? Does he think somebody's going to come and try to steal whatever he has in those crates?"

"I don't know," Russ said, shaking his head. "But it certainly makes me wonder just what I've got out in my garage."

"I hope he's not in any danger," Deanie frowned.

"Just keep on praying. I'm sure he's taking the necessary precautions though. You know Mark. It's probably why he asked me to move the items to a safer location."

"Let's hope that's all it is," Deanie replied.

"In any case, he says he'll probably be coming to get them himself some time soon."

"Did he say when?"

"No. I don't think he wanted to be too specific."

"Hm," Deanie mumbled, looking worried.

"Don't worry, honey," Russ assured his wife, reaching to put his arms around her. "Mark's smart. He won't do anything stupid."

* * *

With no further incident, the casket of the mysterious king was brought to the surface. It was the moment of triumph Mark had been straining toward for weeks. He thought he might burst with it.

"Okay, people," he called out to the crowd of onlookers. Every single person who was part of the archeological team had gathered at the entrance to the tunnels. "Make way. We need to get the king to the lab for some initial analysis."

With great care, the heavy casket was placed on the back of a flatbed truck and carted the short distance to the makeshift laboratory.

"I want all the initial stats, pronto! Photos, measurements, skin and hair samples— everything within the next hour! And don't forget a sample from the reptilian headdress," he barked.

"What's the rush?" Laura asked, frowning. "I thought the chopper wasn't coming until the day after tomorrow?"

Mark smiled slyly. "That's what I led everyone to believe. It might actually arrive as early as this afternoon."

"What?" Laura practically choked on the word. "What kind of game are you playing here, Doctor Graham?"

"I told you before. I'm worried that the government authorities are going to put the clamp down on removing artifacts from the country. A little innocent mix up in paper work is my insurance that I get him back to New Mexico in one piece for some proper analysis."

"This is ridiculous! You're becoming as paranoid as Rocco, for heaven's sake. This isn't some spy movie, Mark. We're scientists and this is an archeological dig. Remember?"

He gave her an icy stare. "Get to work, please, Doctor Sawchuk. We might not have all day."

The team worked efficiently to get the requested statistical information and samples and the casket was resealed and readied for transport. It was first vacuum sealed in a protective, heat, fire, and moisture resistant shroud. Then it was placed in a large wooden crate, surrounded with several feet of foam. Once air lifted by helicopter to Harare, it would be placed inside a metal container and flown the rest of the way to New Mexico. Mark was packed and ready. He wasn't about to let this find get out of his sight. He planned on making the trip right along side the king.

At present, the crate was resting on the back of the flat bed truck, awaiting the arrival of the helicopter. The tension around the camp was palpable. There was still a lot of work to be done, but everyone seemed preoccupied with anticipation.

Mark gathered together the crew chiefs to give them some final instructions before his departure. "Laura, you'll be in charge of the final cataloguing and crating of the artifacts. Joey, you and Rocco look after getting that tunnel sealed off so no would-be raiders come and disturb the site after we're gone. Hopefully the government will do a proper refit and will make the site accessible to the public. We've already got the schematics of the site mapped out and catalogued, but there might be a few additions now that the initial tunneling has been disturbed. If any government officials come by asking questions, plead ignorance. But I want this site ship shape, sealed off and ready to leave in their hands with no glitches by the time the dead line is up."

"Aren't you coming back?" Rocco asked.

"I'm not sure. It's my intention to," Mark answered, "but I'm just not sure what's going to happen once I get to Albuquerque. I want everything wrapped up nice and tidy just in case I don't."

"Great. So you're leaving us to deal with irate government

officials," Laura said. "Once they find out we've hauled everything off to the States, they're not going to be happy."

"I'll deal with it," Mark assured. "You must see that there's no other way?"

Laura just shrugged.

"So? Any other questions or concerns?" Mark asked, looking around the group. A slight smile suddenly turned up the corners of his mouth as he cocked his head to one side. "Is that a helicopter I hear in the distance?" he asked, shielding his eyes from the sun as he scanned the sky.

The rest of them heard it too. The distinct double chop-chop of the huge propellers on a military type helicopter used for transporting cargo to remote locations. The crowd gathered again, as the giant locust came into view, scattering just enough for safety's sake once the beast was close to touching down.

Mark waited with anticipation as the whirling knives at the crown and tail of the vehicle slowed and the door was thrown open. He walked forward to greet the pilot, a trusted member of the underground opposition. Suddenly, the smile that had formed on his lips froze. Several men in green camouflage army fatigues stepped out, automatic weapons trained and ready.

They advanced forward with crouching gait, sweeping the area with their eyes, weapons never straying from the locked in position by their sides. Mark blinked nervously, raising his hands slightly for lack of a better idea. Finally, a well-suited official from the Zimbabwean government, a man whom Mark had dealt with quite pleasantly on several occasions, stepped down from the now immobile chopper. He surveyed his surroundings and with a raised hand gave the signal for the soldiers to lower their weapons.

With a sigh of relief, Mark lowered his own hands as well. "Mr. Sangeruka," he called out, trying for pleasant nonchalance. "This is a rather unexpected surprise. Don't you think the armed guards are a little much, considering this is a government sponsored archeological dig?"

The official glared back at Mark, his eyes never wavering, his mouth never cracking a smile. "We need to talk, Dr. Graham."

"Fine. Shall we step into one of the shelters, out of the sun?" Mark suggested with a gesture.

Without warning, an engine roared to life. All eyes swung in the direction of the sound as a cloud of dust and rocks sprayed up from spinning tires. Someone had commandeered the truck that held the casket! Shouts and gunshots rang out but the truck was already swerving crazily around the side of the mountain and out of sight.

Mark sped toward another jeep and vaulted inside, searching frantically for the ignition keys. Another spurt of machine gun fire pelted the air and he looked up to see the government official with his hand in the air, gesturing for calm.

"Let him go," Mr. Sangeruka yelled. "He won't get far on these mountain roads. We'll cut him off before he gets down the side of the mountain."

"But the casket!" Mark shouted frantically. "What if it gets damaged? What if he has an accident?"

"That is out of your hands now," Mr. Sangeruka said pointedly. "It is not your property. It belongs to the people of Zimbabwe."

"But . . ." Mark surveyed the crowd of frightened, gaping spectators. His eyes searched and catalogued every face. Who was missing? Then it came to him. Rocco. His mouth became a grim line. He unfolded himself slowly from the jeep and stepped out onto the dusty ground.

"We would ask that your crew pack up their personal belongings as quickly as possible. Transport trucks will be arriving tomorrow to take them from the site."

"What's going on here?" Mark asked, his eyes steel.

"The government of the people is taking over the rest of the operation of this sacred and holy site," Mr. Sangeruka explained quite calmly. "Any equipment that belongs to you or your governments will be shipped to you at a later date. We will also be launching an official requisition order. All missing artifacts must be returned immediately to their place of origin. As for you, Dr. Graham, you are under arrest."

Chapter Twelve

It was like a terrible nightmare. Soldiers watched Mark as he unpacked his personal belongings for their perusal and then repacked it all again. At one point he tried to make eye contact with Laura to try to tell her to get the skin and hair samples out - somehow. But he was never given the chance. Before the eyes of the rest of the team, he was hand cuffed and pushed unceremoniously up into the waiting helicopter. Several soldiers were dispatched to stay behind until the rest of the transportation trucks arrived. But in the meantime, Mr. Sangeruka was anxious to get his prisoner safely back to Harare. Not to mention the fact that they still had a thief to catch.

With a deafening whir of propellers, the helicopter lifted off. Mark watched out the window as the archeological site became a tiny cluster of doll sized tents and roped off squares. The people below scurried about like ants. Soon they were out of sight all together as the chopper gained altitude and swung around to the north.

The treacherous alpine road leading to the nearest air strip wound around the sides of the mountain like a snake. Mark strained forward to see if he could catch any signs of Rocco and the flatbed truck. Where did Rocco think he was going with that casket, anyway? Didn't he know there was no way he could outrun them? And even if he managed to hide in the hills for a few days, he was still going to need to surface at some point. He'd never be able to transport a package that size anywhere without alerting the authorities somehow. Whatever his former friend and colleague's plan, it wasn't very well thought out, that's for sure.

They spotted the errant vehicle a few moments later, just up ahead, still creating a cloud of dust in its wake as its driver careened along the side of the mountain. The helicopter swooped down to overtake the truck. Mr. Sangeruka signaled for one of his soldiers to fire on the vehicle. Mark protested loudly, but his voice was caught in the combination of the chopping of the propeller and the battery of gunfire that spewed from the armed man's weapon.

This was no action movie, Mark realized with sickening clarity. There would be no near misses as bullets inexplicably ricocheted off their intended target. No. With the very first ejaculation of the automatic weapon, the tires on the truck blew apart, sending the vehicle swerving uncontrollably on the narrow roadway below. Then, with the grace of a slow motion replay, the truck veered off the edge of the cliff, bouncing and bumping like a toy, end over end. Mark caught a glimpse of the crate flying gracefully through the air and disappearing into the brush below. He thought he might pass out.

"Don't worry, Dr. Graham," Mr. Sangeruka shouted above the din. "We'll send a crew to recover the remains. For now, I think we'd be better off getting you to Harare."

Idiot. Didn't he realize the priceless nature of the cargo he had just sent off the cliff? Not to mention, another man's life. Rocco had some quirks, that was for sure, but Mark felt more certain than ever he had just been trying to protect the discovery from getting into the wrong hands. Apparently, he was correct in trying to do so.

Once the helicopter touched down at the military airport on

the outskirts of Harare, Mark was practically thrown from the aircraft and pushed, headfirst, into a waiting dark blue Escalade. His duffel bag full of belongings, along with the saxophone case, were thrown in beside him on the back seat.

Didn't people learn how to drive in Africa? he wondered. The government official in the front seat seemed unfazed by the way the driver careened through the streets of the city, nearly missing pedestrians and other vehicles alike.

"So what am I being charged with?" Mark asked flatly. He was still reeling from the knowledge that Rocco was dead and the casket probably lost forever.

"Malpractice, substandard working conditions, breech of trust," Sangeruka replied.

"Although I object to all of those accusations, they are hardly grounds for arrest," Mark stated.

"How about theft of public property?" Mr. Sangeruka suggested, never changing his expression from one of stony coolness.

"That's ridiculous," Mark argued quietly. "I did nothing that wasn't specifically laid out in the agreed upon contract with your government."

"Really, Dr. Graham? What about the secret shipment of artifacts to the United States without the express permission of the proper authorities?"

"Sending artifacts out for analysis is standard procedure on most archeological sites."

"Without proper paperwork documenting their departure?" Mr. Sangeruka asked skeptically.

"Your government was placing such unrealistic time constraints on us that we couldn't take the time. Besides, a general release waver was signed at the beginning of the project. It covers any odds and ends that might get missed in the initial shuffle."

"Artifacts of such importance could hardly be classed as 'odds and ends'," Sangeruka replied sardonically.

Mark frowned but remained silent.

"As I suspected. That type of unethical procedure constitutes a definite breech of contract."

"I wasn't going to steal anything," Mark countered. "A find of that . . . delicacy . . . requires specialized care and attention during analysis. There's always a danger of deterioration when dealing with something that ancient."

"Or that valuable," Sangeruka stated.

"Are you suggesting that I was out for personal gain from this find?" Mark asked incredulously. "My track record speaks for itself. I'm interested in scientific discovery, pure and simple."

"You wouldn't be the first," Sangeruka shrugged. "The promise of wealth has turned more than one altruistic head."

Mark glowered. "And what have you gained, Sangeruka? Not only have you lost, or at least irreparably damaged, possibly the greatest archeological find of this century, but you wasted an innocent life doing it."

"Innocent?" Sangeruka laughed humorlessly. "I hardly think so."

"What do you mean?"

"Rocco Cortez had connections to an underground smuggling operation which dealt in rare artifacts. All old, priceless—and stolen."

This information shook Mark to the core. He had known Rocco for years and considered him a personal friend. He'd had no idea . . .

"I can see that this information shocks you," Sangeruka noted. "That will probably bode well for you. Perhaps you will be given a lighter sentence. In any case, shed no tears for Mr. Cortez. He was a 'bad apple', as they say, and needed to be discarded before he tainted the entire barrel."

They rode the rest of the way to the Police Station in downtown Harare without any more conversation. Mark was still trying to wrap his mind around this new piece of information. If Rocco was involved in an illegal smuggling operation, there may be others. If he couldn't trust Rocco, who could he trust? Joey, Anthony . . . Laura? Maybe nothing and nobody was safe anymore.

"We have arrived at your hotel," Sangeruka quipped as they pulled up to the police station. It was a large stone building, several stories high with reddish streaks of rust bleeding down onto the stone from the iron bars on every window. Sangeruka disembarked and allowed two armed guards, heavy artillery still in tact, to escort Mark into the building. It was muggy, close, and dusty grey on the inside. Apparently they were expecting him. The uniformed officer at the front counter waved them forward without even a greeting.

Another officer joined them, a jangling ring of keys at his waist and with a brisk nod at Sangeruka, he led the way through a door, down a dark hallway and into the section of the building that housed the jail cells. The man swung one of the iron doors open with a creek and gestured for Mark to enter. He had little choice but to comply.

"I'm a Canadian citizen," he offered. "You can't just lock me up without specifying the charges against me." The door to the cell had already been firmly shut. "What about legal council?" he asked, grasping the cold steel of the bars.

"All in due time," Sangeruka said, smiling for the first time since the horrific trip had begun.

"I also have working visas from the US government that provide protection," Mark added for good measure.

"Need I remind you you're not in the US or Canada at the moment, Dr. Graham? While in this country you are subject to our law."

"I have special protection under the International Archeological Agreement," Mark said desperately. "I stuck to the letter of the law in fulfilling my end of the contract, and I've got documentation from the University of New Mexico to back me up."

Sangeruka waved dismissively. He turned and was about to leave when Mark called out one last time.

"Sangeruka! Who's breaking faith now? I demand to know who is behind this and what I'm being charged with."

"You will demand nothing," Sangeruka said calmly. "Enjoy your stay, Dr. Graham. Oh, and dinner is served at . . ." He consulted his watch and then looked up pleasantly. "I'm sorry. I guess you've missed dinner." With that he turned and retreated down the dark hallway, his shoes clicking resoundingly on the cement floor.

Mark rested his head against the bars for a moment, utter dejection seeping through him like poison injected into a vein. With a sigh he turned and surveyed the small cell. It was dimly lit, the only light coming from the single bulb in the hallway, and consisted of crumbling concrete walls, ceiling, and floor. The only furniture was a porcelain toilet, a sink, and a wooden bench with no mattress. *So much for five-star amenities,* he thought glumly. How long he would have to endure it, he didn't know.

Another thought struck him with sickening clarity. His personal belongings had not been deposited with him. There was nothing of great value in the duffle bag, but Jack's saxophone . . . It was the only remaining tie he had to his grandfather. He just hoped he'd get it back when all this got straightened out.

Dreams of Pterodactyls swooping down to capture unsuspecting men, women, and children, plagued Marks sleep. Among the victims were various family members including his sister Harmony, his parents, and other family friends like Amy

Walters. Presiding over the crazed mob was the grizzled face of the ancient king, smiling with the toothy grin of the dead, yet very much alive in his gestures and mannerisms. Hovering over everything was Grandpa Jack, glibly playing his saxophone for all he was worth, oblivious to all the grisly mayhem below.

What could one expect, sleeping on a hard wooden bench in a musty African jail cell? Especially with the only other occupant of the place, in another cell farther down, groaning all night long. Mark got to his feet slowly and stretched his aching body. His stomach protested with a loud growl. It had been a long time since he'd eaten and his gut was crying out for some sustenance. Not to mention the fact that he was parched with thirst. He was afraid to drink the tap water for fear of contaminants, but was getting close to taking just a sip anyway.

A clanging noise brought his attention to the door at the end of the hallway. Someone was opening it. Hopefully it was breakfast. He rubbed his chin absently, a night's growth of stubble shadowing his face.

It wasn't breakfast. "Come with me," the uniformed officer said, opening the cell door.

"Where are we going?" Mark asked. The officer didn't answer.

Mark just shrugged and followed the man down the narrow hallway. There was no point in pressing his luck. At least he was out of the confines of that cell. He squinted slightly when they emerged into the main part of the building.

They continued through a maze of desks until they reached an office door. Two armed guards, vaguely familiar in appearance, stood guard. The police officer rapped on the door with his knuckles and was answered by a sharp "Enter!" from within. The officer opened the door and held it ajar for Mark's admittance.

"Sangeruka," Mark said, nodding to the government official who was sitting in the room, along with a man that Mark assumed to be the chief of police.

"I trust you slept well," Sangeruka said.

Mark grunted a noncommittal reply.

"You may take a seat," the police chief said, gesturing to an empty chair on the other side of his desk. Mark complied just as his stomach growled loudly.

Sangeruka raised an eyebrow, but said nothing.

"So? Have you figured out that you've made a big mistake yet?" Mark asked.

Sangeruka's reply was cool. "Don't press me," he said, his look one of steel. He stood lazily, sauntering to where Mark sat across from the chief. "You are in no position to negotiate."

Mark took that statement for what it was worth. There was no arguing one's rights in a third world dictatorship. He rubbed the stubble on his chin thoughtfully, waiting for Sangeruka to make the next move.

"Chief Ganges, here, has offered you police protection during your transport to the State Penitentiary," he informed, gesturing to his stern and silent cohort. The chief's expression never changed.

"The State Penitentiary—" Mark blurted.

"I'm not finished, Dr. Graham," Sangeruka said patiently, much as one would speak to an unruly child. "The charges against you have not been dropped," he explained. "We believe it necessary for security reasons to move you to a more secure facility."

"You've got to be kidding," Mark shook his head in disbelief. "If I only knew what the charges against me were, I could—"

Sangeruka silenced him with a raised hand. "I think I must warn you, however. The accommodations at the State Penitentiary are far less . . . comfortable than here."

Mark's eyes narrowed. "Oh?"

"Of course, I might be able to find a way to alleviate that

situation . . . shorten your stay, so to speak."

"So . . . what are you getting at, exactly?" Mark asked, studying the other man warily.

"Absolute silence about your discoveries," Sangeruka replied.

Mark frowned. "I . . . I don't see how that's possible."

"Anything is possible if you choose it to be so," Sangeruka stated.

"But why? This could be the biggest scientific discovery of—"

"I know," Sangeruka cut him off. "Of the century. So you said."

"You can't expect me to just pretend nothing was discovered. What about all the samples, the artifacts already sent away for analysis? The rest of the crew? You've got up to fifty people who have in one way or another been exposed to that information already. You can't expect to arrest and threaten each one in order to keep them quiet."

"You are the head of the operation. People will listen to you. Follow your lead." He leaned back against the desk, folding his arms.

"No. It's unethical. It's—"

"It's a potential disaster," Sangeruka slid in with a sardonic twist to his mouth. Mark blinked uncertainly. "Come, come, doctor. We both know what a devastating career move this could turn out to be. You'll be the laughing stock of the scientific community. Everyone on that crew is probably looking for a way out. You should be thanking me."

"Hardly."

"You can do things the easy way or the hard way," Sangeruka shrugged, turning away from Mark momentarily as he pushed away from the desk. Suddenly, without warning, Sangeruka swung around and landed a crashing backhand to the side of Mark's head. Mark hadn't been expecting the impact and he reeled sideways,

145

almost falling out of his seat. It took a minute for him to regain his equilibrium, and as he did so he caught a glimpse of the police chief. His expression of cold hard steel had not changed. Mark focused instead on Sangeruka, who was continuing his discourse, almost pleasantly. "Either way, the site will be shut down and all the evidence confiscated or destroyed. It will be up to you whether your crew, as well as your own name, are discredited."

"And if I refuse?" Mark asked, looking directly at Sangeruka. He still held one hand tenderly on his jaw, noting the taste of blood in his mouth, and steeled himself for another potential blow.

"I don't see that you have much choice. Chief Ganges has men waiting to take you right now to the State Penitentiary." At a nod from Sangeruka, the chief stood up, crossing his arms. Mark surveyed the lawman. Sangeruka could throw a punch, no doubt about that, but the police chief was truly gorilla like in proportions, and Mark had no doubt that a blow from him could put him to sleep permanently.

"This is blackmail," Mark muttered. "Isn't this against the law or something?" he asked, turning to the lawman.

The chief was silent. Unwavering.

"I am the law," Sangeruka said in no uncertain terms.

Mark sighed heavily, torn between what he knew was right and the possibility of rotting in an African prison where they might throw away the key. "But why, Sangeruka?" he asked, shaking his head in disbelief. "Why cover it up? This is a great find for your country. For all mankind."

"I don't expect you to understand," Sangeruka replied.

"Try me."

"Those burial grounds are sacred. Tampering with the long dead is taboo among my people."

"So this is about superstition?" Mark asked, trying to understand.

146

"Our religious practices are more than just superstition." Sangeruka glared at Mark for a moment and then swatted the air with impatient disgust. "I knew you wouldn't understand," he snapped.

"If that was the case, why did your government agree to the excavation in the first place?" Mark reasoned. "You knew right from the get go that we would be digging through a potential burial site."

"There are some of our politicians who are not as vigilant at keeping the old ways," Sangeruka said.

Mark's eyes narrowed. "Like the president, maybe?"

Sangeruka just shrugged.

"So, you're not really acting on behalf of the government at all. This is elected official Sangeruka acting as solo vigilante."

"I would watch my mouth, doctor," Sangeruka warned, raising his hand again as if to strike. Mark tried not shrink back, waiting, but the second blow never came. "There are many in the government—and out of it—that see things the same way."

Mark looked at the ceiling speculatively, talking more to himself than anyone else. "So, if I took my chances with the truth, I might get an audience with the president himself. I'm sure he'd be interested to know that one of his trusted advisors has resorted to kidnapping, bribery, even murder. Not to mention undermining a very specific directive coming right from his own desk . . ."

"Don't worry," Sangeruka laughed mirthlessly. "You would never get that chance. Many unfortunate things can happen in prison. Especially to a white foreigner seen as a power hungry oppressor. Besides, there is enough evidence of malpractice on your part, that I'm surprised the president didn't give the order to shut you down himself, long ago. Let's see . . . cave-ins, dangerous working conditions, disappearing artifacts, discrepancies left and right. What kind of operation were you running out there anyway, doctor?"

"Perhaps the site is cursed," Mark suggested with a shrug. He thought for a minute. "What about the media? They're sure to get a hold of this and make something out of it."

"It's up to you to make sure they don't."

"And if I don't?" Mark asked.

"Believe me when I say that would not be wise," Sangeruka responded. "Remember, the rest of your crew are still packing up out at the temple grounds. It would be extremely unfortunate if one or more of them met with an accident similar to your renegade friend, Rocco Cortez, now wouldn't it?"

"You wouldn't dare," Mark breathed, his eyes narrowing.

Sangeruka laughed, a sharp, mirthless sound. "As I suspected. You have no regard for your own personal safety, but your crew . . . now that's another thing, isn't it?"

"How would you explain the deaths of innocent scientists who were entrusted to your country's care?"

"The mountain roads can be treacherous, as you well know," Sangeruka shrugged.

"What if the findings get published anyway?" Mark countered. "Is murder really worth that chance? This discovery can't be kept secret forever."

"North America is not that far away. I'm sure your family means as much to you as your friends . . ."

Mark let out a sharp gust of air. "That was definitely a threat," he observed tightly, more to himself than to Sangeruka.

"A friendly warning," Sangeruka corrected. He refused to remove his icy stare from the hold it had over Mark's own eyes.

Finally Mark lowered his gaze and sighed. "This is a tough one, Sangeruka. You know you've got me between a rock and a hard place, but the only way you'll keep me quiet is to lock me up." He turned to the chief. "I guess I'll need that ride after all."

"A very foolish decision, doctor," Sangeruka said. "Although, I could have predicted as much. Perhaps you'll change your mind in a few weeks once you've had the benefit of, shall we say, reflection." He smiled cruelly.

"What about my personal effects?" Mark asked, rising warily. "A duffle bag and a small black case?"

"Ah, yes," Sangeruka nodded, surprisingly congenial. "They have been thoroughly searched, so I see no reason to retain them. Chief Ganges will see to it that you receive them on your way out. There's nothing like lost luggage to sour one's memories of a trip abroad." He walked to the door and opened it.

Mark took a step forward, but quickly realized his way was blocked by the two guards who had entered the office. Before he could do anything to prevent it, the men had grabbed his arms, holding them back behind him in a vice like grip. He tried to stiffen himself for the blow that he knew was soon to follow, tightening his stomach muscles. Instead, a blinding light of pain shot through his core as Sangeruka jerked his knee upward sharply to the groin, doubling Mark over, gasping in agony.

"Enjoy your stay," Sangeruka quipped mercilessly.

"I'm not afraid of you," Mark ground out between clenched teeth. "Beat the hell out of me all you like, but the truth will be told."

"We'll see about that," Sangeruka replied. This time his fist connected with the side of Mark's head. Everything else went black.

Chapter Thirteen

Deanie sat bolt upright in bed. Her heart was pounding loudly in her ears.

"What is it?" Russ asked groggily, trying to prop himself up on one elbow.

"I . . . I don't know," she replied with a frown. "A bad dream, I guess."

"Go back to sleep," her husband said, settling back down into the comfort of the bed.

"I think we should pray," Deanie stated.

"Yeah?" Russ asked sleepily.

"No, I mean it. I think we should pray for Mark—right now."

"Okay," Russ agreed, pulling himself up again. It wasn't the first time his wife had had such a feeling. She was usually right about these things. He had long since quit arguing.

* * *

Mark opened his eyes slowly and allowed the room to come into focus. He was back in his cell—at least he was pretty sure it was the same cell—but had no idea how long he'd been there. It could have been minutes, it could have been hours. He had no clue.

All he knew was, he had a splitting headache, every muscle ached from the hard surface upon which he'd slept and his mouth tasted like crap.

You've really done it this time, he chided himself. The excavation was probably already in ruins. And the crew . . . he didn't even want to think about what might have happened to them out there. Sangeruka could not be trusted, that was one thing he knew for certain, and to think that his crew—his friends—might be in danger . . .

The image of the flatbed truck careening over the cliff edge, Rocco inside, flashed across his mind. He could see the casket too —so carefully wrapped for transport—catapulting into the air and down out of sight. There was no way it could have survived intact. He felt suddenly sick and jerked upright in an attempt to get to the open toilet. He didn't make it, his brain screaming out in pain as a blinding light overtook his senses for a split second. Good thing he hadn't had much to eat recently, he observed wryly. The acrid stench of bile assaulted his nose, but he didn't even bother trying to wipe it off his shirt. He lay back down instead, slowly this time, hoping that the nausea—and the images plaguing his brain—would dissipate.

What about the threats that Sangeruka had made against his family? Surely he wouldn't pursue them. Was it really worth that much to the African man? All that talk about superstition and religious beliefs was probably a load of crap anyway. Sangeruka couldn't be trusted, he'd learned that much. He just hoped he hadn't put his parents in any jeopardy.

He snorted mirthlessly. Probably nothing to worry about anyway. His own situation looked pretty grim, as it was. He would probably starve to death within the next few days, if he was lucky, or get dysentery, or die of some random act of violence once transferred to the State Penitentiary.

152

He heard the rattling of keys and the creak of squeaky hinges somewhere down the hall. Heavy footsteps advanced and he propped himself carefully up on one elbow.

He recognized the same guard who had let him into the cell yesterday. A lifetime ago. The guard jerked his head, signaling for Mark to exit the cell.

They walked down the dark corridor, shoes clacking hollowly on the concrete floor; Mark in front, his hands secured behind his back with handcuffs, while the guard brought up the rear. Mark readied himself for the bright assault on the eyes that was sure to come once they entered the front of the building. However, they made a quick detour to the left, through an unfamiliar doorway. Several more security doors later, they emerged onto a darkened parking lot. Two more armed guards were waiting, along with Chief of Police Ganges. It was a lot later in the day than Mark had suspected and he glanced questioningly toward the chief.

"Whisking me away under the cover of darkness?" he asked, just a tinge of sarcasm in his voice. The chief did not answer, but just looked at him long and hard with his penetrating stare. Mark's mouth felt even drier, if it were possible, than it had. He swallowed with great difficulty. Better watch it, he thought to himself. They could do away with me right here and no one would be the wiser.

The guards marched him to a waiting police van, and before shoving him roughly into the back seat, a blindfold was tied securely over his eyes.

"There's really no need," Mark protested, a new and more intense wash of fear spreading through him.

"Quiet," was all someone said. Mark couldn't tell if it was the chief or one of the guards, but he did as he was bid. No point in totally pressing his luck, even in such a grim situation.

The vehicle sped away and Mark could do nothing but allow his body to sway with each curve. The handcuffs were still in place, making it very uncomfortable to sit properly. The horrible ride seemed to take hours—whether it really did or not was another question. At one point he dozed off, utter exhaustion overtaking his tensed up nerves.

Suddenly the vehicle came to a stop and Mark almost pitched forward into the seat in front. He could hear the familiar whine of a small plane engine—probably a Cesna—as he was hauled unceremoniously from the car.

"Can I get the blindfold off now?" he asked hopefully. There was no reply as he was half pushed, half pulled closer to the sound, tripping a couple of times along the way. Good thing the guards had a strong grip on his arms, or he would have pitched headlong into the gravel. Up the stairs, bumping down the narrow isle, shoved into a seat . . . The blindfold was retightened for good measure and before he knew it, he could feel the small craft moving forward, the engine revving up to a near scream. Soon he felt the sensation of take off and the plane was air born.

There were other passengers on this flight, two that he could make out distinctly besides the pilot. He strained his ears, listening for any clues as to who they were or where they were headed. The voices were deep, ribald laughter cutting into their words sporadically. Except for the odd word in English, they were speaking a language he didn't understand and he couldn't make any guesses about their identity. Other prisoners? Probably not. They seemed too jovial for that. Government officials? Probably not that either. It didn't make sense for them to be escorting him anywhere. He knew he wasn't merely being transported to the State Pen. They must be miles from Harare by now, and he doubted that the rebels—even Sangeruka—would go to this kind of trouble or expense on his account. Unless there really was something even bigger out at the site, something even he hadn't known about.

The plane touched down and much to Mark's surprise, the blindfold was taken off and he was allowed to descend from the plane unaided. A feeling of disorientation washed over him and he stood still for a moment, steadying himself. It was pitch black out now, but he could see that they must have landed on some deserted landing strip—if it could even be called that—out in the middle of nowhere. The men, presumably those from the airplane, were unloading cargo from the plane into a square, canvas covered army truck. The pilot didn't seem to be inclined to lift a finger, and the driver of the truck stood guard with an automatic rifle. Who were these people and why had he been sent with them? As if in answer to his unspoken question, one of the men looked at him and laughed, a toothy grin spreading across his pock marked face. He was tall, but lean and wiry. The other man was broader and less friendly. Arms dealers? Drug smugglers? Some other type of contraband?

They were finished now. The pilot was closing the cargo doors and one of the men—the lean one—was climbing back into the plane. Mark wasn't sure what he was supposed to do next.

"Uh . . . what do I do now?" he asked no one in particular.

"Town's that way," the lean one said, pointing with his finger into the blackness of the night. "About forty miles." He laughed. "Of course, the lions are out so it's doubtful you'll get there in one piece."

Mark blinked, his stomach tightening. Was that the game? Leave him out in the wilderness to be attacked and eaten by wild animals? That would be one way of disposing of him without a trace.

"Or, you could catch a ride," the man continued, still grinning. "I'd hurry, though. I think they're ready to leave."

Mark looked toward the frowning burly man, who had just finished securing the flaps on the back of the truck. Mark scurried

155

toward the passenger side and awkwardly climbed in ahead of the other man. It was a tight fit with the driver on one side and his flight comrade on the other.

"The cuffs? Can I get them off now?" he tried.

"No." The answer was brisk and to the point. There really was little use in arguing, Mark decided. It was better than taking his chances out there with the wild life.

They bumped along the track for about an hour, every movement jarring Mark's already aching body. Finally he saw lights in the distance. Civilization.

Sticking to the outskirts, they wound their way past ramshackle evidence of industrialization. Soon they were immersed in the tangle of streets—narrow and dirty—obviously not the best area of town, Mark noted. Much to his dismay, the truck pulled over on one particularly seedy looking street and came to a halt.

"This is where you get out," the driver said.

Mark blinked. "Here?" he asked uncertainly. His other traveling companion slid from the truck and waited while he scrambled out.

"Wait," the big man spoke. Now what? Was he going to be shot after all? After all he had endured already?

"The cuffs," the man stated, gesturing toward Mark's back.

Mark felt his hands being released as a wave of numbness coursed through his arms all the way from the elbows down. He was sure that the circulation had been totally cut off for quite some time and the sensation was almost surreal, like he had huge stumps for hands that were not really connected in any way to the rest of his body.

"Thanks," Mark said, circling his wrists and trying to rub the feeling back into them. The other man went around to the back of the vehicle and a few minutes later, threw a couple of bags at

Mark's feet. Mark blinked in surprise, at a loss for words. It was his duffle bag and saxophone case.

The big man caught Mark's eye for a moment, sending some kind of unspoken message that Mark could not quite interpret. Then he turned and got back into the vehicle.

"Um, is that it? Are you just going to leave me here?" Mark asked, frowning. The other man simply nodded.

"But . . ."

"Good luck," was all the other said as the vehicle rolled forward. Mark watched it turn the corner and trundle out of sight. Okay. So maybe this was Sangeruka's next best tactic. Abandon him in some African ghetto where he would get mugged and stabbed to death. But then why give him back his luggage?

He looked around uncertainly. It was pretty deserted, and for that he was thankful. He spotted a narrow doorway with an alcove off to one side. It was just big enough to curl up in for the night. He headed that way, clutching the duffle bag and sax case close.

Noise. Honking, shouting, bustling. Mark opened his eyes, squinting at the brightness of a new day. He groaned as he struggled into an upright position. Was it possible for anyone to feel more like crap? Every bone ached, every muscle cried out in pain, and the sandpaper in his mouth was enough to make him want to gag. Not to mention the gnawing hunger in his belly.

Okay. What to do first. Find out where in the hell he was, that's what.

"Excuse me," he tried, greeting a rather large black woman dressed in a brightly printed dress. "I was wondering—" The woman glared at him as she made a wide berth around him.

Mark threw up his hands and turned to another passer by, this time approaching a man in a loose fitting cotton shirt. Again, no response as the man hurried past.

Mark frowned. What was up? Did he look like an escaped

convict who hadn't eaten in two days?

"Ma'am? Ma'am!" he cried, almost sounding desperate as he stepped in front of the next person on the street. "I just—what city is this?" She stopped momentarily, surveying him as if he were deranged. "What city is this?" he repeated.

She stepped back. "Pretoria," she stated, as if he were dense. She shook her head condescendingly before continuing briskly on her way.

Pretoria. Okay. That was good news. South Africa was a fairly safe country to be in at the moment. If he could find his way to a hotel or something and get cleaned up, get some food and water in his system. Simple enough.

He squatted down on the sidewalk and opened his duffle bag. Change of clothes, deodorant . . . His heart sank. Naturally. No wallet, no passport, no cell phone. He should have expected as much. Whoever helped him escape was obviously not that altruistic.

He needed some cash, but there was really nothing of value that he could pawn. He stopped short. Well, there was one thing. He looked at the battered black case that held Jack's saxophone. He couldn't part with it. He just couldn't. It was out of the question.

What else was he supposed to do? Beg? Starve to death? Die of thirst? With resolve he stood erect, clutching the case firmly in one hand. Jack had told him the story of how the saxophone had saved a life once before. His stepmother Deanie's life. She was attacked by a former boyfriend and another one of her friends used the sax to hit the guy over the head. Jack had the instrument repaired, but you could still see the traces of dents on its gleaming surface. Well, it looked like the instrument was going to have to pull double duty again. Only this time, his was the life on the line.

Twenty minutes later, Mark emerged from a pawn shop,

158

burden lighter, but definitely with a heavy heart. Another half hour passed and he'd satisfied his thirst and wolfed down some food from a local market. Next on the list was finding a decent washroom where he could clean up a bit, and then it was off to find the Canadian Consulate. With any luck, he'd be able to get some temporary documents and access his bank account. Then it would be straight back to the pawn shop to retrieve his beloved sax.

He knew better than to even consider trying to make it back to Zimbabwe. That was just asking for trouble. He had no idea who had arranged for his escape, or if it was all part of some elaborate plot arranged by Sangeruka himself. In any case, he'd be watching his back for the next little while, that's for sure.

In the mean time, he needed to find out what had gone down back at the site. He needed to get a hold of Laura somehow. And he needed to get back to New Mexico ASAP. There was just too much valuable information floating around out there.

Sangeruka's words of warning rang in his mind once again. He needed to be smart about all of this and not put anyone else in danger. He also knew he couldn't ignore the truth.

Chapter Fourteen

Mark sat at his work station, microscope in front of him, as he contemplated his next course of action. He had been back in New Mexico for exactly a week. He debated long and hard about what his next move should be. With the artifacts he had sent to his father and the lab in Albuquerque, as well as the correspondence he had continued with his friend and colleague, John Bergman, he should have more than enough evidence to present his findings. But Sangeruka's threats continued to haunt him. It wasn't his own personal safety that he was worried about, but until he was sure the rest of the crew were safely out of Africa, he wouldn't—he couldn't—do anything. And his family . . . the possibility of harm coming to them was so preposterous, and yet so frightening, that he couldn't even allow his mind to travel down that road.

He couldn't believe what he had gone through in the last week. It almost seemed like a dream, now that he was back in familiar surroundings at the university. After visiting the Canadian Consulate, he had stayed in Pretoria for the next several days, trying to make contact with Laura or anyone else who might have any information about what had happened after he'd been removed from the archeological site. He had also left a short message—very short—with his father. He skipped the part about abduction and jail, simply informing them that he was on his way to New Mexico to continue with the next phase of his work there.

His friend and colleague John Bergman was at the airport to meet him when he arrived in Albuquerque and they had set to work on analyzing all the data that he had gathered.

"Graham! Still hard at it, I see," John said as he strolled into the lab where Mark was presently working. John was about Mark's age, smaller in build, but with a wiry, athletic frame. He had sandy brown hair which he kept closely cropped and wore thick rimmed glasses. He was wearing his usual white lab coat, which flowed out behind him when he walked.

"Hi, John," Mark answered, only looking up briefly from his microscope.

"When is the rest of your team coming, again?" John asked, propping himself on the edge of the work table. "You've an awful lot of samples to scour yet."

"I told you. Laura and the rest need to finish closing out the site."

"Any timeline on that?" John queried curiously, examining a pencil he had picked up.

Mark frowned slightly. What was up with John anyway? "Not exactly. But should be soon. Any reason?"

"I know I told you I didn't mind helping until the rest of your crew arrived, but I've got some other research I need to finish up myself," John offered, almost apologetically, putting the pencil down.

"Thanks for all your help, John. I appreciate it," Mark said, surveying his friend. So far he hadn't shared Sangeruka's directives with anyone. He wanted to wait and see just what kind of final analysis they came up with first before alerting anyone else to any potential threats. And of course, he wouldn't do anything until he knew Laura and the others were safe.

"Man oh man, you've got some pretty interesting stuff here, Graham," John whistled. "Kind of all over the map in terms of geologic dating, but interesting none the less. You think seismic activity accounts for some of the discrepancies in age?"

"Um . . . could be," Mark answered noncommittally.

"Must be something," John said, shaking his head. "I've never seen a more perfectly intact Pterodactyl wing before. When you sent me the first sample I was impressed, but what you've sent since . . . " He whistled again. "Beautiful."

"You should have seen the headpiece," Mark offered. "The one I sent pictures of?"

"Too bad you weren't able to send one over as well. I would've liked to take a look at that baby first hand," John nodded.

"Right. The first ones we found were pretty fragile, although I think Laura was packing some fragments. At least I hope . . ."

"And that last one? The one on the mummified specimen. That's still on its way, right?" John asked.

"We ran into some glitches with the government. It was considered sacred and not to be removed from the country." It wasn't really a lie. Just a bit of spin on the truth.

"Too bad," John said, shaking his head again. "I suppose you'll be going back to do your analysis on it there?"

"Uh, I'm not sure about that yet," Mark hedged.

John raised his eyebrows in surprise. "Why not?"

Mark sighed. Maybe it was time to confide in John about the actual events that took place before he arrived back in New Mexico. So far John had proven to be a helpful and enthusiastic ally. If there was a conspiracy, he doubted that John would be part of it.

"Listen, John. There were some pretty . . . strange . . . things taking place out at that site and afterwards. I wasn't going to say anything, but I guess it's time I was straight with you about it, especially since you're putting so much time and effort into helping me."

John looked at his friend with a sideways frown. "What is it, buddy?"

"I was arrested and forcibly removed from the site," Mark said.

"What?!"

Mark nodded. "The last I heard, the army was coming in to move everyone else off site as well. I haven't heard from any of them since. Not Anthony, not Laura. I don't even know if they're okay."

"But why? How?" John sputtered. "I don't get it, man. What else did you find out there?"

"You've seen it," Mark replied. "But apparently somebody doesn't want the information to go public."

"Why not?"

"I'm not quite sure. Could be political. Somehow I think there's more to it than that."

"Yeah? Like what?"

"Well," Mark began hesitantly. "Just some theories. Kind of way out there. Never mind."

John laughed. "No way, Graham. You can't feed me a lead like that and just leave me hangin'."

"Remember you mentioned something about the discrepancies in geologic dating?" Mark began tentatively.

"Yeah," John nodded.

"There's a theory out there that suggests those aren't discrepancies at all. That dinosaurs and man lived contemporaneously and the world was subsequently exposed to a catastrophic flood that wiped out the dinosaurs."

"You're kidding, right?" John said with half a grin.

"No. We found evidence of massive sedimentation that

corroborates that theory. It cemented off the burial tombs and created almost a vacuum-sealed environment to preserve the artifacts within. That, and the advanced technology used to bury the king himself, preserved the specimens—both man and reptile. And remember that antechamber and the plaster chip I sent you for analysis?"

"Mmhm."

"Very advanced technology. The Bible speaks about just such a time before the flood—"

"Whoa! Wait a minute," John stopped him. "So we've suddenly made this quantum leap to the Bible?"

"I told you it was just a theory," Mark said defensively. "Anthony and I have both been doing some research and it is a plausible explanation."

"Okay, okay. Back up here for a minute. Let's just leave the religion out of it and get back to the site itself. So you found all this evidence of dinosaurs and man and an advanced civilization, but you still haven't told me how this ties in with why you got shut down and arrested."

"Right. The theory goes that there is this international conspiracy to discredit all finds that could possibly back up the creationist model. The first I heard of it was from Rocco, but I've been doing my homework, and it appears to be true. There's all kinds of unpublished, slanderized evidence out there that is just not making it into scientific journals, while at the same time people are bending over backwards to make the evolutionary model fit the evidence."

"Rocco Cortez, you say?" John asked.

Mark nodded.

"I remember hearing something about that guy from another dig I was doing some lab work for. From all accounts, most people thought the guy was a bit nuts."

165

"Exactly my point," Mark responded. "Nobody wanted to believe him. He's dead, by the way," he added quietly.

John looked over at Mark in surprise.

Mark nodded. "The day I got arrested and taken off site—at gun point, I might add—we had the casket all crated and ready for transport. It was sitting on the flatbed waiting for the transport helicopter when all of a sudden one of the government officials stepped off the chopper. Rocco highjacked the truck and the chopper took off in pursuit, with me on board. I saw it happen, John. These guys mean business. They shot him down and the truck went flying off the road into a steep ravine, casket and all. There's no way Rocco could have survived that crash, and I doubt that they'll be able to recover the casket either." Mark paused for a moment in reflection. Rocco had been his friend, despite what Sangeruka had said about him. There was no point in sharing that other information with John. No use tainting his memories of the man any further.

John shook his head, taking in what Mark had just said. "So you think this conspiracy is so deep that they'd resort to killing for it?"

"Maybe," Mark shrugged. "Look, there was lots of other stuff going on at the site as well, before that. Stuff going missing, cave-ins, deletions on the computers, analysis getting lost in the mail . . . You name it, it happened. It was just too much to be a coincidence."

"You know what it's like working in these backwoods countries," John said.

"I know. But this was way above and beyond that."

"And that's why they arrested you?" John asked.

"They tried to make it sound like they were shutting down the site for safety reasons. Malpractice and breech of contract or something, although I was careful to stick to the letter of the law.

166

As for my arrest, it was completely bogus. Mr. Sangeruka, one of the president's advisors and a member of the government assembly, apparently had his own agenda for scaring me off the job."

"And that was?" John asked.

"He says that tampering with the ancient dead is taboo in his culture," Mark scoffed.

"Maybe it is," John shrugged.

"Maybe, but Sangeruka doesn't strike me as a man who cares much for culture if it doesn't benefit him personally. I think there's more to it than that."

"Your conspiracy theory," John stated.

"He warned me not to publish my findings. Not to pursue it in any way, in fact. If I didn't agree, they were going to slam me in a Zimbabwean jail indefinitely—not a fun experience, I can tell you. He also warned me that if I did try to make any of the discoveries public he would see to it that my entire career and credibility would be ruined. He even threatened me personally, as well as the crew. It's why I'm a bit concerned that I haven't heard from any of them yet, and also why I haven't mentioned any of this to you earlier. I need to make sure everyone is safe before I can go ahead and publish my findings."

"What kind of threats?" John asked.

"The worst kind," Mark answered simply. "I don't think Sangeruka's arm is really as long as he tries to make out though. At least I hope not. However, if he is involved in some kind of international conspiracy, I could be wrong."

"And you think he might be?"

"It seems to me he was going to awfully great lengths if it was just a matter of preserving cultural taboos. I mean, I hope that's all it is, because then I think we're pretty safe in pursuing this thing. But if it's something bigger . . ." He trailed off.

167

"Looks like you may have dug yourself a pretty deep hole this time, my friend," John said.

* * *

Two days later Mark was back at his usual station, analyzing more samples when John breezed into the lab.

"Look what the cat dragged in," John called.

Mark looked up and his eyes widened in surprise when he saw who accompanied John. "Laura, Anthony!" Mark stood and grabbed Anthony, slapping him soundly on the back a few times.

"Got something for you," Anthony whispered before Mark let him go.

Mark's eyebrows shot up in question, but Anthony shook his head, almost imperceptibly. Okay, what ever it was, it would have to wait for later. He turned to Laura. Their embrace was more like a gentle, lingering squeeze. "But you didn't call. You didn't even email me!"

"Sorry about that," Laura apologized, pulling back from Mark's arms. "I was having some trouble sending messages while on site. They kept coming back to me." She looked down sheepishly.

"We knew you'd love the surprise," Anthony added with a wink.

"I'm just glad to see that you're safe," Mark stated, gesturing for the group to find a seat somewhere. "So tell me everything."

"You first," Laura countered. "Believe me, we were worried sick for quite a few days until we actually got back to Harare ourselves. Then we were told you had already flown back to the States."

Mark shook his head. "It wasn't good." He looked over at his colleagues, calculating just how much he should tell them. "The casket got destroyed," he informed bluntly.

A look of utter shock crossed both Anthony's and Laura's

168

faces. "How?" Anthony asked.

"The truck went over the side of the mountain," Mark replied.

"And Rocco?" Laura asked sharply.

"Dead."

Anthony let out a gasp. "Oh God."

"Sangeruka said everything was looked after," Laura said quietly. "He never mentioned this."

"Figures," Mark said under his breath.

"I don't understand . . ." Laura said frowning.

"So what happened?" Anthony asked. "We thought you were under arrest. Then, when we got to Harare, Sangeruka said it was all a mistake and that you had left the country already."

"Is that all he said?" Mark asked.

"He had a little chat with most of the crew members. Individually," Anthony replied.

Laura's eyes flickered momentarily toward John before squarely focusing on Mark. "Maybe we should talk about it later," she said.

"I can leave you folks alone, if you'd like," John offered, rising from the stool that he was occupying.

"It's okay," Mark said, gesturing for John to take his seat. "I've already filled John in on everything, as far as I know it, anyway. He's been helping me with this thing all along. He deserves to know the truth." Laura frowned, looking uncomfortable. Mark persisted. "Did he threaten you?"

"He made some insinuations about my future employment opportunities, so to speak," Anthony laughed. "But I wasn't too worried. Everyone pretty much thinks I'm a screw ball, anyway."

"Laura?" Mark directed at her.

"Um . . . the same as Anthony, I guess," she said lightly. "Let's get to what happened to you."

"Not yet," Mark shook his head decisively. "I need to know

what else happened at the site."

"Well, we started packing up the minute you took off," Anthony explained. "But I think it took a lot longer than they were expecting. Obviously, they didn't realize the extent of the equipment and artifacts we had to deal with yet, not to mention the dig site itself. Anyway, a whole battalion of army trucks showed up the next day. They were actually pretty friendly. Helpful even. Wouldn't you say, Laura?" He looked over at her for confirmation. "Anyway, the guy in charge, I forget his name, seemed genuinely interested in preserving what was already discovered, so I wasn't as worried as I had been about leaving things in their hands. Unfortunately, there was no more shipping of the rest of the artifacts. They are now the sole property of the people of Zimbabwe. It took quite a while to pack up all the equipment, though, as well as finish cataloguing what was there. They took copies of our records, so the government will be expecting the return of all missing artifacts that are documented as going overseas for analysis."

Mark nodded thoughtfully. "At least that is something. There is enough documentation to prove where each and every artifact was found. Nobody can deny their existence."

"Who would want to do that?" Laura laughed. The sound was stilted, almost nervous sounding.

Mark scowled, looking at Laura speculatively. "After all we've been through, I'm surprised you even have to ask that question."

She turned to John and rolled her eyes slightly. "He's become a bit paranoid over the last few months," she laughed apologetically.

"With good reason," Anthony piped up.

"Don't worry. He's filled me in on his latest theory," John responded with a grin. "A bit too much time in the African sun, I'd

170

say."

"Exactly," Laura nodded.

"Although," John continued, "In the good doctor's defense, the lab results are pretty damn intriguing."

"I can hardly wait to see what's come out of that," Anthony enthused.

"Um, guys," Laura said hesitantly, looking from John to Anthony. "Do you think Mark and I could spend just a couple of minutes together? Privately?"

The two men glanced over at Mark questioningly.

Laura continued, "You know. We haven't seen each other in awhile . . . " she trailed off with a tiny laugh and shrugged her shoulders.

"Oh, right," John nodded knowingly. "I forgot about that. I'd heard that you two had hooked up on site."

Mark scowled. Anthony rose from his seat. "Come on, John. You can show me some of those lab results."

John led the way from the room and shut the door behind them with a click. There were a few moments of awkward silence before Laura spoke up. "Mark, what really happened after you got taken away in that helicopter? I know there's more to it. I can always tell when you're hiding something from me."

Mark surveyed her irritably for a second or two. "Same here. I don't think you've been completely forthright about your conversation with Sangeruka either."

Laura sighed. "He said you had decided there was nothing worth pursuing at the site. That you had just taken off for the States and left it all behind because you didn't want to ruin your reputation in the archeological field. I knew it wasn't the truth. I know you better than that and it just didn't sound like you. What really happened?"

He furrowed his brow more deeply. "I'm surprised you even

care after that shot back there with John."

"Oh come on," Laura protested. "It was a joke. Now you're sounding childish."

"Why do you insist on denying the facts when they're staring you right in the face?" Mark asked accusingly.

"I'm not denying the facts," Laura defended. "You know as well as I do that there is a plausible—and scientific—explanation for everything we've discovered."

"So how do you explain the shut down? Sangeruka? The army?"

"Obviously there's something going on, but I don't see that the two are related. Shutting the site down because of some kind of plot to stop the advancement of creationists—well, it sounds as lunatic as it is."

"Now I'm a lunatic."

"I didn't say that." Laura stopped for a moment, watching Mark as a muscle moved rhythmically in his jaw. "Mark, come on. You're entirely too tense. You're paranoid."

"Who wouldn't be after what I've been through?" he countered.

"Exactly. Which brings me back to my original question," Laura said more gently. "Just what did happen?"

"Let's see," Mark began cryptically. "After I witnessed Sangeruka kill Rocco in cold blood, and completely destroy the most valuable archeological find of the century, I endured a night in a dark prison cell with no food or water. Then I was interrogated, threatened, beaten up, and finally blindfolded, handcuffed and transported to Pretoria, where I was dumped and left to fend for myself. Hmm . . . Did I miss anything?"

"Oh Mark, I'm so sorry," Laura tried to console. "He—they beat you and threatened you and then let you go? But Sangeruka said—"

"Sangeruka is a lying bastard," Mark interrupted. "He can't be trusted. I have no idea if it was him who arranged for my release and if so, if it was done just to solidify his threats. Or it could be somebody else working against him for who knows what purpose. All I know is that this is no game, Laura. We're dealing with something bigger than any of us thought. And for some reason, they don't want us to share the information."

"What kind of threats did he make?" Laura asked.

"Against me, my family, the crew," Mark listed. "He said not to publish the findings from the dig or else."

"Or else what?"

"What do you think?" Mark quipped. "After what he did to Rocco, I don't think he meant a slap on the wrist."

"Did he really—kill Rocco?" Laura asked in shock. "You said before Rocco's truck went off the cliff."

"After Sangeruka purposely blew all four tires."

"Oh," she said softly.

"And what exactly did he say to you?" Mark demanded. "You never did say."

"Nothing quite so lethal," Laura offered.

"Meaning?"

"He said he'd ruin you. All of us. Our reputations, I mean."

"Bastard," Mark breathed vehemently. "Who does he think he is? The public has a right to know."

"What? You're not thinking of doing it, are you? Going public with this?"

"What do you propose I do?" Mark asked. "Lie? Make something up? People know I've been working on that dig for quite some time. Not just the actual field work, but I've got a couple of years of research into it as well. Now all of a sudden, I'm not interested any more?"

"It's not worth that much. This is your entire life's work we're

173

talking about," she argued. "Not to mention the rest of us. Have you thought about that?"

"Worrying about your own tush again, I see," Mark quipped with sarcasm.

"Now you're being selfish," she countered.

"Maybe," Mark shrugged. "It's when we start bowing to terrorists like Sangeruka that we're really in trouble."

"You used to be so solid. Logical. Now you're ready to throw away your career—"

"What about the evidence," Mark cut in. "Huh? You can't deny what we all saw."

"The evidence was very sketchy. Almost like it had been contaminated, tampered with. And with all the mishaps on site it's probably best just to shut down quietly and say it wasn't worth the effort," Laura reasoned.

"Why Laura? Why so reluctant to face the facts?" Mark wanted to know.

"Facts? The fact is we're in possible danger, here, Mark. Not to mention the fact that we could all become the laughing stock of the scientific community."

"So we're back to that."

Laura sighed heavily. "Mark, I care about you. I know we haven't been getting along that well lately, but once this is behind us things will go back to the way they should be."

"And how's that?"

"You know. Us. Together."

"I don't think I want any 'us together' if it means lying about what we've found."

"I didn't say lie."

"Oh right, you just said pretend it didn't happen. In my books that's a lie. I know what I saw, Laura."

"Your seeing and other people believing are two different

174

things. You need evidence. And what kind of credible evidence do you have left to back it up, huh? Think about it Mark. Sangeruka's already been busy tampering with the documentation. You can bet on that. And all the documentation, and all the records mean nothing without the specimens themselves."

"I've still got specimens," Mark said irritably.

"Fine. A few bones and other samples, but no real proof that it was found where we said it was found. And the most important piece of evidence is destroyed."

"I've still got some other evidence tucked away in a safe place. Remember I told you I was taking precautions."

She closed her eyes for a moment and shook her head. "You're just not getting it, are you?" she breathed.

"I'm not going to roll over and play dead, Laura," he stated firmly. "You know me better than that."

"No?" she asked. "Maybe you won't be playing." She looked at him with candor. "Okay, Mark. Listen. I wasn't completely truthful just a few minutes ago. He threatened me too. He said it was up to me to make sure you didn't publish any of your work from the temple site. If you did, he said he'd kill you. And if I told anyone else about it, he'd kill them too."

Mark closed his eyes, letting out a gust of breath. "I . . . I just don't know what to do," he finally responded soberly.

"Don't you?" Laura asked candidly.

"I can't just back down," Mark argued. "Surely you must understand—"

There was a light rapping on the closed door and John stuck his head in. "Excuse me, you two, but I forgot something in here. Anthony's waiting out in the hall. I've got another appointment I need to make." He slipped inside and headed to one of the cupboards.

"It's okay," Mark said. "We were through anyway."

"This conversation is by no means over," Laura said under her breath as John left the room.

Anthony peered around the door frame. "Safe to come in?" he asked.

"Of course," Mark replied with a slight edge to his voice. "What did you think we were doing in here?"

Anthony raised his hands in a sign of surrender. "Hey, that's not up to me to speculate." Laura rolled her eyes. Anthony continued. "Laura, you'll want to take a look at some of the stuff John's been working on. I think even you will be impressed."

"No thanks," Laura said in a clipped voice. "I think I've seen and heard enough for one day." She turned to Mark. "Just remember what I said and don't do anything stupid. At least not for awhile anyway, until the rest of us have had time to distance ourselves."

"Thanks for being so compassionate," Mark quipped.

"It's your life," she countered angrily, tears in her voice. "If you're set on throwing it away, I can't stop you. Just don't expect me to follow along."

She turned and strode from the room.

"What was that all about?" Anthony asked in surprise, his eyebrows raised. "Lover's quarrel?"

"Hardly," Mark said under his breath.

"So, uh, Mark . . . " Anthony asked tentatively. "Is it true that you're not going to publish your findings?"

"Who wants to know?"

"Whoa! Buddy!" Anthony exclaimed. "This is me, remember? It's what Sangeruka claimed. I told you that already. I asked John, but he seemed pretty uninformed."

"I haven't decided for sure yet," Mark replied.

"By the look of what you're sitting on, I'd say you'd be hard pressed not to. I mean, we all saw what was in the burial chamber with our own eyes. Now that you and John have been crunching the numbers, I'd say it's your duty to tell the truth just the way we found it."

Mark surveyed the other man closely. "You finish reading that book I lent you?" he asked.

Anthony nodded. "My feelings on the subject are—mixed. It all makes perfect sense and what we've seen in the last few months certainly seems to verify that an international cover up against creationist theory is definitely at work. I'm just not sure I'm ready to believe in all that Bible stuff again. It would mean eating some humble pie with my folks and I'm not much for the taste of that."

"I see. But you do think it's part of the conspiracy?" Mark asked. "All of the glitches, the mishaps, getting run out of the country. Everything?"

Anthony nodded. "It's got to be. What else could it be?"

"And Sangeruka? What do you make of his involvement?"

"Now that's one I haven't quite figured out yet, although I'm sure he is involved somehow. I just didn't buy his whole story about wanting to preserve the traditions of his countrymen."

"Me neither," Mark agreed. "He blackmailed you too?"

"What do you mean 'too'?" Anthony asked.

"He threatened the lives of the crew if I didn't promise to keep quiet. Not to mention my own life as well as my reputation."

"Hm. He didn't go that far with me," Anthony said. "He just tried to appeal to my intellectual side. My training as an expert in folklore and the importance of keeping the sacred trust of the local people. He said their rituals demanded that the ancient dead be left undisturbed and that it was also taboo to even talk about it. He made me swear to secrecy. As a scholar, I guess he figured he could safely take that route without going any further."

"But you didn't buy it," Mark observed.

"Are you kidding?" Anthony scoffed. "He was obviously

forgetting that as an expert I do have some background knowledge about these things. I've never heard any such references to such things in that area of the world at all."

Mark nodded in understanding.

"So?" Anthony asked again. "Are you going public or not?"

Mark let out a heavy sigh. "I'm leaning in that direction."

"That's the spirit," Anthony said enthusiastically. "I'd hate to see the bad guys win, you know what I mean?"

"What makes you think they won't?" Mark asked soberly.

"Well, I suppose that is a possibility," Anthony conceded. "But we can't let them win without at least putting up a fight. Say, you want to know what I got you?"

Mark raised his eyebrows. He had almost forgotten. "Sure."

Anthony put up one finger as a signal to wait for a minute. He went to his backpack, which he had deposited on the counter by the door. After a few seconds of rummaging, he pulled out a slim, silver cylinder.

"What is it?" Mark asked with curiosity.

Anthony brought the container over to where Mark sat and popped off the lid. Inside were several small plastic bags. "I got those skin and hair samples, just like you asked," he said with a grin.

Mark blinked in disbelief. "You what?"

"The skin and hair samples," Anthony repeated. "To be more specific, skin, hair, and a nail sample from the king himself, and some scales and leather from the Pterodactyl headdress as well as a fragment from the beak."

"But how did you . . ." Mark trailed off as the probable method of smuggling the evidence dawned on him. "You didn't, did you?"

"Don't worry," Anthony replied glibly with a smile. "I had the cylinder itself wrapped in plastic with a coating of Vaseline.

Absolutely no contaminants reached the samples themselves."

Mark squeezed his eyes tight, trying not to let a picture form in his head. He couldn't help the smile that crept across his face until he suddenly burst out in full-fledged laughter. Anthony joined him good naturedly. "I can't believe you actually did that," Mark muttered.

"Anything for the cause, right?" Anthony grinned.

"What if you'd been caught?"

"I didn't plan on it," Anthony shrugged. "In any case, I wasn't, now was I? I know it can never replace the real thing, but at least it's something."

Mark shook his head. "You're a real trooper, you know that? Now how can I not go forward?"

"I was hoping I'd convince you," Anthony nodded with another grin.

Mark slapped Anthony across the back. At least he knew he had one solid ally.

Chapter Fifteen

Now that Anthony was back, new hope seemed to rise to the surface for Mark. Any threats from Sangeruka, any warnings from Laura—even his own doubts—seemed miniscule and he dismissed them in order to single-mindedly pursue the publication of his findings. John, whose help had been so valuable at first, was unable to help as much now, since he had projects of his own to work on. But Mark had known this was the case from the beginning and was not dampened in spirit. Anthony was making valuable contributions to the project, adding his knowledge of the connections with ancient legends, including the Biblical accounts, and it was now up to Mark to put it all together in some kind of format that would explain all the data and be acceptable for publication in a scientific journal.

"Anthony, how are those specs coming?" Mark asked, looking up from his laptop as Anthony entered the room. His smile faded when Anthony didn't answer. The look on the other man's face was grim and sounded an alarm bell in Mark's brain. "What is it?"

"I just heard a rumor," Anthony replied. "The specimens are already packed for shipment back to Africa."

"What?" Mark asked, eyeing Anthony sharply. "So soon? Who told you?"

"The lab receptionist," Anthony answered.

"That can't be," Mark said, rising from his chair. "I was just in the vault yesterday. The university made all the arrangements so that we could wait to ship after my presentation. The date has already been set. It's a done deal."

"Well, if I were you, I'd check again," Anthony advised.

Mark did just that. He strode with purpose down the hall and stopped at the reception desk. "What's this I hear about artifacts—my artifacts—being shipped back to Africa without my knowledge?" he asked the girl at the desk abruptly.

She raised her eyebrows defensively. "You can check with the Dean of Archeological Studies yourself, if you like. I just happened to mention to Anthony that I had heard something to that effect." She glared purposely at Anthony.

Without any further acknowledgement, Mark swung his body down the hallway to his right, Anthony scuttling after him. He bypassed the Dean's receptionist with a dismissive wave and rapped briskly on the wooden door leading into the office. As soon as the muffled 'Yes?' was heard from within, Mark barged into the room.

"Are the African artifacts getting shipped back?" he asked without preamble.

The other man took off his glasses with deliberate calmness and gestured to the available chair in front of his desk. "Doctor Graham, have a seat, won't you?"

"Just answer the question, Taylor," Mark replied, not budging. His eyes were blue daggers as they searched the Dean's face.

Dean Taylor was a man of about fifty with steel grey hair and a neatly trimmed goatee. The Doctor of Archeology and Anthropology, with honorary degrees from several of the most prestigious institutions in Europe and North America, matched Mark's gaze with unwavering determination. "An agreement was signed with the Zimbabwean government. You know that."

"Yes, I know, but I thought we had agreed to wait until after my presentation," Mark countered. "Institutions like this university have an overriding responsibility to make sure that the world's priceless artifacts are properly preserved and cared for. You can't just turn them over to some other entity whose reputation is questionable at best. Not until we're sure they'll be properly preserved and housed. Those artifacts are priceless. Once they're presented publicly we'll have a better bargaining tool to make the Zimbabwean government see that. Keeping them here at least until then could buy us the time we need to—"

"Um, about your presentation . . ." Taylor cut in.

Mark narrowed his eyes. "What about it?"

"It seems we may have to postpone that for awhile," Taylor hedged. "Strictly a scheduling issue."

"Oh really," Mark snorted skeptically. "Why doesn't that surprise me?"

"You know that we're sitting on a bit of a hot bed, Dr. Graham. The last thing this institution needs is the kind of controversy that could lead to funding cuts. As it is, we're just holding on to many of our corporate sponsorships."

"So this is about money?" Mark asked. "What ever happened to scholarly excellence?"

"I don't think you realize the gravity of this situation," Taylor countered. "Dealing with foreign governments can be very tricky."

"Nothing you haven't handled before," Mark said with exasperation.

"This is a matter of legality. They have a legal right -"

"Legal right!" Mark exploded. "This institution has an obligation to preserve history!"

"Governments can be fickle. We can't take the chance of a law suit," Taylor continued reasonably.

"I was there, remember? Those government officials are steeped in bribery and all kinds of questionable practices. We have an obligation to do what's right, not just on moral grounds, but on scientific grounds."

"Sometimes it's best just to back down rather than push an issue that could end up bringing bad publicity to the university."

"Oh, so this is about publicity," Mark stated flatly. "You don't want any bad press."

"That is part of my job," Taylor reminded.

"How can you be so nonchalant about this?" Mark asked incredulously. "You do realize what we're sitting on here?"

Taylor hesitated for a moment and looked down at his fingers, which he had steepled in front of him. "Um . . . I've been meaning to have a discussion about that."

Mark surveyed Taylor suspiciously. "What do you mean?"

Taylor cleared his throat uncomfortably and sat up straighter before meeting Mark's gaze. "I've been hearing some rather . . . alarming things about the way you are presenting your findings, Dr. Graham."

Mark's eyes narrowed. "Yeah? From whom?"

"That's not the point. The point is, this institution is not interested in any bad publicity over a questionable archeological dig. The fact that we are already running into difficulty with the local governing body is bad enough and now, to find out that our premier archeologist on site is twisting the data for some kind of personal agenda . . . well, I don't need to spell out for you how bad that makes us all look."

Mark was stunned. He couldn't even formulate an immediate reply. Twisting the data for his own personal agenda? What in the world was Taylor talking about? And who was feeding him this information? Laura? He knew she was angry with him, but he would never have expected that kind of retaliation.

184

"Actually," Taylor continued, "what I was going to suggest to you was a brief leave of absence."

"A leave of absence," Mark repeated flatly. "What does that mean, exactly, Dean? Am I being dismissed?"

"Only temporarily. Until this unfortunate situation blows over," Taylor said with a placating smile. "You're a world class scientist, Doctor Graham, known in your field. You wouldn't want to taint your reputation with the type of questionable speculation I'm afraid you've fallen into."

"So you're telling me to drop everything I've been working on for all these months. Just abandon the evidence because you're afraid it might bring some bad press to this institution?" Mark shook his head in disbelief.

"You've obviously gotten way too involved personally," Taylor shrugged.

"Personally involved? Of course, I'm personally involved!" Mark puffed angrily. "It's my life's work. My passion. You know that. It's what makes me good at what I do and one of the reasons you wanted me on board at this institution in the first place, in case you don't remember. You can't expect me to just abandon everything I've been working on?"

"You can work on your dissertation all you like, but just not under the auspices of this institution," Taylor stated.

"Meaning, if I publish anything, you won't verify or back up any of my findings."

Taylor just shrugged in agreement.

"Tell me something," Mark asked, leaning forward. "Your contact from Africa wouldn't happen to be a guy named Sangeruka?"

"I'm not obliged to share that information with you, doctor," Taylor stated, pressing his lips together.

Mark nodded. "Yep. I should've known. So it probably didn't

take much convincing for you to pack up all the artifacts. The farther they are away, the easier it will be to distance yourself." He laughed mirthlessly. "People are going to wonder, you know. There was enough sharing of information that it won't just disappear."

"I know that. That's why I'm going to get someone else to compile the findings."

"Who?" Mark asked with suspicion.

Taylor hesitated, as if he was debating with himself whether to reveal that information to Mark or not. "I've got Doctors Sawchuk and Bergman already working on it."

Mark felt numb. Laura and John. Laura he could understand. She had been threatened herself and probably thought she was saving him somehow. But John? He had been so helpful, so supportive . . . so interested in every detail. Now he knew why. The betrayal was almost too much to swallow.

"And what if I publish my own findings separate from theirs?" Mark asked.

"I can't stop you," Taylor replied. "It's a free country. But don't expect to be welcomed back under the umbrella of this institution ever again, or any other reputable institute of higher learning, for that matter."

Mark was silent for a moment. To sever himself from the university in New Mexico was more than just an act based on moral principle. It could mean the end of his career. But the thought of out and out lying—pretending none of it had ever happened and that he had not seen with his own eyes what he knew he had . . .

What would Jack do? He'd always had an answer. Mark wished now that he had spent more time with him in these last years. With all of them, really. He had been so preoccupied with making his own discoveries that he had neglected the one thing that was most important. Family.

And now it was too late—for Jack, at least. He would never see him again.

A small voice inside whispered. That's not what Jack believed.

Mark blinked. That's right. Jack had given his life to Christ. If there really was a God, and Jesus was it, Jack was safely in heaven, waiting for the rest of them. It was the hope of his entire family— his father, Deanie, Harmony, his grandmother . . .

If he had ever wished he believed like the rest of them, now would be the time. He needed all the help he could get with this situation.

"Well, Dean Taylor, it's been good working with you," Mark said calmly, stretching out his hand to shake the other man's. Taylor looked surprised and didn't reciprocate the gesture immediately. Finally, he grasped Mark's hand tentatively.

"I'm not sure I understand," Taylor said.

"I doubt we'll be seeing one another again," Mark replied. "Even if I do lay low for awhile and drop this whole project, I don't think I could remain under the directorship of a man who would exchange undeniable evidence for the easy popularity of a lie."

Taylor's eyes narrowed. "I'll expect all of your personal belongings off the property by the end of the day," he said coolly before adding, "And don't even think about going near the storage vault—you or your sidekick."

Mark's jaw worked angrily, but he dared not open his mouth again. He swung from the room, almost bumping into Anthony on the way, who had been loitering near the door, listening to the entire exchange. Anthony turned to follow. "You don't have to ruin your own career, Anthony. I would totally understand if you just jump ship right now. It would be the smart thing to do," Mark said as they maneuvered their way back to the lab where he had been stationed at his computer earlier.

187

Anthony waited until they were inside the lab and the door was shut before replying. "I suspect the damage has already been done," he shrugged.

"Guilty by association," Mark nodded in a clipped tone.

"I was thinking, though," Anthony mused. "Maybe you could use a man on the inside."

Mark had already started gathering books off the shelf and piling them in a haphazard stack on one of the work counters. "Why would anyone trust you?" he asked.

"I could convince them, no problem," Anthony assured. "Say I just got caught up in the excitement of the legendary aspects of the dig, but now I realize how foolish it is. Something like that."

"And what good would that do?" Mark asked.

"I could let you know what angle they're taking as they write up their findings. You could counter attack, maybe even publish simultaneously. I also might be able to track the artifacts themselves. Even though they're supposedly packed for shipment, there is a chance they might not get shipped right away. I'm pretty good at smuggling, as you already know," he smiled with a twinkle in his eye.

Mark considered this then asked the obvious question. "How do I know you're not part of the whole conspiracy?"

Anthony blinked and then frowned with a hurt expression on his face. "Hey, that's not the response I was expecting."

"Sorry," Mark sighed, rubbing the back of his neck wearily. "But you've got to admit I have reason to be suspicious. Everyone else I trusted has turned against me."

"You do have a point," Anthony nodded. "There's probably not much I can do to convince you otherwise, although you ought to know I feel as strongly about making sure the truth comes out as you do. If I do stick around here, I'll be trying to see that it happens, one way or another."

"You go ahead and do whatever you think you have to do," Mark said. "I think it's best if I just make a clean break and decide what to do from there. Not drag anyone else into the quagmire I seem to have created for myself."

"You never know," Anthony observed, "our paths might cross again over this thing before it's all said and done. But maybe you're right about distancing ourselves for a while. We can come at this thing from more than one front, maybe take them by surprise."

"You make it sound like a military operation," Mark chuckled.

"It is," Anthony affirmed. "It's a war, man, don't you know? A spiritual battle."

Mark surveyed Anthony with a slight frown, but didn't say anything.

Anthony smiled sheepishly and explained. "You can't be raised by a Baptist preacher and not know something about spiritual warfare."

"Right," Mark replied sardonically. "Anyway, I better get my stuff packed. Taylor gave me till the end of the day and I don't think he was kidding."

"I'll help you," Anthony offered.

"It might blow your cover," Mark warned with a grin. "You wouldn't want to appear too sympathetic."

"I'll take my chances," Anthony replied and slapped Mark on the back before turning to survey the room. "Okay, I'll scare up some packing boxes and then you can just order me around from there."

Chapter Sixteen

Once again, Doctor Mark Graham found himself back in his home city of Winnipeg, Manitoba. Where else would a potentially discredited archeologist find refuge except back where it all began? The first thing he did was find his own small apartment. Although he loved his parents, just a few days in their home convinced him that his own accommodation was a necessity if he wanted to preserve their strong relationship. He had a considerable savings from which to draw and had also made some good investments over the years, so he wasn't too worried about how he would provide for his needs. But there was no use being foolish. He ended up taking an apartment close to downtown in an older three-storey house that had been converted into separate dwellings.

It was late August, still very hot in the prairie city, although outside its limits the land was taking on the characteristic golden ochre of fall. As Mark climbed the creaking staircase up to his new dwelling (there were no elevators) his cell phone bleeped in his pocket.

"Hello?" he said into the phone as he held it between his ear and shoulder. One hand was occupied with a plastic grocery bag, the other he was using to undo the somewhat stubborn lock.

It was Deanie. "Hi, Mark. Can you come over for dinner

tonight?"

Mark hesitated, maneuvering into the dim interior and shutting the door with his foot. "Um . . . I just came home with some groceries. I was going to work a bit on that dissertation I was telling you about." He hadn't told them everything about it—like the fact that he was no longer working for the University of New Mexico. As far as they knew, he was just choosing to work in Winnipeg so that he could have some solitude.

"Oh. That's too bad," Deanie replied, obvious disappointment in her voice. "I've invited the Walters over. You remember Brent and Holly?"

"Yes, yes of course. I saw them at Jack's funeral a couple months back."

"I've invited Amy and Bryan too, but I'm not sure if they're coming, Maybe Amy, since Harmony is here, but Bryan might have other things to do. He'll be starting his first year at the university next week, you know."

"That's nice," Mark answered absently.

"Oh well, maybe next time," Deanie said, preparing to end the conversation.

"What time did you say, again?" Mark asked suddenly.

"I didn't," Deanie laughed. "You changing your mind?"

"Maybe. Depending on what you're making, that is."

"Now, that will be a surprise for both of us. Your dad is barbequing and said he'd handle everything, so I've taken him at his word. We'll be ready to eat around six. That suit you?"

"Sure. Sounds fine," Mark affirmed. For some reason, the prospect of a quiet evening alone wasn't as appealing as it was earlier.

Mark arrived at the home of his parents around five thirty that evening. Deanie greeted him at the door with a hug and directed him to the kitchen where his father was busy preparing salad and

192

garlic toast to go with the steaks he had marinating.

"Hi son," Russ greeted Mark. "Settling in to your new place?"

Mark nodded. "Yep. It's small, but I don't need much room. As long as I've got room for my computer, I'm set."

"You'll have to tell me some more about that paper you're writing," Russ said. "So far, you've been fairly tight lipped."

Mark shrugged. "I know. It's kind of complicated. You'll get to read it soon enough," he hedged.

"I'll be very interested to do that. It's fascinating that so many of your findings support the Biblical record. It's about time the scientific community started taking the idea of intelligent design seriously." Mark didn't say anything, but occupied himself with a celery stick instead. If his father only knew the truth, he wouldn't be so quick with his enthusiasm. "You're awfully quiet," Russ observed. "What's up?"

"Nothing you need to worry about," Mark assured with a slight shrug.

"You're too much like me to hide things very well," Russ laughed.

"I suppose, eh? Well, to be honest, things aren't going as smoothly as I had hoped."

"No?"

Mark nodded. He debated whether he should tell his father more. "You know those artifacts I asked you to keep safe for me?" he asked.

Russ nodded.

"Well, I might be moving them to a different location soon."

"Oh?" Russ's eyebrows rose in question.

"Mmhm. Actually, I've run into more than just a bit of opposition over this project, dad, and quite frankly I'm not sure where to turn next."

Russ set the knife he was using to chop vegetables down on

193

the counter and turned his full attention to his son. "You want to talk about it?"

Mark sighed. It was killing him—not being able to verbalize his doubts and frustrations to anyone. "Let's just say I'm wrestling with the evidence I've found and it's got me questioning some things that I thought were already settled in my own mind. Not just on a scientific level, either, but here," he stabbed at his chest. "And I don't mind admitting I'm not comfortable with some of my own conclusions."

"God's truth hasn't changed," Russ stated. "It's our own way of seeing it that changes."

Before Mark could say any more, Harmony came bouncing into the room. She embraced her brother enthusiastically. "Mark! I'm so glad you decided to come over for dinner. I like having you in the city again. It feels just like old times."

"Except you're about two feet taller," he laughed.

"But just as spoiled," Russ observed affectionately

"Oh whatever, daddy! You're the one who spoiled me if that's the case. Anyway, I'm especially glad you've come, Mark, because I have someone special I want you to meet."

"Oh? Your latest flame?" Mark asked with a grin.

"You could say that," Harmony replied with a coy smile.

"Anyone I know?"

"One of Toby Rantt's grandsons," Deanie informed, coming into the room.

"Oh, I see," Mark nodded. "Keeping it all in the club, eh? So when did this take place? I don't recall you having anyone particularly special the last time I was here."

"You were hardly here long enough to notice," Harmony observed.

"Cory is a very nice young man. Isn't he, honey?" Deanie directed at Russ. He just grunted his assent and went back to chopping the celery.

"Seems to me I may have noticed you two together at the funeral," Mark said.

"We've always been friends, but we kind of started going together shortly after Grandpa Jack's funeral," Harmony explained. "He was very good at listening."

"And he's a believer," Deanie added her approval.

The doorbell rang.

"That's probably him now," Harmony said, scurrying into the hallway on her way to answer the front door.

Deanie's eyes followed her daughter's retreating figure with affection. "Now if we could only find you a nice girl, Mark," she said.

"You make it sound like Harmony and Cory are getting married," Russ observed. "They've only been going together a few months. Besides, I'm sure Mark is more than capable of looking after his own love life."

"Thanks, dad."

"So do you have any one special, Mark?" Deanie asked, obviously digging for information.

"Um . . . actually I was seeing a fellow archeologist for a while, but we've decided to go our separate ways," Mark explained uncomfortably.

"Mom! Dad!" Harmony called from the entryway. "It's the Walters."

Deanie went to greet her guests, leaving Mark and Russ alone in the kitchen.

"Don't mind anything Deanie might say about you and your relationships. She just wants the best for you," Russ explained.

"I know," Mark replied with a smile. "She's been asking the same question since high school. You need any help in here?"

"No," Russ shook his head. "I'm almost ready to throw these

195

steaks on the grill. Why don't you go and say 'hi' to the Walters instead and tell them I'll be right with them. Maybe everyone can go out on the back deck. Why don't you see if they want a soda or something?'

"Okay," Mark agreed, turning to exit the kitchen.

"Oh, and Mark?" Russ stopped him. Mark turned back to face his father.

"When ever you're ready to talk about that other situation—you know, your own spiritual journey—I'm more than willing to listen."

"I know, dad," Mark nodded. "Believe me, I think we'll be having a talk about quite a few things really soon."

He turned and walked down the hall to the living room where Harmony, Deanie, and the rest of the guests had gathered. Mark's insides clenched unexpectedly when he saw Amy Walters among the group.

"Hi," he said with a general wave. "Good to see you again."

"Likewise," Brent said, standing to shake Mark's hand vigorously. "And under better circumstances."

"True," Mark agreed. "I guess Bryan decided not to come?"

"He already made plans to go out with some of his friends," Holly explained.

"Mark, you remember Cory Rantt?" Harmony stepped up, pulling a somewhat shy Cory with her.

"Of course," Mark nodded, not really remembering too well, but faking it nonetheless for Harmony's sake. He shook the younger black man's hand. "Good to see you, Cory. Dad said we should go out onto the deck, if that's okay? Can I get anybody a drink?"

"That's okay, Mark. I'll get the drinks," Deanie offered. "There's iced tea and lots of pop." She took everyone's request and headed back into the kitchen while Harmony led the way through

196

the family room and out the patio doors onto the back deck, Cory in tow. Mark found himself bringing up the rear.

Russ was already out on the patio lighting the barbeque. He waved a greeting to all the guests and proceeded to place eight large steaks on the grill. "Mark, there are a few of those stacking lawn chairs in the corner. You might need to grab a couple."

Mark nodded and went to the side of the house where he found the molded plastic seats. Harmony had already claimed the one padded lounge chair, and the others had pulled up the other deck chairs that went with the table and umbrella. He took three chairs and placed them near the table.

"So Mark," Brent Walters began conversationally. "Your folks say you made quite a find in Africa. I'm looking forward to hearing all about it."

Mark lowered himself onto the molded seat. "Um . . . right."

"So what exactly did you find, Mark?" Holly asked. "Deanie said something about dinosaur remains and human remains found together."

"Isn't that cool?" Harmony interjected. "I mean, we all know the flood is a fact anyway, and of course it makes sense that God created dinosaurs along with everything else, but to actually find real, undeniable evidence! And by my own big brother, the skeptic! Bet you're not so quick to deny the Bible now, eh Mark?" she teased.

Mark frowned slightly, trying hard not to show his own discomfiture. "It's definitely quite a find, that's for sure." He cleared his throat. "I wonder what's taking Deanie so long with those drinks? Maybe I should go and see if I can help." He rose swiftly and headed back into the house via the patio doors.

"What's gotten into him?" Harmony asked no one in particular. "He usually can't wait to talk about his latest discovery."

197

"Maybe he's just tired of talking about work," Holly suggested. "It's all new and fascinating for us, but he might need some down time away from it all."

"I suppose," Harmony shrugged. "Although it's really not like him. It's more like he's struggling with the way the evidence points to the existence of God. He's running scared, that's what I think. Good. It's about time he made a decision for Christ!"

"Let's not get on his case too much," Russ advised from his position over the grill. "He needs time to process his own feelings about that without too much pushing."

"We've all needed our space at one time or another," Brent agreed.

Deanie opened the patio door and stepped out onto the deck, followed by Mark who was carrying a tray laden with pop cans and glasses filled with ice. He set the tray on the table and started handing out drinks while Deanie took a seat. "Thanks Mark," she said.

"No problem." The conversation switched to the relative safety of the weather as Mark continued. "Iced tea, right?" he asked Amy, ignoring the general chatter going on around him. She nodded. He opened the can with a spurt and poured its contents into the waiting glass of ice cubes. When he handed it to her their hands touched briefly.

"Thanks," Amy said, taking the glass. Their eyes locked momentarily over the rim of the glass as she went to take a sip of the sweet tea, then her eyelashes fluttered downward.

Mark took the last remaining can of soda from the tray and snapped it open as he took his own seat. Somehow he had managed to place his own chair right next to Amy.

"You heading back to school soon?" he asked after taking a long swig of his drink.

She nodded. "Mmhm."

198

"As I recall, you weren't that enthusiastic about it last time we talked," he commented.

"I'm getting more used to the idea," Amy shrugged. "Especially when I think about the opportunities I'll have on the mission field if I have my degree in nursing. It will open up so many more doors."

There it was again, Mark thought irritably. *Always some reference to God.*

"And you?" Amy continued. "After you finish writing up your latest report, what's next? Some other exciting adventure in a far off country, no doubt."

"Time will tell. Sometimes I think it might be nice to give up the field work for a while and settle down—at least for a year or two. It gets tiring after a while, living on site all the time."

"But what would you do?" Amy asked.

"I'm not sure. Research, write . . . teach, I suppose. There might be some small university somewhere that would be willing to take me," Mark said with half a smile.

"What about the University of New Mexico?" Harmony asked, overhearing their conversation. "I thought you already worked for them?"

"I might be looking for a change of scenery," Mark hedged, not really wanting to get into the details in front of guests.

"Really? Why?" Harmony persisted. "I thought you liked it there. And besides, you've had pretty much your choice of digs to work on since being associated with them. Why not just teach there if that's what you want to do?"

"Steaks are almost done," Russ called from the barbeque. "Mark, you want to come inside and help me get the rest of the fixings?"

Mark rose from his chair, again glad for the reprieve.

Once inside the kitchen, Russ came right out and asked the

question. "Are you in some kind of falling out with the university?"

Mark sighed heavily, knowing he couldn't hide things very well from his father. "You could say that. I was going to tell you all about it at a more opportune time."

"Does this have anything to do with your discoveries in Africa?"

Mark nodded. "It has everything to do with them."

"What's happened exactly?"

"Let's just say, the scientific community isn't always interested in new discoveries—especially if they don't fit into their preconceived notions of how things are supposed to work."

"Meaning the theory of evolution," Russ supplied.

"Exactly," Mark affirmed.

"And how do you feel about all of this?" Russ asked.

"I'm still feeling my way," Mark admitted. "Don't expect an instant conversion, if that's what you're hoping for."

"Fair enough," Russ replied. "But . . . ?" he prompted.

"I can't ignore the evidence, Dad. It's all there."

"And that institution wants you to do that? Ignore the evidence?"

Mark nodded. "Or get black listed."

"And what did you decide?" Russ asked.

"I can't ignore the truth," Mark stated simply.

"That's my boy," Russ smiled.

"Oh yeah?" Mark grinned sheepishly. "Except now I'm out of a job, with no backing whatsoever from the institution that commissioned me in the first place."

"What are you going to do?"

"Write that dissertation," Mark stated firmly. "What else can I do? People deserve to know the truth."

Russ nodded in agreement.

"Except, now that my credibility is shot, I might find it difficult convincing anyone to believe me, but I've got to try. That's why it's so important that I keep those artifacts that I sent you safe. I need some real, credible evidence to back me up. I can't let anything happen to those items. I just don't want to put you and Deanie in any danger."

"And you think something could happen?" Russ asked. "That we could be at risk?"

Mark sighed and rubbed the back of his neck wearily. "This is a lot messier than you know. Not only is my career in jeopardy, but there have been threats as well. I don't want to drag you into this, but I have to do what I know is right."

"However we can help . . ." Russ offered. "You know we back you 100 percent."

"I know."

"Just tell us what to do."

"Don't do anything for now," Mark advised. "I've been trying to lay low, so to speak, but soon, when I'm finished writing my dissertation, I'm going to have to make quite a bit of noise. I just hope there will be somebody out there listening."

"Too bad I hadn't known about this sooner," Russ mused.

"Why?"

"I heard about a temporary position at the university here in Winnipeg," Russ replied. "They're looking for a professor in the archeology department to fill in for someone who is on temporary leave due to an accident."

"You don't say," Mark said, raising his eyebrows with interest.

"Maybe it's not too late," Russ suggested. "It wouldn't hurt to stop by and ask."

"Maybe I'll do that tomorrow. I could use the credibility," Mark mused. "I just won't tell them what I'm working on."

"In any case, we better get this food out on the table before those steaks get burnt to a crisp," Russ said.

"Right. I hope everyone likes well done . . ." Mark answered with a grin.

Chapter Seventeen

The office was small, tucked in the back corner of the building, but it was his. At least for the time being, anyway. The university had been more than happy to welcome back one of their own for a short-term position on staff. He'd be lecturing twice a week, have a few papers to mark, and have plenty of time for his own research. Perfect. And he'd be getting paid besides. Mark couldn't ask for a better arrangement.

He'd been looking into his Bible a lot lately, trying to line up some of the questions he had with the scientific evidence. Naturally, he had begun to research the whole creation theory quite extensively. There was a lot of information out there that was not making it into regular scientific journals.

Questions about astrophysics and time travel were just some of the latest items to cross his path. The theory that time sped up when traveling at the speed of light was nothing new—it had been estimated that a person traveling at the speed of light for only a few weeks would actually arrive back to earth hundreds of years later. So it made sense that the stars could be a lot younger than most scientists were willing to admit. Then there was the problem with current radiometric dating techniques. A scientist from the states had been studying microscopic halos left from radioactive material in granite. In order for the halos to form, it had to be crystallized within three minutes of formation, not the millions of years assumed by most scientists.

Mark sat pouring over this most recent batch of information he had unearthed. How could the scientific community choose to overlook such a large volume of documented evidence? He was astounded that someone, somewhere, didn't blow the whistle on this tightly guarded club. Well, maybe he was the man to do it.

There was a knock on his office door. He looked up as the receptionist popped her head inside. "Excuse me, Dr. Graham, but there's a woman outside who seems especially insistent on seeing you."

"Who is she?" he asked absently, still perusing the documents before him.

"She says she's your sister," the woman shrugged.

Mark smiled and nodded. "Send her in," he said dismissively. It was just like Harmony to interrupt whenever the whim overtook her. Oh well. He had some things to share that he was sure she'd be interested in. This stuff was right up her alley.

He carefully marked his place with a sticky note as he heard the door opening and looked up. The ready greeting that was on his lips stayed right where it was.

"Uh . . . hello," he offered tentatively. "Maybe you have the wrong office. The receptionist told me my sister was here to see me."

"Oh," the young woman laughed nervously. "Dr. Mark Graham, right?"

"Yes," he replied, waiting.

She stepped further into the room and shut the door behind her. She reached forward and stretched out her hand. "Hi. Sorry to just barge in on you like this. My name is Charlene Howard."

He half stood and barely touched her finger tips in a pseudo handshake before sitting back down.

"May I?" she asked, gesturing to a chair on the opposite side of his desk.

"Go ahead."

She perched on the edge of the seat, obviously nervous about something. She looked to be in her mid to late twenties, pretty and blonde, and was wearing a trendy, yet tasteful outfit. Probably a student wanting advice about something, but afraid she wouldn't gain admittance without an excuse.

"Can I help you with something?" he prompted.

She looked down at her hands, which she was twisting in her lap. "I'm a lot more nervous than I expected," she admitted with a little laugh.

"Um, okay . . ." he responded uncertainly.

"I mean it's not every day I get to meet thee Dr. Mark Graham."

He frowned, suspicion birthed after so many weeks of tension, now rising to the forefront. "Oh?"

"Oh dear," she muttered to herself. She looked up with pleading in her eyes. "You see, you are . . . or rather, I am . . . actually we're brother and sister," she finally blurted.

"Pardon?" Mark asked, not sure he heard correctly.

"We have the same mother," Charlene explained. "Miranda Riley?"

Mark felt like he had been gut punched—again. He couldn't seem to find any words for a few minutes as he tried to digest the information. Finally he managed to fumble, "Ah . . . I don't know what to say."

"I'm sorry," Charlene offered. "It came as quite a shock to us too."

"Us?"

Charlene nodded. "Me and my younger brother Scott. We had

no idea we had an older brother or that our mom had been married before she met dad. She'd kept it all secret."

Mark didn't know how he felt about that bit of information. The little boy that still resided within him somewhere was suddenly very hurt. "I see. So how did you find out?"

"Mom secretly kept a scrapbook full of all kinds of articles about this famous archeologist named Dr. Mark Graham. I was helping her pack after she and dad split up a few months ago, and I found it. When I asked her about it, she wasn't going to tell me anything, but I could tell there was something up. She finally broke down and told me everything about her first marriage and how when her husband got custody, she just decided to up and start a new life altogether."

Not exactly the way I'd heard it, Mark mused blackly. *And what is up with everybody keeping a scrapbook?*

"I can see this is quite a shock for you," she said again.

"Yes. To put it mildly."

"I was really choked at first, you know? Like I felt betrayed or something," Charlene said. Mark knew the feeling. "But then I started thinking I wanted to meet this famous brother of mine. And so, after I did a little more research of my own, I flew out here and here I am."

"Just like that," Mark stated.

"Um, yeah. I guess I could've called first, but I didn't know if you'd see me . . . " she trailed off.

"No, it's . . . fine." Mark cleared his throat and sat up straighter. "So you flew here. From where?"

"Calgary," Charlene replied. "That's where I live with my husband, Tom. Mom and dad still live there too. And Scott." She hesitated. "Um, you want to see some pictures?" She didn't wait for a response, but began digging in her handbag.

An unreasonable fear clutched Mark's heart. He wasn't sure he wanted to see any pictures . . .

Charlene already had them out of her purse and was handing them over as she pulled her own chair in closer to the desk. He willed himself to look down.

"This one was taken about a month ago at my son's birthday party. See, there's my husband Tom, and that's your nephew Cade. He's two." She smiled proudly and looked over to measure Mark's reaction. He just blinked. He had a nephew. Charlene continued, "And this next one shows my . . . I mean our brother Scott holding Cade on his knee. Scott's twenty-one. Cade was born on his birthday."

The same age as Harmony. "How nice," was all that came out of Mark's mouth.

"Yep. He's a pretty proud uncle."

"And how old are you?" Mark asked.

"Me? I'm twenty-five."

"I see." So he was just eight years old when she was born, he calculated. Still a boy wondering why he didn't have a mother, or at least get cards and gifts like the other kids he knew whose parents had split up.

"Here we all are watching Cade and Scott blow out the candles," she went on, referring to the next photograph. She waited for him to peruse the picture before adding, "Oh, and that's Mom there on the right."

Mark swallowed hard, his eyes feeling suspiciously prickly. She was a nice looking woman for her age. She was probably in her early fifties with auburn brown hair done up in a fashionable style.

Mark cleared his throat and handed the pictures back to Charlene. "Yes. Well, thank you for showing me."

"I can send you some more if you'd like. On Facebook . . . " Charlene offered.

"I don't really do Facebook," Mark said.

"Oh." There was an awkward silence as Charlene looked down at her hands.

"Um, but perhaps by more conventional means?" Mark added quickly, seeing her distress.

Charlene nodded. "Okay."

"So . . ." Mark looked down at his watch. More awkward silence. The minutes seemed to stretch on and on.

"She's not really a bad person," Charlene finally whispered. "Whatever her reasons for giving you up, I'm sure she's thought lots about you. Look at the scrapbook she kept. And she was a good mother to Scott and me."

"That's . . . that's fine," Mark said, nodding mechanically.

"I'll be in town for a few days," Charlene said. "Tom and Cade came along for moral support. We're staying downtown at the Ramada."

Mark wasn't sure what she expected. "Oh. I see."

Charlene persisted doggedly. "I thought maybe you'd like to meet them. Especially the baby."

"Um," He looked down at the stack of papers on his desk. How was he supposed to concentrate on work when he'd just been thrown a bomb?

"I know you're probably a very busy man," Charlene went on breathlessly, "but we're only in town for a few days . . ." She trailed off. She looked as if she might cry.

"Of course," Mark said quickly. "I'm still just in shock, that's all. I would love to meet your husband and son."

Charlene smiled with relief. "Oh, good. I was pretty scared there for a minute. Like you might just kick me out or something."

"No, no. I wouldn't do that."

"Um, and you probably have other family in town. You can bring them along if you like. A wife? Kids?"

208

"I'm not married," he supplied.

"Oh," Charlene said.

There seemed to be nothing more to say other than to pick the time and location for their next rendezvous.

"So where should we meet?" Charlene asked tentatively.

"You pick," Mark said.

"I don't really know Winnipeg that well," she said hesitantly.

"How about the hotel dining room at, say, seven?" Mark suggested.

"Okay," Charlene said, "but . . . "

"That's probably too late for Cade," Mark surmised.

"No, it's not so much that as . . ."

"What?"

"The dining room at the hotel is awfully fancy. Maybe somewhere a little more family friendly? You know how two year olds can be."

Actually, he didn't, but he smiled anyway and nodded. "Okay. How about one of those family restaurants? There's a good pancake house on Main that serves kids meals," he suggested.

"Perfect," Charlene agreed with a grateful smile.

"Alright then. See you there at seven."

Charlene rose from her chair. "Thanks for being so . . . I don't know. Down to earth, I guess. You're nothing like I was afraid you'd be after reading all those articles about you. I felt pretty intimidated because you sound like such a genius."

Mark just shrugged. "I'm just a plain ordinary man like everybody else." Just an ordinary man with too many problems to count on both hands at the moment.

* * *

"So what's your brother up to these days?" Amy Walters asked casually as she and Harmony sat out on the deck, catching some of the last warm weather before autumn swooped down in earnest.

209

"You know. The usual," Harmony shrugged. "Digging up the past. I haven't seen much of him lately, but I think he's enjoying his time at the university."

"Oh."

"Why?" Harmony asked, surveying her friend closely.

"No particular reason," Amy hedged.

"You like him, don't you?" Harmony speculated.

"Well . . ."

"I knew it!" Harmony blurted with a wide grin. "I just knew it. This is awesome! My brother and my best friend."

"Harmony, don't go, you know, spreading it around or anything," Amy pleaded. "I mean, yeah, I like him, kind of, but he probably has a girlfriend already. And besides, he's so . . . I don't know. He's kind of out of my league."

"What? Don't be ridiculous," Harmony said dismissively. "He's nowhere near being out of your league. This is Mark we're talking about, remember? And as for a girlfriend, I have it on very good authority that he broke up with the most recent one, Doctor whatever her name was."

"See? He's used to dating doctors. Smart people. People in his own field. What could he and I possible have to talk about?"

"Quit being such a pessimist," Harmony frowned. "Now, we're going to have to stage a few more meetings between you two. We can't wait for the parents to keep inviting both of you over. Besides, that's not kosher."

"Harmony, I don't think—"

"Trust me, Amy," Harmony assured. "You just leave it all to me."

* * *

"I'm with another group," Mark informed the restaurant hostess. He could see Charlene and her family sitting at a booth across the room and gestured in their general direction.

"Oh!" Charlene said with relief when she saw Mark approaching. "I thought maybe you decided not to come."

"Of course not," Mark assured stoically. He nodded at the man he presumed to be Charlene's husband.

"This is my husband Tom," Charlene introduced. "And this is Cade." She smiled indulgently at the two-year-old, who was presently stuffing crackers into his mouth.

The two men shook hands and Mark sat down. He had one side of the booth to himself since Cade's high chair was at the end of the table in the isle.

"I, uh, had some last minute calls to take care of," Mark explained. "Sorry I'm a bit late." *More like last minute excuses,* he thought. He wasn't sure how comfortable he was with this whole situation.

"That's okay," Charlene said. "I'm sure you're awfully busy. Cade was getting kind of hungry though. Hope you don't mind that we already ordered."

"Of course not," Mark dismissed. He surveyed his own menu and made a quick decision, ready to catch the next waitress that went by.

"So Tom," Mark ventured conversationally. "What do you do for a living?"

"Electrician. In the patch," Tom answered.

"Oil industry's going crazy these days, eh?" Mark continued.

"Yep. Pretty crazy."

"Cost of housing is high too, I hear."

"Mmhm." The slightly younger man seemed fairly quiet, Mark noted. He was big and burly, not quite overweight, but not skinny either, with closely cropped brown hair and glasses.

"Tell us more about what you're doing," Charlene interjected.

"Oh, research. Always lots of research," Mark replied noncommittally.

211

"You've sure been to some fascinating places," Charlene said. "I was astounded when I read all the articles mom's been keeping."

There was an awkward moment of silence. "Um . . . yes."

Charlene looked down at her hands. "I'm sorry. This must be especially . . . uncomfortable for you. I mean, we know all kinds of things about you and you had no idea we even existed." Cade started to fuss and Charlene's attention was momentarily drawn elsewhere.

Mark was glad for the timely distraction. Of course he was uncomfortable. Uncomfortable didn't even come close to what he was feeling. Shock, betrayal, anger– all mingled together into one indescribable emotion.

"Our, uh . . . our mother. Does she have other relatives close by?" Mark asked.

"Grandma and Grandpa—her parents—both passed away. They used to live in Winnipeg I think, but they moved out to the west coast before I was born. We have an uncle out there too. In Vancouver."

Mark nodded. "I see."

"I should have brought pictures of them too," Charlene apologized.

"No, that's fine," Mark said with a shake of his head. Knowing he had other siblings was enough. Too much, in fact.

"So, you said you weren't married, but do you have other family? Did your dad remarry or anything?"

"Yes. Yes he did," Mark supplied. "I have one other sister."

"Oh. That's nice."

There was more awkward silence. Mark was glad when the food finally arrived and they had something to occupy themselves with besides straining for conversation.

"Hey, bro! Fancy meeting you here." It was Harmony.

"Harmony." Mark looked up in surprise. "What are you doing

here?"

"I'm meeting Cory, but he's late as usual," Harmony shrugged. "Mind if I join you for a sec?"

"Uh, no. Go ahead," Mark said awkwardly as Harmony was already sliding in beside him. "Um . . . Charlene, Tom, this is my sister, Harmony. Harmony—Charlene and Tom. They're . . . from Calgary," he finished lamely.

"Hi," Harmony greeted with a friendly smile. She was her usual bubbly self and didn't seem to notice the tension her arrival had caused. "So, I was actually going to call you later. I'm moving into my own place on the weekend and I need your help. Mom and Dad are going out of town."

"You're moving out?" Mark asked. "Why?"

"I am twenty-one," Harmony reminded. "Don't you think its time I got my own place? Besides, you moved out by the time you were my age."

"True, but I was going on to graduate work in the States. It makes more sense to stay home and save the rent money until you're finished with school."

"I was thinking of quitting anyway," Harmony shrugged. "I mean, I've wasted enough of the parents' money as it is and I still don't know what I'm doing with my life. I think I just need some time off. Some space to try and get my act together, so to speak. That, and some privacy for a change."

"Because of Cory," Mark noted with a disapproving scowl.

"Oh please!" Harmony laughed. "You're one to talk! Besides, I'm a Christian remember? I don't believe in sex before marriage, so just chill, okay? Big brothers," she said sarcastically to Charlene and Tom. "Hey, I see him. I gotta go. Nice meeting you two, and I'll call you to remind you about the weekend." She planted a quick kiss on Mark's cheek and was up out of the seat and heading toward the entrance where her boyfriend was surveying the crowd expectantly. Mark watched as they embraced before following the hostess to a seat.

"You're a Christian too?" Charlene asked enthusiastically. "So are we. Wait till I tell Mom!"

"Pardon me?" Mark asked, almost choking on his water.

The smile faded on Charlene's lips. "I just assumed . . . I mean, your sister, she said . . ."

"She often spouts off at the mouth without putting much thought behind it," Mark quipped.

"Oh. Have I offended you? I'm sorry, if I have," Charlene apologized.

"Don't worry about it," Mark said dismissively. "I should've guessed as much. Seems I'm being bombarded every which way by Christians these days."

"Oh. Sorry," Charlene apologized again.

"It's okay," Mark said.

"I didn't mean to make you uncomfortable," Charlene offered.

Uncomfortable? That was an understatement if ever there was one. Everything about this meeting was uncomfortable.

"Sorry."

"Quit apologizing."

"Oh. Sorry."

"We're kind of new to this Christian thing ourselves," Tom came to his wife's defense.

"We all got saved together," Charlene explained. "Me, Tom, and Mom."

"Then I guess I'm the only hold out on both sides of the family," Mark shrugged.

"Sorry about that."

"You're apologizing again," Mark noted. "Besides, I'm used to it. The rest of the family is 'saved', as you put it. I haven't much choice but to put up with it."

"I suppose you two are really close," Charlene said off hand, fiddling with her spoon.

Mark frowned. "You mean me and Harmony?"

"Yes," she nodded wistfully.

"Uh, well, we did grow up together. She's twenty-one. Same age as your—our—brother Scott, right?"

Charlene nodded. "Scott would really like to meet you too sometime. He couldn't get time off work."

"I see."

"Maybe sometime you could come out to see us?" she suggested.

Mark didn't know how to respond.

"Hey, honey, let's not jump the gun," Tom put in quietly.

Mark wasn't sure what Charlene was expecting. Sudden attachment for an unknown sister was not something he could just manufacture. And as for some kind of family reunion—that was beyond what his current state of mental health could even fathom. It all added up to an emotional rollercoaster ride that he would just as soon avoid.

"Look, it has been really nice," Mark said. "Surprising, yes, and a bit disconcerting too. But I can see you two are good people. You just need to know that I am really, really busy right now. I might not have time . . ."

"You don't need to say anymore," Charlene cut in.

"I'm not trying to put you off," Mark offered. "I am seriously busy on a dissertation from my last dig."

"Look at you!" Charlene exclaimed suddenly, turning her attention to her son, Cade. "Mommy better take you to the washroom and clean you up. What a mess!" She fiddled awkwardly with the safety strap on the highchair for a moment, and then scooped Cade up into her arms. Mark and Tom both watched her retreating figure as she scurried away.

215

"I'm not trying to hurt anyone," Mark stated in a low voice. "It'd just—"

"She'll be alright," Tom answered. "I'm just glad you agreed to meet us in the first place. It would've crushed her if you hadn't."

"I wouldn't have done that."

"I was worried about this meeting from the moment she got it into her head," Tom admitted. "I'm just glad you turned out to be half decent."

"Only half?" Mark asked with a small grin.

Chapter Eighteen

"Anthony," Mark said into the receiver. "How are things going at your end?"

"Excellent," Anthony replied. "I am a genius, if I do say so myself."

"Okay genius, what've you got?" Mark asked with a laugh.

"I've been able to keep tabs on everything—every scrap of so-called data that Laura and John have used to put together their report on the site. It's so full of holes it even smells like Swiss cheese. As soon as they publish, I'll have a counter attack all ready to go."

"Great, but will anybody be listening?" Mark asked.

"Of course, cause here's the good part. You ready?"

"Spill it."

"I've got verification from that university in Texas I was telling you about. They are very interested—and I mean, very—in backing our study and housing the archeological display. As long as you can deliver the specimens like you said, they're all over it," Anthony relayed enthusiastically.

"Don't worry about my end," Mark reassured. "You just make sure nobody else gets wind of this until we're ready. I don't want this to come out on anybody's timetable but my own."

"Got it."

"I'm actually pleasantly surprised to find out that there are some reputable institutions willing to go out on a limb for true scientific research. Not just to try to fit things into their own narrow definitions of what could and couldn't take place."

"Intelligent design is gaining in popularity," Anthony agreed. "Of course, this is a university with a definite Christian bend. Hopefully, the world won't be too put off by that factor and will sit up and take notice."

"We'll take what we can get," Mark agreed.

"Say, actually, while we're on the topic, did I tell you that I visited my folks last week?" Anthony asked casually.

"No, you didn't. Well, that's good news."

"Yeah . . . uh, did I tell you I kind of, like, rededicated my life to God?" There was silence on the other end. "Mark? Hello? You still there?"

"I'm here," Mark replied curtly.

"It's not a curse, man," Anthony defended. "It's actually pretty cool."

"Well, just don't let it go to your head," Mark cautioned. "I want that display strictly scientific. No reference to faith whatsoever. You got it? We want to remain credible here, not be dismissed as a bunch of religious crackpots."

"Of course," Anthony replied. "I wouldn't do anything to jeopardize the work we've been doing. You know that. Besides, you're the one writing the dissertation, so what's your worry? Anyway, I've got to go. Laura can be a real taskmaster. Keep in touch."

Mark frowned slightly. He'd just as soon forget about Laura. And John for that matter. And as far as Anthony's new found faith, it hit just a little too close to home right now. He'd been feeling the draw of it himself, lately, despite what he'd said to Charlene and

Tom. But it wasn't something he would allow himself to succumb to—not yet anyway. He had to keep his head clear and his mind focused on the task at hand. Vindication.

* * *

"So, Cory's got his dad's truck and with my parents' van we should only have to make two trips," Harmony was saying to Amy.

"I thought your parents were away?" Amy asked.

"They are," Harmony replied. "They took my dad's car, but they left the keys for the van. It's so old! But my mom likes it for grocery shopping."

"I can drive it if you want to ride with Cory," Amy offered.

"Okay. Unless Mark wants to drive," Harmony added. "You know how men are."

"Mark's coming to help?" Amy asked.

"Of course, silly. You didn't think I'd pass up an opportunity like this, did you? I mean, not only can we use the muscle power, but you two will have lots of time to bump into one another."

"I'm so embarrassed," Amy groaned.

The door bell rang. "That'll be Cory. He still rings the door bell. Imagine! Mark wouldn't, that's for sure."

As predicted, Cory Rantt was standing patiently outside when Harmony answered the door.

"Well, we might as well get started," Harmony directed. "The sooner we start, the sooner we're finished."

Mark arrived just as Cory and Amy were coming out of the house with Harmony's double mattress. Harmony was bringing up the rear with part of the disassembled bed frame.

"Here, let me help you with that," Mark offered, coming to take over for Amy. Their bodies brushed briefly as he secured his hold on the somewhat floppy cargo.

They spent the next half hour making trips in and out of the house with boxes, suitcases, and pieces of bedroom furniture.

"There's more room in these two vehicles than I thought," Harmony mused. "Maybe we can squeeze it all into one trip. Unless I find some other odd furniture that the parents wouldn't mind getting rid of."

"Better ask first," Mark cautioned.

"You're no fun," Harmony quipped with a grin. "I think I can fit the rest into my own car later. I'll have to bring the van back anyway."

"I can bring it back," Mark suggested. "I'll have to come back for my vehicle when we're through. Why don't you just take your car now?"

"Cause I want to ride with Cory," Harmony stated matter-of-factly.

"Oh. Right."

"You and Amy can ride together," Harmony called, already jumping into the passenger seat of Cory's borrowed truck.

"You know the way, I presume," Mark said to Amy as they followed in the van.

"Yeah. I've got the address right here." She handed Mark a slip of paper that he read quickly before turning his eyes back to the road.

They chatted about school, the weather, and the Blue Bombers chances of winning the Grey Cup as Mark maneuvered his way through the streets. Amy turned out to be a diehard football fan and went to every home game the Bombers played.

"I never would've guessed," Mark said with a short laugh. "I mean, you just don't look like the type to follow football that closely."

"Are you kidding? My dad is a Bomber fan from way back. He used to take me to games when I was little. I thought you knew that."

"I guess there's lots we really don't know about each other."

"I guess," Amy replied softly and turned to look out her window.

Mark glanced over at her for a moment. She really was very pretty. Soft and feminine—almost cherub like. And young. Very young. His jaw clenched slightly and he kept his eyes on the road for the rest of the trip.

The foursome unloaded both vehicles expediently enough, hauling everything up the one flight of stairs into Harmony's new one bedroom apartment. They were all exhausted by the time they were finished. Harmony flopped down upon the carpet.

"You're going to need more furniture," Mark mused, surveying the room as he lowered himself onto the floor.

"You wouldn't let me, remember?" Harmony quipped and stuck out her tongue.

"We should've brought some drinks to put in the fridge," Cory said, still breathing heavily.

"We can go out," Harmony suggested. "There's a pizza joint just around the corner."

"We should help you unpack a bit, first," Mark said, always practical.

"Naw, I don't feel like it," Harmony said, shaking her head. "I'll do it tomorrow. Although it might be kind of nice to have the bed put together. Mark, why don't you and Amy work on that while Cory and I get the entertainment system back together? The rest is all stuff I can do on my own."

Mark agreed nonchalantly, although on the inside he felt decidedly awkward about the task. The last thing he wanted was to make up a bed with Amy Walters.

* * *

"And that's when I burst out laughing and spit my coke all over him," Harmony finished her story with gusto. "Isn't that right, Cory?" She leaned into him playfully as the others laughed. The

221

foursome had gathered at the pizza restaurant as planned and were sitting in a booth. Mark had no option but to sit next to Amy—not that he minded—since Harmony and Cory were cuddled up across from them.

"That still doesn't explain why you started dating," Mark said. "Sounds more like a nasty cold shower to me."

"Seriously, I felt so bad. I ruined one of his best t-shirts, so I had to start being nice to him," Harmony explained.

"Instead of teasing him all the time," Amy added.

"Funny, I don't remember any of that," Mark mused. "I mean, you two not getting along so well when you were younger."

"You were so much older and definitely too preoccupied. Or gone already," Harmony shrugged.

"Right," Mark nodded. He looked down at his plate for a moment, feeling ancient.

"You know," Amy said conspiratorially. "Maybe Cory didn't mind all that much."

Cory just shrugged, and the rest of the group laughed. The good-natured banter continued, Harmony carrying most of the conversation.

Mark snuck a sidelong glance at Amy. Her face was framed by her blonde curls and she was smiling and laughing easily. She was definitely not affected by his presence the way he was being affected by hers.

He turned back to the conversation and laughed along with Harmony's next anecdote. He really needed to get a grip.

"So?" Harmony asked her friend later as they both lay stretched out on her newly assembled bed.

"So what?" Amy asked with feigned innocence.

"So, didn't you see the way Mark kept looking at you in the restaurant?"

"Are you kidding? He purposely avoided looking at me the

whole time," Amy sighed.

"Not true," Harmony said with a shake of her head. "He just didn't want you to see, that's all. He's shy."

"Right," Amy scoffed. "Doctor Mark Graham, world traveler and internationally renowned archeologist gets tongue tied around the girl next door. I don't think so!"

"I know my own brother, okay, and he definitely likes you," Harmony stated emphatically.

"He still sees me as a little kid," Amy disagreed. "The annoying little girl he had to baby-sit. He's said as much a few times now."

"Then it's up to you to show him that you're not that little girl anymore," Harmony reasoned. "You're all grown up."

"Harmony," Amy gave her friend a withering look. "Just what are you suggesting?"

"Well, look at you," Harmony said, sliding off the bed and scrutinizing Amy closely.

"What?"

"Your clothes for one thing. Up to your neck! And your makeup and hair. Maybe it's time for something a little more, shall we say, enticing?"

"I'm not liking the sound of this," Amy interjected. "I'm a Christian, remember? And so are you, for heaven's sake!"

"I didn't say anything bad," Harmony defended. "Just something—risque."

Chapter Nineteen

"Hello," Mark addressed absently after picking up the receiver. He was actually much more interested in the information displayed on his computer screen and hoped whoever it was would be quick.

"Mark? Hi, how are you?"

Mark blinked momentarily and then frowned as recognition dawned. "Laura?"

"Who else? You haven't forgotten me that quickly, I hope."

"What do you want?" he clipped, exiting the site he was using.

"Goodness. That hardly sounded very friendly."

He let out a pent up breath. "What were you expecting? We hardly parted on good terms."

"True," Laura noted. "I thought maybe we could get past all that. John and I have almost finished up here. The exhibition is opening soon. I thought you might like to be there for it."

"Exhibition?" Mark's heart leapt in his breast. "I thought all the artifacts went back to Africa already."

"Oh, yeah. Most of them did, but we've got great digital photos of everything and a power point presentation like no other. Amazing what one can do with technology these days."

"I'll bet."

"So? You interested?"

"What do you think?" Mark asked sarcastically.

"You're being very juvenile, Mark."

"What?" Mark snorted. "I'm supposed to be happy about the fact that you sabotaged my work—you and someone I thought was my friend?"

"Better friends than you are to yourself," Laura countered. "In fact, you should be pleased that John and I took over when we did. Your credibility as an archeologist is still intact. If it'll make you feel better, your name is still very prominent in all the findings."

"I don't want my name associated with a lie," Mark grated.

"Mark, be reasonable," Laura said, as if talking to a child. "Nobody is lying. It's simply a different interpretation of the findings than what you wanted. But in the end, it's the most plausible. I had hoped that you'd see that now that you've had a little time to think it through."

"My time to think about it, as you say, has only convinced me that the international cover up is even more deeply entrenched than I thought."

Laura laughed. "Now you're sounding positively melodramatic."

"Whatever."

"In any case, I wanted to let you know that there are no hard feelings on this side of the border, and we would really like to see you at the opening, if you can see your way to coming. I . . . I miss you."

"Don't hold your breath."

There was a moment of silence before Laura spoke again. "You never used to be so petty. So unfeeling."

"Maybe you never really knew the real me," Mark quipped.

"Apparently not."

"Although, I must say, I'm surprised at you, as well, Laura. I never thought you could be bought so easily."

"What is that supposed to mean?"

"We both remember Sangeruka's threats, but you don't seem to be too bothered by that right now. I suppose your findings line up perfectly with whatever he told you to say."

"That's ridiculous," she scoffed. "Time and distance have put Sangeruka well out of the picture. Not to mention a change in authority back in Harare."

"Oh?" Mark asked, his curiosity pricked.

"I'm surprised you hadn't heard. Sangeruka is out. We're dealing with a much friendlier official now."

"The man at the top is still the same."

"Mugabe?" Laura sighed heavily into the receiver. "He was never going anywhere and you know it. I forgot just how paranoid you've become. Look, sorry for bothering you. The invite still stands, in any case, not that I'm expecting anything."

"Thanks, I guess."

"Alright, then. See you around," Laura clipped and hung up.

Mark held the receiver aloft for a moment before slowly lowering it to its cradle. *Definitely not the best start to the day,* he mused. He went back to his computer screen, trying to regain his earlier train of thought. Easier said than done, apparently. The sentence he had just read made absolutely no sense and he had to read it again.

With a sigh he sat back and rubbed his eyes. How did he feel? Angry, betrayed . . . a bit nostalgic. That should be his presentation, his day in the spotlight. Instead, here he was holed up thousands of miles away, hoping that someone—anyone—would listen to his version of the story. And if he did tell it, would he be safe in doing so? Sangeruka's threats still rang quite clearly in his head, no matter what Laura said.

And what about her declaration that she missed him?

227

Thankfully, he felt decidedly neutral on that score. If he'd ever had any feelings for Laura Sawchuk, they'd been put to rest. Unfortunately, he still had not reconciled his present feelings for a certain someone else or the wisdom of pursuing the object of his affections.

The telephone cut abruptly into his thoughts. So it was going to be one of those days. With a sigh he answered it.

"Mark, good news!" Anthony fairly panted with excitement on the other end of the telephone receiver.

"Yeah? What might that be?" Mark asked sardonically.

"The faculty at the university wants you to be there for the opening of the exhibit," There was silence for a moment on the other end. "Mark? Buddy? You still there?"

"I'm here."

"So? What do you think?"

Mark shrugged. "Big deal. I'm not coming. Besides, I knew that already."

"You did?"

"Mmhm. Laura contacted me earlier."

"Laura?!"

"Yeah. She was very friendly—quite civil. She says they're still giving me credit. Probably just trying to save face, since the whole archeological community knows I was in charge of that dig. It wouldn't look too good to let people know there was mutiny among the ranks."

"What did you say?" Anthony asked.

"I told her to shove it," Mark replied. "In a manner of speaking."

"I don't know," Anthony mused. "We might be able to use this to our advantage."

"Really? How do you figure?"

"Got a minute?" Anthony asked.

"I'm all ears," Mark said, sitting up straighter.

"Let's just say you accept the invitation," Anthony said. "All nice and legit-like so when you do show up, they can't turf you."

"I already told you I wasn't going to that opening. Under any circumstances."

"Even if it comes after your own presentation in Texas?"

"Just what are you getting at?" Mark asked.

"They want the whole spiel—you and whatever artifacts you've got," Anthony hesitated a moment. "You did say you had some actual artifacts?"

"Yes . . ."

"We'll have to keep your dissertation under wraps as much as possible. The university has already agreed not to mention your name in any of their publicity until after the event. I told them it would add to the hype and all that. People are so gullible these days. Always looking out for whatever will get them the most dollars."

"Whoa, whoa, whoa! Hold on a minute! You're getting way ahead of me here, buddy," Mark blurted. "Sounds like you have the whole thing planned. And what's this about dollars?"

"Oh, I told them you had an anonymous sponsor that was willing to fund the project under the condition that the publicity was low key until after the opening," Anthony explained.

"Great, and just who might that be?"

"I'm still working on it," Anthony replied easily.

"I'm not liking the sounds of this," Mark sighed.

"Don't sweat it. I've got it all under control," Anthony breezed. "Besides, now that I'm a Christian and all that, would I lie to you?"

"You're really not making me feel any better," Mark replied. "Okay, so then what? We present our findings in Texas, the world gets a hold of it and . . . "

"Your name gets attached, then you show up in New Mexico —if they still have the balls to go through with their presentation— and kind of rub their noses in it."

"Or start one hell of a lawsuit."

"A bit of controversy never hurt anyone."

"So you say," Mark quipped.

"Okay. Difference of opinion never hurt anyone," Anthony conceded. "Dialogue is healthy."

There was silence on the other end of the phone as Mark considered everything Anthony had said. "You think we can be ready in time?" he finally asked.

"Ready when you are," Anthony replied. "How soon can you pack?"

* * *

Okay, this was getting down right ridiculous. *Just how many phone calls are going to interrupt my train of thought in one afternoon,* Mark wondered. This time it was Harmony, and she wouldn't be put off.

"Mark, I need you to be there, okay?" Harmony pleaded on the other end of the line.

Mark pinched the bridge of his nose and adjusted the telephone receiver to the other ear.

"That's silly, Harmony," he said logically. "It seems to me that a nice romantic dinner for two is more appropriate for your anniversary, don't you think?"

"But that's just it," Harmony explained on the other end of the line. "It's a surprise, and I need you and a bunch of other people there so Cory doesn't suspect."

"Look, I'm really busy, okay?" Mark tried again to get out of it. "It's been a crazy day all around and I've got some pretty important new developments to work on . . . "

"But poor Amy! This will make her feel terrible," Harmony

230

wailed.

"Amy?" Mark repeated curiously. "Why will she feel terrible?"

"I told her you'd be there to kind of look out for her, you know?"

"No, I don't know," Mark laughed. "What on earth are you talking about?"

"Well, there is a bunch of other people coming that she doesn't really know that well, except for this one guy that I know has a crush on her. The only problem is, she can't stand him. She was afraid he would be trying to hit on her all night or something, but I said you'd be there for her to talk to and that she could kind of pretend like you were kind of going out or something."

"Harmony!"

"Not like she'd be falling all over you, or anything like that, but just like, if she needed to, you know, call on you for moral support or something," Harmony explained, adding just a touch of pleading to her voice. "I mean, she is an old friend."

Mark shook his head, a smile playing on his lips. "Harmony Graham, you can be a real pain sometimes, you know that?"

"Why?" Harmony asked quickly. "I mean, its not that bad, is it? Pretending to like Amy, I mean."

It was absolutely the opposite of bad, but he couldn't let his little sister know that he was the one who actually had a crush on Amy Walters. "No, no of course not. That's not what I meant."

"Good. Then you'll be there?"

Mark hesitated for another second or two, looking over at his computer screen. "Sure," he decided. "I'll be there. Just let Amy know I might need to call in a similar favor one of these days."

"Oh?" Harmony asked, all curiosity. "What do you mean?"

"Nothing," Mark laughed. "Now get off the phone so I can get some of this work done before I have to meet you."

"Thanks Mark," Harmony replied happily. "You're the best. Oh, and I forgot to tell you. You should dress up."

"Dress up," Mark repeated.

"Yeah, you know, a suit or something."

"Whatever you say," Mark shrugged. "Sounds like you have it all worked out."

"Absolutely," Harmony agreed.

Okay, Mark admitted to himself after hanging up the telephone. The prospects of seeing Amy Walters again so soon were not that bad. In fact, it was probably just what he needed to rid him of any niggling doubts about his upcoming presentation.

Chapter Twenty

Mark entered the dim interior of the upscale restaurant and scanned the room for his sister. No sign of her. She could be running late. That wouldn't be unusual for Harmony. He had managed to leave the university a bit earlier than expected and had time for a shower and change before driving over himself. He didn't much like suits, but he did own a couple. Doctors of Archeology had to make speeches on occasion and they came in handy once in awhile. The last time he'd worn this one, though, was at Jack's funeral. Probably not the best comparison for tonight's event.

"This way, sir," the hostess said, leading him further into the interior of the building. The restaurant was famous for its steak and lobster and was a favorite for romantic dinners for two since it had many small alcoves that provided privacy, even in the midst of the busy restaurant.

Mark was surprised when the hostess stopped and he was confronted with Amy Walters. Alone.

"Hi," she waved nervously and smiled.

"Um . . . where's everyone else?" Mark asked, looking around.

Amy shrugged in ignorance, then spoke quickly. "Harmony just called. She said they'd be late. Cory's car wouldn't start or something."

"They could always take a cab," Mark suggested, more to himself than to her.

"Oh, yeah. Well . . . won't you sit down? They probably won't be that long," Amy ventured.

Mark did just that. He looked at Amy closely for a moment and frowned. There was definitely something different about the way she looked. Her hair was swept up off her neck in an elegant style and the dress . . . spaghetti straps, low v-neck—nothing indecent, but definitely not the demure type of clothing he was used to seeing her wear. He cleared his throat and fixed his gaze on the table top instead. He definitely had to keep the eyes off the dress . . .

"Is everything okay?" Amy asked.

"What? Oh, absolutely," Mark replied quickly and tried for a relaxed smile. "I was just—I mean, you look different this evening. That's all."

"Oh." The syllable sounded flat.

"I mean, in a good way. Nice . . . but different."

There was more awkward silence. Amy let out a long and heart felt sigh. "I, um . . . I don't think I'm very good at this," she admitted.

"Oh? And that would be . . . ?"

"This," she stated again. The candor in her eyes held his. "Look, Harmony and I planned this whole thing. It was her idea really, cause I told her that I liked you, but I thought you didn't even notice me because of, well, just because. The dress, the makeup, everything, it's not really who I am, you know?"

Mark's eyebrows rose slightly as he took this information in.

"I feel kind of silly right about now and if you want, we can just leave," Amy said, looking down.

A slight smile started to curl the corners of Mark's mouth.

"There's no hurry. Now that we've got that out in the open, let's have dinner."

"Then you're not mad?" Amy asked hopefully, looking up.

"Should I be?"

Amy looked down at her cutlery again. "I am so embarrassed," she admitted. "Now you'll really think I'm a juvenile."

"Hardly."

Now Mark was the one to feel embarrassed. He had been thinking about Amy Walters—more than he liked to admit—and the context was definitely not juvenile.

"In any case, I should've known Harmony would be up to something," Mark shook his head, trying to lighten his own intense emotions. "I'm a little ashamed to say I fell for it so easily. I hate to think of all the teasing I'm going to have to put up with."

"Sorry," Amy said sullenly. "We don't have to stay."

"I didn't say it wasn't worth it," Mark stated with a gleam in his eye. "Let's order."

"Okay," she nodded and ducked behind her menu.

* * *

"Who's Charlene Howard?" Deanie asked her husband while sorting through the mail that had piled up during their few days away. They had gone to see an old friend, Chris Nambert, in Brandon. He and his wife had just moved back to Manitoba after several years' absence. Chris had been the drummer in Deanie's former rock and roll band and had even saved her life once. But that was another story.

"I don't know," Russ shrugged, barely looking up from his newspaper. "Doesn't ring any bells. Where's it from?"

"Calgary. It's addressed to Mark."

"Probably a colleague or something," Russ shrugged.

"It's funny they'd send it here," Deanie mused. "It almost

looks like pictures or something."

"Curiosity killed the cat," Russ warned. "They probably just didn't know his new address. If it's pictures, it could be something important though. I'll call later and tell him it's here. Did you talk to Harmony today?"

"Mmhm," Deanie nodded. "She's getting settled in nicely."

"Maybe we should go over later and see if she needs anything," Russ suggested.

"She and Cory were going out tonight," Deanie informed her husband. "It's their anniversary. Isn't that sweet?"

"Hm," Russ grunted. "I hope they're not getting too serious too soon."

"Spoken like a true father," Deanie teased, squeezing him from behind. "Don't you remember what it was like when we were young and in love?"

"Only too well," Russ responded seriously. He turned around to take his wife fully in his arms. There was a slight smile playing around the corners of his lips. "Which is why I'm so worried."

* * *

The rest of their evening at the restaurant went smoothly. There were lots of things to talk about—safe things—like family and football and warm fall weather. When the conversation began to wane and they'd had as many refills of coffee as either could stand, Mark offered to drive Amy home.

"You just need to turn up here," Amy pointed as they neared her street. "Third house in with the blue door."

"I know the way," Mark said with a smile.

"Oh. Right," Amy laughed slightly.

Mark pulled up in front of Amy's parents' home and put his SUV in park, letting the motor idle. There was a moment of awkward silence before Amy made a move to get out of the vehicle.

"Hold on," Mark said, grabbing her hand.

Amy blinked, hardly daring to breath. The atmosphere in the confined space was electric.

"Amy, you must know I want to kiss you," Mark stated.

She worked her bottom lip and nodded.

"But I can't help thinking about the difference in our ages. I mean, you're young. You don't want to get entangled with a fossil like me."

"You're hardly a fossil," she breathed.

"And you're not a little girl," Mark went on. "And believe me, I noticed—even without the recent make over."

"Oh."

There was no more questioning the wisdom of the inevitable. They leaned toward one another and allowed a first tentative kiss. Mark hated to draw away, but knew, for both their sakes, he had to take it slow.

"You know, my sister told me I had to come tonight to protect you from some guy who had a crush on you," Mark said with a small laugh.

"Oh?" Amy asked, blinking.

"Yeah. She said you wouldn't appreciate his advances, so we might have to pretend to, you know . . . like each other."

"I didn't know she said any of that," Amy offered.

Mark looked at Amy candidly. "I'm not pretending," he said quietly. She didn't say anything. "And I hope you don't mind . . ."

"No, no I don't," Amy whispered.

"Good." He leaned over for another kiss, this one slower and more deliberate. When they separated, both were breathing more heavily.

"I have a message I want you to give to my sister," Mark said, a slight smile spreading across his face.

"Oh? What's that?"

"Tell her that her services are no longer needed."

Chapter Twenty-One

"I brought that package by," Russ said, stepping into Mark's office.

"Hm?" Mark asked, looking up.

"The package," Russ repeated. "The one that came to our house by mistake. From . . . " he read off the package, "Charlene Howard."

"Oh that," Mark grunted. "Just put it there." He gestured to a pile of other unopened correspondence on his desk.

"Oh. Guess I needn't have bothered then if it's not important," Russ shrugged. "I thought it might have something to do with the top secret what ever it is you're working on."

Mark looked up in surprise. "It's not top secret. Well, maybe kind of, but . . ."

"Nothing you can share with your old man," Russ stated, clearly fishing.

"Look Dad," Mark explained. "You already know from what I told you that I'm going to run into some opposition. I just don't want to put you in a compromising position, that's all."

"Who am I going to tell?"

"No one, but . . ." He sighed. "Look, I might as well tell you. I'm planning to head to Texas next week. I'm still working on putting together an air tight dissertation on that excavation site in Zimbabwe. Only now it's got to be sooner than later."

"That sounds like good news," Russ offered.

"It is," Mark nodded. "But I still need to be careful. There are some people out there that won't take kindly to what I have to share."

"Are you being threatened?" Russ asked with concern.

"In recent enough history that I don't want to take any chances," Mark admitted. "I just want to be safe, all right?"

"Are you sure you should go through with this?"

"Not a doubt in my mind," Mark nodded. "Look, I'd love to tell you everything, but I think it's best for everyone if I just keep it under wraps until the actual day of reckoning."

"Sounds ominous."

"Don't worry, okay? Everything is going to turn out alright. I just think it would be better for you and Deanie to know as little as possible. Once everything is out in the open, you might see my reasons, but for now, you'll just have to trust me."

"You know I always do," Russ said, surveying his son for a moment. "Just be careful." He cleared his throat as if to move onto the next subject. "Okay. Well, there's the package anyway." He patted it where it sat on Mark's desk and turned to leave.

"Dad," Mark stopped him.

"Yes?"

"There's something else on my mind, if you have a minute." He smiled sheepishly.

"Okay. Sure," Russ responded, eyeing his son as he sat down.

Mark took a deep breath. "So what was it like for you when you first met Deanie?"

Russ just blinked in surprise.

"When you first knew you might have feelings for Deanie," Mark rephrased. "How was that for you?"

"I don't even want to tell you what I thought of Deanie the first time I saw her," Russ responded.

"Love at first sight?" Mark asked with an amused grin.

"Hardly. I thought she was a little tramp," Russ laughed.

"Okay. So once you figured that part out, then what?"

Russ leaned back in his chair, considering. "Sometimes she made me so mad. I couldn't really sort my own feelings out at first, but I knew I couldn't live without her. Why all the questions all of a sudden?" He squinted speculatively.

"And what about the difference in your ages?" Mark persisted. "Was that a problem for either of you? How did you reconcile that in your mind?"

"This doesn't have anything to do with Amy Walters, does it?" Russ asked pointedly.

"How did you know?" Mark asked with a slightly embarrassed grin.

"Your sister isn't that good at keeping secrets," Russ stated dryly. "How old is Amy now anyway?"

"She'll be twenty-one pretty soon," Mark replied.

"And you are?"

"Thirty-three."

"Thirty-four next month, if I remember correctly," Russ added.

"Yeah. Right," Mark nodded flatly.

"So that makes you thirteen years older than her, give or take a few months."

"I know," Mark said with a grim sounding sigh. "I don't know what's gotten into me."

Russ just shrugged. "Seems to me you're like your old man in more ways than we imagined. We Graham men just take a little longer to decide on a mate, that's all. We're choosey, but when the right one comes along, there will be no other choices."

241

Mark thought about that for a minute. Amy Walters was his choice. Now he just had to convince her of that fact.

"Thanks. That helps a lot."

"Good. Well, I better get going," Russ said, rising.

"Um, one more thing," Mark stopped him again. "About that package. I was debating whether I should say anything or not, but I think maybe I need to."

Russ frowned. "What is it?"

"Maybe you should sit down again," Mark suggested.

Russ did as he was told and waited patiently for Mark to continue.

"I've been contacted by this Charlene Howard person. Actually, she came here with her husband and child not that long ago. I was going to tell you then, but I chickened out."

Russ just raised his eyebrows, but didn't need to prompt any further.

"Yeah . . . she's actually my sister," Mark said. He could see the change in his father's countenance. His expression hadn't changed, but all the color had drained from his face. "She's Miranda's—my mother's—daughter," Mark continued quickly. "Apparently she remarried and never told any of them about me—or you. There's a boy too. Harmony's age."

"And how do you feel about this?" Russ asked tightly.

"Confused, angry, indifferent . . . how should I feel?"

"I suppose she wants to meet with you," Russ stated. "After all these years."

"As far as I know, Miranda doesn't know Charlene made contact. It was an accident that she even found out about my existence when she ran across a scrapbook Miranda had been keeping about my career."

"I see," Russ nodded. He rose abruptly from the chair. "Well, you do whatever you want to. I won't stop you. You're a man, after

242

all."

"Dad . . ."

Russ shook his head and gave a self-deprecating laugh. "After all these years. I thought I was completely over it. I'm surprise at how . . . vulnerable I feel right now."

"Me too."

"I'm not sure what I'm going to tell Deanie," Russ mused.

"You don't have to say anything if you don't want to."

"Are you kidding?" Russ laughed. "Your stepmother has this uncanny sense—like radar. She can spot when something's troubling me from a mile away. I'm afraid I'm not that good at keeping secrets. At least not with her."

"Sorry, Dad. For upsetting you," Mark offered.

"I'll get over it," Russ quipped. "She hasn't made me totally soft you know."

Chapter Twenty-Two

Amy Walters turned and gave her sideways reflection a good scan. Did these jeans make her look fat? Was the t-shirt too low cut? Maybe she should change. She definitely wanted to look good tonight. It was her first real date with Mark—well, if you didn't count the other night. They were just going to a show, but she really, really wanted to look right. Not too juvenile, but not frumpy either. With a sigh, she turned away from the mirror. It was getting late and she'd just have to settle for the way she looked, imperfections and all. Next week she was definitely going to work out at the gym.

"Mom, have you seen my grey sweater anywhere?" she called as she skipped down the stairs and entered the kitchen. Her mother, Holly, was sitting at the table in front of her laptop computer.

"I'm afraid not," Holly replied, clicking away.

Amy frowned. "I wonder if I left it over at Harmony's. Oh well, I'll just have to wear something else."

"Going somewhere?" Holly asked, peering over the tops of her glasses.

"Um, yeah," Amy shrugged. "Just to a movie."

"That's nice. Who's going?"

"Mark should be picking me up any minute."

"Oh? Are Harmony and Cory going along?" Holly asked casually.

"Not that I know of," Amy replied. "Why? Does it matter?" she added somewhat defensively.

"Of course not," Holly defended quickly. "Should it?"

"Mom, we've been friends with the Grahams for forever. Harmony is my best friend."

"But you aren't going to the show with Harmony," Holly pointed out. "You're going with Mark."

"Is that a problem?"

"Well, no . . . it's just that . . ."

Amy stopped in her tracks and frowned, placing her hands on her hips. "Just what, Mom? Yeah, I like Mark, okay? Of all the guys I could choose, I thought you'd approve since he is an old family friend and all."

"He is quite a bit older than you," Holly offered. "And more . . . worldly."

"Oh, I get it," Amy's voice held a sarcastic bite. "You don't trust me."

"I never said that."

"Then what?" Amy asked.

"Well, you must admit you have lived a more sheltered life than he has, and well, I worry. Maybe you're getting in over your head."

"See? You don't trust me," Amy repeated emphatically. "I'm not exactly a little kid anymore, you know. And as for living a sheltered life, that much might be true, but you're forgetting that I am a Christian. My faith is solid. I'm not going to do anything stupid."

"How do you know?" Holly asked, a worried frown crossing her brow. "I just read some rather disturbing statistics recently. It said pre-marital sex among believers was almost as high as among

246

non-believers."

"Mom!" Amy groaned and rolled her eyes. "You don't need to worry, okay? Besides, this is Mark we're talking about, remember? He was raised in a Christian home."

"Ah ha!" Holly seized on the point. "Which means absolutely nothing. There's no guarantee he'll follow his family's faith."

"Mom!"

"In fact, Deanie and Russ have asked for prayer along those lines on more than one occasion."

"Which doesn't mean he doesn't believe," Amy defended.

"Have you asked him?" Holly asked pointedly.

"Well, no, but . . ."

"A conversation you should have very soon, I would think," Holly stated. "There's no point in pursuing a relationship that is not based on mutual faith. The Bible warns us about becoming unequally yoked."

"You make it sound like we're getting married!" Amy exclaimed. "This is like, our first real date."

"Oh really?" Holly queried skeptically. "What about the other night?"

"Um, well that really wasn't a date . . . "

"Oh? I saw you two when he dropped you off."

"Mom!" Amy spouted. "You were spying on us?"

"Not spying exactly," Holly defended. "I just happened to glance out the window when I heard the car drive up. I wasn't trying to spy. But, well, I couldn't help but see what happened next."

"Mother!" Amy cried again, her face turning a healthy crimson.

"Sorry," Holly shrugged.

"In any case, it's all really new and I'd appreciate it if you didn't read too much into anything," Amy declared huffily. "Like I said, we're not getting married or anything."

"What's the point of it then?" Holly asked. "As a Christian, it doesn't make sense to become emotionally attached to someone if you aren't thinking about that conclusion. What else are you in it for?"

"Now, that is sounding positively archaic." Amy rolled her eyes.

"Really? Just think about it. What do you want out of this relationship?" Holly persisted.

"Friendship?" Amy stated with a shrug. "Companionship?"

"And is that all Mark wants?" Holly asked.

Amy didn't have an answer for that.

"Amy," Holly tried to sound gentle, "men aren't like us. Eventually, he's going to want to go further. And then you're going to have to decide whether that's something you're willing to give up. Either way, you could end up losing. Once you've given yourself away to a man, there is no getting that part of you back again. You've attached yourself emotionally, like it or not. And the alternative is a marriage where you don't share the most intimate bond—that of a spiritual union."

Amy interrupted her mother with anger. "You're a fine one to talk! Dad wasn't a Christian when you first met him."

"That much is true," Holly agreed, "but that doesn't mean I recommend it. The Lord was gracious to us and it all worked out, but stepping outside His boundaries is never a good idea. Besides, as you said, Mark was raised in the church and knows. Sometimes people like that are harder to reach. They're skeptical. I just don't want to see you get hurt."

Amy let out a deep sigh. "Trust me," she said, reaching to give her mother a squeeze. "I'm not that stupid. Now, I've got to get going if I'm going to make the bus."

"He's not picking you up?"

"He was working late. It just made more sense to meet at the theater," Amy explained.

"Oh," Holly said with a frown. "I'm not sure how I feel about that. If he's too busy for you now, how will it be in the future?"

"Mom," Amy warned with a grin. "Don't start, okay? I love you and I won't be too late." She gave her mother a quick peck on the cheek and scurried toward the front door.

Okay, so just what was she expecting, Amy wondered? She wasn't sure. She only knew she had a whole chorus line of butterflies high kicking their way up and down her insides.

* * *

Blue light from the TV screen flickered across Russ's face as he sat on the couch watching the evening news. Deanie surveyed her husband from the doorway to the family room. She saw the same chiseled features that she loved so dearly, lines of age only adding character and depth. He had never been one to show emotion very easily, his composure seeming almost stoic and unfeeling to those who did not know him. But to Deanie, he was the caring and sensitive man she had grown to love so completely. Even after all these years, the emotion had not faded, only grown stronger. And she had learned to read his face, too, like a book. Something was up. She knew it.

"Hey, anything interesting happen in the world today?" she asked, settling down next to him on the couch.

He just shrugged. "Same old. War, famine, floods."

She nodded, snuggling in closer. "What about in your world?" she asked.

"What do you mean?"

"Oh, I don't know. You just seem—quiet."

"I'm a quiet guy," Russ countered.

"I know, but this is different. A different quiet. Like something is bothering you," Deanie stated. "Is something bothering you?"

Russ paused for a moment, then chuckled softly under his breath before switching off the TV with the remote. He turned to face his wife. "I told Mark you had some kind of sixth sense. I can't keep anything from you."

"And why would you?" she asked. "Now, spill it."

* * *

"So what did you think of the show?" Amy asked as she and Mark strolled hand in hand down the darkened downtown street.

Mark shrugged, allowing a slight smile to play at his lips. "Okay, I guess. I must confess I haven't been to a movie theater in a long time."

They had left the theater and were headed toward Mark's apartment. It was only a short stroll and he'd left his SUV parked in his designated parking stall so he wouldn't have to worry about parking at the theater.

Their hands had been intertwined almost from the beginning of the movie. As soon as the lights had dimmed, Mark had reached over and taken her hand into his. It fit so perfectly, felt so comfortable. He hadn't ventured to kiss her though, a fact that left Amy decidedly disappointed. But on the other hand, she sensed a growing anticipation for the moment when it did come. The wind whipped past, opening the bottom flap of Amy's coat and whipping it across her legs.

"Now let's see," Mark frowned, stopping by his vehicle as he dug in his jacket pocket. "I was sure I brought the keys with me when I left."

"Hope you didn't drop them at the theater," Amy offered, not really sounding all that worried.

"They're probably just up in the apartment," Mark said. "You might as well come up for a minute while I go get them. You

250

wouldn't want to stand down here on the street."

Amy nodded. Mark took her hand again and they approached the building. He led her up the steep flight of steps and unlocked the entrance to his own dwelling. "Not very elegant, I'm afraid," he apologized. "And excuse the mess. I've been a bit preoccupied with work."

Amy glanced around the dim interior. It was rather cramped and certainly not new, but as far as any mess went, it looked pretty orderly for a bachelor's pad. It was basically one room, except for a door that she assumed went to the bedroom and bath. It was the first time she had been in Mark's private dwelling. She felt a shiver —no, more of a tingling sensation, run over her body.

"I'll just be a minute," Mark was saying. "I think I left them on my dresser." He disappeared into the bedroom and was back in just a moment. "Ready to go then?"

"Hm? What's that?" Amy asked absently, bringing her attention back to Mark's form, framed in the bedroom doorway.

"I was just wondering if you're ready to go," Mark repeated. "Unless you'd like to stay for a bit. I could make coffee . . ." he trailed off.

"Coffee would be great," Amy nodded.

"Okay. You can just throw your coat over that chair if you like."

She nodded again and did as she was told, then lowered herself onto the sofa that was one of the few pieces of furniture in the compact room.

Mark busied himself with the coffee maker in the adjacent kitchenette and then turned with a smile. "That should only take a few moments." He crossed to the sofa and sat down beside her. "So. How was your day at school?"

"Fine," Amy said. "Yours?"

"Fine."

"Good."

There were several minutes of tension filled silence. Amy felt as if her lungs were about to burst until she realized she was holding her breath. She smiled tentatively.

"You're awfully tense," Mark noted.

She nodded and laughed nervously. "Sorry."

"There's no need, you know," Mark assured in a low voice. His arm had crept around the back of the sofa. "Did I tell you how very beautiful you look this evening?"

Their lips met in an explosion of light and stars. Amy wasn't the only one breathless now. Mark's own world was shaken by the kiss. He moved in for more.

"Wait."

The one syllable was so small, so tenuous, that he almost missed it. He pulled back slightly. "It's okay. Don't be afraid."

"But I am."

Mark pulled away fully now, keeping his arm protectively around her shoulder but giving her the space she needed. "I would never hurt you," he stated. "You must know that."

"I know," she whispered. "It's not you I'm worried about. It's me."

"If it's the sex thing, we can wait if you want to," Mark continued. "For as long as you need." He stroked her cheek gently with the back of his index finger.

"Thanks. I—I appreciate that," she said, looking down. "You must think I'm awfully old fashioned. Or naïve."

"I think you are very, very beautiful." He bent his head for another kiss. Their lips met gently this time, tenderly, until the hunger took over again. This time it was Mark who pulled away.

"What's wrong?" Amy asked in a small worried voice.

Mark laughed slightly. "I'm only human. I think I better go check on that coffee." He stole another quick kiss before standing

252

up. He went over to the counter, found two mugs, and filled them. "Take anything?"

"No thanks," Amy said, smoothing her hair with her hand.

Mark returned with the steaming mugs and set them down on the coffee table in front of the sofa. "Now, if we keep these between us we should be safe," he joked.

Amy took a sip, keeping the mug close enough to her lips to hide their trembling. Mark wasn't fooled. "What's wrong?" he asked. He surveyed her closely, then with deliberateness he set down his own mug and took hers from her hands, placing it beside his on the coffee table. "Amy, what's the matter?'

She shook her head mutely.

"Talk to me, Amy," Mark pleaded. He took her hands in his and placed a kiss on each one before returning his gaze to her distraught face.

I'm . . . I feel so, so silly," she finally said with a shake of her head.

"Silly? Why?"

"Because you're so . . . so worldly and I'm such a naïve little duck."

Mark laughed outright at that. "A duck? Now that's a good one."

"I'm serious," she said. "I mean, you've been around the world. Probably, you know, been with lots of women. And well, you know. I'm not like that. I believe in saving myself, I mean. But you make me want to forget about all of that."

"I told you. I can wait."

Amy shook her head. "Maybe my mother was right. It's too dangerous to be in a relationship with someone who isn't a Christian."

Mark felt his jaw tighten. "So that's what it's about, is it? Religion?"

"It's important," Amy offered quietly.

"I know, and for all intents and purposes, I believe the same way you do. I was raised in the church. You know that," Mark stated.

"That's not good enough, Mark. I want you to accept it for yourself. Accept Jesus."

"How do you know I haven't?" Mark countered.

"Have you?"

There was a telling silence.

"I see," Amy said.

"I don't object to your faith, Amy. I know how important it is to you. I don't see how it's an issue."

"Because you don't know Jesus the way I know Jesus. If you did, you'd see where I'm coming from."

"And if I agreed to your terms?"

"It has to be for real, Mark. It has to be sincere."

"Okay. So, say I was sincere. Then what?"

"I still wouldn't sleep with you."

Mark considered this a moment. "Hm. You drive a hard bargain, you know that?" His mouth twisted up at the corner in a boyish grin.

Amy turned away. "I think I want to go home now," she stated.

"Sorry," Mark apologized. "Now I've offended you. I was only teasing. I won't pressure you to have sex. When we make love, it will be strictly on your terms."

"I don't think you've been listening to a word I've said," Amy said with exasperation. "There will be no sex without marriage." She paused for a moment, her eyes welling up with tears. "Oh, I feel so absolutely stupid now. I just want to go home. This was such a bad idea. Take me home, please." She stood abruptly, dashing at her eyes.

"Amy, wait," Mark said, standing also. "I'll take you home—in a minute. But I think we need to have a talk first. A real, honest conversation about what matters to us and our future."

"I don't see a future," she stated sullenly, but allowed Mark to push her gently back down onto the sofa.

"Because now you're the one who's not listening," Mark teased. He sobered slightly, letting the smile in his eyes be replaced with an intensity of raw emotion. "Amy Walters, you may not realize this, but you are a very powerful woman."

"Stop. If this is about sex, I don't want to hear it. You're making fun of me now."

"It's not about sex," Mark clarified. "Well, not directly anyway. I mean, eventually, yes, I hope it is."

"Mark!"

"What I'm trying to say is this. You have, quite honestly, swept me off my feet," Mark admitted. "And you keep saying how naïve and inexperienced you are! Well, let me tell you, I am so grateful for that. The thought of any other man, now or in the future, ever laying a hand on you—well, it puts me in a rage! When I make love to you for the first time, I want to be the only man to ever do it again."

"There you go talking about sex again. I already told you—"

Mark sighed, lifting a hand to silence her. "Look, this is not going at all like I had imagined it."

"I'll bet."

He continued undaunted. "I was going to give you more time. Court you. Woo you. You're young and I didn't want you to feel rushed into anything. It's important that you know your own feelings, that you don't feel pressured. That you're sure. As sure as I am already."

"What are you saying?" Amy asked, frowning.

"I would think it's fairly obvious," Mark laughed.

Amy blinked back tears. "Don't you dare be making fun of me."

"I'm not, honest," Mark said, stroking her cheek again. He kissed her gently on the trail made by his finger.

"Mark, don't," Amy pleaded. "I can't think straight."

"Good," Mark said with a satisfied grin. "Exactly how I want you when I ask you. Now, I do have to admit, I have been around a time or two. And yes, I have slept with other women—a fact I have never regretted up until this moment. Now I wish I could give you the same gift that I hope you'll give to me. You have captivated me, Amy, and if waiting for marriage is the only way I can have you all to myself, then I'm asking you. Will you marry me?"

"Mark, you don't know what you're saying."

"Stop telling me what I know and don't know!" Mark exclaimed. "Actually, I am well aware of every word that just came out of my mouth. My dad said it best. We Graham men are kind of slow, but when we find what we're looking for, we fall hard."

"You talked to your dad about us?" Amy asked incredulously.

"That a problem?" Mark asked. "By the sounds of things you've been talking to your mom . . ."

"But that's different!"

"Why?"

"Well, it just is! Besides, we haven't addressed the issue of your spiritual beliefs."

"I'll believe whatever you want me to," Mark said.

"Mark—"

Mark pulled her to her feet and cupped her head between his hands. "I mean it, Amy Walters. I love you. I've fallen hard. Whatever it takes, I'll do it." He sealed the declaration with a kiss.

Amy felt herself melting into the haze of desire that could so suddenly overtake her body wherever Mark Graham was concerned. She responded with a matched urgency, slipping her arms around his neck.

"You don't have to say yes right away," Mark said when they parted for air. "In fact, maybe you need time to think on it, take it all in." She opened her mouth to respond, but he quickly covered it with a finger before she could utter anything. "Actually, I don't even want you to say anything right now. Just think on it and in the meantime, know that my intentions are honorable. Take as much time as you need. I'll wait."

Amy ignored the warning bells that were going off in her head and reached upward for another kiss. Mark gave her what she wanted.

"And now," he said, extracting himself gently from her embrace. "I better take you home before you make a liar out of me. Much more of this and I won't be able to keep you a virgin until the wedding."

* * *

"I think Mark should meet his mother," Deanie stated with no uncertainty.

"I don't know," Russ said with a frown.

"Of course he should," she declared. "No matter how much time and distance, it's still an area of his life that is unresolved. He needs to meet her, meet his other siblings, and whether or not they get along together or continue with any kind of relationship isn't the point. He needs to lay that particular demon to rest."

"You seem very opinionated on the subject," Russ noted humorlessly.

"Of course. In fact, you should probably go with him."

Russ almost choked. "Pardon me?"

"You heard me," Deanie said. "Despite all your declarations to the contrary, I think you still have some demons to exorcize as well."

"That is absolutely out of the question," Russ stated, disentangling himself from his wife's loose embrace.

"I don't understand what you're so afraid of. I mean—"

"I said no." Russ stood abruptly. The steel in his voice made Deanie jerk her head up. She hadn't seen that look in his eyes for years. Intense hatred mixed with a cool detachment that made her cringe with only the slightest amount of fear.

"Well, it was only a suggestion," Deanie tried for lightness.

"This conversation is officially over," Russ said. With that he strode from the room. Deanie knew that he meant it.

* * *

Mark pulled up in front of the Walters' residence and put his vehicle in park, letting the motor idle. He leaned over for another goodnight kiss. Amy shied back slightly.

"Um, my mom might be watching," she said, slightly embarrassed.

Mark raised his eyebrows. "Oh?"

"Yeah," Amy laughed nervously. "She mentioned something about the last time you dropped me off."

Mark considered this for a moment and smiled. It had been awhile since he had to worry about overprotective parents waiting indoors. "I see."

"Um, will I see you again tomorrow?" she asked hopefully.

"I'll try," Mark said. "It might not be for very long though, I'm afraid. I have a mountain of work I need to get finished up in a really short while."

"Oh." There was no mistaking the disappointment in her voice. "Well, good night then." Amy leaned over and gave him a peck on the cheek before turning to open her own door.

"Wait a second," Mark laughed, grabbing her arm gently to stall her departure. "Is that it? Seems pretty cheap to me."

"My mother," Amy protested. Anything else she had to say

258

was squelched by the persuasive pressure of Mark's lips on her own.

"If your mother is watching, we might as well give her something to look at," Mark countered when he finally let her go.

"I better go now," Amy said. "Call me tomorrow?"

"Um, yeah." Mark responded somewhat flatly. "Actually, can you wait a minute?" he added.

"Sure."

"I'm going to be leaving town for a bit next week. Got some business that I have to take care of. When I said I was going to be really busy for the next little while, I meant it. Not because I want to be. But I really need to finish up some work before I leave. I wanted you to know that if I seem a bit preoccupied, it's not because of anything you did, or didn't do."

"Oh. Thanks." Amy looked down at her hands, embarrassed.

"If I could, I'd spend every waking moment with you."

"What kind of business?" Amy asked, avoiding the intensity of his gaze.

"Archeology stuff."

"Of course. How long are you going be gone? Where are you going?"

"I can't tell you that, and I'm not sure," Mark responded. He noticed the hurt expression on her face. "Sorry. I don't mean to be secretive, but I really can't tell you just yet what it's all about."

"Oh. Okay." Her voice sounded small.

He reached for her again. "Hey, no long faces." He kissed her tenderly on the mouth. "I'll call you tomorrow, I promise."

She nodded mutely. Why, oh why did she suddenly feel so forlorn?

Chapter Twenty-Three

Mark glanced up from his desk as Harmony walked in after only a preemptory rap on the door. She hadn't waited for a response, just entered. He repositioned his cell phone to the other ear and waved her in. "Yeah, I know that, but I thought I told you to be more careful about who you talk to about our relationship." He was talking to Anthony again. He paused, looking over at his sister who was now loitering near his desk. He stood up, speaking more quietly. "We need to be discreet. Absolutely so." He smiled tentatively to Harmony as he listened and then motioned to her that he was going to slip out into the hall.

Harmony nodded, just catching another phrase that sounded intriguingly secretive. She smiled. That was her big brother. She swung around behind his desk and settled herself comfortably in his chair, leaning back, pretending to be a world famous doctor of something or other herself. Her eyes strayed to the open email on his computer screen.

'Looking forward to your visit. Very glad you reconsidered. Do I flatter myself that you might miss me after all? No hard feelings on my part. John and Anthony say hi. We'll have a celebration party, just like old times. Love, Laura'

Harmony frowned. Laura . . . no, not just Laura, but love Laura. The name rang a bell. Wasn't she the archeologist? The one that Mark had been dating back in Africa?

Her mind jumped to the secretive conversation she had just overheard. *"Be careful who you talk to about our relationship . . . we need to be discreet . . ."* She glanced back at the computer screen, her mind fitting the pieces together like a puzzle. How could he? After he had stolen her best friend's heart—with some coaxing from her, she had to admit. They were so perfect together, and Amy was so trusting, so naïve . . .

Mark came back into the office with a relaxed smile on his face. Harmony jumped up from his chair guiltily and tried to match his nonchalance. "So you coming out for lunch or what?"

"Lunch?" Mark repeated absently. "Oh, I better not. I've got way too much to do here."

"I'm meeting Amy," Harmony added persuasively.

Mark considered this a moment then shook his head. "Convincing, but I'm afraid the answer is still no. I'm leaving the day after tomorrow and I'm nowhere near ready."

"You sure?" Harmony tried again.

"Absolutely. But say 'hi' to her for me."

"Hi?" Harmony repeated disparagingly. "Is that it? Just 'hi'?"

Mark laughed. "I distinctly remember telling you that your services are no longer needed, remember?"

"Oh really? I'm not too sure about that, big brother. For a man who just declared his undying love, you've been awfully stand offish this last week."

Mark scowled, feeling slightly ashamed by his sister's words. "Firstly, my love life is really none of your business—"

"Of course it is. Amy is my best friend," Harmony countered.

"And secondly," he continued, "I have explained to both of you that it's imperative that I finish my work."

"Fine, Mr. Doctor Big Wig. You're so busy you can't even take an hour off for lunch with your own sister or your girlfriend? I'll tell Amy."

"There's a lot riding on this that I don't expect you to fully understand."

"I just don't want to see her get hurt," Harmony said. "She's really gone off the deep end for you, you know."

Mark ran his hand through his hair. "You're not making this easy, you know that?" he said with a sigh.

"Who's Laura and why are you meeting her?' Harmony asked pointedly.

Mark's eyes narrowed. If he'd been reconsidering, he had changed his mind. "You've become far too nosy for your own good, you know that?" he quipped. He strode to his chair and sat emphatically.

"Oh really? Why? Because you're off on a rendezvous with a former girlfriend while you leave my best friend waiting by the phone in your absence?"

"That's absolutely juvenile," Mark laughed mirthlessly. "You've obviously been watching too many movies."

"Well? What am I supposed to think? What am I supposed to tell Amy?"

"Nothing," Mark said. "There is absolutely nothing to tell," Harmony didn't look convinced. Mark sighed again. "Look, Laura Sawchuk and I were an item at one time, but that is long over and done with. Okay? Honest. Now, if you wouldn't mind, I really do need to get back to work." Without another word, he began clicking away on the keys.

Harmony was about to say something else, but decided against it and clamped her mouth tightly instead. She turned and strode from the room.

* * *

Mark leaned back in his chair and stretched his arms backward to cradle his head. He surveyed the computer screen with satisfaction. He was ready. Along with the written dissertation, which was persuasive and well researched, he had a power point presentation that contained dynamic graphics and photographs. But this was about far more than just empirical evidence. The real kicker was still waiting in his father's garage—the artifacts and samples that he had smuggled off site. Nobody could dispute their existence; nobody could dispute the painstaking care he had taken in testing and identifying each one. The only problem would be the legal ramifications once their existence, and the method in which they were secured, became public knowledge. He would just have to cross that bridge when he came to it. Both he and Anthony were working on an angle, but there were no guarantees.

The tricky part was going to be crossing the U.S. border with the cargo. He still had copies of the original documentation he had received from the Zimbabwean government back when the project had started. And, under the auspices of the university, he had secured immunity to transport certain otherwise contraband items for scholarly purposes. The fact that the said items were not exactly as listed was another matter. He would just have to convince the guards at the border that his cargo could not be opened or tampered with in any way.

Of course, advance permission had already been secured, which was a bit of a worry. The fewer people that knew about his plans the better. Even though it had been some time since Sangeruka's threats, as well as the fact that he no longer seemed to have the influence that he once did, Mark couldn't help but feel a few pangs of anxiety over the safety of his loved ones. It was one of the reasons that he had been so tight lipped about his actual itinerary, even to his father. The less anyone knew, the better off they would be.

Mark glanced down at his watch. It was late—probably too late to call Amy, but he felt euphoric somehow. He needed to share his excitement with someone. All the preliminary work was finished. All that remained was the anticipation of telling the world —and the possible danger of traveling to the appointed destination.

"Hi Amy," Mark said into his cell. "Did I wake you?" He kept his voice low, as if it would help somehow.

"No, it's okay. I couldn't sleep anyway," she replied.

"I finished up here," he offered, as if that explained everything.

"Oh. That's good news."

"I was wondering, is it too late to meet me somewhere? For a coffee or something? I know it's kind of late, but I was thinking, I haven't had much time for you these past few days, and since I'll be leaving soon . . . " he trailed off.

"Um, I guess so. I'm not sure what buses are running this time of night . . ." she added hesitantly.

"Of course," Mark chided himself. "How stupid of me. I'll come by and pick you up."

Amy came out the front door of the Walter residence as soon as Mark drove up. All the lights were off and it struck him how ridiculous it was for a man his age to be sneaking around his girlfriend's house after hours. Like he was doing something illegal or something. Maybe he should suggest that Amy move into her own place for awhile, like Harmony. Or even move in with Harmony.

Wait. Strike that thought. The last thing he wanted was his little sister nosing about his affairs even more than she did now.

"Hi, you," Mark greeted as Amy slid into the passenger seat. A rush of warmth washed over him and he felt definite regret that he hadn't been able to spend much time with her over the past several days. "You look nice," he said and leaned over to kiss her. His lips barely touched hers before she was pulling away, busying herself with buckling the seatbelt. He frowned slightly, but brushed it off. "Where to?"

"Um, where ever," she shrugged.

"Somewhere close, I suppose," he said, and pulled away from the curb.

"Or we could just go down by the Forks," she suggested. The Forks, as it was called, was a large park-like area in the middle of the city where the Assiniboine and Red Rivers met.

"Forks it is," Mark nodded. He reached over and took her small, soft hand into his larger one. "I missed you."

"Me too."

They were content to ride that way for some time, satisfied in the physical contact without the necessity of words. Finally, Amy spoke up.

"Mark?"

"Hm?"

"Why can't you tell me more about what you're doing?"

He glanced over at her and smiled. "If I told you, it would be telling. Which I can't." He noted the slight furrowing of her brow. "Just trust me, okay? I'll tell you all about it someday. I promise." He gave her hand a squeeze.

There was silence again for a time before Amy piped up again. "Mark? Tell me about Laura. Did you love her?"

He scowled. "You've been talking to my sister again, haven't you?" He released her hand as he turned sharply into the parking lot near the Forks.

"Um . . . sorry. I shouldn't have brought it up," Amy apologized timidly.

Mark put the SUV into park with a jerk. "It's okay. I should know better than to trust my sister to get things right." He turned to look squarely at Amy. "Whatever I had with Laura is over and done. Understand? It's finished. Over. Kaput. I thought I made that clear to you the other night."

"Well, yes, but . . ."

"And about you sharing our personal lives with everyone," he continued. "I'm a pretty private person, and I don't appreciate being the subject of gossip."

"I didn't say anything to anyone," Amy replied, tears very close to the surface now. "Well, except Harmony, and then I didn't mean to say anything."

"Ah, but you did," he stated.

"You know how hard it is to keep anything from her," Amy defended.

"She couldn't wait to see my reaction," he went on, almost as if he hadn't heard her defense at all. "I felt like my love life was being written up in some teen magazine. I'm not interested in that, so you and my sister can stop any time." The moment the words had come out of his mouth he realized exactly how hurtful they sounded. Amy blinked. Her nostrils flared with the effort of keeping the tears at bay. "Amy, I'm sorry. That was utterly uncalled for," he apologized.

"I'll try to act more grown up from now on," she managed to choke out sarcastically.

"Oh man," he breathed, closing his eyes and pinching the bridge of his nose between his thumb and forefinger. "I didn't mean that the way it sounded."

"No?"

"No. I just don't want people interfering. I didn't mean anything else by it."

"I suppose you think I'm too immature to be trusted with your secret mission, whatever it is."

"Amy," he pleaded. "That's just—" he was about to say childish, but stopped himself in time. "Silly," he finished.

"Silly," she repeated. "Because I'm just a silly little girl."

Mark sighed. "Okay. What do you want from me? I said I was sorry and I meant it. And I'm sorry that I can't tell you where I'm going or what I'm doing, either. But it's for your own safety and the safety of other people. I know that sounds pretty lame right about now, but it's the best I can do."

"Safety?" Genuine concern replaced any former churlishness. "Why? Are you in some kind of trouble?"

"Amy . . ." he warned. He surveyed her features and reached to run the back of his finger down her cheek. "Even when you're mad you're beautiful, you know that?" he said softly. She didn't reply, but he could see that her features were softening. "Forgive me?"

She nodded, suddenly mute with conflicting emotions.

"Good. And I'll take all the questions as a sign that you care, that's all."

Somehow they managed to find themselves in each other's arms, their kisses urgent with pent up emotion and the knowledge that they would be apart for some time in the near future.

"I'm really going to miss you," Mark breathed. "I wish we'd been able to spend more time together." Their mouths and bodies locked in another heat filled embrace.

"Mark?" Amy whispered against his mouth.

"Hm?"

"Did you mean it? The other night, I mean."

"Of course. Every word." He nibbled his way around her ear and down her neck.

"Then I was thinking," she said tentatively. "Maybe we should go over to your place."

Mark stopped what he was doing and pulled back slightly, just far enough to see her face fully. "Why? What are you saying?"

"Just that maybe I don't want to wait after all," she replied, her voice sounding small and not quite convinced. She looked down, avoiding his gaze, as heat infused her cheeks.

Mark was silent for a moment before adjusting himself further away from the temptation of her body. Instead, he took her hand safely in his own. "I don't think that's a very good idea."

"Why?" she asked sharply, anxiety catching in her voice.

"Not because I don't want to, believe me," he chuckled. "But because I know how important it is for you. To save yourself for marriage, I mean."

"But I thought . . . I mean . . . the other night you said you wanted to marry me," Amy said.

"Right. But you haven't answered yet. And I don't want you to just yet, either."

"But I've already made up my mind," Amy replied quickly. "The answer is 'yes'. Yes, I want to marry you."

"That is like music to my ears," Mark smiled. "But I'm leaving for awhile. You might feel differently once I get back. Things have been pretty intense between us, not to mention the fact that everything has happened so fast. A little time away from me will help you put things in perspective."

"Or help you put things in perspective," Amy countered. "Maybe you're just hoping that I'll fall out of love with you so that you don't have to get stuck with me."

"Now that was utterly ridiculous," Mark laughed. "If any one is getting stuck with anyone, it's you. I'm practically a senior citizen."

"Hardly." She reached for his collar and pulled him closer for another heated kiss.

"I must admit, you're getting very good at that," Mark mused.

"I'm a fast learner," Amy quipped.

"So I see."

"We could make love right here. In the car," Amy suggested

between kisses.

"Not a chance," Mark laughed huskily. "Now that would be down right degrading . . . You're not making this very easy, you know," he breathed.

"I want to make sure you come back," Amy said provocatively.

Mark stopped his ministrations abruptly. "Is that what this is about? You think if you sleep with me I'll be sure to come back to you? Amy, I told you already that I love you. I don't know what kind of crazy notions you've got running around in your head, but let me assure you that it takes more than sex to secure a man's heart. If that were the case, I'd be married already by now."

The words stung and Mark could see the change in her countenance once again. He let out a gust of frustrated breath. "Man, I just keep putting my foot in it, don't I? What I mean is, you've already got my heart. Don't you know that already? So much so, that I'm willing to wait for you. And if I spoiled that now, even for a wonderful night with you in my bed—something I want more than you can imagine—well, I'd be mad at myself for the rest of my life. You're worth it, Amy. Don't you see? I want to do this thing right, for a change. I want it to be different for us, with no regrets."

"I guess I really am pretty naïve," Amy whispered. "Oh, I'm so ashamed!" she turned away, a tiny sob escaping her lips.

"Come here, honey," Mark soothed, taking her into his arms. He smoothed her hair. "Don't worry about anything, okay? I meant what I said. I'm coming back. I promise."

"And I meant what I said," she murmured into his shirt. "The answer is yes."

He gently bent his head and sealed the declaration with another kiss. "I believe you. Now, I better get you home." He shifted in his seat and started the car.

270

Amy nodded mutely.

"So, this might be it for awhile until I get back," Mark said, steering out onto the street. "Sorry. Again."

"What do you mean?" Amy asked. "I thought you were leaving the day after tomorrow."

"I was, but since I finished up early, I figure there's no point in hanging around."

"Oh," Amy responded flatly. "I guess there's nothing here to keep you an extra day."

"That's not what I meant. Of course I'd like to stay and spend an entire day with you. But, on the other hand, too much time with you and we might end up doing something we'd regret." He glanced over at her and gave her a gentle smile. "Besides, the sooner I get going, the sooner I get back, right?"

"Can I at least come and see you off?" she asked.

"My plan is to pack up first thing tomorrow, and leave as soon as possible after that."

"I could help," she offered.

"Out of the question," he replied in no uncertain terms. Amy was silent. "Tell you what. As soon as I'm ready, I'll call you. Okay?"

"Okay." Every doubt that had plagued her thus far came rushing back.

Chapter Twenty-Four

Mark arrived very early at his parents' home the next morning. He'd only gotten a couple hours of sleep, anticipation making it almost impossible to relax. He had already secured the permits needed. All that was left was to load up and leave.

Russ greeted his son at the door, dressed casually in jeans and a sweat shirt, his hair still looking tousled from sleep. "Come in," Russ waved with his free hand. In the other he held a steaming mug. "Coffee?"

"No. I already stopped at Tim's," Mark replied. "Deanie up?"

"Are you kidding?" Russ laughed. "This is even early for me." He downed the rest of his coffee, setting the cup down on a side table by the door before stretching and yawning. "Well, let's get at it then."

They headed out to the garage. "Is there room for me to back in?" Mark asked.

"If I take my car out, I suppose," Russ shrugged.

"Okay. I think that's the best idea."

Russ surveyed his son speculatively, but said nothing. In a few moments they had made the switch and Mark had opened the back door of the SUV. "I sure hope you know what you're doing," Russ commented.

"You know me," Mark joked. "Always got a plan, and if not, I fake it anyway."

"Will you contact us?" Russ asked. "Once you get wherever you're going so we know you're safe?"

"Probably not," Mark replied. "Not right away, anyway."

"I see," Russ nodded stoically.

"It's better this way," Mark explained.

Father and son loaded the vehicle in relative silence. Three sealed crates in all were safely stowed in the back and covered with a dark blanket.

"Well, that's it then," Mark said as he closed the back hatch with a firm click.

"Take care, son," Russ offered, holding his hand out.

Mark shook his father's hand firmly. "I will."

"We'll be praying," Russ added.

"Thanks, I appreciate that." He actually meant it. "Well, I guess I better get going, then. Say bye to Deanie and Harmony for me."

"I will."

"Oh, and tell Harmony no hard feelings."

Russ raised his eyebrows.

Mark laughed. "It's complicated. She'll understand."

Next stop, the Walters' residence. Russ pulled up in front of the house. He'd called Amy on the way over, waking her. He'd offered to just say goodbye over the phone, but she insisted that he stop by instead. He just hoped her parents were still asleep.

He approached the front door and was about to knock when the door swung open. Amy beckoned him inside and shut the door quietly behind him. She was wearing a terry robe and her feet were bare.

"Hi," he greeted awkwardly.

"More like bye," Amy said, her voice already becoming

wobbly. Tears glistened in her eyes.

He pulled her into his arms and just hugged her, letting her bury her face in his jacket. "I'm coming back. I promise." He felt his own throat constricting.

She pulled back slightly. "When?"

"I don't know for sure . . ." He searched her face—that beautiful face that had captured his heart. Why hadn't he made more time for her over the past weeks? He had been so single minded in his need to finish his dissertation that he'd neglected the thing that had become most important—even more than the most intriguing archeological find of the century. "Amy, I love you," he whispered urgently. "You know that, don't you?" She nodded and their lips sought each other in a feverish embrace. He could feel her body, soft and pliable, against his own. At that moment he wished he had taken her up on her offer the night before. He needed her now. He needed to show her, in a physical way, just how much he loved her.

They heard the noise simultaneously, a quiet tinkling of dishes, and parted reluctantly. Someone was in the kitchen making coffee. Mark looked down at Amy and mouthed the words 'I love you.' She took a shuddering breath and stepped back.

"Come on," she said quietly, taking his hand. "We might as well go in since they know you're here anyway."

Both of Amy's parents were in the kitchen, still wearing robes. Holly was busying herself near the coffee maker while Brent sat at the island counter, reading. They both looked up when the younger couple entered.

"Good morning," Holly greeted. "Coffee'll be ready in a minute."

"Morning angel," Brent said to his daughter, rising to give her a peck on the cheek. He turned to Mark. "Mark. Nice to see you again." The atmosphere was artificially nonchalant, like they

275

greeted their daughter's boyfriends every morning while still wearing their bathrobes. It was decidedly awkward.

"Um, Mark's on his way out of town," Amy offered as explanation. "On archeology business."

"Oh? This about that big find you made last spring in Africa?" Brent asked.

"Partially," Mark responded.

"Very interesting, from what I recall," Brent offered. "What was it all about again? Dinosaur and human remains found together?"

"I . . . I'm not really at liberty to talk about it just yet," Mark hedged.

"Oh. I see. Well, good luck with it anyway," Brent nodded congenially.

"Thanks."

"Take anything in your coffee?" Holly asked as she busied herself pouring four mugs with the freshly made brew.

"Um, no thanks," Mark shook his head. He took the coffee mug from Holly with thanks, and raised it to his lips. There were a few minutes of silence as the group sipped their steaming drinks.

"So, I take it you and my daughter have taken up with each other," Brent said suddenly.

"Daddy!" Amy rolled her eyes.

Mark cleared his throat uncomfortably. "Yes. Yes, that's true." He paused, considering his next words. "I was planning to have a talk with you in the near future, but I was going to wait until I got back from my trip."

"Oh?" Brent asked, taking another sip and surveying the younger man over the rim of his mug.

"Um, yes. Just so you know my intentions are . . . honorable."

"I see, and what might that mean exactly?"

"Daddy! This is embarrassing," Amy repeated.

Amy's father obviously wasn't going to make this easy on him, Mark mused. "Just that, even though I'm a lot older, I'm not going to take advantage of her, so to speak."

Brent nodded. "Good, good."

"More coffee?" Holly piped up.

"I'm fine," Mark said, placing his hand over the top of his cup. "Actually, I really need to get going now though. Thanks." He rose from the stool he had occupied.

They said their goodbyes in the kitchen and Amy walked Mark to the front door once again.

"I'm really sorry about that," she whispered. "I'm so embarrassed."

"It's okay. I'll probably be the same way if I have a daughter." He stopped and looked intently at Amy. "Especially if she looks anything like you." He bent for a kiss. It was hard to keep the intensity at bay, even knowing that the parents were seated in the next room. He extracted his lips. "I've got to go."

"Will you call me?"

"I can't say when, but I'll try. Definitely." He gave her another quick kiss and turned.

She watched him stride down the sidewalk to his waiting SUV. Her heart beat with a strange mixture of elation, uncertainty, and fear. *Oh God,* she prayed. *Keep him safe.*

She turned to head up the stairs to her bedroom to get ready for the day. "Amy? Can you come here a minute?" she heard her mother call from the kitchen. With a sigh, she turned and headed back in that direction. She had been hoping for some reprieve, but apparently not today.

"Sounds like you and young Graham are pretty serious," Brent mused when Amy re-entered the kitchen.

"Um, yeah."

"This seems rather sudden," Holly commented. "I hope

you've given some thought to our conversation from before."

Amy sighed. "Yes, mom. I have."

"And?"

Amy thought for moment, considering her words. She was an adult now. It was time she started acting like one. She looked up, catching her parents' gaze squarely with her own. "Look, I really love you guys, you know? I respect your opinions, but I'm an adult now, and this is my life."

"Nobody said it wasn't," Brent countered. "We're just concerned, that's all."

"You might be getting in over your head," Holly added.

Amy laughed at that. "Yeah, well, I guess that much it true. I love him, okay? There. I said it. I love him."

"Don't be silly! You can't know that for sure after such a short time," Holly scoffed.

"No? Well, it's true. And he loves me too. He asked me to marry him!" Amy cried. There was a moment of stunned silence. "Yeah. And I said yes."

"But Amy! It's so sudden!" Holly blustered. "You've hardly even been dating!"

"Mom, I'm not a baby anymore, remember?"

"But you're so young. What about school? What about his work? Does this mean you'll be traveling? Oh dear!"

"Mother, relax!"

"And what about his commitment to Christ?" Brent asked pointedly. "Did you talk about that?"

"Of course," Amy said defensively. "He believes."

"He said so? Point blank, 'I am saved'?" Holly asked.

"Yes," Amy said. She tried hard not to show the uneasiness that had crept into her stomach.

"Are you sure about this?" Brent asked. "His intentions, I mean? Sometimes men say things—do things—in order to, well, you know, entice a woman, when they have no real intentions of following through."

"This is Mark we're talking about, remember?" Amy pointed out.

"True," Brent nodded, thinking.

Holly surveyed her daughter skeptically for a moment. "Well, you're absolutely right, of course. You're a grown woman now and we can't run your life for you. At least I know you'll be well provided for."

"You make it sound like you're trying to make the best of a bad situation," Amy observed.

"I'm sorry, dear. I like Mark. I really do. The age difference is one thing though, and then there's the fact that his conversion seems rather sudden."

"I love him, mom, and he loves me."

The pleading in her daughter's eyes silenced any other criticisms Holly may have had. "I know you do, Amy, and I'm happy for you." She went to her and embraced her.

"Come here, kid," Brent said, holding his arms out for his turn at an embrace.

"I just need your support, you know?" Amy said. "And your prayers."

"You'll have that," Brent said wryly. "No doubt about it."

Chapter Twenty-Five

Mark glanced in the rear view mirror and noted the dark green sedan. It had passed him, he was sure, about an hour ago. Probably stopped for gas or something, he mused. He shifted in his seat, trying to stretch as much as possible while still driving. It was getting dusk, now. He'd been driving pretty much non stop for the past ten hours and his body was starting to stiffen up.

Thankfully, he had made it through customs earlier that morning with very little inconvenience. Seems his documentation was enough to wave him on through, a blessing for which he was very thankful. He may even have prayed, come to think of it, in a manner of speaking. These days, crossing the border had become a regular comedy of errors. The fact that things had gone so smoothly was truly a miracle.

The landscape across the line was very similar to that of his native Manitoba—flat and dry expanses of farm land, sectioned off with fencing and dotted with small towns and farm yards. He had traveled south on Interstate 29 through the Dakotas and would have to veer west into Nebraska on a secondary highway that would connect him with the Interstate heading south through Kansas and on into Texas. Of course, that would have to be another day's adventure. He'd be lucky to make it to Kansas tonight.

He was tired already, he knew, but the need to make as much progress as possible kept him going. That, and way too much coffee. By tomorrow night, he'd be in Texas.

The green sedan was accelerating again, pulling past him on the left. Apparently, the driver didn't care much about rising gas prices. *I guess we've all got places to be,* Mark mused.

He had contacted Anthony once during the trip. Everything was a-okay and ready to go, Anthony had said. All clear with no suspicion on the part of Laura or anyone else connected with the University in New Mexico. Anthony was scheduled to meet him at the University in Texas the day after tomorrow, first thing.

That his presentation was so under publicized was somewhat irksome, to say the least. A find of this nature deserved all the hype available, but Mark realized that would have to come later. For now, he must be satisfied that the truth was going to be told.

It was dark now, the days becoming shorter now that fall was half way through her cycle. Mark turned off the interstate, heading west and then south again, through Nebraska. It still reminded him a lot of home— the rural setting, the open landscape. He was traveling straight south through the very heart of the continent. The thought struck him as awe inspiring. He must be tired.

Several hours later he pulled into an overnight rest area. Unlike the highways back home, the U.S. seemed to have outfitted their rest stops quite thoroughly—bathrooms, plenty of parking, some even had small coffee bars. He'd considered getting more coffee and just carrying on, but decided against it. He had already developed a headache and a slight feeling of nausea from too much caffeine. He'd be better off taking a break and starting fresh tomorrow. Of course, getting a room for the night was absolutely out of the question. He couldn't leave his precious cargo alone in the car unattended.

After using the restroom, he hunkered down as best he could

in the back seat of the SUV and tried for some shut eye. Fortunately, despite the inordinate amount of coffee and inadequate accommodation, exhaustion finally took over and he did, indeed, sleep.

Not enough sleep though. He groaned as he struggled to sit up several hours later. The crick in his neck would not allow further repose.

The morning was clear and he stretched expansively once out of the confines of the vehicle. He would just use the facilities and be on his way to the next town for breakfast.

He stopped in his tracks, frozen for a millisecond with sudden alarm. The green sedan. It was parked just three vehicles over from his. He took a deep breath. *Don't jump to any conclusions,* he chided himself. Lots of people traveled these highways. There was bound to be someone—probably several people—going in the same direction at the same general pace. It was just coincidence.

He took a deep breath. Despite his own assurances, he turned back to his own SUV. He could wait to relieve himself. For now, he was hitting the road.

Another hour down the road and Mark felt himself relaxing a bit. The first thing he would do once the cargo was safely unloaded was take a shower. And shave. A full day and a night in his vehicle and he was beginning to feel like he was out in the field again. Out there, they got used to roughing it and hardly even noticed the aura of body odor that must have surrounded them. Funny how that kind of thing didn't seem to matter much. But here, back in western civilization, he was very conscious of the fact.

Another hour and he was looking forward to connecting with the next southbound interstate again. You could always make good time then—those highways were meant for driving. He glanced in his rear view mirror and nearly swerved. The same green sedan was tailing him.

This had to be more than mere coincidence. Mark accelerated slightly and watched with dismay as the green car did the same. That was a definite signal. Apparently, his uninvited traveling companion was no longer trying to be subtle. Okay. What now? The possibility of losing him by taking some other route held little appeal. The last thing he wanted was to end up lost. And judging from yesterday's track record, the driver of that car seemed to know exactly which direction he was headed.

The tension grew more palpable with each passing mile. Mark glanced down at his gas gauge. At some point, he was going to have to face the music. He couldn't travel on fumes. According to the overhead signs, he was approaching the next town. Now might be his last chance.

Mark swerved off the exit ramp without slowing down or signaling. He kept both hands on the wheel and held his breath as he maneuvered the SUV around the clover leaf and onto a city street. He gunned it through the intersection just as the traffic light turned red and noted with satisfaction that the green sedan was several cars behind, stopped at the light.

Okay. Now to find some side streets and try to get lost. He needed gas, but decided it would be better to wait for a while in some back alley somewhere. He turned into one such likely hiding spot and parked beside a delivery truck. The truck shielded him from one side, but still allowed him to view the intersecting street. He waited.

Mark noticed the pounding in his head—his own heartbeat had accelerated and adrenaline was coursing through his body. If that green car had any connection to Sangeruka, he needed to warn Anthony. He needed to check on his family back home.

Mark waited for several more minutes, listening to the shallowness of his own breathing. Okay. That was probably long enough. He needed to find a gas station and get the hell out of here.

He was about to put the SUV in gear when he spotted it again—the green car passing slowly by on the street. He swore under his breath.

He took the cell phone out of his jacket pocket and punched in Anthony's number. They had been trying not to contact one another too often via that method for fear that someone would be able to track their communication. This was an emergency.

Pick up, pick up! Nothing. He wasn't about to leave a message. Well, there was nothing else to do now, but take his chances. Mark crawled out onto the street and took a right. Hopefully there would be a gas station nearby and he could be on his way. He spotted one two blocks down and drove cautiously in that direction, glancing this way and that for any sign of his 'friend'.

Once at the gas station, he went quickly inside to prepay for the gas and then began filling his tank. He watched the meter on the pump as the numbers seemed to click by interminably slow. He was just replacing the nozzle when he saw the car again.

He tried to jump into his seat as quickly as possible, but the car was already pulling into the station at break neck speed, blocking his exit. Horns honked as several other motorists made their displeasure known. Well, maybe this was as good a place as any for a confrontation. Sangeruka's thugs wouldn't try anything too drastic right here in broad daylight, would they? And in front of so many witnesses.

He waited as the driver of the car extracted himself from the driver's seat. There was only one person in the car. That was good. Maybe he could actually take him if it came to hand-to-hand combat.

The man was approaching Mark's vehicle now. Wait a minute. He looked vaguely familiar somehow. Mark held his breath as his brain struggled to compute.

"Rocco?" Mark asked uncertainly, rolling his window down slightly.

"Geez, boss. You're not the easiest guy to flag down."

"But . . . how? Why—what are you doing here?" Mark sputtered. "I thought you were dead!"

"I think we need to find a place where we can talk," Rocco suggested. "That lady don't look too happy about our reunion."

Mark took note of the frustrated face in the next car. "Right. You lead the way."

"Sure you're not going to take off on me?" Rocco asked.

Mark laughed. "Get going."

Rocco backed his vehicle out onto the street and Mark followed behind. They drove another few blocks to a small diner. Inside, a waitress seated them at a booth where Mark could keep an eye on his vehicle from the window.

"I'm telling you, you really led me on a chase," Rocco said, shaking his head.

"Me? You had me scared to death. I thought Sangeruka had sicced his thugs on me."

"I was going to wake you up last night and talk to you, back at the rest stop. But then I thought I'd take pity on you and let you sleep a bit first. When I came out of the can this morning, you were already gone."

"So? Tell me everything," Mark demanded. "Right from the moment the truck went off the road. Man, I thought you were dead. How could anyone survive a crash like that?"

"Luck?" Rocco shrugged. "Or maybe providence. I baled as soon as the truck went over the edge and somehow managed to hit some brush that cushioned my landing. The truck exploded on impact at the bottom of the ravine and I guess they figured I got toasted with it. I was pretty scratched up and sore as hell, but no broken bones. Just walked away."

"And the casket?" Mark just had to ask.

"It got hung up in some brush further down, just teetering over an embankment. It took some convincing, let me tell you, to get some locals to help me retrieve it."

"You mean it survived?" Mark asked in disbelief. Renewed hope soared in his breast. "This is fantastic! This is the best news yet! With that as evidence, no one will be able to dispute our findings."

"Hold on there," Rocco cautioned. "I said it survived, but I didn't say I have it in my possession."

"So who does?"

"Now, that is where it gets complicated," Rocco replied. "See, once we got the container safely down from the mountain, there was a lot of curiosity about what it contained. I was afraid that Sangeruka's gang would come after it if they found out it survived, so I had to lie—just a little bit—in order to keep it safe."

"What did you say?"

"I said it contained my grandmother's remains," Rocco replied sheepishly. "I told them she was a missionary in Africa and it was her greatest desire to be buried among the people she loved so well."

"And they bought it?" Mark questioned skeptically. "Surely the markings on the casket itself would bring up some suspicion."

"Only two other men saw the casket itself," Rocco explained. "It was still well sealed inside the shipping container. I told them she had been fascinated by the old legends and requested her casket be modeled after them. I don't think many people have actually seen artifacts from that far back anyway. I mean, the legends were there, but as far as actual evidence goes, nobody has really seen it with their own eyes."

"And you don't think there might be some suspicion since we were working on the site that housed the actually evidence? That somebody might put two and two together?"

"I did the best I could under the circumstances," Rocco defended.

Mark shook his head doubtfully. "I'm sure by now somebody has heard about the military take over of the site too. I can't believe it won't go unnoticed."

"Listen, these people are very superstitious, especially when it comes to the dead," Rocco explained. "Nobody will want to disturb a dead missionary. They believe strongly in ancestral spirits, and a missionary would have some special connection with God. Nobody will want to risk the Almighty's wrath by desecrating her bones."

"So it's buried somewhere?" Mark asked.

Rocco nodded. "A secret location. Only the two guys I mentioned know where."

"And they can be trusted?"

"I went over that already," Rocco sighed. "Besides, the fact that I survived a near fatal crash, along with my grandmother's remains, must mean something, right? God must really want her buried there, and who's going to risk arguing with the Almighty?"

"I don't know. I just don't feel good about this," Mark mused.

"I guess there's not much you can do about it, is there?" Rocco quipped.

"Hm. True. But it's safe for now," Mark repeated. "You're sure of that?"

"Nothing is sure these days," Rocco stated. "By now the international conspiracy might have got a hold of the fact that I survived, along with the casket."

"International conspiracy?"

"Excuse me for being paranoid," Rocco said sarcastically, "but when you've been shot at and assumed dead in order to keep a world changing find from coming to light, well . . . "

"That could just have been Sangeruka," Mark said. Somehow he didn't believe it though.

Obviously, neither did Rocco. "Believe me, I've seen enough in my time to know, beyond a shadow of a doubt, that this is much bigger than one wayward African official. I told you before. There's all kinds of evidence out there that has never been shared with the public at large, or has been twisted so much that anyone who tries to say otherwise sounds like a stark raving lunatic."

Mark nodded in agreement. "I know. I've been doing my homework and it's pretty alarming."

"Tell me about it," Rocco snorted. "I have the scars to prove it."

"Right, but we need real proof. Proof that would stand up to the kind of scientific scrutiny that we're sure to face."

"I'm glad you said 'we'." Rocco replied. "Because you just might be the man to shake up the old boys' club once and for all."

"I'm going to try," Mark acknowledged, "I just hope someone is listening. Now, though, if we can actually get access to the casket—get it brought somewhere secure where proper analysis can be done—well, we just might have a chance at blowing this whole thing wide open."

"You better go ahead with your plans as they are," Rocco advised. "I wouldn't wait any longer. Doctors Sawchuk and Bergman are just chomping at the bit to release their own version of events."

"How do you know that?" Mark asked, frowning. "And how do you know about my plans?"

"I've still got contacts," Rocco said secretively. "I make it my job to know these things."

"Which is why you were able to tail me," Mark observed sardonically. He wondered how many other people knew about his plans or his whereabouts.

289

"Don't sweat it," Rocco shrugged. "I have good intelligence that says you're still safe."

"Okay, now you're really starting to make me worried," Mark laughed nervously. "Good intelligence? You make it sound like you work for the FBI or something."

Rocco considered his next words carefully. "I guess I can trust you with this much. There really is an international conspiracy out there—men and women who control the scientific community like so many puppets, releasing what ever information they want to release; feeding them data and facts that support their own agenda. Most scientists are like you—completely unaware that they're being manipulated—played. There are a few of us, guys like me who've been in the field and know better, who have gotten together and are trying to combat this thing."

"How come this is the first I've heard of it?" Mark asked.

"See, it's like this. We have to be really careful what we say and who we say it to. Otherwise, we look like a bunch of crack pots."

"I've been accused of that, myself," Mark nodded. He looked squarely at his friend. "It's still small comfort, though, you know. Knowing that someone has been tracking my movements."

"Consider it free protection," Rocco stated.

"You really think I need it?" Mark asked.

Rocco shrugged. "Who knows?"

"Well, you certainly had me thinking along those lines," Mark laughed. "Don't ever scare me like that again."

"I just hope you're ready once you actually drop the bomb."

Mark sobered instantly. "So you think there might be danger? Even after the fact?"

"I'd just watch my back."

"Makes me wonder if it's really worth it," Mark mused.

"Of course it is," Rocco stated firmly. "That's the whole point.

If someone is willing to go to those lengths—even try to kill someone—well, you know it must be worth it."

"Right. I was just joking, anyway. I plan on going ahead. You know that. I've come too far to back down now."

"Just keep that in mind," Rocco nodded. "We're counting on you."

"So, what's this about Laura and John?" Mark asked curiously. "You said you've got some info on their operation too?"

Rocco laughed humorlessly. "Yeah. Now, those two are puppets if ever there were any. Totally bought into the conspiracy's game, if you know what I mean."

"Well, I suppose that's some comfort," Mark mused. "At least they're not the real bad guys."

"Don't fool yourself," Rocco warned. "Neither one of them are exactly innocent. Did you know that John was working to undermine you with the university brass right from the beginning?"

"I can't believe that," Mark denied with a dismissive laugh.

"No?"

"We've been friends for years," Mark stated firmly.

"Suit yourself," Rocco shrugged. "And your girlfriend. She was the one sabotaging the site all along."

"You have proof?" Mark asked.

Rocco gave him a withering look. "Remember the cave in? The data collection problems? Delays in sending and receiving important documentation . . . even all the mix-ups with the government officials. All her."

"Says?" Mark probed. "Oh, right. Your intelligence network. Look, I know there were problems, but I can't believe it was all on purpose."

"That's your problem," Rocco noted. "Always too trusting. I suppose it's hard not to when you were into her pants."

"Hey! Now that was crude," Mark defended. "I always tried to remain professional, you know that. Besides, I had my doubts a time or two, I must admit. But I just can't believe it was so wide spread and so . . . insidious. That's all."

"Remember that missing wing bone?" Rocco asked. Mark nodded. "Just ask her about that yourself, sometime. See what she says."

"I'm not planning on that opportunity," Mark responded dryly.

Rocco shrugged. "Just don't say I didn't warn you. Sometimes these skirts can really pull the wool over our eyes."

"Talking from experience again," Mark asked, trying to lighten the almost combative attitude that Rocco had adopted.

"You know it," Rocco winked.

"Anyway, I really think we need to carry on," Mark said, looking at his watch. "There's still a long way to go tonight."

"Now that I finally caught up to you, I'm veering off in another direction for a day," Rocco said. "Say 'hi' to Anthony when you see him."

"You know about Anthony?" Mark asked. Of course he knew about Anthony. The guy seemed to know about everything.

Rocco just nodded. He stood up and threw sufficient money on the table to cover both their drinks and the tip. "Drive safe, and don't make any more stops off the main highway."

"Why not?"

"You just need to get your butt safely to Texas in one piece," Rocco grinned.

Mark nodded. That was one piece of advice he was definitely going to listen to.

Chapter Twenty-Six

Mark arrived at the university campus in Texas well past 2:00 a.m. He'd already stopped for a stretch not far back, so his plan was to just stay put in his vehicle until morning and try to get some shut eye. It wasn't going to be easy. His mind was racing—and not just on account of tomorrow's prospects. How could he have misread Laura and John so badly? The sense of betrayal cut deep. Very deep.

Somehow, he must have dozed off. He woke with a start to somebody rapping on his window. Light was streaming in and he could feel the warmth of the Texas sun. He squinted, shielding his eyes for a moment as they adjusted themselves to the onslaught.

"Hey! Wake up in there!" It was Anthony. "What you gonna do? Sleep the day away?"

Mark shifted himself into a full sitting position and rolled down the window. "I see you made it too," he said amid a huge yawn.

"I rolled in last night about seven o'clock," Anthony nodded. "What time did you get here?"

"About two," Mark replied.

"So you gonna sit in your car all day or what?" Anthony asked with a grin. "Come on inside. You look like you could use a coffee."

Mark glanced down at his watch. 8:00 a.m. local time. He really had slept. "I'm not going anywhere until this thing is safely unloaded," he stated.

"Sure. Let's go meet the team, and then they can help us unload," Anthony suggested.

"No, I mean I'm not leaving the vehicle unattended," Mark clarified.

Anthony stopped for a moment, surveying his friend. "Okay," he shrugged. "How about if I go find somebody to show us where to unload and then we can get right on that."

"That would be good."

"You seem a bit . . . tense," Anthony observed. "Paranoid, even."

"You wouldn't believe who I met up with on the way," Mark replied.

"Oh? Who?" Anthony asked, eyebrows raised.

"Rocco." By the look on Anthony's face, he was as shocked by the news that Rocco was still alive as Mark had been. "So I take it he hasn't contacted you?"

Anthony shook his head. "You sure?" he asked doubtfully. "I mean, by all accounts, there's no way he could have survived . . . "

"Believe me," Mark stated in no uncertain terms. "I'll tell you all about it later. For now, we really need to get these specimens safely unloaded."

They did just that. Mark was directed to an underground parking area where brief introductions had taken place. Doctor Tim Hazzard and his assistant George Krasinsky were very excited about the prospects of what this find could do for the credibility of their institution. Mark felt a small pang of anxiety at that. Why did everything have to boil down to some kind of political gains?

They unloaded the precious cargo and took it up to the lab.

294

"We are very honored to have you present your findings at our institution," Dr. Hazzard was saying. He was a man who looked to be in his early fifties, with jet black hair that was swept back in a definite retro style. He also looked to be in good physical condition. His colleague was younger, but with much less hair, and he sported large glasses that definitely gave him the air of 'geek'. "This could be the biggest break through for creation theory yet. It's wonderful to have someone with your credentials on our side."

"Excuse me?" Mark asked, blinking back to reality. He had been staring at Dr. Hazzard's mop of hair. "Creation theory?"

"Of course," Dr. Hazzard responded. "We are a Christian university. We teach some very innovative interpretations of the creation model though, I must say. We've got a very well trained staff with wonderful credentials." He stopped, looking puzzled. "Is there a problem?"

"I . . . um, no," Mark said, shaking his head.

"I told you it was a Christian institution," Anthony reminded quietly. "He's probably just a little foggy after such a long drive," he offered to the two other men.

"I hope there isn't a problem," Dr. Hazzard went on. "We pride ourselves on doing everything above board and we certainly wouldn't want you to feel like you've been duped somehow."

"I was just hoping to present the facts in a non partisan way," Mark explained.

Dr. Hazzard nodded his head in understanding. "It's exactly what we do here. Most theory that backs a different timeline for the universe or a different sequence of events than what we've all been told, bases its model on religious creationism. Even though we believe that here, we do try to present all our scientific arguments in just that way—scientific. We don't want to scare people off any more than you do. Of course, we do have specific classes that teach our findings in conjunction with our religious

295

beliefs. But you needn't worry about that. You can be as non partisan as you want." He stopped for a moment and surveyed Mark closely, the friendly smile never leaving his face. "I was simply under the impression from talking to your friend, here, that you were a believer also. I didn't mean any offense."

"None taken," Mark replied.

"Well, let's get at it, shall we?" Dr. Hazzard suggested brightly. "How about a tour, Dr. Graham? Mr. Krasinsky would be happy to oblige, I'm sure."

"That would be fine," Mark nodded. He stopped and added hesitantly. "I was wondering if I might go somewhere to clean up first though? I've just spent two full days and nights in my car and . . ."

"Of course," Dr. Hazzard blustered. "How negligent of me. We have a room booked for you at the Ramada. Why don't you go and clean up, have some breakfast or whatever, and we can get started after lunch. Does that sound okay?"

"I'll probably be ready long before that," Mark laughed. "I'm kind of anxious to get started myself."

"Excellent," Dr. Hazzard stated. "Don't rush yourself. Just take whatever time you need."

Mark arrived back at the university two hours later. He and Anthony had met for some breakfast in the hotel restaurant after he's showered and changed. During that time he'd been able to fill Anthony in on his little encounter with Rocco.

"I still can't believe it," Anthony was saying as they emerged from the elevator next to the lab. "Not only that Rocco is alive, but all that other stuff about a conspiracy. I mean, sure, there are lots of people out there with an agenda, but do you really think it's that well backed, or that deeply entrenched?"

Mark shrugged. "I don't know what to think any more. Maybe it would be interesting to get Dr. Hazzard's take on it."

"You think that's safe?" Anthony asked with a grin. "He might be in on it."

George Krasinsky was waiting for them in the lab. "Dr. Hazzard had a few other things to attend to this morning. I can take you on that tour now, if you like."

Mark hesitated, anxious to get started putting his presentation together.

"Come on," Anthony said persuasively. "It'll be fun. And informative," he said brightly looking in George's direction. "Right?"

George nodded. "Uh . . . right."

As it turned out it was both. Mark was glad he'd agreed. Despite George's rather bland delivery, he was fascinated by what Dr. Hazzard had earlier referred to as 'very innovative interpretations of the creation model'. There was a whole gallery set up for that purpose. Some of the theories, backed up with corresponding evidence, he had already come across in his own research on the subject. Some of the others were new.

He stopped in front of one particular display. "Explain what's going on here," he said to George, pointing. Inside the glass cabinet was a large replica of the earth with several cut away sections. The Earth's atmosphere was shown as a clear canopy that encased the globe. The label said "Creation in Symphony."

"Ah," George nodded. "The work of a fellow Texan, Dr. Carl Baugh. Very convincing research into pre-flood atmospheric conditions."

"Another young earth model," Mark offered.

"Yes, as most creationist models are," George agreed. "This one speculates that the earth was encased in crystalline hydrogen."

"Wait a minute," Mark interrupted. "Crystalline hydrogen? How is that possible?"

"Quite simple, actually," George replied. "Several Soviet

scientists have been able to confirm the possibilities through quantum algebra. The superconductivity of such a substance would also relate to its suspension." He gestured to the model as he continued to explain. "The 'rakea' effect would have intensified colors as well as magnified objects beyond. It would mean that everything outside the atmosphere; stars and so forth, would have been much bigger and brighter to the naked eye. Also, the fiber optic transfer of light and energy would conduct sound waves much like a short wave radio signal. So, solar sounds would have been broadcast during the morning hours—thus the name 'Creation in Symphony'. It's quite fascinating since the Bible does record such examples in Genesis. The ancients seemed to have been very well versed in astronomy for not having the benefit of modern technological instruments."

"Interesting," Anthony mused.

"It also accounts for the greenhouse conditions that would have been necessary to grow the large specimens that are evident in the fossil record, as well as explain the presence of tropical plants near the poles, etc."

"I suppose so," Mark nodded. "I have done a bit of reading on that myself. It's hard to ignore some of the discrepancies in present evolutionary theory."

"That it is," George agreed. "Of course, once the canopy began to collapse, a whole series of cataclysmic events would have followed. The hydrogen would have liquefied, the great fountains of the deep would have opened as earth quakes racked the earth and what we know as Noah's flood occurred."

"My favorite story," Anthony nodded. "Did you know that almost every society has its own version of a worldwide flood?"

"Yes, I knew that," George said matter of factly. He turned away. "Come. There's plenty more to see."

Mark and Anthony looked at one another and grinned. "Lead

the way," Anthony quipped.

What George lacked in delivery, he made up for in knowledge. "Here is some fascinating research done by a very respected scholar, Dr. Robert Gentry. He found that halos in granite, found in the black flakes called 'mica', show evidence of radioactive material that could only have been recorded within minutes of formation—not the millions of years suggested by other scientists. Once again, evidence for a young earth."

Mark nodded. "I have read enough recently that it's hard to dispute, although I must admit, I'm still a bit uncomfortable with the idea."

"Why dispute something when there is so much evidence in its favor?" George asked candidly. "Here's more proof. The geomagnetic field is decaying exponentially, making it impossible for life to exist on the planet past a much younger age. The magnetic field would simply have been too strong."

"I know," Mark responded. "I guess it's just hard to totally throw everything out the window that I've come to hold true for so long."

"Once presented with the truth, it is hard to go back to believing a lie," George responded.

"Now, that is true," Anthony offered.

"Over and over again, the fossil record shows plants that extend through several layers," George continued. "Look at this. A whale was even found vertically on its tale."

Anthony moved in for a closer look at the display. "Would you look at that? Now if that isn't something else. Poor Moby Dick would've had a hard time hanging out in that position for a few million years."

"Hey, guys," Mark interrupted. "I think I really need to get back to my own work now." He turned to George. "Thanks for the tour. It was fascinating."

299

"There is a lot more to see. We've only just started on this section. There is still radiometric techniques, stellar-light velocity and time travel, Pangea . . . "

"Thanks, but I think it'll have to wait until later," Mark begged off. "You could continue the tour with Anthony, here, if you like. Then he could fill me in on the highlights later."

"Can we get to the section dealing with mythological creatures?" Anthony asked.

George looked confused for a moment. "Mythological creatures?"

"Dragons and so forth?" Anthony clarified. "I know there must be some scientific as well as Biblical explanation for that. Almost every culture also has dragon like mythology."

The two men had already wandered off, George seemingly more than happy to satisfy Anthony's curiosity. Mark wasn't sure why he'd felt so suddenly uncomfortable. He had been reading and researching many of the same things himself and had come to basically the same conclusions: that the earth was a much younger place than most people would like to admit and that there were serious flaws in the present model of how the universe came to be. But there was something different here. Something else that had him feeling antsy, somehow. Probably just tired, he reasoned.

It all made such sense, even though it sounded far fetched. Well, far fetched as far as most of his former colleagues would see it, but it was making more and more sense to him with every new piece of evidence he was presented with. Why the hesitation to just give in and 'believe' as his parents did? He couldn't quite pinpoint the answer to that question. All he knew was, there was still something holding him back.

Chapter Twenty-Seven

It had been a long but satisfying day. Mark had met with Dr. Hazzard once more to go over the logistics of his presentation, and was able to get everything in order for the next day's event. Then he and Anthony had spent some time together, going over any last minute details. As far as he could tell, everything was on track and running smoothly. It almost seemed silly that he had been worried about anything bad happening. The university staff was very accommodating and he was as ready as he'd ever be. If only he could shake the warning sound of Rocco's voice, everything else would be fine.

He unlocked the door to his hotel room and stepped inside. He switched on the light by the door, untying his tie at the same time.

"Finally. I was beginning to think I had the wrong room."

Mark started. "Laura?"

She smiled, nodding pleasantly as if it were perfectly natural for her to be waiting alone in his darkened room. "You're looking good. I guess a regular shave and a shower can do wonders."

"How did you get in here?" he demanded.

"It really wasn't all that difficult," she shrugged, not moving from her comfortable position in the one armchair. "They should really think about upping their security. I would mention it to the manager if I were you."

"I will, don't worry," Mark quipped. "Now, may I ask, what in the hell are you doing here?"

"Oh, come off it," Laura scoffed. "You didn't think you could keep your little bomb a secret, now did you?"

"Meaning?"

"Don't play dumb. I know all about the presentation you're giving tomorrow, Mark."

"And? What are you planning to do about it?" Mark asked.

"I haven't decided yet," Laura replied, cocking her head to one side. "Nobody else from my team knows. Yet. I guess it all depends on you."

Mark sighed heavily. "Okay. Interpret that, please. I've had a pretty exhausting day and I'm not really in the mood for word games. Just what are you doing here and what do you want?"

"I think I should be asking you that question." She rose and moved toward him as she spoke. "Obviously this whole thing is a ploy to ruffle some feathers back in New Mexico. Honestly, I thought you were above that kind of petty need for revenge. You must know that nobody within the scientific community is going to take you seriously. I mean, an obscure university with a misfit bunch of pseudo scholars for backing, artifacts that are questionable in origin at best, and a definite falling out from the institution that commissioned you in the first place."

"The truth needs to be told," Mark said quietly.

"Right. I forgot how altruistic you'd become." She sighed. "I miss the old Mark. The sensible scientist." She looked at him coyly. "Not to mention one terrific lover."

He felt his insides tighten. Was she trying to come on to him? After all this time and all that had transpired? "I'm going to ignore that last comment," he stated carefully. "Just know this. I will present my findings."

"I can't persuade you?" She put her hand on his arm and stepped closer.

"Um, I thought I made it clear that I wasn't interested. In that way." He took a step away, further into the room.

"Really? I'm not convinced." She followed him, coming up behind him and kneading his shoulders.

Mark shrugged her off. "Stop."

"Why? You're so tense . . ."

"I said stop," he grated, "before I call security."

She dropped her hands. "Look, I'm not that good at playing games either. Forget the findings for a minute. I'm here because I still care, Mark. Despite everything, the fact that you abandoned us —"

"I abandoned you?!" Mark spat, swinging around.

"Yes! Abandoned everything we'd been working on for—for some religiously motivated fantasy."

"Okay, just stop right there," Mark snapped.

"Don't you see? I'm here because I still care, Mark. Plain and simple. I can't stand by and watch you throw your entire career away. Come back to New Mexico with me. We can make a new start there. Together."

"I don't think you get it," Mark shook his head. "There is no chance of 'together' for us. Despite the fact that we're operating from totally different frames of reference, I'm not interested, Laura. I'm seeing someone else."

Laura blinked. "Oh." She laughed self depreciatingly. "I guess I should be more careful about checking my sources."

"Who've you been talking to?"

"Never mind," Laura shook her head. "I just had a tip that maybe you were still, you know—free. In any case, I need to make you understand the importance of canceling. Don't go through with this. Please."

303

"I already told you, I have to."

"Mark, if I can't persuade you any other way, think about your own safety and the safety of your loved ones. Including that someone you're seeing now."

"Whoa. Now you've got my attention. Just what are you getting at?"

"My 'sources', so to speak," Laura laughed nervously. "I have it on, well, reasonably good authority that Sangeruka is still out there. If you do this you could be putting all of us in danger."

"He wouldn't do anything after the fact. Once the information is out there, what would be the point? And as far as your sources go, why should I trust you? I've got some sources of my own."

"I have absolutely nothing to hide," Laura scoffed.

"No? What do you have to say about that wing bone? The very first one found that went missing while I was away?"

"I . . ." Laura fumbled for words, clearly not expecting the question. "I'm not sure. I forget. Which one was that?"

"You're lying," Mark stated calmly. "You claimed that you knew nothing about its disappearance. That's not true, is it?"

"I—I did send it away without waiting for your go ahead," she finally admitted. "But only because I knew it was important and couldn't wait."

"Then why did you lie about it?"

"I was scared when I saw how angry you were. I . . . things hadn't been going exactly as I'd hoped between us. I was afraid you would just call it quits."

"And how did you suppose I would react when I did find out?"

"I don't know. I guess I wasn't thinking straight," Laura conceded, shaking her head. "Maybe I was afraid of what it actually might be, and I was trying to shelter you. All of us. Look, I think I've made enough of a fool of myself, already, don't you?"

"That's no excuse," Mark grated. "I trusted you."

"I know you did," Laura nodded. "And now, in retrospect, I can see that not telling you was a big mistake. But that was it, Mark, I swear. None of the other stuff that happened on sight was me."

"How can I believe that?" Mark asked.

"I don't know. I guess I don't expect you to. I just wish I could make you see. Everything I did—back in Africa and afterwards, was because I care. I love you, Mark. I know I'm a fool to be telling you that, especially now after everything that's happened. But it's true. I love you and there's nothing that can ever change that."

Mark felt his insides tighten, but it wasn't with desire. It was pity that he felt for Laura. She was a pathetic creature and he wished he could release her from the hold that she claimed he still had of her heart. "I think you better leave," he said quietly.

"Mark—"

"I mean it. Leave now," he repeated firmly.

* * *

Mark woke with a start. It was pitch black in his room and his eyes were slow at adjusting to any light that may have been creeping in below the door or beneath the drapes. He had been started out of his sleep by what he thought was a noise. But now, listening intently, there was nothing. Probably just edgy after what Laura had said earlier. He highly doubted that Sangeruka or any other would be thugs were a threat.

He settled back into the comfort of the large bed. Just as he was drifting off again, the telephone rang shrilly.

"Hello," he said into the receiver. "Hello?" he tried again when there was no immediate response. He was about to hang up when he heard breathing on the other end of the line.

"Hello? Who's there?" he demanded.

"Your girlfriend has a nice—" followed by some unmentionably crude remarks concerning the female anatomy.

"Who am I talking to?" Mark cut in, enraged. "Coward! If you so much as dare—"

"I'm just watching—for now."

Click.

Amy. He had to call to make sure she was alright. He dialed the number and waited impatiently as it rang several times. He swore under his breath. Maybe she had her cell phone turned off. It was late there as well. He'd try again first thing tomorrow.

Now what was he supposed to do? Going back to sleep was impossible. Who was behind such a threat? Sangeruka? Laura? He hated to think that she would stoop that low, but he wouldn't be surprised by anything anymore.

Maybe he should phone his father. He would at least be able to look out for Amy.

He dialed the number. This time, someone picked up. "Dad? Mark here."

"Mark?" There was a slight pause, as if his father was still half asleep. "You're okay? What's going on?"

"I know it's late—or early, whichever the case may be, but I need you to check on Amy for me."

"Now?"

"Um, look. Someone just called here. They made some crude comments about her. It's probably just hot air, but I need you to make sure she's alright. I can give you her cell number and you already have her parents' number at the house."

"Oh. So what do you want me to do? Go over to the Walters' and wake the entire household?"

Mark considered this. "Uh, well, what do you suggest?"

"I can drive by if you like, see if there are any lights on. But I'm not sure about waking them in the middle of the night. If

306

anything has happened to her, we would've heard."

"Right. I know." Mark sighed heavily, running his free hand through his already disheveled hair. "Probably overreacting, right?"

"I'd say."

"I'll call again tomorrow," Mark said.

"I take it you made it safely then. To where ever it was you were going."

"Yeah. I'll be able to tell you more about it after tomorrow. Just make sure Amy is safe. And the rest of you."

Mark hung up the phone. His worst nightmares were coming true. It was going to be one long wait for morning.

Chapter Twenty-Eight

Mark squinted as he stepped out of the hotel foyer and into the light. He had a nagging headache already—not the best start for the day of his big reveal. He had called Amy the earliest he dared and had been relieved that she sounded normal. There was no mention of anything untoward, and when he cautioned, casually of course, that she be careful and not go out anywhere unaccompanied, she seemed miffed. She took it to mean he was treating her like a child again, and it had ended up in what could technically be called their first real fight. He didn't want to tell her the truth—that he had received threatening phone calls concerning her, and so he had to leave it at that. Then he'd called his father, and had to endure a brief discourse on the wisdom of putting others in jeopardy. It all added up to a wonderful beginning.

He reached the spot where he had parked his SUV and stopped. It wasn't there. Maybe he'd parked elsewhere. He looked around the parking lot. He felt a sinking feeling in the pit of his stomach. Stolen? Surely not today of all days. That would be just his luck, on top of everything else.

He reached for his cell phone, ready to punch in Anthony's number and tell him the 'good' news. Then he'd have to go inside and report it to the hotel staff and the police.

He stopped abruptly on his way back toward the lobby. There was a vehicle just peeking its nose out around the back corner of the building. It looked to be the same color as his.

He pocketed the cell phone and strode in that direction. *What in the world is going on here, he wondered.* His pace slowed as the entire vehicle came into view.

"What the—?"

Someone had taken what looked to be a baseball bat to the body of the car. Huge dents to the roof and side panels, a crumpled grill, and slashed tires greeted his eyes like yawning wounds. Anger, mixed with a touch of fear, welled up inside. He wondered if the motor still ran.

He approached the vehicle, about to pop the hood, when suddenly he was jumped from behind.

What happened next was a blur of blows. He was punched, kicked, and kneed by some unknown assailant with vice like arms and quick movements. He never got a good look at him, although he did note the ski mask over the face and the grunts of breath being expelled. By the time he came to on the pavement, lying next to his equally battered SUV, the perpetrator was long gone.

With a groan, Mark pulled himself into an upright position. No doubt about it now. This was no random act of violence. Somebody was out to play hard ball.

* * *

"You're late." Anthony stopped in his tracks. "Oh my God, what happened to you?"

"I'm thinking of canceling."

"What?! You can't do that. After all we've been through."

"Look at me," Mark said ruefully, gesturing to his blackened eye. "It was no phantom that did this."

"What happened?" Anthony asked.

"I was jumped coming out of my building this morning. I think I got one good shot in before I got the shit totally kicked out of me," Mark mused. "Somebody took a baseball bat to my car besides. So . . . let's see. By the time I called the cops and then went down to the hospital, well . . . I'd say I did pretty well to show up at all."

"But you did," Rocco nodded with satisfaction. He slapped Mark on the back, causing the younger man to wince. "Oh, sorry, amigo."

"Rocco?" Mark asked. "Who let this guy in?" he joked, looking around.

"He just showed up off the street," Anthony grinned. "Not long before you arrived, in fact."

"I knew you wouldn't let them stop you," Rocco said.

"Who?" Anthony asked.

"The international conspiracy," Mark supplied glibly. "I'm not sure it's worth it."

"You can't let them win," Rocco stated. "Not when we're this close."

"This isn't it," Mark said, gesturing at his bruised face. "Last night I received some threatening phone calls."

"What kind of threats?" Anthony asked.

"Against my girlfriend back home."

"You've taken up with somebody special?" Rocco asked curiously.

Mark just nodded. "My dad's looking out for her. In the mean time, I'm just not sure it's really worth it. I don't care so much about my own safety, but if anything ever happened to her . . ."

"This just sucks," Anthony spouted.

"Don't you get it, man?" Rocco asked. "This is exactly why you need to get that information out there, and fast. If it means that

311

much to the international conspiracy, then it must be worth sharing. You're the man of the hour. It's up to you to blow the lid on this thing once and for all."

Mark let out a deep sigh. "Right."

* * *

Mark stepped out of the lecture hall where the presentation had been scheduled for seven o'clock that evening. It was six thirty-eight. He had just needed one last sweep of the place to make sure everything was in order. He felt nervous, but ready. There was little more that could be done now, except hope for the best. That and pray for the safety of his loved ones.

He rounded a corner and noticed Anthony and Rocco engaged in what appeared to be some kind of heated debate. As he approached, he could definitely detect the sound of anger in their whispers.

"Hey, you two. Everything alright?"

"Um, absolutely," Anthony replied quickly. "Just another one of our debates. You know how it is."

Mark nodded. He did know all about it, especially with these two. "Rocco?"

Rocco grunted something unintelligible and turned without excusing himself. Mark and Anthony watched him stalk away.

"He's frowning so hard his eyebrows almost touched his mustache," Mark joked. "What did you do to ruffle his feathers now?"

"Nothing important," Anthony waved dismissively. "You know how he is. Sometimes, I tend to agree with Laura on the subject. The guy is definitely not stable." Anthony sighed and then his countenance brightened. "So? You all ready?"

"Ready as I'll ever be," Mark replied.

Anthony nodded. "Good, good. I hate to admit this, but as much as I've been having a good time, with all the subterfuge and all that, I'll be glad when it's all over."

"Amen to that," Mark agreed.

"Shall we?" Anthony asked, gesturing toward the lecture hall doors.

"After you," Mark said.

* * *

"And now, without further adieu, may I present to you, Dr. Mark Graham." Dr. Hazzard stepped back from the podium to resounding applause. Even though the event had been practically kept under wraps, there was still a good crowd. News traveled fast, apparently. Mark was seated in the front row and stood slowly. It was now or never. As he approached the podium, he scanned the crowd. He wasn't sure what he was looking for. Potential assassins, perhaps? He put that thought well away. Besides Anthony and the faculty members he had met, there was no one else familiar. Just do it, come what may.

"Good evening, ladies and gentlemen, esteemed colleagues, and fellow scientists. I hope you're ready to be amazed, for that is what I was, and still am, after discovering what I am about to share with you tonight. For some of you, it may seem like the stuff of legends; it may rock some firmly entrenched ideas about the history of our planet, as it did for me. For others it will solidify what you already believe to be true. In either case, let me assure you of the most painstaking and meticulous methodology possible. Let me take you now on a journey, to a far away place in a far away time . . ."

More applause. Congratulations, handshakes, questions, schmoozing. It was all a blur as Mark was circulated through the room. There was no doubt that the presentation was well received, but then again, this was a Christian institution. Only time would tell how the rest of the scientific community responded.

"Excellent job, partner," Anthony enthused, slapping Mark on the back. Mark winced, still feeling the bruises from earlier that morning. "Oh, sorry. I forgot already."

"I haven't, believe me," Mark said with a grin.

"So? When do you think we'll hear from the opposition?"

"You tell me," Mark quipped. "You're the one who's been hanging around with them all these months." He hesitated. "Did I tell you Laura was in my room last night when I let myself in?"

"No way," Anthony breathed. He seemed genuinely shocked. "For serious?"

Mark looked at Anthony closely. "You mean you really didn't know?" He wasn't sure whom he could trust anymore. He would like to think that Anthony was trustworthy, but he had been fooled more than once in the recent past.

"What is that supposed to mean?" Anthony asked, clearly offended. "You think I tipped her off or something?"

Mark just shook his head dismissively. "Sorry. I guess I'm still smarting over Laura and John. Especially John."

"Okay. Apology accepted," Anthony shrugged. "If that can actually be classed as an apology. So why didn't you tell me earlier that you'd seen her?"

"I was otherwise occupied, remember?" Mark replied, gesturing at the bruise on his cheek.

"Good thing field archeologists of your caliber are supposed to look all rugged," Anthony mused, peering more closely at the damage. "So, I'd say that if Laura already had the tip off, she'll be publishing her rebuttal as we speak. Funny she wasn't here herself."

Mark nodded. "My thought exactly, but I didn't see her

anywhere in the crowd. Did you?"

"I already said I didn't," Anthony replied sardonically. "But if Rocco is right, there will be plenty of other spies just waiting to fill them in."

Mark nodded. "Speaking of Rocco, I didn't see him either. I fully expected him here, you know?"

"Who knows with that guy," Anthony shrugged.

Mark frowned. "What were you two fighting about earlier anyway?"

"I think I offended him when I questioned his secret intelligence sources a little too closely. I mean, I agree that there is definitely something going on that is not above board, but he makes it sound like some kind of 'mission impossible' operation."

"Whoever attacked me and wrecked my car was real enough."

"True."

"Which reminds me, I need to make a phone call."

"Want me to come along?" Anthony asked. "You might need a body guard."

"No, that's okay," Mark laughed. "I'll just find a quiet corner. I won't go too far." He noticed another enthusiastic audience member approaching with more questions. "Take these ones for me, will you?"

"Gotcha," Anthony saluted. "I'll add question deferrer to my list of credentials."

Mark slipped from the room and found an empty corner in a nearby hallway to make his call.

"Amy!" His heart flooded with relief when she answered.

"Mark?"

"I can't tell you how good it is to hear your voice," Mark said into the phone. "You're . . . okay? Everything is okay?"

"Um . . . yeah."

"I really miss you." He waited but she didn't respond. "About this morning . . . I'm sorry it seemed like I was being over protective. It's just, well . . . when I get home I can explain everything."

"I should hope so."

Mark frowned. There was a definite edge of annoyance to her voice. Apparently she was still angry. "Listen, Amy. I know you don't want to hear it, but just be careful, okay?"

"Just what is going on, Mark?" she asked point blank.

"I gave a presentation today on my findings in Africa," he tried to sound enthusiastic. "It went well, I think."

"Oh right. You and your archeologist friends."

"Um, right . . . It is what I do for a living." There was silence on the other end for a moment. Mark thought he heard the distinct sound of a sob. "Amy? What's happened? Are you alright?" he asked anxiously.

"Why can't you just come right out and say it?" Amy cried. "I thought you had at least that much integrity."

"Amy? What are you talking about? If it's the fact that I haven't told you much about my trip, I promise I'll fill you in when it's safe to do so."

"I'll just bet!"

"Pardon me?"

"When were you going to tell me about her, Mark?" Amy asked, her voice full of despair. "Or were you planning on keeping both of us? A woman in each country, so you'd never have to sleep alone!"

"Whoa! Hold on a minute! Now you're making no sense at all," Mark sputtered. "Have you been talking to Harmony again? I swear when I see her next—"

"Don't lie to me, Mark. You're better than that. Just tell me, honestly. Have you seen Laura since you've been in Texas?"

"Well, yes, but—" Renewed crying on the other end drowned

out whatever else he might have said. "Amy, it's not like that. We're former colleagues. Of course we're bound to meet up with one other on occasion."

"But you invited her to your room!" Amy cried. "And to think I almost slept with you!"

"Amy! That's not true. Who told you that? It's ridiculous! It's —"

"Was she or was she not in your room with you—alone?" Amy asked.

"Okay, now I'm getting angry," Mark said. "Just who have you been talking to?"

"Answer the question."

"Yes, but—"

"I never want to see you again, Mark," she stated with grim finality.

"Amy, you don't know what you're saying," Mark tried desperately. "Did Laura tell you this? Is that it?" He let out a frustrated growl. "I can't believe she would stoop that low. I told her flat out that I was not interested in her anymore and that I was seeing someone else now. You."

"Goodbye Mark," Amy whispered.

"Amy, wait," Mark pleaded. "Please, just let me explain."

Click. She'd hung up on him.

All the elation he'd felt after his presentation was now as flat as a deflated balloon. It meant very little when his heart was breaking.

The urge to redial was strong. If he could just get her to listen to reason. Her phone rang until the voicemail picked up. He listened intently to the sweet sound of her voice telling him to leave a message. What could he say? He snapped his phone together and used his shoulder to push off the wall where he had been leaning. Just as he turned, he saw Dr. Hazzard approaching, and nodded.

"Well done!" Dr. Hazzard enthused. "Your colleague said you had just slipped out to make a call. Everything all right?"

"Um . . . a family emergency," Mark supplied.

"Oh? Not too grave, I hope?" Dr. Hazzard asked with concern.

"Well . . . no. It'll keep till tomorrow," Mark hedged.

"Good, good. So many people have so many questions. Your findings are absolutely ground breaking. Shall we go back inside?"

"Yes, of course," Mark replied woodenly.

"About that incandescent lighting in the antechamber . . . "

Mark followed the professor back into the room, nodding like an automaton to the well wishers that he passed, as he tried to concentrate on what the doctor was saying.

"Dr. Graham?"

"Yes?' Mark snapped himself back to attention.

"I thought I had lost you there for a moment," Dr. Hazzard laughed good naturedly.

"Oh, sorry," Mark apologized.

"Thinking of that family emergency?" Dr. Hazzard asked sympathetically.

"Uh, yes," Mark agreed with a sheepish grin. "And the irony of this whole evening."

"Irony? What do you mean?"

"Well, it does seem a tad ironic that a fence sitter like me should be the current hero at a Christian university."

"Ah," Dr. Hazzard nodded knowingly. "Of course, the difficulty with the creation model for most people is not the logic behind it, or the evidence, for that matter. Quite simply, if one believes in the creation model, then one must also believe in a Creator. And there, as they say, is the rub." Dr. Hazzard's eye's twinkled.

"Indeed," Mark agreed flatly.

318

"No pressure," Dr. Hazzard said kindly. "Just think on it later after you've enjoyed your accolades."

Mark nodded. "Um, do you mind if I excuse myself for just a minute? I find I'm in need of some fresh air."

"No problem," the doctor said. "This party isn't going anywhere."

Mark pushed his way through the crowd, avoiding eye contact that might lead to more questions. Once outside the building, he let out a pent up breath. What had he expected? He believed it himself, deep down. Of course all the evidence pointed to God; to the Biblical model. It was wearing him out trying to justify his findings and still not put his faith in the one who created it all. So why was he still resisting? It's what his family wanted; what Amy wanted. Why was he so stubborn in not just doing it? Accept Christ now, idiot! He looked up at the night sky, glowing orange with the artificial light of urbanity. It was a far cry from the African sky, bejeweled each night with diamonds from heaven. It was a far cry from what the ancients would have seen, magnified tenfold under the canopy of crystalline hydrogen.

What would it have been like? he wondered. *To live back then, so close to the beginning of creation?*

Men were as evil then as they are now. They didn't believe, even though the evidence was right before their eyes.

Mark blinked. Okay, so it wasn't an audible voice, but if ever he'd felt like God had just talked to him . . . He shivered.

"Okay, God," he said aloud. "I can't deny your existence any longer, but like Dr. Hazzard said, if I believe in the creator, I have to take the whole package. You know I'm kind of stubborn though, so you're going to have to help me in that department. P.S. Can you help me win Amy back?"

He smiled, a very surreal peace coming over him. Should he go back inside and field more questions? Naw . . . he'd talked enough for one night. He just wanted to go back to his hotel room and mull this new faith thing over a bit. Wait until he told his folks. Until he told Amy, if she would listen.

He dialed the cab company he had used earlier that day.

Let whomever come and beat him to a pulp while he waited. He didn't care about much right at the moment, except basking in this strange light that had nothing to do with the urban glow.

Chapter Twenty-Nine

Mark opened his eyes gradually to greet the morning light that was filtering through the partly opened drapes in his hotel room. He hadn't slept this well in weeks, he realized. With a satisfied smile, he stretched languorously and relaxed back against the pillows, arms behind his head. It was his first day as a brand new person. Despite all that could happen, he felt strangely peaceful about the future.

He should probably call his folks. Then he would work on Amy. Or maybe he should wait until he got back home and deliver the good news in person. Yeah, that seemed like a better idea. But Anthony—now, that guy deserved a bit of gloating time, even if it was way too early in the morning. That would be half the fun. Mark smiled at the thought of what Anthony would say, and reached for the phone.

After trying both Anthony's room and his cell, Mark called the front desk. "Did Anthony Vanguard check out by any chance?"

There was a pause as the woman consulted her computer. "No. He's still in room 309."

"Oh. Okay. Did he leave any messages for me?"

"I'm afraid not, sir," the woman at the front desk replied.

"Thanks," Mark said and hung up. *Maybe he's back at the*

university already, Mark mused, *although it doesn't seem like Anthony to be up and about this early in the morning.*

For his own part, there was no going back to sleep. He was ready to face this new day and was anxious for it to begin in earnest. Dr. Hazzard would be pleased by his newfound faith, he was sure. Now he just needed some help in remembering what to do next. He knew reading his Bible and praying was part of the deal. His parents had drilled that in to him. There was probably one of those Gideon Bibles somewhere in a drawer. He'd start with that.

He found the Bible in the bedside table and opened it to a random page. Romans 8. He scanned the page and noticed a break in the text at verse 26 with this heading: "Our Victory in Christ." Sounded good . . .

"And in the same way the Spirit also helps our weakness; for we do not know how to pray as we should, but the Spirit Himself intercedes for the saints with groanings too deep for words; and He who searches the hearts knows what the mind of the Spirit is, because he intercedes for the saints according to the will of God."

Hmm. That was good. He certainly didn't know what to pray right at the moment, or even how to pray, for that matter. "Okay, God. I'm taking you at your word. Help me out here. I want to do your will, so you're going to have to show me how to do this. " He continued reading.

"And we know that God causes all things to work together for good to those who love God, to those who are called according to His purpose. For whom He foreknew, he also predestined to become conformed to the image of His son, that He might be the first born among many brethren . . ."

Mark stopped reading and thought about that for a moment. He'd heard that verse before—the one about God working all things out for good. His parents had quoted it often enough. Did

322

that mean all things? Even all the mess with the archeological dig? Getting mugged? The present falling out with Amy? He looked at the verse again. It said *all* things. And it was pretty awesome to think that God knew about it all, even before it happened. He was predestined to be a child of God; to be counted among "the brethren." Yes, he could believe it. It was what he had been moving toward his whole life.

He closed the Bible and said another quick prayer, this time for guidance in approaching his career in this new frame of light. God knew everything, including what his next step should be in that regard.

Just as he was putting the Bible back into its nest, the telephone rang. Probably Anthony.

"Hello?"

"Mark?"

Mark smiled. He'd been right. "Wait until I tell you the news," Mark began.

"Hang on," Anthony interrupted. His voice sounded weak and far away, like he was gasping for air.

Mark frowned. "You alright, buddy? You don't sound too good."

"Can you come to my room right away? And maybe call an ambulance first."

* * *

"It's okay if I don't make it," Anthony whispered. "I know where I'm going."

"Stop being melodramatic," Mark chided good naturedly. "The doctor says you'll be fine. A couple of broken ribs, a few bruises. You'll be fixed up in no time and outta here."

Anthony lay on the emergency room gurney, waiting his turn

in the already busy ward. "Doesn't feel like it. I'm glad I'll be seeing you in heaven though. That's good news."

"Just stop it. Nobody is going to heaven today."

"How do you know? The cost just might kill me."

"You've got insurance," Mark said, then looked Anthony square in the eye. "You do have insurance?"

Anthony nodded, and then winced. "Geez, that smarts. Not like you spoiled Canadians and your Medicare."

Mark ignored the gibe. "Where are you going to stay? I'm sure Dr. Hazzard won't mind putting you up for awhile until you can travel."

"I hate to put him in danger."

"Quit being a martyr."

"And you? How long will you stay?"

"Just until I can get packed up. I've got some—business to take care of back home."

"Lady business?" Anthony asked.

"None of your business," Mark clarified with a grin. "Man, for a guy with multiple injuries, you sure talk a lot."

Anthony smiled, before groaning in pain once more. "I feel like crap. You sure I'm gonna live?"

Mark nodded. "Doctor said so. He should be turfing you shortly."

"Did you check the papers yet? I wonder what the reviews say. Or if there's any rebuttal from New Mexico."

"I haven't had time," Mark replied. "I've been otherwise occupied," he added with a grin.

"Yeah. Likewise . . . Did I say thanks for rescuing me?" Anthony asked.

"Yep. What are friends for?" He sobered. "This is getting kind of scary. Maybe Rocco's theories aren't all that off. You got a good look at him, right?"

Anthony nodded. "Too good."

"Oh? You told the police?"

"Yep."

"And you think it might be the same guy who beat me up?"

Anthony hesitated. "I think there are a couple of things I should tell you."

"Like what?" Mark asked, his eyes narrowing.

"I should've said something earlier, but I didn't want to worry you unnecessarily right before your presentation."

"Just spill it."

"It's about Rocco."

"I'm listening."

Anthony took a breath and winced again. "That argument you saw between me and Rocco. He was asking me some pretty funny questions."

"What kind of questions?"

"Questions about you and your girlfriend. He seemed to think she might be a distraction. I told him it was none of his business."

"Which is exactly true," Mark responded. "How does this have anything to do with what happened?"

"I'm not sure. Just some other stuff he said. Random stuff about you and Laura and the conspiracy . . ." Anthony looked squarely at his friend. "I think the guy has gone loco, Mark. Like, stark raving mad."

"Whoa. I'm not really following you . . ."

"I think Rocco is the one who beat me up. Who beat us both up," Anthony said.

"Why?"

"I recognized his voice," Anthony replied. "At least I think it was him. And even with his face covered, he had the same build."

Mark thought for a minute, grasping for a shred of recognition that was trying to form in his own brain. "Yeah . . . there was something familiar about the guy. It all happened so fast, but . . .'' He snapped his fingers. "He said something in Spanish! The guy who beat me up. It was just the kind of thing that Rocco would say when he was frustrated."

Anthony nodded.

"But why?" Mark asked, his brow furrowed. "I thought he was on our side."

"I think he was trying to scare us. Scare you, anyway, to make sure you were taking his conspiracy theory seriously. And me? Maybe he thinks I'm still on their side, a double agent, so to speak."

"Do you think he's on his own?" Mark asked. "That this whole conspiracy is a fabrication and he's just a vigilante trying to take matters into his own hands?"

"I'm not sure," Anthony replied. "But I'm worried about Laura."

"Laura?" Mark asked. He glanced over as the attending doctor approached. "What about her?"

"I'm not sure," Anthony said. "Just something he said the other day during our argument. Maybe you should check into it. Warn her. She might be in danger."

Mark nodded. "I will." He stepped back as the doctor greeted them.

"You're very lucky, Mr. Vanguard. One rib came very close to puncturing a lung." He held up the x-rays for inspection.

"But he's going to live, right?" Mark asked with a grin.

"A long life, I would suspect," the doctor agreed with a smile. "Now, I'll make a final wrap on those ribs, write you a prescription for the pain, and you can be on your way."

Mark helped Anthony out of the cab in front of Dr. Hazzard's home. It was a gracious Southern two-story with large trees in front almost hiding the house from the street.

"Pretty easy for a guy to cloak himself in the trees, if he wanted to try to break in," Anthony mused.

"Yeah. We should warn Dr. Hazzard," Mark agreed.

The man himself appeared in the doorway. "Come on up. You need a hand with your belongings?"

"Everything's back at the hotel," Mark replied. "I'll have to go back for it and check out."

"No use spending money on a cab," Dr. Hazzard said. "I'll drive you over later myself, or I can lend you my car, for that matter."

"Thanks," Mark replied.

"My goodness," Dr. Hazzard clucked. "If I didn't know better, I'd say you boys have made some enemies along the way. First, Dr. Graham's car accident and now this. What exactly happened anyway? Did you trip on the stairs or something?"

"Um, maybe we should go inside," Mark advised. "We didn't want to alarm you with the details over the phone, but I think there are a few things we need to straighten out . . ."

* * *

"This is grave indeed . . ."

"We should have been up front with you right after I was attacked," Mark said. "Before that—well, I didn't want to alarm you with mere speculations. But afterwards, well, I apologize. You had a right to know the truth."

"We didn't want you to cancel the presentation," Anthony offered.

"I wouldn't have done that," Dr. Hazzard replied. "Maybe taken some extra precautions with security . . ."

"But now I don't know what to think," Mark continued. "If there really is some kind of international conspiracy to hide the

327

truth about creation, then you and the university could be in danger. Not to mention, the artifacts."

"I doubt that's a problem," Dr. Hazzard said. "We've dealt with this kind of thing before. We have a very tight security system. Besides that, now that the truth is out, the opposition wouldn't dare sully themselves further with anything too obvious."

"You mean there really is a conspiracy?" Anthony asked.

"In a manner of speaking, yes," he replied. "Although, I'm not sure it's quite as insidious as your friend Rocco says. It's more a war of words. There are certain factions that have out and out lied on more than one occasion. Changed the facts, rewritten the texts, taken evidence completely out of context. It's a mega game that the opposition takes quite seriously. There are millions of dollars of government funding at stake. Evolutionists can't afford to have the truth come out. It would mean an end to their steady pipeline of money."

"That's just not right," Anthony said, then gasped.

"Maybe you should lie down," Dr. Hazzard suggested. "My wife Mabel has already made up the guest room. You should be comfortable there."

"Maybe you're right," Anthony nodded. "Those meds are starting to make me feel pretty drowsy."

"Just down the hall and the first door to the right. The bathroom is right across the hall. Do you need help?"

"No, I should be fine," Anthony said, rising from the sofa with difficulty.

"You sure?" Mark asked, jumping up to lend a hand.

"No, I'm good," Anthony replied, waving his friend off gingerly.

"I'll bring your stuff over as soon as I can," Mark called after Anthony's retreating figure.

"Just watch your back," Anthony mumbled.

The two doctors watched him disappear around the corner.

"Did you see the morning paper?" Dr. Hazzard asked.

"No, I didn't," Mark replied. "The reviews are in already?"

Dr. Hazzard nodded. He reached behind his chair and retrieved a jumble of newspaper that was already in several pieces. "Let's see. Here's the section. Quite a good piece, I would say. Certainly not the kind of thing the 'conspiracy' would appreciate. The facts are quite well represented, I'd say."

Mark took the paper. The headline read, "New Finds In Africa Lend Credence to Noah's Flood." He scanned the article, noting the mention of his own credentials and the 'good work' he'd done in the past. It outlined the find in most of it's particulars, including the Pterodactyls and "giant men" found together, the advanced technology in the antechamber, and the fact that it was sealed off by layers of sediment that helped preserve the specimens.

"So what do you think?"

"Generally very accurate," Mark conceded with a satisfied nod. "It almost makes me suspicious. There were no major details left out and not even a hint at sarcasm. I was at least expecting a small dose of skepticism."

"My feelings exactly. I'm surprised the opposition hasn't come out with a rebuttal yet. I checked on line and there was nothing so far. All in due time, I suppose."

"Yes. I'll be interested in what my former colleagues back in New Mexico have to say." Mark hesitated for a moment, remembering Anthony's warnings about Laura. "Um, actually, speaking of which, would you excuse me while I make a phone call?"

He let Laura's cell ring until her voice mail picked up. What kind of message could he leave? 'Watch your back?' He clicked his phone shut instead. He'd try again later.

"So tell me more about this Rocco fellow," Dr. Hazzard said.

"He was always a hard worker. Very knowledgeable. Up until recently, I trusted him completely, but now . . . Anthony seems to think he's gone crazy. I know he talked to me before about people out in the field not telling the truth and it really frustrated him. He says he hooked up with some others who wanted to rectify the injustice, but to do the things that we think he might be doing . . . I just don't get it. It makes no sense. It's working against us, if anything, not for us."

"People can commit heinous acts, all motivated by good intentions. Take, for instance, the attacks on abortion clinics over the years," Dr. Hazzard mused. "Harming those involved doesn't stop the killing of babies. It probably furthers their cause, if nothing else."

Mark nodded in agreement. "Two wrongs never make a right."

"And as for your friend Rocco, I guess we'll have to leave it to the police to find out whether he's involved. In the meantime, you and Anthony should probably both stay here."

"I don't know," Mark said hesitantly. "I really do want to get back . . . "

"The family emergency?" Dr. Hazzard asked with a twinkle.

"Just what has my colleague been telling you?" Mark asked suspiciously.

Dr. Hazzard shrugged. "Something about a love interest, that's all. If it's real, it can wait. I would think the young lady in question would rather have you home in one piece."

"Once Anthony recovers, I'll kill him," Mark laughed. He sobered slightly and added, "I wouldn't want to put your family in any danger."

"Don't let the open hominess of my property fool you. I've got my own security system in place," Dr. Hazzard assured. "I think we should alert the police though, so they can check around periodically."

330

"Great," Mark commented sardonically. "And you're sure everything will be safe at the university?"

"Absolutely. You can rest assured that the artifacts are completely secure."

"Okay. I guess I'll have to take you on your word, doctor."

"True enough, and since you'll be my guest for the next few days, please call me Tim."

"Right. Tim it is, as long as you call me Mark."

"Agreed. Now, may I suggest that we go over to the hotel and retrieve your belongings?"

* * *

Two days passed and still no rebuttal from New Mexico. Other scientists and interested individuals entered the fray on line, some for and some against. Some tried to downplay the creationist connection and explain the findings in other more "plausible" ways, while others attached their own religious biases to such a degree that it made Mark cringe. Even though he was now a believer himself, it was down right embarrassing the way some fundamentalists carried on. At the least, his presentation had generated some debate, which meant it hadn't gone completely unnoticed. But the fact that there was nothing—not a peep from the University of New Mexico—had him worried.

Maybe it was their way of distancing themselves, shunning him, so to speak. If they didn't even bother to reply, then it would show the world that they really didn't put any credence in what he had to say. Or maybe there was a more sinister reason.

Mark had tried Laura repeatedly since Anthony's warnings, but there was still no answer. He'd even stooped to leaving a message for her to call him back. He hadn't quite steeled himself to call John, though. That betrayal was still a little too raw.

There was little more that he could do here. The debate online continued and he had even received a request to talk on the local

331

radio station, which he had done earlier that day. But now he was anxious to go home. He had more important things on his mind that needed reconciliation. He planned to head out first thing tomorrow.

He was lying in bed in the room that Tim and Mabel had prepared for him. It wasn't that late, but he felt the need for some solitude. He kept going back to that passage he had read in Romans the other day—the one about God working everything out for good. He was clinging to that promise right now. He also liked what it said a little further down in the chapter, in verse thirty-one.

"If God is for us, who is against us?"

It seemed like God's hand had been with him so far in presenting his findings to the world. There was very little opposition, which still surprised him. He just hoped it didn't fade into obscurity, just another quack Christian trying to tout his own beliefs.

His reflections were cut short by the ring of his cell phone. He almost let his voice mail answer it, but decided against it.

"Hello."

"Amigo! Congratulations! I see everything has gone off well with your presentation. Now maybe those skeptics will take us seriously, eh?"

"Rocco?" Mark asked, sitting up fully.

"Of course it's me. Who else?" Rocco laughed.

Relief and fear mingled inside Mark's gut. Rocco wouldn't be calling if he was actually guilty, would he? But then again . . . "Hey, buddy," Mark said with forced cheerfulness. "Where have you been these last few days? I thought you'd want to be here to celebrate."

"Sorry about that, amigo. I had some other business to take care of."

"We missed you. Both me and Anthony." Mark paused to see

if the mention of the other man's name had any effect. Nothing. "Anthony met with a bit of an accident, I'm afraid."

"Oh?"

"Yeah. Kind of similar to my accident, if you get my drift."

Rocco chuckled; an unexpected response. "About time that mama's boy got toughened up a bit."

"Excuse me?" Mark questioned in disbelief.

"He'll mend," Rocco continued. "A couple cracked ribs never killed anybody."

There was silence for a moment as Mark digested what Rocco just said. "How . . . how did you know about his ribs?"

"I've got my ways, remember?"

Mark didn't like the sound of that. "So you said."

"So, I've been keeping up on the debate. I'd say we're coming out on top about 80 percent of the time."

"Yeah right," Mark responded blandly.

"Hey, you don't sound too pleased," Rocco noted. "What's the matter?"

"I'm just a bit concerned about who our supporters really are," Mark responded. "If there really is an international conspiracy, why aren't they more vocal? And who exactly is on the other side? How do I know I can trust them any more than the opposition?"

"I'd say it's pretty obvious that the conspiracy is alive and well. Look what they did to you and Anthony," Rocco reasoned.

"Did they?" Mark asked point blank. "Was it really 'the conspiracy', as you call them, or was it some other well meaning vigilante trying to convince us of a conspiracy?"

There was hesitation on the other end for a moment before Rocco laughed again. "Whoa, now! I'm not sure what you're getting at, but don't bite the hand that feeds you."

"What is that supposed to mean?"

"Look, things are working out perfectly for our cause. Who

333

cares how it came to be? Just bask in it, amigo. Grasp it and run with it."

"Did you or did you not attack Anthony?" Silence. "I see."

"It was for his own good. He was playing a double game, you know. It just helped to put the fear of God in him, so to speak. I don't think he'll be wavering over to the opposition again any time soon."

"Did it ever occur to you that that was all part of our plan?" Mark asked.

"Either way, no harm done," Rocco reasoned. "It still makes the bad guys look worse and the good guys look better."

"In some people's minds," Mark said, shaking his head. "Okay. So you admitted that much. What about me? And don't try to deny it. I know it was you." There was more silence. "Rocco? Answer me, damn it!"

"Look man, you don't even know half of what I've done for you," Rocco said, his voice sounding hard and foreign. "You should be thanking me for spurring your ass into action. For saving you from distractions—"

"You mean Amy?" Mark cut in, his throat constricted. "It was you that told her I was still seeing Laura?"

"Hey, I couldn't look that kind of a gift in the mouth. When I tipped Sawchuk off about your presentation, I had no idea I could use her for more than one purpose."

A chill ran down Mark's spine. "You tipped her off. But why?"

"Lots of reasons. It would keep her close by; where I could keep an eye on her."

"Rocco, tell me once and for all. Is there really an international conspiracy—the kind you've been warning me about? Or is this just some giant fabrication that you've come up with to further your own cause?"

"Oh, it's real enough," Rocco responded. "I'm just helping

bring it to light a little quicker, that's all."

Mark closed his eyes. The man really had gone loco. "Look, Rocco. Thanks for all your help, but I think you should just back off for awhile now, okay? We don't want anyone else to get suspicious."

"I was planning on it anyway. That last job got a little messy. I'm going to disappear for awhile, myself. I think you can handle the rest from here."

"What do you mean?"

"Don't worry about it," Rocco laughed. "I took care of everything. You won't be hearing any slander from New Mexico. Gotta go now. Take care, amigo!"

"Rocco? Rocco!" Mark called into the receiver. Nothing. The man had already hung up. Mark slowly clicked his cell together. Oh God. What had his former friend done now?

Chapter Thirty

Laura Sawchuk and John Bergman were added to the missing persons list and a warrant was issued for Rocco Cortez's arrest. Three days later, Laura's body was found in a shallow grave near the university grounds in Texas. Another four days went by, and John's body was found floating down the river.

My God, my God, why have you forsaken me . . . It pounded through Mark's brain like a mantra after each grisly discovery. Several weeks of a fog filled existence moved Mark forward through time, each day making the necessary motions to eat, sleep, and talk with the police. Tim and Mabel Hazzard became the solid foundation upon which he and Anthony relied. In all, it was like a dream, surreal in its clarity, but distorted beyond reason.

"I'm really sorry it's turned out this way," Tim was saying. They were standing at the doorway of the Hazzard home, Mark and Anthony both ready to take their leave.

"Yes. You and me both," Mark nodded.

"And you?" Tim turned to Anthony. "You're sure you're fit to travel? You're welcome to stay on longer if you'd like."

"No, it's about time the prodigal son made his way back home again," Anthony grinned. "Besides, I miss my Mom's cooking, no offense to your wife."

"None taken," Mabel smiled. "It's been a pleasure to have you both, even under these trying circumstances."

"Just remember, God is still in control," Tim declared.

"I'm trying to remind myself of that daily," Mark nodded.

"Hopefully we'll both make it home in one piece," Anthony noted. "I mean, Rocco is still at large."

"I'm sure the police will ferret him out soon. He can't hide forever," Mabel reasoned.

"His type don't stay underground long," Tim agreed. "Always looking for publicity. It's unfortunate that we've gotten some bad reviews out of it, though. The connection between you and Cortez has certainly shed some questionable light on your discovery. Not in my mind, of course, but the critics are getting a hold of this and eating it up, I'm afraid."

"I guess Rocco's plans back fired pretty badly," Anthony speculated. "Looks like he's played right into the 'conspiracies' hands."

"If only it was just our reputations that were lost," Mark added.

The others nodded.

"Yes. A very sad outcome," Tim offered.

Sad could not nearly describe what Mark was feeling. Despite what had taken place in the recent past, these people had been his friends, his colleagues. John had been his most trusted confident, and Laura . . . well, she had even shared his bed. His stomach turned inward with another spasm of inner pain. It was time to go home.

"Thanks again for everything," Mark said, shaking Tim's hand solemnly.

Mabel gave him a heart felt hug instead. "Anytime you're in Texas, feel free to look us up."

"I'm sure we'll want some follow up on your work once the

dust settles a bit," Tim added.

"If my reputation isn't in complete tatters," Mark said with half a grin.

"Trust," Tim advised, looking Mark straight in the eye. "Sometimes God puts us through the refiner's fire to make us more useful."

"I'll keep that in mind."

The quartet waved their final good byes and Mark and Anthony got into the waiting cab. Mark settled back into the seat, shutting his eyes in an attempt to block out the rush of emotions that continually threatened to overtake him when he thought about recent events. Maybe he never should have pursued this thing in the first place. If he had only listened to Laura, to the Director of Archeology back in New Mexico—to any voice of reason, maybe none of this would have happened. Maybe then, Laura and John would be alive. Was telling the truth really worth such a cost?

"Hey, you awake?" Anthony nudged Mark in the shoulder.

"Hm?" Mark responded, opening his eyes.

"Check out the car behind us," Anthony urged. "Or should I say, the driver of the car."

Mark turned around and peered out the back window of the taxi. He let out a gust of air. "No way. It can't be."

"The guy certainly has balls, I'll give you that," Anthony mused.

"Hey, driver," Mark leaned forward. "I think we're being tailed. You got a police band on your radio?"

The driver looked in his rear view mirror. "Who are you? I don't want no trouble," he barked. He moved into the far right lane. "I'll drop you off. That'll be eleven fifty. I don't want no trouble."

"Whoa! Wait a minute," Anthony interjected. "We don't want trouble either. Just keep going. But faster."

"I don't want no trouble," the cabby repeated, warning in his voice.

"Then keep going," Mark advised. "I'll call the police myself." He dialed the number.

Rocco had pulled up beside them on the left and was gesturing for them to pull over.

"Ignore him," Mark said, waiting for the police to answer. "Hello? Yeah, I've got a location on a guy named Rocco Cortez. There's a warrant out for his arrest." There was a pause. "Yeah. He's headed down the freeway now, going south toward the airport. Right. He's in a green sedan . . . " The police took the rest of the pertinent information and Mark hung up the phone.

"Okay," he said more to himself than anyone else. "If we can just keep him with us, the police should be able to head him off at the next overpass."

"I don't want no trouble," the cabby said again, almost whining as if he was trying to convince himself now.

"You're doing a great job," Mark assured.

"Yeah. Consider it your civic duty. The guy's a nut case. A criminal."

The cab driver gripped the wheel even tighter as he rounded the next bend, Rocco staying close by on his left. Suddenly, Rocco swerved toward them, side swiping the cab with enough force to make it momentarily veer into the sidewall and bounce off again. "I don't want no trouble!" he shouted, almost in tears.

"Keep driving," Mark shouted back. He looked at Anthony, who was holding onto his side. "You okay?"

Anthony nodded, grimacing. "I just hadn't braced myself, that's all. I'll be ready next time."

"There better not be a next time," Mark said through clenched teeth. "Can't you go any faster?"

There was a next time. This time he could see the sparks fly with the impact. "He's crazy, I tell you," Anthony muttered.

"I know," Mark nodded.

They were rounding another curve, this time to the left, when Rocco hit the taxi once again. This time, the force of the impact sent the cab over the edge, airborne for a millisecond, before landing with a jarring thud on a grassy section amid the spaghetti factory called freeway. Rocco's green sedan bumped after ward, coming to an abrupt halt ten feet away.

The cab driver ejected himself as quickly as possible from the driver's seat and took off running. Anthony lay slumped in the back seat. For his part, Mark had taken a bump to the head, which was already forming into a goose egg, but was none the worse for wear. He checked Anthony's pulse. His friend let out a groan. That was a good sign. Glancing to the side, he saw Rocco's stalky figure looming in the back window.

"Get out, turncoat," Rocco growled as he jerked the rear door open.

Mark had no choice but to comply, being half jerked out of the back seat by one of Rocco powerful forearms. He held a pistol in the other.

"All I did for you," Rocco ranted, waving the gun. "Everything. And you turn on me. What kind of a friend is that?"

"You turned on yourself," Mark countered, raising his hands slowly to chest height. "How could you do it, man? Laura and John were innocent."

"Innocent?!" Rocco spat. "How can you say that after what they did to you? To all of us. To the cause."

"I don't know what cause you're talking about," Mark said. He tried to keep his voice calm, though everything inside of him was screaming with adrenaline. "Maybe they had different views, but that doesn't mean they deserved to die."

"We all die one day," Rocco countered philosophically. "Some just sooner than others."

Mark shook his head. "I thought I knew you. Thought you were my friend. But this—this monster that you've become! What happened to the Rocco I knew?"

"He got stomped on one too many times. Oh yeah, you were my friend—when you wanted to be. But do you know what it's like being bossed around by a bunch of young intellectuals that think they know more than you just because they got a piece of paper that says 'Doctor' on it? Man, I been around longer than any of you, and I know my job too. But, I always had to bow to what the 'experts' had to say."

"So that's it? You were jealous?"

Rocco snorted. "Jealous? Naw. Just fed up. I've been on too many sites where the truth gets covered up with fancy theories that don't add up. It was time someone told the truth. I thought you were the man."

"I was. I am," Mark said. "You heard it. The truth was told, so why did you have to go and commit murder?"

"It wouldn't be long before they twisted everything you had to say and made it sound like a fool's fairy tale. I know how these things go. I had to stop them before they had a chance."

"But there are other ways, Rocco. Legal ways," Mark reasoned, as if talking to a child.

Rocco snorted. "I've tried that. Doesn't work in the end. The only way is to eliminate the problem."

"By committing murder," Mark restated.

"I do what I have to do," Rocco shrugged. "And I'm really sorry, Amigo, but I'm afraid you're going to have to join them." Rocco had steadied himself and was now pointing the gun straight at Mark's head.

"What would that prove?" Mark asked. "You're just digging yourself in, deeper and deeper."

342

"You think you're pretty smart, don't you, Dr. Graham? You think I've gone off my rocker and you can somehow sweet talk your way out of this one, don't you? Well, let me tell you a little secret. You're not as smart as you think you are. I was able to keep pretty close tabs on everything—even your secure files."

"Really?" Mark asked. "What files are we talking about?"

"Everything. Back in Africa; in North America . . . It wasn't very hard, my friend. You should really have chosen more obscure passwords. I mean, how hard was that to figure out? 'Jack' and 'Sax'? For a doctor, I'd say you're not too bright."

"Okay. So what was the point of that? I would have told you anything you needed to know."

"Ah, really? For one thing, I found out that the government was getting a little too nosy. That Sangeruka fellow was starting to push his weight around."

"Sangeruka," Mark repeated. "Just what exactly did you have to do with him?"

"As little as possible," Rocco admitted. "Although I did try to throw him off the trail just a bit."

"Meaning?"

"Missing artifacts, the cave in . . . my own little insurance should he and his cronies come snooping around."

"What?! I don't see how that helped—"

"Of course you don't," Rocco cut him off in a reasonable tone of voice. "That's because you're not seeing the bigger picture. I was looking forward to what I knew would be the next great cover up. Oh yes, I knew as soon as I laid eyes on that first wing bone that we were heading down another one of those trails. I just had to make sure that when the time came, you'd have enough first hand experience to believe me."

"That doesn't make any sense," Mark said. "You're sick."

"Watch it," Rocco laughed. "This sicko is the one holding the gun, remember?"

"So what about my arrest? Did you mastermind that as well?"

"That didn't go quite as planned," Rocco admitted. "Especially not the part about me getting chased and losing the casket."

"So that part is true?" Mark asked. "The casket is still intact and buried somewhere?"

Rocco nodded. "Of course. Why would I lie about that?" he asked. "Too bad you won't be around when I retrieve it."

Why indeed. "So how did I manage to get released?" Mark asked.

"That I don't know. Maybe the good Lord was looking out for you even back then," Rocco shrugged. "In any case, it's time for you to meet your maker now." He was momentarily distracted by the distant sound of sirens.

Mark heard it, too. "Give it up, Rocco. The cops'll be here any minute. You'll never get away with another murder."

Rocco shrugged, focusing on his victim once again. "Might as well go out with a bang, then." He laughed at his own joke; a sickening maniacal sound. "Any last requests?"

Wham! Rocco toppled to the ground as the simultaneous sounds of Anthony's grunt and the bark of the gun mingled inexplicably. Anthony had snuck out of the car and circled around behind Rocco, hitting him over the head. He grabbed the gun from where it lay on the ground and trained it on Rocco's sprawled form.

"Mark! Mark, you okay?" Anthony rasped, holding his side with one arm as he tried to keep his other arm steady. Mark lay beside the cab in a heap. "Buddy! Say something."

Mark groaned. "I've been hit," he groaned. "I think it's my shoulder."

The sirens blared in their ears now, as several police cars

344

arrived on the scene, bumping their way over the rough terrain.

"Put your weapon down!" a commanding voice shouted over a megaphone.

Anthony dropped the gun and put his hands in the air as far as he was able, bending forward slightly with the effort to his injured ribs.

"He's not the one," Mark tried to shout. His own voice sounded disturbingly far away. Suddenly everything went black.

Chapter Thirty-One

Here he was, back in Winnipeg, in the comfort of his parents' home. With his injured shoulder, and all the other trauma he'd suffered recently, it didn't take much convincing on their part for him to stay with them for awhile. Besides, he could use the pampering.

He sat in the family room, in one of the large cushioned chairs, cradling his arm, which was in a sling, with his good hand. There was something on TV; noise that he really wasn't very interested in, but that helped keep his mind occupied.

"How's the shoulder today?" Russ asked, coming into the room and sitting in the chair beside Mark.

"Mending, I suspect," Mark responded.

"What's on?"

"Um, I'm not sure," Mark said honestly. "I guess I wasn't paying much attention."

Russ nodded. They were silent for a few moments, staring at the TV with glass eyes. "You know, son," Russ finally said. "You did the right thing. Telling the truth about your find, I mean. No one could have predicted what would happen after that."

Mark nodded. "I know, but I'm still coming to terms with that, I guess. It just seems so senseless now."

"God's truth is never senseless," Russ stated.

"Even when innocent people die?" Mark asked.

"I don't pretend to know all the answers. Just know that in his sovereignty, God does."

"I know that, too," Mark nodded. "Really. I'm very grateful that you and Deanie never gave up praying for me."

"That's what parents do," Russ smiled.

"It does hurt though, that the dig back in Zimbabwe is getting so much bad publicity. I mean, I could handle it if it was just my own reputation that was getting slammed, but the whole dig is being discredited. It makes Laura and John's deaths seem even more pointless."

"Satan will have his day," Russ mused. "But I believe that what Satan means for harm, God can still use for good. Someday you'll be vindicated. And there are still lots of people out there that believe you."

"Anyone that will give me job?" Mark asked with a sardonic grin.

"Give it time," Russ advised.

"True. Dr. Hazzard is still on my side anyway, although I'm afraid he's taking some flack for it."

"God works all things out—"

Mark cut his father off and finished the sentence. "For good to them that love the Lord."

"You got it," Russ smiled.

"Don't you two just look cozy, sitting in here together having a man to man chat?" It was Deanie, standing in the doorway to the family room.

"Well, hello there," Russ said. "Come sit with me. There's room for two." He gestured to his lap.

Mark smiled. He had hoped that some day he could share that kind of lasting relationship with someone. With Amy. They had only spoken once since his return, and despite his revelations about his new found faith, she seemed distant at best.

"Actually, I was just coming to tell you that we have company," Deanie said. "Amy Walters," she added, giving Mark a knowing look. "Her car just pulled into the drive."

"In that case, I better leave you alone," Russ said, standing up. "We'll send her right in."

Mark's heart was pounding in his chest. Amy had come to see him. It was the first time they would meet face to face since his arrival back in Winnipeg. He straightened himself in the chair a bit and then winced with the effort.

"Mark," Amy greeted, entering the room. Mark made a motion to stand and grunted. "No, please! Just stay sitting. I was so worried when I heard you'd been hurt." She perched on the edge of the seat that his father had just recently occupied.

"Were you?" Mark asked, raising his eyebrows. Hope soared in his breast. He settled back down into the comfort of the cushions.

"I was," she stated. "I was grateful when I found out you'd be okay. And when I heard everything else, too . . ." She trailed off, looking away.

"Amy, you have to believe me when I say there was nothing going on between me and -" he almost choked on the last word. "Me and Laura."

"I believe you," she said quietly.

"And, well, now she's out of the picture anyway."

"I know. I'm so sorry, Mark," Amy offered. "About everything."

He nodded, unable to speak for fear he would burst into tears in earnest. What must she think of him? That he really cared for Laura in that way? Somehow he needed to reassure her. "Honestly, Amy. It was long over between us. But that doesn't mean she

349

deserved to die."

"I know that, Mark. It must be very hard for you."

He nodded again.

"And I was very happy when I found out you had given your life to Christ," Amy went on. "Sorry if I sounded kind of—distant —the other day when we talked on the phone. I guess I was still in shock over everything that has happened."

"I wondered about that," Mark said, trying for a feeble smile. "I was going to call the very night I accepted Christ, and then I decided I'd wait and tell you in person. Probably not that smart, considering everything else that took place in between."

"But the bottom line is, you've made a decision for Christ," Amy stated.

"Yes. Yes, I have, Amy. It's the genuine thing, not just a way to get you to marry me."

Amy looked down at her hands, clearly flustered. "Mark—" she said hesitantly.

"Amy, you must know, my feelings haven't changed. I still love you and want you to marry me. If you'll have me, now that I'm a bit defective." He gestured at the wrapping on his arm.

"It's not that," Amy shook her head.

"Then what is it?" Mark asked. "I get the distinct impression that this is not going the way I had hoped. Is there someone else? Is that it?"

"No. Of course not," she denied. She sat up straighter, steeling herself. "Look, Mark. I still care about you, but I've had some time to think about things while you've been gone. And well, maybe I am too young to know my own mind about something so important."

"Who told you that?" Mark interjected.

"Nobody," she defended. "I've come to that conclusion all on my own. See, that's part of the problem. You treating me like a child. And maybe in some ways, I am. I'd like to grow up, Mark, on my own terms. Not because you tell me to."

"I see. You think I've been over bearing."

"No. You were sweet and attentive and made me feel desirable —"

"Because you are," he interrupted again.

"Let me finish! I just feel like I need to see the world. Follow my own dreams before I settle down. You've traveled the world; followed your dreams. Surely you of all people must understand how I feel."

"What are your dreams, Amy?" Mark asked quietly.

"To be a missionary. To help people. To tell people about Jesus," she replied just as softly.

Mark surveyed her angelic young face. Tenderness overwhelmed him. "Then you should follow your dreams, Amy Walters," he said finally. "I won't stop you."

"Thank you," she barely whispered. She jumped up and rushed to his chair, kissing him on the forehead, the way a schoolgirl would kiss an aging elder. Then she swept from the room on a sob.

Mark sat for a moment, blinking back his own tears. It was the most profound act of love he had ever shown her—setting her free.

Was this how God worked all things out for good? Two friends dead, another criminally insane, and utter rejection from the love of his life. And yet . . . he couldn't help going back to the next part of Romans 8.

But in all these things we overwhelmingly conquer through Him who loved us. For I am convinced that neither death, nor life, nor angels, nor principalities, nor things present, nor things to come, nor powers, nor height, nor depth, nor any other created thing shall be able to separate us from the love of God, which is in Christ Jesus our Lord.

351

Chapter Thirty-Two

"Um, Dad? Can I talk with you a minute?" Mark asked from the doorway of his father's study.

Russ looked up from the book he was reading. "Sure. Anytime. Come on in." He removed his reading glasses and placed them on the desk.

"I've been in contact with Charlene Howard again, since I've been back." He scanned his father's face for recognition. "My . . . sister in Calgary," he finished, hesitating on the word.

Russ nodded contemplatively. "I see."

"I was thinking I might like to go out there. To meet with her and . . . and the rest of the family." He stopped, holding his breath for his father's reaction.

Russ steepled his fingers, rocking back and forth in his chair.

"I know you don't approve," Mark rushed forward, "but I think I might need the closure myself after all these years and—"

Russ silenced his son with a raised finger. "Mark, I think you should know that Deanie and I have talked about this. We knew it was coming. And . . . well, we both think you should go." He looked squarely into his son's eyes.

"You're sure?" Mark asked, surveying his father closely.

Russ nodded. "Absolutely. Whatever demons I need to

exorcize in relation to your mother are mine and mine alone. You shouldn't be held hostage by my own shortcomings."

"But—"

"And besides that," Russ cut him off, "it's time I faced up to the facts anyway. I was not totally blameless in my first marriage. I wasn't the husband I should have been. I was controlling and bitter and I see that now. I've been carrying this offense way to long. It's time I gave it over to the Lord once and for all. You deserve to know the rest of your family. It's simply the right thing to do."

"Thanks, dad. I appreciate it."

* * *

Mark paid the driver then stepped out of the cab. Another wave of anxiety hit him as his stomach tightened into a hard ball. Dr. Mark Graham, big wig archeologist, world traveler and scientist; a man who had seen more than his fair share of trouble these days—shaking in his boots.

He was in Calgary, where the other half of his "family" lived. Charlene had given him the address to her home and the rest of the family would be there, waiting. Charlene, Tom, little Cade, Scott, the brother he hadn't met yet, and—her. The woman who had given him birth. He took a deep breath. Well, no use in stalling any further. Might as well face the music.

It had been a long journey around the world and back again, but somehow it seemed that this was the culminating moment, when all the questions about his own worth as a person—his own purpose on this earth—would be answered. No matter what the outcome of the meeting, he knew God could use it for good as he put his new found faith to the test once again. Perhaps it was symbolic of his life in general. He had no idea what his future held. It certainly was not what he had expected or even hoped. And yet . . . in the midst of all the devastation, he had felt the hand of

354

God, and for that, despite everything else that had happened over the past year, he was grateful. Maybe that was all that really mattered.

Epilogue

Despite the khaki hat, the African sun beat down mercilessly on his head as Mark strode down the sidewalk. Mid afternoon was no time to be out in Harare. He needed to find some shelter. He spotted a small sidewalk café across the street, and headed in that direction, dodging the slow moving traffic that clogged the street.

He ducked under the awning, feeling the immediate reprieve from the punishing rays of the sun. Most of the tables were occupied already. He spotted one with a lone woman – a white woman at that, off against the brick of the building.

"Excuse me? May I join you?" he asked. His heart literally stood still as recognition dawned. "Amy? Is that you?"

She looked up, clearly as taken aback as he was. She nodded mutely, then managed to squeak out. "Please sit down."

He did, the chair scraping along the cement as he pulled it out before sitting.

"What are you doing here?" they both asked at once and then laughed.

"You first," Mark said politely.

"I'm working at an orphanage for victims of AIDS," Amy informed.

Mark nodded. "Of course. And telling the children about

357

Jesus, no doubt," he added with a grin.

"Naturally," she said with a smile of her own. "And you? Are you working on location somewhere near?"

"Sort off," Mark said. "I'm not really sponsored by anyone in particular. I'm just here on my own to do a little follow up."

"Oh? What about?"

"Just a tip off a friend gave me once," Mark supplied. "About a certain casket that might be buried somewhere in the mountains."

"I see."

"I can't believe I've run into you after all this time. In Harare, of all places," Mark shook his head. How many years had it been now? Four? Five? He'd lost track. But Amy . . . Amy Walters was as beautiful in his eyes as ever. He stole another glance and noticed she was surveying him just as intently.

She looked down. "Yeah. Imagine."

There was a moment of silence before Mark spoke up again. "Harmony and Cory had a son. He's about six months old or so."

"Yes, I heard."

"Of course."

"You must be a very proud uncle."

"Indeed I am."

"I'm sorry I didn't make it to their wedding. I was working with 'Doctors Without Borders' at that time, and was somewhere on the Pacific."

"You were missed," Mark commented. "By more than one person," he added, trying to catch her eye.

She kept her gaze down. "Oh. Um . . . I'm still trying to get used to the African sun. It's so intense."

"Amy, look at me, please," Mark said. She looked up, her breath catching in her throat. "You know, you are still as beautiful as I remember you."

"Mark, don't," Amy pleaded. "After all this time—"

"I've never stopped loving you, you know," Mark continued despite her warning signals. "There has been no one else since you, you know that? I've pretty much resigned myself to a life as an eccentric old bachelor. But now, seeing you again, I feel this small glimmer of hope. Tell me there's hope, Amy."

"I . . . I don't know what to say," Amy faltered, clearly flustered. "I mean, I've grown up a lot in the past five years, Mark."

"It's been that long?" he asked. "It seems like only yesterday I was gazing into your beautiful eyes."

"Things have changed. I have changed."

"I see." He looked down at his hands. "Then life as an eccentric old bachelor it is."

"I mean, I've matured, both as a woman and as a Christian," Amy continued. "I'm not the shy, naïve little girl you knew back then. I've traveled the world for myself, Mark. I've seen things, some of them pretty horrible. And yet my faith is still strong. I've been able to make a difference in the lives of these people. And I can't believe that God would want me to sacrifice all of that to satisfy my own feelings."

Mark looked up. "You still have feelings?"

Amy hesitated before nodded her assent.

His eyes filled with tears; uncharacteristic and yet fitting. He let one roll unchecked down his cheek. "I'm a believer too, Amy. Remember? I told you that way back when I got home from the States."

"I know. I guess I just needed to know that it was for real. Not something you said or did just to satisfy my requirements."

"No Amy. It's for real," Mark reassured. "I've been through enough to know that no matter what; whether you take me back or not, God will never leave me or forsake me."

"Is that what you think I did? Forsake you?" she asked,

choking on her own words.

"It felt like it. But I think God had a plan. He knew you needed time to grow up, to live life on your own and to make a difference in the world. And I needed to grow up, too. Spiritually. I needed to make my faith my own, not just something my parents handed down to me."

"But what about my career?"

"What about it?"

"I like what I do," Amy said defensively. "I don't want to give that up."

"And why should you," Mark responded logically. "I mean look at us. Here we are, meeting up in Africa of all places after all these years. I'd say we both have a bit of the wander lust in us. Surely God must have a niche somewhere for us, where we can work together."

"Do you really think so?"

"God works all things together for those who love Him," Mark quoted. "My favorite verse. I think he can do the same for us, Amy."

"I'd like that," Amy smiled.

"Then I take it your answer is yes."

"To what?" she replied coyly. "You haven't asked a question yet."

"Right. Okay, Amy Walters, for the second time—or is it the third time? Anyway, Amy will you do me the honor of becoming my wife?"

"I thought you'd never ask!"

After a prolonged kiss, Amy pulled away with a giggle.

"Now what are you laughing about?" Mark asked. "I haven't lost my touch, have I?"

"No, that's not it. I was just thinking how worried I was that I was destined to be an old maid missionary."

"You're kidding, right?"

"No. I guess you weren't the only one who had resigned to life as a single. I mean, I kept telling myself that I was still young, that some day someone else would come along and sweep me off my feet. That I was too young when I fell for you, anyway, and it was probably just a crush. But deep down I knew. There would never be anyone for me besides Dr. Mark Graham."

"Now, that is music to my ears," Mark laughed. "If Jack were here right now, he'd be playing a celebration tune on his saxophone."

"Maybe he is here," Amy mused. "Looking down on us from heaven with his own four thousand piece jazz band."

Mark nodded. "Yeah. And somehow, I think he approves."